"Readers will remember Trana Mae Simmons's romances long after the last page has been read."
—Michalann Perry

KISS ME NOT

Caitlyn tilted her chin up an inch. "Of course there's a few other things about you a woman could admire. Silas said you kept a clean camp and didn't kill anything you didn't need to eat. And the times you're not snarling at me, you're sort of pleasant to be with."

"The snarling comes from fighting the urge to kiss you," Jon admitted.

"Quit thinking about kissing me; then you won't be snarling like a wounded puma cat all the time."

"Quit thinking about it? Good idea," Jon murmured.

He slipped a hand around her neck and bent his head slowly, giving her time to react if that was what she wanted to do. Her eyes widened like a startled fawn's and her lips parted, but she didn't pull away. Capturing her lips with his own, he gently kissed her, struggling with all his might not to give in to the raging desire the feel of her lips immediately touched off in him.

MOUNTAIN MAGIC

TRANA MAE SIMMONS

LEISURE BOOKS **NEW YORK CITY**

A LEISURE BOOK®

September 1995

Published by

Dorchester Publishing Co., Inc.
276 Fifth Avenue
New York, NY 10001

Copyright © 1995 by Trana Mae Simmons

Printed in the United States of America.

To my best friend and soul mate—Linda Smith.
Thanks for always being there for me, lady!
And to the rest of my extended family:
Duane Smith, Lori, Lisa and Leslie Hales, and
Maggie Naud.

Prologue

Please don't cry! I'm coming. . . .

Stay there, Caitlyn! Whatever happens, you stay there!

No, I want to go with you! He's crying, and I'll help you with him. He's so little.

Stay. I love you, Caitlyn. Always remember I love you.

Caitlyn sat up with a start, covering her ears and burying her face on her knees. Still the horrible cries that always followed the voices rang in her head: war whoops of victory and the terrible, gut-wrenching keening of a woman's scream. Somehow even more ghastly was the voice missing from the cacophony of sound—the tiny, crying voice she'd been struggling to go to.

Why did this dream keep visiting her? Who were these people?

A soothing hand caressed her shoulders, and Caitlyn flung herself into a warm embrace. Shudders racked her body, but after a moment, another voice chased the dregs of the dream back into the blackness. It would spring on her again, catching her unaware. It always came back.

"My daughter," the voice said, "it is over now. You are awake."

The calming words finally made sense to Caitlyn, and she lifted her face, staring into the concerned gaze of the only woman she could ever recall treating her as a mother might.

"Why, Sky Woman?" she pleaded. "Why is it always the same—never different? What does it mean?"

The Nez Perce woman smoothed the hair back from Caitlyn's forehead. "I do not know, my daughter. One day it may become clear to you. Or it may never be. It will be as the spirits intend."

Chapter One

Rendezvous
Wyoming Territory—July, 1829

Jonathan stared blearily at the pile of Indian gambling bones and took a sip from the tin cup in his hand. The sun slipped again, and his shadow crawled another inch toward the fire, intermingling with the dark silhouette cast by a nearby wigwam. With a disgruntled snort, the Nez Perce Indian across from him raised his eyes and tossed the fine-bladed knife on the growing pile of plunder at Jonathan's feet.

Jonathan gave a curt nod and left the knife where it landed. He'd already had his chance to examine it when Tall Man pulled it reluctantly from his belt in a final attempt to recoup some of his losses. Rising shakily to his feet, he returned his elderly partner Silas's nod of satisfaction regarding Jon's gambling prowess, then grimaced at the strain the unaccustomed squat had put on his legs. How these Indian men could stay like that for such long periods was beyond him.

And how could anyone stomach much of the rotgut whiskey that half filled his cup? Silas had warned him about it—said it was cut with diluted alcohol several times over, treated with red pepper to give it back its kick. Then twists of tobacco, along with sorghum, were thrown in for some semblance of its former color.

The traders justified their doctoring of the brew by the long distance they had to carry it on their pack trains in order to reach rendezvous each summer. The pack mules and traders made yearly treks from St. Louis to the eastern edge of the Rocky Mountains, where the annual gatherings of mountain men, Indians and traders took place. But this whiskey wouldn't even be fit libation at one of the dockside taverns Jon used to frequent in Richmond, Virginia. Still, he drank another swallow.

He'd traveled that same trail himself last year, after finding himself in St. Louis following a few weeks of aimless wandering. But despite the thousand-plus miles he'd put between himself and Richmond this summer, he still hadn't escaped the memories. They seemed to have hitched a permanent ride in his mind. Now, following a winter spent in the high country with nothing to dull the pain of his reflections, he welcomed this chance to dull the memories for a little while—whatever the vile taste of the sedative.

The tin cup missed its mark the next time Jon lifted it, and he clumsily swiped at the trickle of whiskey running down his chin. A sudden pain knotted a leg muscle, and he staggered a step.

"Whoa," Silas said with a chuckle as he placed a steadying hand on Jon's shoulder. "Guess I better pick them things up for you, else you might end up on your ass, boyo."

"I'm not drunk—not yet," Jon amended.

"Well, anyway, looks like you're gonna have to find another wigwam with richer pickin's," Silas said. "And there's hundreds more for you to choose from. Didn't I tell you every Indian and mountain man west of the Mississippi would be here at rendezvous? It's like one of those fairs they have back east."

"Yeah," Jon admitted. "But I think I'll wait until after we eat to do any more gambling. Hell, Silas, my belly's rubbing my backbone. Thought you said there'd be some food tents here, where we could get decent meals. I'm sick and tired of beans and those hard biscuits you make. While we're here, why don't you get someone to show you how to cook?"

"Me? Who said I was the meal maker in this here outfit? You were damned glad to eat whatever I put in front of you all winter! Why don't you get some lessons yourself, so's I don't have to spend all my time tryin' to fill that bottomless pit you call a belly?"

A cry from inside the wigwam echoed in the air. After glancing at the spot where Tall Man had been sitting to find him gone, Jon turned toward the buffalo skin structure. The flap flew back and Tall Man emerged, pulling a slight figure behind him. Tall Man's woman, whom they'd only had a glimpse of when they first arrived, followed the other two figures out, her furious voice spitting Nez Perce words.

"What's she saying, Silas?" Jon asked.

"Something that's gonna get her a beatin' if she don't shut up," Silas said grimly. "Watch, and keep out of it."

Tall Man halted and swung around. He spat one word at his woman and raised his free arm, bringing it down in a swinging arc. Since the Indian man was even drunker than Jonathan, the woman easily evaded the blow and ran back toward the wigwam. At the entrance, she shook her fist and fired a last invective at Tall Man before ducking inside.

Tall Man stood swaying and staring at the wigwam for a second, then shrugged his shoulders and stumbled to the fire. He jerked a small, deerskin-clad figure from behind him and placed his hands on her shoulders. She straightened her slight stature and glared at Jon and Silas, refusing to bow her head when Tall Man clapped a huge palm against it. Instead, she tossed her long hair angrily and swept a matted black hank over her shoulder, moving a step away from the Indian.

"What the bloody hell . . . ?"

"Hush, Jon," Silas said softly. "Let me handle this."

Jon glanced uneasily at his wizened old partner. Silas had taught him a lot this past winter, probably even saved his life. The agreement between them was for the most part unspoken. Silas took Jon under his wing and passed on his vast store of trapping knowledge in return for Jon's acceptance of Silas's superior experience. The first, inviolable rule was that Jon allowed Silas the lead in dealing with any Indian they came across—anywhere.

Jon nodded his head and stepped back, draining the last swallow of the almost unpalatable liquid from his tin cup. He stifled a burp and swept his hand up to push back a blond curl that had fallen over his face. Focusing his somewhat blurred eyes on the three figures in front of him, he settled himself to watch the confrontation.

Tall Man pointed at the female figure standing near him and began speaking to Silas. He'd already figured out that Jon did not understand the Nez Perce language, but he glanced now and then at Jon, obviously indicating for Silas to translate his words. While Jon waited for Silas to explain things to him, he moved closer to better study the bedraggled woman Tall Man held in his grip.

Woman? Barely more than a child would be more like it. She couldn't have been much over five feet—a good 12 inches shorter than he was. He moved a few steps closer, squinting in order to see past a flame that danced high when a log shifted. She had turned slightly to watch Silas and Tall Man, apparently ignoring him.

He revised his estimate of her age upward a little. The ragged buckskin garment outlined some fairly shapely curves. Proud breasts rode high, straining against the worn deerskin, and a rope was tied at her slender waist, probably in an attempt to hold together a long rip at the side of the garment.

She still appeared younger than Roxanne, the woman who by now had been his brother James's wife for almost a year. Damn Roxie to hell, anyway. She had become the mistress of that grand manor house in Virginia after all. What story had she cooked up to try to convince Charlie she'd never had a man before their wedding night?

Jon shook off his lingering thoughts and slid his eyes down the woman to where her dirty feet were planted in the sandy soil, at least a good 12 inches beneath the jagged hem of her garment. He had a hard time discerning the feet from the dirt—in fact, dirt and mud encrusted the entire expanse of legs exposed below the hem. Strange. Most of the Indians they had met in the mountains had seemed fairly clean. He and Silas had even shared a winter sweat lodge at a Sioux camp one week.

"Jon! Damn it, are you listenin' to me?"

"Huh? Sorry, Silas. What'd you say?"

"I said," Silas repeated, "that he wants you to look her over. You know, feel her muscles and check her teeth. Says she's small, but she's strong."

"Why the hell should I . . . ?"

"Do it, Jon," Silas said sharply. "Just do it!"

Jon hesitated another second, his eyes drawn again to the woman. This time he studied the set profile of her face. She stood staring away from them, her slender neck straight beneath a rigid chin. Her face wasn't nearly as dirty as her legs, and the dying sun's rays gave enough illumination for him to make out full lips set in a grim line, along with a delicate nose in good proportion to her other features. Her eyes were shuttered, and he hadn't been able to determine their color yet. They were probably brown, like those of other Indians he had met.

"Jon!" Silas repeated in a warning voice.

"All right, all right," Jon grumbled as he walked toward the woman. "But I'd still like to know what the hell this is all about."

As soon as he got close, he could smell her. A fortunate wind had blown her scent away from him at first, but even the breeze couldn't carry away this noxious odor. The smoke from a thousand cooking fires permeated her garment and rose from her gnarled black hair. Grease spots stained almost every inch of her ragged dress. And something else—she smelled as if she'd gotten mixed up with a skunk sometime in the near past.

"Damn it, Silas, she stinks," Jon grumbled. He glanced

over at Silas and missed the almost imperceptible further tightening of the the woman's mouth and lift of her chin.

"Then hold your breath," Silas growled.

"What am I supposed to do?" The odor penetrated the whiskey fuzz of Jon's brain and he lifted the tin cup, mighty displeased to find it empty.

Tall Man gave a grunt and moved over beside Jon. He grabbed one of Jon's hands and placed it on the upper portion of the woman's arm, covering Jon's fingers with his own and urging him to squeeze. Nodding his head, he spoke a few guttural words and looked to Silas to translate.

"Feel her arm, Jon," Silas said. "Up and down along the muscles, then do the same to the other one."

"Silas, I can't. . . . "

"You damned sure can and you damned sure better," Silas returned.

Jon gave a sigh and tried to breathe back in through his mouth as he complied. During his examination, the woman held herself even more rigid, if that were possible. He turned her toward him in order to reach her other arm and she closed her eyes. After a cursory examination of that arm, Jon dropped his hands and glanced at Silas.

"Now, open her mouth and look in," Silas ordered.

Jon reached a tentative hand toward the woman's face and she jerked her head aside as soon as his fingertips touched her. Beside him, Tall Man surged forward and grabbed the woman's chin, his fingers crushing cruelly. Jon's arm flew up and he knocked the Indian's hand away, turning on Tall Man with a snarl.

"There isn't any damn reason to hurt her," Jon spat. "I'll do this my way!"

Tall Man understood the tone of Jon's voice, if not his words. His eyes narrowed dangerously, but he glanced at the pile of plunder Jon had won from him and gave a shrug. With a wave of his hand, he indicated for Jon to continue.

The woman's head was bent finally, her shoulders burrowed forward and her arms clenched across her chest. Jon's heart went out to her and he spoke softly as he brushed back a clump of hair from her face. The back of his finger inadvertently touched the side of her neck, and the silky feel of her skin surprised him. But he'd already noticed she kept her upper body a lot cleaner than her lower.

"I'm not going to hurt you like he did," he assured her, hoping she'd be able to understand his tone if nothing else. "Look, I don't know what's going on here, but I do know that if I don't do exactly what Silas says, we'll have this whole camp of Nez Perce after our scalps. Bear with me, will you?"

The woman shuddered and clenched her arms tighter.

"Damn it, Silas." Jon turned toward his partner. "I'm not gonna paw this woman like some horse I'm tryin' to buy. You tell Tall Man to explain why he brought her out here, then we'll talk about it."

"I think you've already figured it out, son," Silas said mildly. "You ain't no idiot. Leastways, you ain't seemed to be so far. Otherwise, I wouldn't've wasted my time with you this past winter."

"You mean—" Jon turned back to the hunched figure before him. Her bowed head would barely reach the top of his shoulder, even raised on that silky-skinned neck. Jon's eyes widened and he felt a desperate need for another drink.

"Here, boyo," Silas said as he reached for Jon's cup. "Reckon we can take care of that."

Not even realizing he'd spoken aloud, Jon nevertheless held out his cup. As soon as Silas filled it from the jug that had never been too far from his side all day, Jon tipped the cup to his lips while he scanned the mountaintops around him. The fiery streaks of vermilion and chartreuse left behind by the now vanished sun reflected the feeling of the liquid burning a path to his stomach.

"Silas, he wants me to gamble what I've won against him for this woman, doesn't he?" Jon questioned.

"Yep. And as long as the loser's got somethin' else to bet, it ain't proper for the winner to walk away with what he's won," Silas informed him. "You ain't got no choice. If you don't do it, we won't be able to trade with none of these tribes for winter supplies. They'll all find out about it, and they won't have nothing to do with anybody they think's dishonorable. And, like I told you when we headed here, we can get some of the stuff we need from the traders. But we ain't gonna make it through another season without the food the Indians'll trade for.''

Jon gulped down the remainder of the whiskey and walked over to the fire without looking at the woman again. He squatted and waited until Tall Man took his place across from him. With a nod at the Nez Perce, he indicated for him to take the bones first.

Tall Man picked up the small stack of white bones and rolled them between his palms. Then, with a flick of his wrist, he tossed them to the ground between them. A satisfied smile tipped his lips when he looked up at Jon.

A shadow fell on the pile of bones. Jon's nose told him even before he made out the shape whom the shadow belonged to. She had moved around to stand by the fire, the flickering flames casting her outline toward them.

Tall Man's head came up and he shouted at the woman.

"Leave her," Jon said in a steely voice, having correctly interpreted Tall Man's order for the woman to move. "She's got an interest in this."

"Not according to Nez Perce rules, Jon," Silas said as he moved over and took the woman's arms. "It's bad luck for a woman to stand near."

Tall Man spoke again, and Jon looked at Silas.

"He says it won't be fair to him for you to hold him to that shake if you beat him, since the woman gave him bad luck," Silas explained. "He'll get another shake, if he wants it."

Jon nodded in agreement and picked up the bones. As Silas moved away with the woman, he imitated the Indian's movements, then flicked the delicate white bones to the ground. He heard Tall Man give a whuff of disgust when the Nez Perce saw the winning layout.

Jon remained squatting while Tall Man gathered the bones again. The Indian let out a whoop when the bones landed on the ground, but his face quickly clouded over when one bone teetered back and forth for a second. The bone fell toward Jon, and Tall Man quickly fixed his face into an impenetrable mask as he stood.

"He says more or less that you won fair and square," Silas interpreted after Tall Man spoke. "He says he's honored to've played the bones with someone as good as you and that it ain't no disgrace for him to lose to such a better player."

Jon stuck his hand out to Tall Man and the Nez Perce grasped it for a quick shake before he started to turn away.

"Hey, wait a minute," Jon said, grabbing the Indian man's arm. "What happens now?"

Tall Man said something to Silas and gestured at the pile of goods on the ground, then to the woman.

"He says you can either take your winnin's and go, or stay and have supper with him and his woman," Silas explained. "I think the first choice is the best one, lessen you fancy roasted dog meat. Me, I ain't never developed a taste for it."

Jon stifled a grimace and dropped Tall Man's arm. "But what about her?" he asked Silas.

"She belongs to you now, boyo," Silas said in an exasperated voice. "Ain't you figured that out yet?"

"But . . . but, Silas. What the heck am I going to do with her?"

"Up to you, I reckon. You can try to lose her to someone else, you want to git rid of her. But she's yours 'til then."

Jon turned to where the woman stood, her back to him as she stared into the fire. The buckskin garment fit snugly across her rump and her matted hair fell down almost to her waist. It would probably reach halfway down her legs if she brushed it out.

"What if I offer to give her back?" he said pleadingly to Silas.

"Wouldn't be perlite," Silas said. "You'd insult Tall Man and we might's well leave rendezvous right now. We'd never get no tradin' done."

"Wait!" Jon called as Tall Man moved away.

The Indian paused and shot Jon a puzzled look.

"Ask . . . Silas, ask him what her name is. We don't even know her name."

Silas spoke to Tall Man, and the Indian's unfathomable countenance changed with a quicksilver movement into lines of sly amusement. He spoke a few words and disappeared into his wigwam.

Silas's roar of laughter split the air. Gale after gale swept over Jon, and Jon's face darkened in anger as he stalked over to the old man.

"Tell me what he said, Silas," he demanded.

Silas straightened and looked at Jon. As soon as his eyes fell on his partner, Silas broke up again, clutching his arms across his stomach. His shoulders shook and he danced around, buckskin fringe bobbing as he whooped his merriment, gasping for breath between whoops.

"Silas! Damn you, quit cackling and tell me what he said her name was!"

"It . . . it's . . . oh, Lordy. I can't breathe! Har! Har, har! Oh . . . ugh . . . hardy har!"

Jon grabbed Silas's shoulders and shook him roughly. "Damn it, shut up and answer me!"

"Make . . . make up . . . your mind," Silas gasped between breaths. "Can't . . . can't shut up . . . and talk, too."

Jon released Silas in disgust and glanced at the woman. To his amazement, he found the first sign of emotion on her face. Her lips were barely uptilted and the eyes beneath her half-mast eyelids confirmed an expression of shrewd mirth. Catching his gaze on her, she quickly froze her expression again into stoniness and turned away.

"I . . . oh, I think maybe I can talk now," Silas said with a loud guffaw. "Got to. Can't wait to see your face when I. . . ."

Silas lost his power of speech again and burst into more guffaws. He wiped at the tears streaming down his plump cheeks into the white beard on his face and snorted. Grabbing a dirty handkerchief from his pocket, he tried to blow his dripping nose, the convulsions from his laughter adding force to his efforts. Finally he took a deep breath and straightened again, but Jon was already stomping away.

"I'll see you back at our camp after you're done making a jackass of yourself!" Jon tossed over his shoulder.

Silas stopped laughing immediately and jerked his wolf-skin hat from his head. Turning to the woman, he clasped the hat against his chest and tried to fix his face into the proper measure of respect.

"I apologize, miss," he said in Nez Perce. "The Indians usually come up with a name to fit the person, though. Guess you've given them some sort of fuss if they pinned a name like that on you."

The woman's lips quirked and she gave a smothered laugh. "Reckon I did," she said in English. "And reckon I can show either one of you why they call me Smelly Woman with Wolf's Teeth below Belly, you get any ideas about seein' if you can get any further with crawlin' in my bed with me than they did. I'll cook your meals and help tan your hides. I won't poison you with my cookin', since I might just end up worse off with whoever else I have to take up with. But I bed down alone at night!"

Silas took a step forward and peered at her face. "Thought so," he mused, this time in English to match her language. "Ain't a drop of Indian blood in you, is there? Bet your skin's white as milk under all that dirt. What's your real name?"

"Caitlyn," she said with a shrug. "But Cat'll do, unless you want to call me Smelly."

"Well," Silas drawled as he raised a hand to scratch at his beard. "Don't seem right to call a white woman Smelly. But ain't never heard of one called Cat, neither, 'cept maybe one."

"If you've let crawly critters start growin' in that beard, old man, you best get rid of them. If one of them hops over here on me, I'll douse you with kerosene while you sleep. I don't hold with lettin' no bugs live on me."

"Hell, Cat," Silas replied, settling the issue of her name. "Take more than six legs on a critter to hold onto that dirt coverin' you. 'Sides, ain't lice, nor fleas neither. I just naturally scratch my beard when I'm a thinkin'. And you surely do give a man a lot to think about."

"As long as that's all you do," Caitlyn warned, her blue eyes flashing a warning in the reflected firelight. "I can't do anythin' about what you think on, but I sure can make you sorry if you try to act on those thoughts. Especially if they ain't tolerable towards me."

"How old you be, Cat?"

"I don't rightly know. Expect it's somewhere between eighteen and nineteen. Pa's been dead nigh on a year now—the only pa I recall, anyway. I kept track of the winters we lived out, and Pa, he said he thought I was probably around five when he got me."

"Great gobs of goose dip!" Silas said in surprise. "You ain't that girl ol' Mad Mick O'Shaunessy drug around with him, are ya? You mean, Ol' Mick's dead?"

Her blue eyes filled with tears and she angrily blinked them away. "Don't too many folks win over a grizzly bear," she said. "Especially when he lets the bear get too close while he's shovin' me up a tree. The bear swiped the rifle away before Pa could get it aimed."

"Ol' Mad Mick," Silas said with a sad shake of his head. "One more of my old pards gone. 'Course I ain't seen him in a few years. You didn't have them bumps on your chest last time I laid eyes on you."

She took a step back and grabbed a piece of wood from the fire, holding it out between them. "You won't be lookin' at bumps on any girl's chest, you keep lookin' at mine."

"Hey there, gal," Silas soothed. "Wouldn't never cross my mind to try anythin' with my old pard Mick's girl. Hell, that man loved you to pieces and reckon you can count on me to pertect you, just like he did. Wouldn't have it no other way. You got my solemn word as a mountain man on that."

She dropped the flaming branch back into the fire. "What about him?" she asked, the flick of her head indicating the direction Jon had taken.

"Well," Silas admitted. "Jon's a tenderfoot from back east, but so far he seems to be one of the rare good 'uns that show up out here from time to time. I wouldn't've took up with him, I didn't think there was somethin' there worth savin'. Watched him for a few days afore I made myself known. He didn't kill nothin' he didn't need to eat and kept a clean camp."

"He's almost as big as Pa was," she mused.

"Yeah, I recall," Silas replied. "Look, you got anythin' in that there tent you want to take along? 'Course ol' Miz Tall Man didn't look none too happy 'bout losin' her slave. Don't reckon she'll be real glad 'bout lettin' you take any thin' with you. And, 'long with my pertection, I'll be sure you don't want for nothin'."

As the reality of her situation began sinking in, Caitlyn glanced at the wigwam, which had been her home for several months. She didn't have much in there—hadn't been able to pack much when she left Pa's cabin. She'd had to depend on Sky Woman's generosity, although she did her share of the work. Now this mountain man was offering her a chance to make another new start.

She believed his promise of protection. She'd lived with these men all her life. Nothing meant more to them than their word—especially if given in an oath as a mountain man. They considered themselves a breed apart from so-called civilized folks, who looked you in the eye and smiled, while they lied and stole you blind.

She shook her head, unconsciously raising her hand to caress the small, leather bound book wrapped in oilskin that rested in her bodice. One day she was going to get someone to read that book to her—or maybe even screw up her courage and ask someone to teach her to read herself, something she and Pa had both yearned for. Then she could see what it said on her own.

"No, nothin'," she told Silas. "And you're right. Sky Woman's not happy about seein' me leave, but it ain't because I'm her slave. She's been pretty good to me. She ain't Tall Man's wife, either. She's his sister, and her and Pa . . . well, a man gets lonesome in the mountains, like Pa used to say. I didn't have anyone else to go to after Pa got killed, it bein' well into the fall and all."

"I see," Silas replied. "And I guess it was Tall Man

who pinned that there moniker on you, when he tried to make you somethin' other than his sister's friend, huh?''

"It wasn't only him," Caitlyn said with a shrug. "I found it was easier to make myself sort of unappealin'. Maybe I ought to see if Sky Woman will let me have my wolf's jaw from my blanket roll, though."

The flap on the wigwam burst open, and Sky Woman came through, slapping at the arm that tried to haul her back inside. She bared her teeth and bit the arm, and it released her. Sky Woman smiled grimly at the yelp of pain that accompanied the arm retreating into the wigwam.

She ran over to Caitlyn and thrust a buckskin-wrapped bundle into her arms. "Take this with you, my daughter," she said in Nez Perce. "It is my gift to you. Soon now, when you find yourself without the desire to hide and instead wish to show your beauty to a man, you will wish to have this."

Caitlyn drew back a corner of the buckskin and gasped. She thrust the bundle back at Sky Woman and shook her head.

"I . . . I can't accept this, my mother," she said in English. "It's the dress you wore when you and Pa. . . . "

Sky Woman closed Caitlyn's hands over the parcel. She replied in Nez Perce again, in the same way she and Caitlyn had carried on many a conversation.

"Do you so soon forget your Indian training, Daughter?" Sky Woman said with a smile. "It is not done—to return a gift. A gift is given with the heart, and you deny the love offered if you return the gift."

"I'm sorry." Caitlyn hung her head. "I . . . oh, Sky Woman, I'm goin' to miss you!"

"And I, you, my daughter. But we will meet again. I feel it here, in my heart, where my love for you will sleep until we find one another again. And the yellow-haired one—the one who thinks he has won you now?"

"What about him, my mother?"

"I see goodness in him, Daughter. He will treat you kindly, as he has done already."

"Yeah," Caitlyn spat without thinking. "And he'll probably be tryin' to get in my britches every time I turn around, just like every other man I've got near since Pa died. Nobody's goin' to tie me down and keep me penned up in a cabin, nursin' babies while they roam the mountains. I grew up here and I aim to die here, where Pa and I were happy.''

Sky Woman reached out and touched Caitlyn's cheek. ''It is not always so when you find love with a man, Daughter. I was happy to wait for Mick to return to me, even without a baby from him to ease my loneliness. It will be so with you some day. You have much love to offer a man who is worthy of you.''

''My love died with Pa,'' Caitlyn said in a flat voice. ''Except for what I've got left for you, I guess. Like I told Pa's friend here, I'll earn my keep. I ain't got much choice, because I ain't got the gear for goin' off to trap on my own right now. But some day I'm goin' to be able to cut free— somehow I'll get back to mine and Pa's cabin, and then I'll have what I need.''

They silently embraced. When Caitlyn reluctantly pulled away from the woman she called mother and joined him, Silas plopped his wolfskin hat back on his head.

''Me and Jon are camped over on the other edge of rendezvous,'' he explained quietly. ''You ready to go?''

''Yes,'' Caitlyn replied. ''I. . . . '' She felt over the bundle as they walked, then paused to look back at the wigwam. Sky Woman had already gone inside, and her furious voice escaped the confines of the buffalo-skin structure as she yelled at Tall Man.

''Somethin' you forgot?'' Silas questioned.

''My wolf's jaw,'' she admitted. ''Sky Woman didn't give it to me with the dress.''

''You won't need it with me and Jon to pertect you,'' Silas assured her as he took her arm and started through the maze of wigwams and camps again. ''We ain't gonna let anyone close enough to try to hurt you.''

But she would be close to these two men, Caitlyn thought to herself. Pa's friend she had no doubts about. Silas—she remembered him now, and the dolly he carved her one year near Christmastime.

The other one, though. Jon. Her neck still tingled where his fingertip had brushed it, and she had opened her eyes in time to see the deadly glint in Jon's when he knocked Tall Man's grip from her chin. He had blue eyes, lighter than her own, reminding her of a clear mountain lake on a summer day.

And she would be in close contact with him, the three of them stuffed into the narrow quarters of a winter cabin for months. There would be barely enough room to move around each other with a man as large as Jon taking up most of the space.

Caitlyn clutched her parcel closer to her chest as they walked. He'd probably make her take a bath, she realized, not entirely unhappy with the thought. She couldn't imagine a man who smelled as good as the one called Jon suffering with the odor clinging to her for long. It offended her own nostrils, too, even if she was the one who'd surreptitiously stolen the glands from the wolverine Tall Man trapped last winter to mix the scent with the mud on her legs from time to time.

Oh, well, she sighed to herself as they approached the small lean-to Jon and Silas had fashioned between two pine trees. Life goes on until a person dies. She had made her adjustments after Pa found her nearly dead of hunger and thirst inside the trading post. She'd even taken Pa's last name, O'Shaunessy, when all she could recall about herself was her first name.

And she'd adjusted when, after years of Pa's loving protectiveness, she had found herself alone again. It hadn't been awfully bad, since she and Pa had lived off and on with the Nez Perce over the years.

Pa had always told her to keep herself free to experience the almost daily new adventures that were part of a mountain man's life—adventures the men lived and breathed for—freedom they would have withered away without.

They'd never discussed the future, even though death was a part of their living. Mountain men died many ways. The Blackfeet were still as wild as ever and would torture to death any man they caught near their hunting grounds—

white or Indian. Seemingly innocuous wounds could fester without proper medication and kill quickly, poisoning a body while he tried to reach a friendly Indian camp for treatment. Snakes, it went without saying. And grizzlies, like the giant that had broken Pa's back with one swipe of a huge paw and carried him off. Heck, she'd even heard of one mountain man who died from a silly old bee sting!

She and Pa had ignored how near death hovered about them in favor of savoring each day they were allowed. Even when Pa fell for Sky Woman, he remained close to her. He probably figured Sky Woman had told her all about the business between a man and woman, she supposed, but Sky Woman hadn't mentioned it. Instead, she had taught Caitlyn by her actions—her caressing touches when she passed Pa, her eyes following him, glowing with her feelings.

When Silas took her arm and pulled her to a stop on the edge of the camp, Caitlyn studied the figure crouched in front of the fire. Jon favored a red, woolen cap over the animal fur hats most of the men donned in the cool, evening mountain air, and his blond hair curled beneath it, falling almost to his shoulders. She'd already noticed that his body put even most of the Indian men she had seen to shame— a flat belly and wider shoulders than any she had ever laid eyes on before. Most of the mountain men she ran across usually had a paunch, even the young ones, attesting to a liking for whiskey or rum.

She'd had a chance to look at his face while he crouched over the bones. It was pleasingly free of a beard, like many mountain men cultivated, and he must use some scent after he shaved. His profile had reminded her of a picture of a man in one of the rare books she and Pa had run across in their travels. The man had been standing in the front of a strange-looking ship with a curved prow, the head of a woman decorating it.

She had dreamed about that man a time or two lately, and it had almost been like her dream stood before her when she first looked upon Jon. It had taken every bit of will power she could muster to calm the flutter in her heart.

She hadn't yet decided what the warmth she felt in her belly meant.

"You might as well come on in," Jon growled over his shoulder. "I can smell that the two of you must be close."

Chapter Two

Surprised at the stab of hurt Jon's words caused, Caitlyn dropped her bundle and pulled away from Silas to stride over to the fire.

"Well, I can smell you, too," she said as she propped her hands on her hips and glared at him. "You better not wear that stuff when you're tryin' to kill some meat. Any animal with a lick of sense could smell you comin' two miles away and hightail it for safety!"

Jon surged to his feet. "You're speaking English! Where did you learn that?"

"Far as I know, I've always been able to speak it," Caitlyn said, for some reason nettled even more at his surprise. "I can also speak Nez Perce, Sioux, Crow and a smatterin' of a few other Indian tongues. I'll bet that's more than you can speak."

"I'm fluent in French and Latin, and I can also read and translate German, as well as Spanish. It's not the pidgin Spanish spoken here in the United States, though. And I converse quite adequately in Italian, too."

"Well, now," Caitlyn said, considering. "Might be

some of that French would help you out here in the mountains. Lots of it's been mixed into the Indian languages.
You might as well use the rest of it to entertain yourself
while you're runnin' a trap line, for all the good it is.''

Jon suddenly wrinkled his nose and stepped away from
her. ''Do you understand the meaning of the words in those
languages you speak? For instance, clean? You're not
spending one night in this camp unless you take a bath
first.''

''I plan to,'' Caitlyn returned huffily. ''As soon as you
lend me a bar of soap.''

Ignoring her, Jon turned an imploring glance on Silas.
''Silas, couldn't you have found someone to take her off
our hands on your way back here?''

''Ain't that simple, Jon. Couple things you ought to
know, and I'll explain them to you after we get Cat over
to the pond for her bath.''

''Cat?''

''Cat O'Shaunessy, meet Jonathan Edward Clay,'' Silas
introduced. ''Just call him Jon, though. He ain't been out
here long enough to earn himself a proper moniker.''

''Oh, you mean like they call you 'Swift Feet'
sometimes?'' Jon said somewhat scornfully. ''Thanks but
I'll stick to Jon. And what kind of name's Cat?''

Silas threw him as haughty a look as he could manage
through all the hair on his face. ''I earned my moniker all
by myself, after I outran a whole pack of Blackfeet one
fall. And Cat's short for Caitlyn, the adopted daughter of
an old and close partner of mine, now dead and gone. You
watch your mouth 'round her, boyo, 'cause I've promised
her my pertection in memory of her dead pa.''

''You?'' Jon asked in an astonished voice. ''I thought I
was the one who won her at bones.''

''No one *won* me,'' Caitlyn informed him. ''I wasn't a
slave to be traded away to begin with. You should've asked
Tall Man what the deal was when he drug me out there.''

''I tried. . . . ''

''Not hard enough,'' Caitlyn informed him smugly.
''You should've made sure just exactly who I was before

you squatted down to shake again. You'd have found out Tall Man was playin' his own game with you—tryin' to win back some of his loot by lettin' you think you'd get me if you won.''

"Silas?" Jon questioned.

"She's right, boyo. I didn't recognize Cat at first, otherwise I might've been a little more careful 'bout the whole deal. 'Course that likker we'd been downin' all day might've had somethin' to do with us not bein' as suspicious as we should've been.''

Jon turned abruptly away and strode over to the lean-to. Ducking inside, he rummaged around in the darkness, then stuck his head back out.

"Bring me one of those branches from the fire so I can see in here, Silas," he called.

"You ain't gonna stick a burnin' branch inside our sleepin' place," Silas called back. "Might catch it on fire, and it's too danged late to have to build another one!"

Jon shrugged and reached inside to drag out both their packs. He dug in his and pulled something out, tossing it to one side, then reaching in again.

Silas and Caitlyn stood silently while he pulled everything he had won from Tall Man out of one pack, then dug in Silas's until he uncovered his elderly partner's spare britches and tossed them on the pile.

"Where's your extra shirt, Silas?" he asked over his shoulder.

"Don't have one," Silas replied. " 'Member, I left that piece of rag at the stream where we washed afore we came on in to rendezvous. What do you want it for, anyway? And what are you gonna do with my britches?"

"She sure can't wear mine," Jon spat. "Here." He grabbed the fine linen shirt he'd worn when he left Virginia and laid it on the pile. Rising, he gestured at the goods at his feet.

"There, Silas. There's clothing and soap and everything I won off that sneaky Indian. She can have it all and buy herself a place with some other crew. You said we could get some new clothing made by the Indian women while we were here, and I'll pay for your new britches out of my share of the furs.''

"Jon, Jon," Silas said with a smirk. "You haven't been listenin'. Cat ain't no slave to be traded from man to man. Fact is, she's not even Indian—she's white as you and me. And I done told you she's under my pertection.''

"Silas . . . !''

"Boyo, you weren't this mouthy all winter. Hell, I couldn't get more'n a word or two out of you at a time. Sure is gonna cut into the peace and quiet I so admire, you keep chatterin' like this from now on. Reckon you wanna give them things to Cat, that's a good idear, though. She's gonna need some things maybe we won't think of, and she can trade for them herself.''

"You're serious, aren't you?" Jon asked. "You really are going to take her with us into the mountains this winter!''

"It's what I been tellin' you, Jon. Now, come along so's we can make sure Cat don't get disturbed while she takes her bath.''

Jon stared at his partner, resolutely ignoring the tattered ragamuffin at Silas's side. If Silas thought he was going to stand close while that little package of contradictions turned herself from five feet of stinking refuse into a clean, soft-skinned, sexy. . . .

Jon's fist clenched at his side, and he rubbed the back of the finger that had touched Caitlyn's neck against his buck-skin-clad leg. How the heck did he have any idea what was under all that dirt? His other hand, which had examined Caitlyn's arm, started tingling, and he wiped it across the front of his shirt.

"You. . . . '' Jon cleared his throat and licked a dry tongue around his lips. Damn, he wanted another drink. "You don't need me," he said. "You just said she's under your protection. Well, you go protect her while she bathes.''

"Four eyes are better than two, Jon," Silas said as he walked over and dug through the pile Jon had gathered, searching for the soap. "Must be over two thousand trappers and Indians here. You don't 'spect me to keep an eye on all of 'em alone, do you?''

"Just give me one of them guns," Caitlyn put in. "I can protect myself."

Jon shot her a disgusted look. Their buffalo guns were as long as she was tall. A little thing like her probably couldn't even lift one.

She shifted her feet, then casually rubbed her legs together, as though the mud bothered her and itched. Her nose wrinkled, too. Good, maybe she had caught a whiff of herself.

"Dash darn it anyway," she said with a stamp of her foot, "make up your minds!" Lifting her foot, she curled it against the back of her leg, flinching when her toenails scraped against the crust of mud. Off balance, she staggered a step toward the fire.

Jon instinctively leapt forward and caught her, whirling her a safe distance from the flames. Damn it, on top of smelling bad, she was clumsy!

Funny, though. The breath that feathered across his face when she turned a grateful gaze up to him didn't stink—it held a hint of mint. Through the slightly parted lips, he could see the straight, white teeth Tall Man had wanted him to examine. And, yes, above that pert nose, blue eyes, not Indian brown—blue eyes that could change color, he thought to himself in awe as those eyes darkened to indigo and he heard her teeth clamp shut with a snap.

"Thank you," Cat growled through clenched teeth. "Now, you've got a half-second to get them damn paws off me before I kick you where it'll make you sing a few high notes until you heal!"

Jon jerked his hand from the rip in her dress, where his fingers had been caressing a smooth, silky back. "Damn it," he snarled. "You're about the most ungrateful piece of baggage I've ever run across."

"You just keep your hands to yourself," Caitlyn spat back in reply. "You ain't brought enough furs in for *that*, even if you offered them all to me! Like I told Pa's friend there, I bed down alone."

"*That*? Good grief, woman, I'd as soon bed down in a buffalo wallow with a wolverine," Jon denied in a half-lie. Touching the silky skin beneath that buckskin dress had already caused a reaction in his groin, but thank goodness the buckskin fringe on his shirt hung down over his thighs. That fringe was good for more than shedding water, as Silas had informed him. But when he made the mistake of a visual check to assure himself, Caitlyn smirked.

"There's always women for hire over on the other side of the rendezvous camp," she said in a snide voice.

Silas's roar of laughter split the air and Jon whirled around to see his partner with his head thrown back. A fiery blush spread over his face, stealing down his neck and even over his shoulders under the buckskin shirt.

He drew a hand across his face, then glared at Caitlyn. "Go get your damned bath! And while you're doing it, think about this! If you keep going around making remarks not proper for a female, some man's going to take you up on it—see just whether or not you know as much as you've been spouting off about!"

"There ain't a whole lot of room in a wigwam, and Pa and I never built a cabin bigger than we needed just to keep the snow off us in winter," Caitlyn said with a shrug. "And sometimes Sky Woman would spend a week or so at the cabin with us. I reckon I know enough to keep my body my own. Let some snortin', snufflin' man too close, you end up saddled with a baby to take care of, though Sky Woman was lucky enough that didn't happen to her."

"There you go again!" Jon shouted. "Didn't I just tell you remarks like that aren't proper conversation for a woman to make?"

"Why not?" Caitlyn asked, a truly puzzled look on her face.

"Because they make a man think of things better kept off his mind!" Jon said in exasperation. "What the heck have I been telling you?"

Caitlyn frowned and cocked her head to one side. "You mean, I wouldn't have needed to smear this mud all over me? If I'd just have kept my mouth shut and not let those men know that I knew why they were tryin' to get in my britches, they would have left me alone?''

Silas bit back another guffaw and thrust a bar of soap into Caitlyn's hand. ''I wouldn't go that far, Cat,'' he said as Jon turned away with an irritated moan. ''You gotta remember, Ol' Mick had himself a reputation in these here mountains. No man was gonna try anything with you while he was alive, leastways not if they figured Mick would find out. He'd've hunted them down and they'd've wished they'd been caught by the Blackfeet instead, by the time Mick got done killin' them inch by inch.''

''Then why's he tryin' to tell me . . . ?''

A blush stole over Silas's face. ''How 'bout we have a visit with Sky Woman afore we leave, Cat? Jon's right 'bout it not bein' proper for a man and woman to be discussin' such. You can ask Sky Woman your questions and let her explain it to you. Just try to remember that there's different kinds of men around. Most of 'em got a lot of respect for a woman and would sooner die themselves than hurt a female, but there's others who ain't so particular.''

''Wish I knew where that 'most of them with respect's' been hidin','' Caitlyn grumbled. ''Guess I'll ask Sky Woman about that, too. Now, are we goin' to get me that bath or not?''

''We damned sure are!'' Jon tramped over to the lean-to and picked up his long rifle. Without a glance at his companions, he strode off through the clump of trees toward where he and Silas had found an old beaver dam still partially holding back a stream from the mountains. Ears sharpened by his past months in the wilderness, he soon picked out the sounds of footsteps following him from among the rustles of night creatures scurrying away at his approach.

The haunting cry of a wolf echoed from a nearby hillside, answered almost at once from the opposite ridge. Jon's fingers instinctively tightened on his rifle, though Silas had told him wolves avoided men—except maybe near the end of winter, when they had empty bellies from poor hunting. The sound nearly always sent a prickle up his spine,

though, and he glanced toward the hilltop, trying to pin-
point the source from among the echoes rebounding around
him.

An ebony sky spread out before his gaze, dotted with
diamond pinpricks until it lightened to charcoal where the
moon was rising. Beyond those faintly-outlined hilltops sat
the mountains where he had spent the winter. Grudgingly
he admitted to himself that he might never have made it
out of there to rendezvous this summer if not for Silas.
Somewhere in that rugged expanse, he had left the cocksure
young man who rode out of Virginia in a rage and found
instead new strengths and attitudes in himself, thanks in
part to Silas.

Now Silas expected him to ignore all the plans they had
made together the last few weeks and accept Silas's "pertection" of that . . . that *kid*, he decided to call her in his
mind. What else could you call a child-woman, who
seemed stuck halfway between acknowledging her own developed body and simple-minded naivete over her effect on
the male population?

His booted foot slipped on a round stone, and Jon cursed
softly under his breath as he righted himself.

"Guess I ain't the only clumsy one," he heard Caitlyn
say behind him.

"Been tryin' to get him into moccasins," Silas replied.
"Maybe you can make him some. Them boots he's got on
are 'bout wore through."

"I can make him some, if you've got some deerskins
with your furs. I probably made me and Pa a hundred or
more pairs over the years. Rabbit or wolf fur's good to line
them with for wintertime."

"Don't catch too many wolves in our traps," Silas said
with a sly look at her. "They're too smart. You'll have to
make do with rabbit, and they ain't got such big jaws."

Caitlyn joined Silas's snickers, and Jon clenched his
teeth over his irritation. The two of them were already acting as though they'd known each other all their lives, effectively excluding him from their mutual easiness with
each other. The hell with them. Maybe he'd just take his

share of furs and get his own outfit for the winter—go on back into the mountains alone. Plenty of trappers led a solitary life without a partner, or so he'd heard.

He had come to love the peace and serenity of the mountains as much as Silas claimed to this past winter. The quiet stillness—air so pure it hurt you to breathe it. Always on the plantation, even at night, sounds disrupted the silence. Horses and cows neighed or lowed. Dogs barked at imagined intruders. Traces of smoke lingered in the air from the smokehouse and blacksmith forge.

And those trips into nearby Richmond. Once he hadn't even noticed the smell from slop buckets dumped into the gutters or the stench from overflowing spittoons in the taverns. But the subconscious memories, set now against the contradiction of the splendor of the mountains, almost made him wonder what the pull in Richmond had been. Besides Roxie.

Jon stopped beside the beaver pond and silently studied the surroundings, assuring himself they were alone. Even his eyes had sharpened over the past months, he realized as he found himself easily able to differentiate between what could have been a man standing beside a tree and the knotted bulge on the trunk it actually was. Satisfied there were no intruders—animal or human—to interfere with that little scamp scraping off those gobs of muck, he turned to see Caitlyn already slipping one arm free from the sleeve of her dress.

Caitlyn froze and tossed him an angry glance. "You were all right just like you were standin'. I didn't come out here to put on a show for you."

A whisper of moonlight glanced from alabaster skin, and Jon choked back a groan. The stupid little minx didn't even have the decency to pull her dress back up over the hint of fullness it had dropped below. Instead, she clutched the fingers of one hand in the sleeve on the opposite side of her body and just stood there!

"Where the hell's Silas?"

"Back over there," Caitlyn said with a short movement

of her head. "Where you're goin' to be before I make another move."

"Think so, huh?" Jon muttered under his breath.

With no warning, he dropped his rifle and surged forward. Disregarding Caitlyn's scream of rage, he grabbed her in his arms and strode to the edge of the pond. With her arms effectively penned in his grasp, her legs wildly bucking against his hold, he stood for a moment by the water.

"You flop-eared son of a knock-kneed jackass!" Caitlyn screamed. "Take your damned hands off me!"

"Gladly!" Jon shouted. With a heave, he tossed her into the water.

"Now!" he yelled when she bobbed to the surface, spitting and sputtering and wiping at her eyes. "Don't even think about coming out of there until you're clean! Here!"

He reached down and grabbed the bar of soap from the pile of clothing Caitlyn had dropped on the bank, then tossed it at her. It hit her between her breasts, and Caitlyn reflexively grabbed it with one hand. Stomping over to his rifle, he bent down just as something whizzed over his head and landed with a thunk against the pine tree ahead of him.

Jon stood and looked down at the bar of soap by his feet for a second. Shrugging his shoulders, he left it lying there and walked away.

"That soap's not going to do you any good out here," he called over his shoulder. "Best you haul your fanny out of that pond and get it yourself. But if I don't hear you in that water again in thirty seconds flat, I'll throw you back myself! And you won't get out again until I've made sure you're clean with my own hands!"

Caitlyn bit back the oath before it could escape her mouth, teeth worrying her bottom lip as her rage faded into panic. He sounded like he meant it. Surely he wouldn't . . . a man didn't wash a woman. Not this woman, anyway.

Shivering horribly, she splashed out of the water and over to the pine tree. Grabbing the soap, she stared at the spot where Jon had joined Silas to stand watch. She could hear the murmur of their voices and supposed Jon was explaining his cockamamie actions of a moment ago. Her fingers gripped the soap until it threatened to squirt out of her hand, and she clenched her teeth in renewed anger.

"I haven't heard you get back in that water yet!"

Caitlyn gasped and scurried to the pond. She splashed into the water, raising her knees higher than necessary and bringing her feet back down with enough force to send waves away from her—and make plenty of noise. At least her movements warmed her body, contrasting with the frigid water. When the water reached her waist, she paused and turned around.

Tentatively, eyes glued on the two figures protecting her to make sure they kept their backs to her, Caitlyn slipped off her dress and tossed it toward the bank. It landed on the rock she had slipped the leather-bound book beneath just before she'd started to undress a moment ago. With a sigh of pleasure, she laid back in the water, luxuriating in the silky feel of it and the weightlessness of her body.

She could feel the gobs of dirt washing away, freeing her legs to kick more easily. The desire for cleanliness, which she had trained her mind to ignore, crept over her.

Caitlyn curved her body and disappeared beneath the surface, imitating the otters she had watched. Legs kicking like scissors and arms moving smoothly, she pulled herself through the liquid silkiness until she had to surface for breath. She cast a surreptitious look toward Jon and Silas. The moonlight gave enough illumination for her to tell their backs were still toward her.

Somewhat reluctantly, Caitlyn swam into shallower water and stood. She lathered the soap between her palms, transferring the lather to her hair. When she was satisfied with the amount of lather in her raven locks, she tossed the soap to the bank and worked her fingers through the black mass of tangles.

Caitlyn retrieved the soap two more times before she felt her hair was sufficiently clean, then plodded through the water to sit on the bank and finish the remainder of her body.

"Silas, I don't care how much older or more experienced than me you think you are," Jon repeated. "It won't cause anything but trouble. Hell, I'll take some cooking lessons, if that's what's bothering you."

"It ain't just the cookin', Jon. Thought we talked about this afore. I'm gettin' old, yeah, and I'm lots older than you. That means I gotta start thinkin' 'bout how I'm gonna take care of myself when I can't trap all winter. I ain't never been able to bring in enough furs to much more than buy myself a new outfit for the next winter. Danged traps break and have to be replaced. Cost forty dollars, they do! You know how many furs it takes to make forty dollars to buy a new trap?"

"Yeah," Jon admitted. "You told me. Thirteen or fourteen, depending on the quality of the furs."

"And that's if you can buy enough traps. Told you, too, the traders got a limit on the number of traps each man can buy, so's it's fair for everyone. Cat's got her own traps in that there cabin she and Mick built. With the three of us, we can run the lines more often—get the skins quicker and not lose as many to varmints. Have help tannin' 'em, too. Be a lot more earnin's for all three of us come next summer."

"You're actually going to ask a woman to help run the traplines? You're out of your mind. You know how dangerous it can be. There's grizzlies and wolves out there. Wolverines. And what about those blizzards that come up without warning? You got lost yourself for almost a week last winter and were half-starved when you got back to camp."

"Cat's run lines with Mick almost since she could walk," Silas informed him. "She grew up in these here mountains, and bet she knows as much as me 'bout takin' care of herself. But who said anythin' about her runnin' lines? She can stay at the cabin, cook the food, tan the hides. Leave us free for other things."

"It makes sense when you put it like that," Jon admitted. "But what about her and me? You can tell neither one of us likes the other. We've been spitting and snarling at each other all evening. What about that peace and quiet you value so highly?''

''We'll be out runnin' lines most of the time, Jon. You won't have to put up with her much. And think how rich we'll be after a couple winters of bringin' in twice as many furs as any other trappers.''

''A *couple* winters! Silas, we haven't even made it through this one yet!''

''Hey!'' Caitlyn called. ''I hate to interrupt, but there's a puma cat lyin' on that rock just above your heads!''

Chapter Three

Silas let out a whoop and dived under the ledge beside them.

"Move, boyo!" he shouted when he saw Jon crouched in the open, his rifle aimed at the rocks above him.

The rifle spit fire, drowning out Silas's shout. A tawny body tumbled toward Jon, amid a shower of rocks and small boulders gathering in the body's path. Jon awkwardly tried to fling himself aside, but one rock ricocheted from the ledge and hit him squarely on the head. He crumpled to the ground, the puma's dead weight landing on his legs.

Caitlyn screamed in dismay and grabbed the white shirt from the pile of clothing as she raced past. Shrugging into it as she ran, she clasped it around her body, her feet flying as she crossed the distance separating her from Jon and Silas.

"He . . . he ain't dead, is he?" she asked Silas as soon as she stopped beside him.

"Who? Him or the puma?"

"I can see the puma's dead, darn it!"

Jon moaned and tossed his head, answering her question.

Between the two of them, Caitlyn and Silas managed to haul the puma off Jon's legs. As soon as he was free, Caitlyn hurried to examine the wound on Jon's head. She found herself staring into his face and froze in her tracks.

"Go get your damned clothes on!" Jon spat at her.

Caitlyn clutched her fist at the neck of the shirt and returned his glare. "I'd have been dressed by now, if you hadn't been stupid enough to shoot at a puma in the dark!"

Jon struggled into a sitting position, shoving away the small pebbles in his lap. "What was I supposed to do? Let it come down here and attack us? You'd have made a pretty sight trying to get away from that lion in the water!"

"Don't you know anythin'?" Caitlyn shook her head. "Pumas hate water, unless they have to swim for some reason. And it would have run away as soon as it knew we'd spotted it. Fact is, it was leapin' away when you shot. I saw it."

Jon gritted his teeth, staring at her, and she froze. His blue eyes traveled over her, and she could literally feel the path they took. They dropped to her bare feet, slithered up her legs and lingered on that place below her belly. They wrenched upward, but instead of climbing to her face, they caught on the fist, where she held the shirt together. They slid to one side of the fist, then the other, lingering over her wet breasts.

Her legs shook, and she glanced down at herself, eyes widening in horror when she saw the shirt clinging wetly to every part of her. With a gasp, she ran back toward the pond, her shaky legs pummeling and her heart pounding in reaction. Grabbing the pile of clothing and linen bath sheet, she scurried behind a pine tree.

Silas chuckled loudly and knelt beside Jon. "Boyo, you sure it ain't somethin' besides *dislike* that's settin' off the sparks a'tween you two?"

"What the hell's that supposed to mean?"

"Nothin'. Nothin'," Silas said with a laugh. " 'Spect the two of you'll work it out sooner or later. Here. Let me see that there head."

Jon flinched when Silas's fingers touched his head, then

rigidly took hold of himself and allowed Silas to probe around the cut. He could feel the blood seeping out and his scalp was already tightening from the knot swelling against it. Distastefully eyeing the puma that had caused the whole ruckus, he tried to concentrate on it while Silas checked the gash on his head. At least it kept his mind off what was going on behind that damned pine tree.

"You're gonna have a sore head for a day or two," Silas mused, "but I've seen worse over the years. We'd best go down to that there pond and wash this out."

"Like hell," Jon muttered. "You bring our *guest* back to camp and I'll go on ahead. I brought some water in earlier, and I'll wash this out back there."

"Whatever you say, boyo," Silas said as he rose. "Best let me load your rifle afore you go. Won't be safe to be trampin' 'round these hills with an empty gun, though probably ain't nothin' left to bother us after that shot."

"What about the lion?" Jon asked as he stood up, swaying slightly and grasping a tentative hand to his sore head.

"I'll come back and skin it after I bring Cat to camp. Ain't a real good pelt this time of year, but no sense lettin' it go to waste."

Silas reached down and picked up Jon's rifle, reloading it from his own powder and shot pouch. He handed it to Jon, a worried look on his face.

"You sure you can make it back all right? Times I've seen a head wound kick up worse a while after it happens."

"I'll be fine," Jon assured him. "You just be careful around that little scamp we got stuck with. Seems like she's caused nothing but trouble since Tall Man drug her out of that wigwam. Hope you make it back to camp in one piece, none of your legs or arms broken."

"She sure is a distractin' little thing, ain't she?" Silas agreed in definite contradiction to Jon's meaning. "Even at my age, it brings back memories."

Jon snorted in disgust and tramped away.

Silas waited until he saw Caitlyn emerge from behind the tree, fully dressed, then walked down to meet her.

Lordy, she was a little beauty, even in that outlandish outfit. Her hair curled wildly now that it was washed, though it still needed a good combing. The white shirt clung in places, but the arid mountain air would dry it quickly. It fell well below her knees, and beneath it, the pantlegs of his old britches were rolled up above trim ankles.

"You feel better now?" he asked.

"Well, I feel clean, at least," Caitlyn replied. "And hungry. We left Sky Woman's wigwam before I had supper."

Silas eyed her indecisively for a second. There wasn't much back at camp to eat—he and Jon had planned to visit one of the eating tents. But he wasn't about to take her with him, especially with her looking like she did and a few hundred drunk trappers wandering around.

"Uh . . . how 'bout you wait at camp and I'll take our plates over to one of the tents and get them filled? Someone needs to keep an eye on Jon," he quickly added when he saw the mutinous look on her face. "You know well's I do that rock might've done more damage than it 'pears to've at first."

"I suppose," Caitlyn said with a sigh. "But he ain't goin' to be too happy about me bein' the one left to watch over him. Maybe I ought to go get the food."

"Not on your life," Silas said grimly. "Come on now."

Caitlyn gathered up her old, ragged dress, surreptitiously slipping her hand beneath the rock to pull out the journal and wrap it among the folds. She followed Silas back down the trail, her apprehension growing with every step.

This wasn't turning out to be one of her better ideas. Darn, it had seemed like the perfect opportunity at first. She'd only gone along with Tall Man's plan because it would give her a chance to break free from him and get back into the mountains. She had enough sense to realize she couldn't make it on her own, and she had earned her way while she stayed with Sky Woman. It really chafed her sometimes how the Indian men expected their women to do all the work—saving themselves for hunting and protecting the women and children, they called it.

Caitlyn snorted softly, and Silas glanced over his shoulder.

"Somethin' wrong?"

"No. Just thinkin'," Caitlyn replied.

And lordy, lordy, she was getting tired of thinking. Dash darn it, it made her head hurt, especially when those dark thoughts tried to push out of the corner where she kept them locked away. Pa had always told her to never mind about them—he'd taken care of her like a baby the few times she woke up petrified with terror, screaming in the night. She wished she could feel those huge old arms around her just one more time.

The mountains always healed her, though. The rugged, wild, peaceful mountains. Beauty so wondrous it almost hurt her eyes sometimes to look at it. How she had resented it five years ago when the mountain grapevine told Pa about the idea William Henry Ashley had of setting up a central place where the trappers could bring in their furs all at once and trade. Rendezvous, they called it.

A drunken, month-long binge was more like it. The only tribe that didn't show up was the Blackfeet. Games of chance sprang up at the drop of a hat—the best shot, the best with a knife. Heck, last year they'd even bet on whose beard was the longest.

And those tall tales she heard around the camp fires at night: Old Gabe, Jim Bridger, and that yarn about a salty lake west of them that a man could almost walk across. That place they called Colter's Hell, because John Colter insisted he had seen bubbling caldrons and a fountain of water gushing up from the ground at such regular intervals that he could set his pocket watch by it.

A haunting melody drifted on the wind from a nearby camp, and Caitlyn paused as she recognized the lovely strains of the "Wayfaring Stranger" lament. She even recognized the voice—old Tom Snafferty, another of Pa's friends. That was probably Dick Adkins with his fiddle, playing along.

Friendships were forged at rendezvous, too, Caitlyn admitted to herself. Lasting friendships between men who only saw each other once a year, yet would give their lives for one of their own. She just hoped Tom didn't decide to sing "Greensleeves," Pa's favorite. Her pain over Pa's death might overwhelm her again if that happened.

"Cat, come over here! I need help!"

Caitlyn swung around toward Silas's voice, her face creasing in concern when she saw Silas trying to lift Jon's body from the log it lay draped across. Flinging aside her bundle, she ran over and grabbed one of Jon's arms, straining to assist Silas until they had Jon propped up, his back against the log.

"Go get that buff'ler hide out of the lean-to," Silas said with a grunt as he caught Jon when he slipped sideways. "Gotta cushion his head."

Caitlyn returned with the robe in record time, and Silas pushed Jon forward into her arms while he adjusted the hide behind Jon's back. Caitlyn gritted her teeth and braced herself on her knees, her slender figure trying desperately to counteract the dead weight. Jon's head lolled on her shoulder, his blond hair wafting against her nose when she took a deep breath against the strain.

Caitlyn sneezed, then tightened her grip on the broad shoulders. Just in time, Silas turned around and helped her position Jon against the buffalo robe.

"What's wrong with him?" Caitlyn asked in a worried voice.

"Must be that there knock on the head," Silas replied. "I warned him this might happen."

Caitlyn's eyes fell on the whiskey jug sitting beside the overturned water pail a few feet away. "Yeah," she said. "Or maybe that there liquor bottle there!"

Silas reached across Jon and picked up the jug. He shook it once, then set it back down at his side.

"Naw. There's just as much in it as when we left for your bath. We're gonna have to get him awake."

"Awake? Just let him sleep, until he gets better."

"Don't work that way, Cat. I picked up a little doctorin' over the years, like I reckon you have. Man gets hit on the head, he ain't supposed to sleep for a while. Supposed to

stay awake, 'til he's sure his sleep don't become permanent.''

"If you say so," Caitlyn agreed doubtfully.

Silas patted his palm against Jon's cheek, calling softly
to his friend, "Jon. Jon, boyo, wake up."

Jon moaned and turned his head away from the hand.

"Come on, boyo," Silas said, shaking Jon's shoulders.
"Wake up."

Caitlyn picked up the wooden water bucket and peered
inside. An inch or so of water remained, and she lifted the
bucket, dribbling the liquid onto Jon's face. He grunted and
swiped at his nose, and she quickly hid the bucket behind
her back when his eyes opened.

"What . . . what are you doing, Silas? Trying to drown
me?" Jon grumbled.

"Just tryin' to get you awake, partner," Silas told him.
"Told you to watch out for that there wound. Don't want
you driftin' off now for a while."

"Look, I'm tired . . ."

"You listen to me, son," Silas said. "We got us some
plans, 'member? You ain't gonna be no good to me laying
beneath a pile of rocks so the buzzards can't pick your
bones."

"I'm not hurt that bad."

"How'd you end up tryin' to sleep laid across that there
log, then?"

"I . . . I don't remember," Jon admitted. "I was trying
to wash my hair—get the blood out of it. Then everything
went black."

Caitlyn stepped closer, reaching out to examine his head.
"You're still bleedin'," she said in a voice softened with
worry.

Jon swiftly turned his head toward her, giving a moan
when the movement obviously sent stabs of pain pounding
through him. She drew her hand back, and he opened his
eyes, blinking them a couple of times as though to clear
his vision. Her frown of concern deepened as she realized
he was having problems seeing, and she carefully brushed
the blood-matted hair apart to peer at the wound.

"It's goin' to need a stitch or two," she murmured in an anxious voice. "Do you have a needle and thread, Silas?"

"Yeah, but you'll have to do it, Cat. Don't bother me none to work on animals, but puts my stomach in an uproar to even think of sewin' on human skin."

Her stomach clenched, but she nodded her head. Jon squinted his eyes again, then lifted a hand towards her. She started to clasp it in comfort, but he swayed dizzily and fell back against the buffalo robe.

"Stay still," Caitlyn ordered as she rose to her feet. "I'll be right back."

"You're not sticking a needle in my—" He made one attempt to rise, but his eyes rolled back in his head and his body went limp.

Chapter Four

"Silas, he's passed out again."

"Yeah. Maybe we should leave him for a minute, Cat, 'til we get him stitched up. Then I'll wake him again. There's another bucket of water over by the fire there."

Caitlyn filled a pan and set it to heat before she picked up the water bucket and retrieved the damp linen bath sheet and soap, then returned to Jon's side. With Silas steadying Jon, she cleaned the wound thoroughly.

"Hand me that liquor jug," she said as she patted the bath sheet over Jon's head.

"Don't use it all," Silas ordered as he passed the jug to her. "Stuff costs two arms and a leg out here."

"Harumph!"

When Caitlyn tipped the jug and poured the whiskey over the wound, Jon's eyes flew open and he let out a howl of pain. She quickly fixed an innocent expression on her face and passed the jug back across Jon's chest to Silas.

"What the hell are you trying to do?" Jon yelled at Silas when he could focus his gaze. "That rotgut's probably worse than dirt in a cut!"

"You're right, boyo," Silas said with a smirk. He lifted the jug and took a deep pull. "It's better in a man's stomach than on his head."

Silas chuckled again and stood. "Seein' as how you're awake again, you oughta be able to brace yourself on your own while Cat finishes up. I'm gonna fetch us some food."

"Not before you fetch the needle and thread," Caitlyn informed him. "Drop it in that pan of water over there first. No tellin' where it's been."

Silas scratched his beard and took another pull from the jug. "Oh, yeah, now I 'member. It's tucked away in my shavin' kit."

"Shaving kit?" Jon blurted in astonishment. "You don't even own a shaving kit."

"Sure I do, boyo. What you think we used all winter to scrape them hides with?"

Silas trudged over to the lean-to and dug in his pack. He gave a satisfied grunt and pulled out a deerskin pouch. After untying the drawstring knot, he removed another, smaller piece of deerskin and unwrapped it. Striding over to the fire, he dropped the needle and thread into the simmering water.

"Silas," Caitlyn called before Silas could walk away. "Leave that jug."

"What for?"

"To use on that needle, too. It might take more than water to get the dirt off that thread."

Silas sighed deeply and set the jug down, then reached for an empty iron kettle. Carrying the kettle with him, he walked back to the lean-to and picked up the smallest bundle of furs lying there.

"I'll be back shortly with some food," he said when he looked over at Caitlyn to see her studying him.

"Yeah, and from the size of that fur bundle, you'll probably have another jug with you," she said with a frown.

"Need plenty of likker 'round," Silas informed her with a grin. "Case you find any more dirt to chase away."

Whistling merrily, Silas strode from the camp.

"We'll probably have to go fetch our own food," Caitlyn muttered as she turned back to Jon. "That might be the last we see of him tonight."

"Leave him be, Caitlyn. He worked hard as hell for those furs all winter. Guess he can spend them on whatever he wants."

"You ain't tellin' me anythin' I don't know. I spent thirteen winters helping Pa scrape together bundles of furs. Just seems like there ought to be a little more to it than only gettin' enough to go back and start doin' it all over again. And the name's Cat."

"You looked like Cat fit you before." His eyes lingered on her. "Now you look more like a Caitlyn. I'll bet you didn't even know that your full name means pure."

"Ain't interested," Caitlyn said, trying to ignore the blue eyes that appraised her appreciatively. "You're bleedin' again. We'd best get that wound closed up."

"Bring that jug back, too," Jon said as she rose. "If there's anything left in it."

Caitlyn reluctantly did as he ordered, handing him the jug and dumping the water from the pan so she wouldn't burn her fingers when she reached in for the needle. When Jon lowered the jug from his mouth, she took it and poured a few drops of whiskey onto the needle.

"You ready?" she asked.

"In a second." Jon took the jug and drained the last swallow before he laid his head back and shut his eyes tightly.

"All right."

Caitlyn brushed at his wet hair, then moved away.

"Now what?" Jon said as his eyes flew open.

"I can't see."

She pulled a branch from the fire and brought it back with her, wedging it into a crack in the log, close enough so the flickering flames gave light for her to see the angry gash on his head. He flinched away from the heat, and Caitlyn sighed and wrapped her fingers around the side of his face to drag his head back.

"How do you keep your hands so soft?" Jon asked in a

gruff voice after Caitlyn released his face to knot the thread on the end of the needle.

"Somethin' Sky Woman showed me to use. She knows lots about the plants and healin' uses for them. It's good for all parts of a person's body."

Jon groaned and raised his left leg, bumping Caitlyn's elbow with his knee. Slitting his eyes a crack, he glanced at his lap and the fringe on his shirt.

"You're goin' to have to hold still," Caitlyn fumed, resisting the temptation to let him know she was aware of his reaction to her closeness again. "Unless you want your scalp sewed to your eyelid!"

He clenched his fists and clamped his eyes shut again. "Just get on with it!"

"Dash nab it, that's what I'm tryin' to do!"

Despite the sternness in her voice, Caitlyn parted Jon's hair with gentle fingers and pricked his skin with the needle. She probably should have shaved a little of the hair away, she realized, but she managed to get two fairly neat stitches in the wound, leaving the thread hanging loose. Bending forward, she snapped the thread with her teeth and leaned back to drop the needle into the pan again so it wouldn't get lost. Needles were scarcer than hen's teeth in the mountains.

Jon opened his eyes just as Caitlyn turned and leaned over him again, then clamped them closed again. "I thought you were done," he gritted.

"Have to tie the thread. Just be a second."

One eye peeped open all on its own. The other one quickly followed. Jon clenched his teeth over the tongue trying to flick from his mouth, toward that tantalizing breast. A long, fragrant lock of silkiness fell across his face, and he curled his toes inside his boots.

"Shit," he muttered.

"Sorry," Caitlyn said as she sat back on her haunches. "I know it probably hurts, but I'm done now."

"Good God, I hope so!"

Caitlyn carried the pan with the needle in it and the

branch over to the fire. She tossed the branch into the flames and turned back to Jon with a frown.

"Maybe we should put a bandage over those stitches."

"Or maybe not," Jon returned with a grimace as he scooted into a more upright position. Damn it, hadn't these mountain women ever heard of corsets? He had to admit, though, the firm breasts outlined by the flames flickering behind Caitlyn didn't look like they needed an ounce of support. And that itsy little waist—why, he could probably span it with his thumbs and forefingers.

Caitlyn shifted uneasily, but Jon couldn't seem to stop his gaze from roving over her body like a starving man getting ready to dive into a steak. Hell, she was covered clear from her fingers, hidden by the too long sleeves of his now dry shirt, to the tops of her bare feet, sticking out beneath Silas's rolled-up pantlegs. But he could still imagine that luscious body beneath the loose clothing.

She glanced down at herself, as though to check whether her shirt was buttoned, then shrugged her shoulders. The strains of the fiddle in the adjacent camp began anew, the tune an aching lament, and the melody swirled through Jon's thoughts as an accompaniment to the pulsation of his senses.

"Think I'll go see where our supper is," Caitlyn said in a nonchalant tone as she turned.

"Get your fanny back here!" Jon surged to his feet and stumbled toward the fire. The pain slicing through his head blinded his vision, and he clasped his hands to his skull, swaying in agony.

"For pity sakes," Caitlyn murmured as she hurried over to help him sit back down against the log. "I ought to just let you starve. And I already told you that I ain't a slave to be ordered around. If I want to get somethin' to eat, I'll do it."

"Please," Jon pleaded. "Don't leave me right now."

"Oh, all right," Caitlyn grumbled. "But it's your own fault your head's poundin' again. You need to rest. Heck, a day or two from now you won't even remember that you hurt yourself, if you just take it easy for that long. When a person's body suffers somethin', it expects a person to take care of it—let it get better and heal itself. A person's only got one body. It ain't somethin' you can trade in when it gets worn a bit.''

"Quit talking about it!"

"What?"

"Your bo—never mind. Look, I think there's some pemmican left in my pack. Maybe that'll hold us until Silas gets back.''

Caitlyn nodded agreeably and walked over to the packs. Tall Man's knife lay beside the one she already knew was Jon's. She dug in it and her fingers encountered a hard squareness.

She pulled out the book and stared in awe. Shifting it to her other hand, she removed three more books of varying sizes, laying them reverently on the flap of the pack so the dirt wouldn't stain them. She found the bag of pemmican the next time her hand delved into the pack, and frowned, plucking something from her sleeve when she pulled her hand back out.

"A comb," she said with pleasure. She glanced over at Jon to see him watching her closely. "Do you mind if I borrow this?" she asked, holding up the comb. "I promise I'll clean it out after I'm done.''

"Feel free."

"Thank you."

She rose to her feet and approached him again, handing him the pemmican. He kept his eyes on her as she settled a little ways from him on the fallen log.

Trying to ignore him, she swung her hair over her shoulder and started working on the ends of it, picking gently at the tangles in order not to break any of the teeth in the comb. While she worked, her gaze went yearningly back to the books she hadn't returned to the pack.

"You're welcome to borrow the books anytime you like," Jon said. "I know how scarce reading material is in the mountains. It's one thing I've missed sorely."

"Have you read all of them?" Caitlyn asked in quiet wonder.

"About ten times over." Jon broke off a piece of pemmican and stuck it in his mouth, immediately spitting it into his palm. "Maybe I'll wait until Silas gets back with the food after all."

Sticking the comb in her shirt pocket, Caitlyn walked back over to the books. Kneeling down, she picked one up and opened the cover. She reached out a tentative finger and traced the tip around the squiggles she found there. They were completely different from the lines in the journal she always kept with her, which she had studied over and over.

"She's my mother."

Caitlyn craned her head over her shoulder. "Who?"

"The person who's name you're looking at. She inscribed the book before she gave it to me at Christmas one year."

"Oh." Caitlyn gently closed the cover and laid the book down. "Figured it was some relative," she said as she walked back to the log. "Same last name and all. Clay, you said, didn't you?"

"I didn't," Jon reminded her. "Silas did. But, yes, it's Clay. You couldn't have figured that out from the book's inscription, though. My mother didn't sign her whole name, just 'Evelyn, your mother'."

Caitlyn blushed and dropped her head. Shifting around on the log so her back was to him, she pulled the comb from her pocket and reached for a snarled tress of hair. Working on it would give her something to do with her trembling fingers.

"You can't read, can you?" Jon asked softly. "Look," he continued when her back stiffened, "it's nothing to be ashamed of. I don't suppose you've had much of a chance to learn out here."

"Pa didn't know how, either, and he got along right well!" Caitlyn said in an injured voice.

"Would you like me to teach you?"

"Would you?" Eagerly, she swung around on the log.

"Oh, *would* you? I'd find some way to pay you back. I can sew up a real nice pair of moccasins for you, like Silas was askin' me to do. And shirts and britches. Heck, Pa never had to get his clothes from the Indian women. I always kept both of us fitted out proper."

"I hope what you had on earlier isn't an example," Jon said with a laugh.

"Naw. I was just wearin' that to try to make Tall Man keep his hands to himself." She saw Jon's eyes narrow at her words, but she prattled on. "That, along with the mud and wolverine scent on my legs. It worked pretty well, too, except when Tall Man made me sleep outside the wigwam at night. Sky Woman always called me in as soon as he nodded off, though. Oh, darn!"

Caitlyn jerked at the comb embedded in the tangle, then quickly slowed her movements. She might never be able to find Jon another comb if she broke this one, and it was snagged in a big clump of hair. The more she worked on it, the tighter her hair wound around it.

"Here," Jon said, reaching toward her. "Let me help."

Caitlyn scooted off the log to kneel beside him, and Jon realized his mistake at once. His fingers froze in the silky strands as she bent her head to watch him work and her scent surrounded him.

He had given her the last bar of scented soap he'd bought in St. Louis before he left with a group of explorers headed for the mountains, but it wasn't soap scent that distracted him. Damned sure wasn't skunk smell, either. It was a special smell, hard to identify. Mountain meadows filled with flowers. Crisp fall days. The very essence of the mountains, everything he had stored in his memory these past months, filled his nose.

The fiddle swung into an even more haunting melody, and Jon gritted his teeth, resolutely working on the comb. It fell free at last, and he handed it back to her.

"Could you help me a little more?" Caitlyn asked innocently. "Sky Woman and I always helped one another. It's sort of hard to reach back behind the shoulders."

"I . . . suppose," Jon agreed, almost biting his tongue over the escaping words.

Caitlyn sighed in pleasure and turned her back again. "Pa used to help me, too," she said when he picked up a tress and started working the teeth of the comb lightly through it. "I threatened to cut it all off one day, and he told me if I ever did, he'd beat me black and blue."

Caitlyn quickly glanced behind her at him, then turned forward. "Pa didn't mean a word of it, of course. He'd have sooner cut off his arm than ever raise it to me, though I expect there was a time or two I pushed him mighty close to losin' his temper."

Jon grunted a silent agreement and worked quietly for several minutes, as the fiddle continued to spill out its mournful ballad. He gently threaded his fingers through some of the larger tangles, then followed with the comb. The damp hair was quickly drying and tendrils curled around his hands, as soft as black silk. At one point Caitlyn dropped her head onto her chest, and he could almost swear he heard a soft purr coming from her throat. Or maybe she was just humming along with the fiddle's tune.

He couldn't imagine doing this for any other woman— not that any woman he had ever known would ask him. They always appeared before him primped and cosseted, straight and proper, covered from head to toe with their hair bound and rolled so tightly he figured the preparations probably took them all day. Couldn't have, he realized, since even his mother had come down to break the fast each morning with the only difference in her appearance being a slightly more modest gown than she wore in the evenings.

Jon had never known a woman so free and immodest. It didn't seem to bother Caitlyn that the borrowed clothing hung and draped on her, miles too large for her slender body. And she obviously wasn't a bit self-conscious about letting him know she enjoyed his ministrations to her hair. That little purr. . . .

"Uh . . ." Jon began. Conversation, even if they started spitting at each other like they usually did, had to be better than the direction his thoughts were trying to take.

"Hum?" Caitlyn purred.

"Uh . . . Silas said, and it seems obvious, that you aren't Indian."

"Huh-uh. At least, I don't think so. There wasn't anybody left alive for Pa to ask when he found me, though."

"I don't understand. If he was your father. . . . "

"Pa just took me in when he found me at that fur post," she explained. "There wasn't much else he could do. The Blackfeet—we supposed they were Blackfeet, anyway, because Pa said the sign looked like Blackfoot sign. They—"

Suddenly she choked on her words and clamped her hands over her ears. But before Jon could voice his concern, she dropped her arms and continued.

"The Blackfeet didn't leave no one else alive. And Pa said he was on his way back from his summer tradin'. He figured he'd bring me with him the next summer and try to find someone to take me in. By that time, though, we were kind of attached to one another."

"How did you escape the attack?"

"I don't remember. I was only around five or so. And I don't like to think about it. Pa was the only family I ever needed."

She stiffened under his hands and a slight shudder ran through her body. She probably did remember, Jon thought, but had buried it deep in her mind. If the stories he had heard about Indian torture were true, the people at the post hadn't died easy. He pictured a small, frightened Caitlyn in his mind, hiding in some safe place while the people she had lived with screamed out their agony and last breaths.

"I'm sorry," he said softly. "About bringing it up and about your father, too. I lost my own father before I was even old enough to have any memories of him. The only picture I ever saw of him was one my mother gave me—their wedding picture. My stepfather didn't allow us to even talk about him."

"That ain't right," Caitlyn said as she shifted to a more comfortable position and raised her head so Jon could reach the hair tumbling around her face. "If a person wants to know, he ought to be able to find out. I just ain't never had no desire.' "

"Isn't, not ain't," Jon said.

"What do you mean?" Caitlyn asked in a puzzled voice.

"The proper word is 'isn't.' You'll understand when you start reading. 'Ain't' isn't really a word."

"I don't see how that can be," Caitlyn replied. "Lots of folks use ain't. It can't not be a word if people speak it. Besides, 'I isn't never had no desire' makes me sound stupid."

Jon's lips quirked and he searched among the tresses of hair for any tangle he might have overlooked, reluctant to admit his task was done.

"In that sentence, you would use 'haven't,' " he explained. I 'haven't' had. And instead of 'no desire,' it would be 'any desire.' "

"I haven't had any desire," Caitlyn repeated. "Huh. Sounds funny, like you talk."

"There's nothing wrong with the way I speak, Caitlyn. Almost everyone where I come from uses proper English. And not everyone out here talks like you and Silas. Proper speech is a sign that people have had at least some education."

"Huh," Caitlyn said again. "I don't know if I want to get educated, if it's goin' to make me sound like you." But then her eyes fell on the books beside the pack, and Jon could see she regretted her words.

"Why don't you try it?" he asked, admitting to himself that he would appreciate having a small part in transforming Caitlyn's butchered English into words more properly suited to the melodious tone of her voice. "You can choose your own style of speech after that."

Caitlyn nodded earnestly in agreement, apparently glad he hadn't revoked his offer to teach her to read. Her movement swayed a tendril of hair around the comb just as the fiddle from the next camp began a new song.

"Oops," Jon said with a laugh. "Turn your head a little so I can get the comb free again."

Caitlyn bowed her head instead, pulling the comb from his fingers. He reached for it and heard a short sob escape Caitlyn's lips.

"Caitlyn, I'm sorry. I didn't mean to pull your hair. You moved your head before I could let go of the comb."

She raised her head, swiping at a tear tracking down her cheek. "You didn't hurt me," she croaked in a tight voice.

"Then, what's wrong?" Jon gripped her shoulders and tried to turn her toward him, surprised at the strength in the small body when she resisted him. "Caitlyn?"

"It isn't you. It's 'Greensleeves.'"

"'Greensleeves?'" Jon instinctively glanced down at his buckskin-clad arms before he realized what she meant. "Oh, you mean the song he's playing."

She nodded, swiping the heels of her palms beneath her eyes. "It . . . it was Pa's favorite."

"Do you want me to ask him to stop?" Jon loosened his grip on her arms, his fingers stroking them as he sought to comfort her.

"No."

She gave a soft sigh and leaned back against him. The music lost its mournfulness all of a sudden, and Jon untangled the comb with one hand, dropping it beside him on the ground when Caitlyn turned her head slightly and burrowed under his chin. She started singing under her breath, and the sound went through him like a languid breeze on a summer day:

> *Greensleeves was all my joy.*
> *Greensleeves was my delight.*
> *Greensleeves was my heart of gold*
> *And who but my Lady Greensleeves—*

"Uh . . . Caitlyn."

"Hum? Sleepy. So darned sleepy."

She cuddled closer to him, and Jon shifted his arm to her waist.

"Silas will be back with the food any minute," Jon said in a distracted voice. "Aren't you hungry?"

"Huh-uh. Sleepy."

Caitlyn's arm settled across his chest, and a soft cheek cuddled against the open vee in Jon's shirt. Faint breath feathered on his skin. A long eyelash quivered once among his chest hairs, then was still. Her body relaxed and curled against his side, and Jon frantically stared into the darkness beyond the camp, hoping Silas would appear. Then hoping not.

Jon's own eyes grew heavy with strain and he blinked them, forcing them back open. A gruff but pleasant male voice joined the strains of the fiddle, singing the words Caitlyn had sung a moment before.

"And who but my Lady Greensleeves. . . . "

Jon's head nodded and he jerked it back up.

"Umm," Caitlyn murmured in a disgruntled tone. She flung one leg over Jon's thigh and nestled even closer, her breasts sending a shiver of pleasure down his body.

Jon groaned under his breath and closed his eyes. His own cheek rested against the top of Caitlyn's head and he yawned, struggling to retain consciousness. It wouldn't do for Silas to find them like. . . .

Silas broke off his merry whistle abruptly as he entered camp, his moccasined feet making not a sound to break the quiet stillness. Jon really shouldn't be sleeping, but Silas had studied Jon's eyes when he'd woken up after Caitlyn poured that whiskey on his head. He hadn't seen any of the signs the Sioux medicine man had told him to watch for.

He carefully set the bucket of stew by the fire. And he wasn't about to go over there and wake the two of them up so he could listen to them spit and spat at each other.

He settled against a log by the fire and pulled the cork from the new jug. More for him, and Jon could have some tomorrow, if there was any left. The stew would keep—the night was cool. They could heat it up for breakfast.

"Looks like you and Cat finally found some common ground," he said with a soft chuckle. He lifted the jug and waved it in a short salute toward the two figures curled together on the other side of the fire.

Chapter Five

"Greensleeves, hum, hum, hum hummmm." Caitlyn's own voice woke her, and she sleepily reached for the warmth she had cuddled against earlier. Her fingers encountered the water bucket instead, and she blinked her eyes open, staring at the bucket with a frown on her face. Where had Pa gone?

No, not Pa. Caitlyn gasped and pulled the buffalo robe around her, peering over the edge to see if anyone else was awake yet.

"Morning," Jon said from his seat on an upturned log by the fire. "Coffee's ready, if you want some. The stew's heating, too, but I was thinking about going over to see if any of the food tents were open yet. Thought I smelled bacon on the breeze a second ago."

Caitlyn scooted up, drawing the buffalo hide beneath her chin. "I . . . you . . . we . . . didn't. . . . "

"Sleep together?" Jon said with a chuckle. "Well, not all night. Silas woke me up sometime after midnight, singing along with the fiddle. He wasn't in any shape to help carry you over to the lean-to, and my head was still making me a little dizzy. I was afraid I'd drop you."

"Where . . . where'd *you* sleep then?"

"Sure as hell not in that lean-to. Silas's breath was enough to curl a person's hair." Jon nodded at a pile of blankets beside him. "Brought my own stuff out here."

"Oh."

"Do you want some stew, or would you rather go with me to one of the tents? Everyone's probably still passed out from last night, so we shouldn't have any trouble. Or maybe I could bring you back something."

Caitlyn blew a curl away from her face and scowled at him. "I don't see why you and Silas want to keep me penned up in this here camp! Every time I even mention steppin' a foot outside it without one of you hoverin' over me like an old hound that's just found its lost pup, you act like I'm goin' to run off. Ain't . . . don't have anywhere else to go, except back to Tall Man, and that's not a possibility in my book. You both know that!"

Jon's face lost its complacent look and he returned her scowl. "You *will* have one of us with you at all times," he ordered. "You are *not* to go wandering around by yourself, do you understand?"

"Not really. Understand, I mean. Ain't . . . it's not like I don't know what's going on out there. Pa and I spent four summers at rendezvous before he died."

"And did your father ever let you go off by yourself?"

"Well, no," Caitlyn admitted. "He made me stay with Sky Woman if he didn't want me taggin' along after him. Mostly that was in the evenin's, though. Pa, he liked his liquor at times, just like Silas. But I'm older now—a grown woman."

Yeah, don't I know it. Jon kept his thoughts to himself and got to his feet. He threw the dregs from his coffee cup into the fire, and the flames sputtered and flared. "Come on then, if you want to go along. We didn't have anything to eat last night, remember? You'll stay right beside me every second, though, or I'll march you back here so fast your feet won't touch the ground!"

Caitlyn rolled her eyes, then tossed the buffalo robe back and scrambled to her feet. She shivered slightly in the cool air and brushed her hair back over her shoulders.

"Well, you're goin' to have to wait a minute. And there's one place even Pa always had to let me go alone!"

Jon nodded his head curtly, acknowledging the fact that she probably had to relieve herself. Some things just had to be discussed that weren't proper drawing room conversations, he admitted to himself.

"Silas and I fixed a place behind that big oak where the trail to the pond starts. Shouldn't take you more than two minutes to get there and back. If not, I'll come looking for you."

"Two minutes? Good grief. A man might be able to do it that quick. All he has to do is pull aside his—"

"Get going!" Jon roared. "You've already wasted ten seconds!"

Caitlyn faced him defiantly before she reached down to snatch up the comb by her feet. Almost strolling, she slowly walked out of the camp.

"You get tired of waitin', I'll catch up to you later on," she called over her shoulder in a sticky-sweet voice.

Jon groaned and dropped back down on the log. Burying his face in his hands, he shook his head, wincing when a stab of pain shot through him. He raised his head again, eyes trained on the spot where Caitlyn had disappeared.

This wasn't going to work. Not by a long shot. She knew as well as he did that he wasn't about to go stomping up that path and risk finding her half-clothed in the brush. She was so damned matter-of-fact and open about everything— her feelings, her bodily needs. She didn't seem to have even an ounce of contrivance or game-playing in her, none of the womanly wiles he had assured himself he would be on the lookout for in women from now on.

And he'd lied when he told Caitlyn he slept in his blankets last night. Hell, what man in his right mind could sleep with that little ball of sweet-smelling femininity curled up almost within arm's reach? Especially knowing full well how that undeniably womanly shape fit just exactly right against the side of his body!

Jon dragged a hand across his face, then stared at the fur

bundles beside the lean-to, where a sudden loud snore from Silas split the air. Silas had told Jon no one would bother the furs while they looked around yesterday. It would be more than a man's life was worth, getting caught with furs carrying another man's mark on them—or no marks at all, if a man tried to get rid of them.

He wondered how many furs those women Caitlyn had mentioned charged. He'd almost tried to find out for himself last night, when he could no longer stand the ache in his groin. Passing out like he had earlier had scared him a little bit, though, and he didn't fancy waking up somewhere stripped of his essentials.

But something had to give. He wasn't about to spend another year without losing himself a time or two in a warm, willing female, even if he did have to pay for the pleasure—something he'd only done a time or two before in his life.

"You tryin' to burn a hole in them furs with your eyeballs, or you goin' to pick out enough of them to pay for our breakfast?"

Jon jerked his head around to see Caitlyn standing beside the buffalo robe, her hair neatly braided, although wisps curled around her face. The one, long braid hung down her back, reaching past her waist. His fingers twitched when he recalled the feel of it, and he clamped his hands into fists.

"Uh—" Jon cleared his throat and began again. "How many will we need?"

"Depends on what kind you take. If it's beaver, probably two apiece for a meal. Mink, one each'll do. You and Silas keep track of what you spend on me, and I'll pay you back this winter."

"Reckon I can afford to buy you breakfast," Jon muttered as he walked over to the fur bundles. "After all, you doctored my head last night."

"How is it this morning?" Caitlyn asked in concern. "Remember what I said. Person's body needs—"

"I'm damned well aware of what my body needs! And right now, it's food!" Jon split open a bundle of furs and ignored the other need crowding his mind.

"These two will do."

Caitlyn's hand came over his shoulder, and Jon jumped away from the close contact of her body behind him. Sprawling on his rear in the dirt, he shot her an angry glance.

"Jeez," Caitlyn said. "You sure are jumpy this morning. I was only tryin' to show you which was mink and which was beaver."

Jon closed his eyes for a second and let out a huge sigh. "I at least learned that much over the winter," he said as he got to his feet and swiped two mink furs from the top of the pile. "Even before that. It might surprise you, but we've got pictures of animals in books back east. I knew a little bit about tanning before I came out here, too, from working on deer hides."

When Jon strode away in irritation, Caitlyn hurried after him.

"I ain't entirely ignorant," she informed him with a haughty look when she caught up to him. "Pa told me stories about what it's like back there. And he said a person can't even walk down one of them streets without bumping elbows with everyone else."

" 'Not' entirely ignorant," Jon reminded her. "Not 'ain't.' "

Just beyond the trees where Silas and Jon had set up camp, they topped a small rise, and both of them stopped in unison to stare at the sight spread out before them.

Hundreds of smoke plumes from smoldering camp fires curled up through the early morning light. A brilliant sunrise streaked the sky to the east, colors so pure they could never be captured on canvas. White, brown and darker shades of wigwams stretched ahead as far as they could see. Scattered here and there were the traders' larger tents, with hastily thrown together counters built from raw wood out front.

"Sure is somethin', ain't . . . isn't it?" Caitlyn breathed. "A person doesn't realize just how full this country's gettin' until he sees all those folks gathered in one place. It's goin' to fill up out here, too, if we're not careful."

"You could set this entire rendezvous down in the middle of Richmond and never find it," Jon told her as he started down the rise. "Of course, you'd always be able to distinguish the people from one another."

A bearded man rose from a nearby bedroll and burped loudly, then scratched his stomach. His hand wandered downward and groped at the buckskin loincloth between his legs. Opening his eyes, the man caught sight of Caitlyn and his fingers froze in their quest. Another burp rumbled from his throat and he dropped one eyelid in a wink.

Jon grabbed Caitlyn and shoved her to his other side, casting a warning glance at the man before he could remove his hand from his loincloth.

"She gits ta be too much for you, sonny boy," the man called after them, "I got somethin' here to hep' you out!"

Jon gritted his teeth. "See why I always want someone with you?" he growled.

"I can't walk around with my eyes closed. Pa taught me just to ignore those that have no manners. And the sights are just as bad on this side of you."

Jon glanced over Caitlyn's head to see a bare-chested man sprawled on his back, one naked leg flung out and a blanket barely covering his privates. The man's arm was clasped around an Indian woman as naked as the man appeared to be under the blanket.

"That does it! From now on, you're eating in camp," Jon said with a groan as he wrapped an arm around Caitlyn and pulled her close to his side.

"I already told you what I think about bein' penned up. There's nothin' here I ain't ... haven't seen before. You try to cage me up like some dancing bear, I'll take you up on that offer to trade what you won from Tall Man for a spot in another crew. I'm not ... I *ain't* gonna be tethered like a dog bein' fattened up for supper!"

Caitlyn's loud voice disturbed the naked man behind them, and he blearily opened one eye. He shot up into a sitting position, slapping at the Indian woman when she muttered and tried to pull him back beside her. His face narrowed in concentration as he watched the two figures walk away.

"Make up your mind," Jon said with a small chuckle. "You want me to treat you like a dancing bear or a dog?"

"Neither, I just said! I. . . . "

"Easy, Caitlyn," Jon said, keeping a firm grip on her when she tried to jerk away. "I apologize. You're right, I guess. You remind me more of an eagle, soaring on the wind drafts over the mountains. It's just that I can't get used to the idea of allowing a woman to look at sights like those back there. But it wouldn't be right to try to keep an eagle caged."

"Do I really?" Caitlyn asked with a shy glance at Jon's face.

"Really what?"

"Make you think of an eagle? They were mine and Pa's favorite animal. Even the Indians don't kill eagles. They just trap them and pull out a few tail feathers for their war bonnets before they turn them loose. I expect the eagles grow new feathers afterwards, since I've never seen an eagle with missing tail feathers."

"An eagle, definitely," Jon agreed. "Wild and free and unspoiled. But an eagle's a bird, not an animal."

"Same thing, ai—isn't it?"

"Not hardly. I'll tell you what the difference is while we do our studying. Right now, isn't that bacon he's frying in that skillet?"

"It is!" Caitlyn agreed, eyes wide with wonder and her delicate nostrils quivering. "And what are those round things in that bowl on the counter?"

"Oranges, Caitlyn. Haven't you ever had an orange?"

"I don't think so. I've never seen anything that color before, shaped like that."

"Well, you can bet your bonnet he's going to want more than just a mink fur for one of those, after carrying them all the way out here. But don't worry. I'll come back later and get you one."

Caitlyn glanced at Jon, this time in gratitude. She

climbed over the bench and sat beside him, eagerly sniffing the aromas trapped beneath the covering canvas.

Fully clothed now, the man ambled over to the bench on the other side of the tent. He sneered to himself. They were so absorbed in each other, they hadn't even noticed him following. He was no match for that blond giant accompanying her right now, with his head pounding from the effects of that rotgut they'd served instead of the fine Irish whiskey he usually imbibed. But he had time yet. From what he understood, this gathering of traders lasted at least a month.

"Caitlyn," Jon said almost an hour later as they walked away from the food tent. "We need to go back and check on Silas."

"Please," Caitlyn begged. "Just for a little while longer. Silas will probably sleep until noon, and everyone's up around here now. We won't stumble across any more naked bodies."

"No, they'll be awake and more ready to cause problems," Jon grumbled.

"You're big enough to protect us, Jon," Caitlyn said. She felt his arm, which he had securely tucked her hand beneath when they left the food tent, slacken its tenseness.

"Please?" she repeated, enjoying this newfound power she seemed to have over Jon when he looked down at her and his steps slowed. She widened her eyes like she had seen Sky Woman do at times when the Indian woman was coaxing Pa for a treat.

"And here I thought you were above trying to use those feminine tricks on me," Jon growled.

Disappointed, Caitlyn dropped her gaze and murmured a hasty compliance that they would return to camp. The sounds around them—women and men murmuring and laughing together, tent awnings flapping gaily in the morning breeze—made her remember how much she and Sky Woman had enjoyed strolling around yesterday, taking in the sights after so many nearly silent months in the mountains. Back at the quiet camp, she would still be able to hear faint echoes of the merrymakers enjoying the rendezvous, which came only once a year.

She kicked at a small clump of grass with one dirty, bare foot, and her lower lip protruded just a scant bit.

Remembering his own somewhat wide-eyed amazement when he and Silas had wandered around the previous day taking in the sights, Jon reluctantly slowed his steps again and pulled Caitlyn to a stop. "You'll stay right by my side," he said gruffly. "You won't wander away."

"I promise," Caitlyn said quickly, drawing an "X" between her breasts with a slender finger. "Cross my heart and hope to die. Let's just look around another hour."

"Half an hour," Jon growled. He changed direction and strode back toward the center of rendezvous, with Caitlyn hurrying beside him to keep pace. It was worth it this once, he guessed, when he looked down and saw her lip back in place and her eyes sparkling with unsuppressed excitement.

At least it was a lot quieter this early in the day than it would be later on, he told himself in an attempt to justify his actions as he led Caitlyn to another tent, this one set up by an employee of one of the trading companies. American traders, rather than British, it looked like from the nature of the goods laid out on the rough wood. Probably the company owned by Jedidiah Smith, whom Jon had heard about back in St. Louis.

The employee approached them, holding out his hand.

"Pete Smith," he introduced himself. "I head this outfit for Jedidiah Smith, no relation to myself. If you're interested in trading, rather than just looking, I'll haul one of my clerks up. They're still lazing in bed."

"Jonathan Clay," Jon returned as he clasped the man's hand. "And this is Caitlyn O'Shaunessy."

"Pleased to meet you, ma'am." Not having a cap to remove, Pete tugged his forelock. "Clay, you say?" he said as he looked back at Jon. "Virginia Clays?"

Jon only gave a curt nod in reply. Just his luck. The first man he ran across had heard of his family. "We're only browsing right now," he said in an attempt to forestall any more questions from Pete. "We'll come back when we've got some furs with us."

"Oh, look." Caitlyn pulled her hand free and bent over the counter. She picked up a figurine and tenderly ran her fingers over the full skirt.

"It's a music box, Miss O'Shaunessy," Pete said. "Here, let me show you how it works."

Pete took the figurine and turned it upside down. He twisted a key on the base and handed it back to Caitlyn. The haunting strains of "Greensleeves" tinkled in the air.

"We brought six of them with us, and that's the only one left," Pete told her. "Two got broken on the way here, even though we packed them in straw. Don't reckon we'll try to bring any more of those with us next summer. Sold the other three yesterday. They all played different songs."

"Thank you for showin' it to me," Caitlyn murmured. She set the figurine back on the counter and turned away.

"How much is it?" Jon asked.

"Six mink or twelve beaver," Pete replied.

"Good grief," Caitlyn said as she swung back to the counter. "That's three or four days' good trappin' for two men, even at the height of the season! You're mighty proud of that there thing, ain't—aren't you?"

"Well, now," Jon mused when Pete shrugged his shoulders. "Seems to me like gold would take up less room going back to St. Louis. Leave room to haul more furs."

"You got that right," Pete said. "But nobody out here has gold to trade."

Jon reached in his buckskin trouser pocket and pulled out a leather pouch. He opened the drawstring and dug his long fingers inside, bringing out a gold coin that sparkled in the morning sun.

"Six mink or twelve beaver come to around thirty-six dollars," Jon said as he held the coin between his thumb and forefinger, turning it to catch the sun's rays. "A double eagle's only worth twenty, but it sure takes up less room."

"Come on, Jon." Caitlyn tugged on Jon's free arm. "Them music boxes is for women, anyway. You ain't . . . don't have no . . . any use for one."

"What do women use them for, Caitlyn?" Jon asked as he smiled down at her.

"How'd I know? I never had one."

"Sure is a pretty tune." Pete picked up the figurine and twisted the key again before he set it down. " 'Greensleeves,' isn't it?"

Caitlyn couldn't stop herself from looking down at the music box again. The wide-skirted woman twirled around on the box this time.

"How's . . . how's it do that?"

"There's another button on the bottom you push," Pete told her.

"Oh. Well, come on, Jon. We don't have much time left, and I want to see all we can."

As Caitlyn walked away, Jon flipped the coin to Pete and raised an eyebrow. Pete caught the gold piece and brought it to his mouth, biting it, then nodded his head as he reached for the music box.

"I'll hold it for you," Pete said with a conspiratorial wink.

Jon whistled a few soft bars of the song as he strode after Caitlyn and caught her arm. "You're breaking your promise already," he said, pulling her close to his side. "You're supposed to stay with me."

"I'm sorry," Caitlyn said in a distracted voice. "I'm just goin' to have to get used to bein' on a leash, I reckon."

" 'Going to,' " Jon said, "not 'goin' to.' In proper English, you also pronounce the g's on the end of the words—like 'being,' not 'bein'. And 'trapping,' 'sleeping,' 'walking.' "

"Going to. Being. Trapping." Caitlyn rolled the words around once more over her tongue, then nodded her head. "Think I've got it now. Look! Look over there!"

Caitlyn grabbed Jon's hand and tugged him after her toward another tent. A lot longer than a half hour passed as they wandered from tent to tent, stopping now and then at the wigwams where the Indian women had spread out their own wares for trade, and even sampling a taste or two from various cooking pots, both white and Indian.

At one point, Jon pulled out another coin from his pouch and bought a few of the smaller goods at a trader's tent, giving them to Caitlyn so she could make her own trades with the Indian women.

Caitlyn's blue eyes glowed with excitement as she accepted the goods with only a slight protest. She traded a small paring knife at the first wigwam they came to for a basket to carry the remaining goods in, then dragged Jon with her over to another nearby wigwam and dickered endlessly with a sour-faced woman sitting in front of it. Finally Caitlyn handed over a small mirror and accepted an exquisite pouch decorated with painted porcupine quills in return.

"Here," she said as she held the pouch out to Jon. "Your possibles bag's about worn through."

"I gave you that stuff to trade for things *you* need," Jon grumbled. But he bent his head and allowed her to place the strap over his head.

"There." Caitlyn patted a small hand on Jon's chest and adjusted the bag slightly. Cocking her head, she studied the bag and gave a nod of satisfaction as she grabbed Jon's hand to continue her quest for bargains.

"Next thing you get better be for somethin' for yourself!"

" 'Something,' not 'somethin,' " Caitlyn returned as they stopped in front of the next wigwam.

Jon chuckled and shook his head as he watched Caitlyn pick up a beaded belt.

"This sure would hold up my britches a lot more comfortable than that rope I got now." Caitlyn started to gather Jon's shirt and lift it above her waist.

Jon's hand snapped out and he grabbed her arm. "Try it on over the top of the shirt for now!"

Caitlyn shot him a quizzical glance, then shrugged her shoulders and wrapped the belt around her waist. She drew it snug, then looked up at Jon for approval.

"Uh—" Jon wrenched his eyes away from the tilted mounds outlined against the shirt material, now drawn tightly against them. "Uh . . . it's a little small, isn't it?"

Caitlyn reached down and adjusted the belt, a frown of

concentration on her face. She loosened it an inch, then moved her shoulders until the shirt hung more loosely over them.

"That better?"

"Much," Jon agreed.

Caitlyn lifted the lid of the basket and pulled out a string of multi-colored beads. She slipped them around the Indian woman's neck and stepped back to study them. Nodding her head, Caitlyn spoke a few words to the woman.

"What did you say to her?" Jon asked.

"Told her they made her eyes sparkle."

The Indian woman picked up the beads from her chest and fingered them, then glanced down and back up at Caitlyn. A smile quirked the Indian woman's lips, and she held up two fingers and spoke to Caitlyn.

Caitlyn laughed and translated the woman's words for Jon. "She says if one string will make her sparkle, she needs two, one for each eye."

Caitlyn nodded agreeably and delved into her basket. Leaving the belt on her waist, Caitlyn grabbed Jon's hand and hurried to the next wigwam, almost dancing along in her excitement.

"Slow down," Jon said with a chuckle. "Those things aren't going to walk away before you get there."

"I was afraid you'd remember you only gave me half an hour," Caitlyn admitted, her eyes twinkling when she slid a sideways look at him.

"All right," Jon agreed in a grumble he had to force into his voice. "We'll stay until noon, then have dinner before we go back to camp."

"That long? Thank you!" Caitlyn gave Jon a brief hug and squatted down to examine the articles on the blanket in front of the wigwam, leaving Jon standing upright with his breath caught in his throat.

Chapter Six

"You paid way too much for it," Caitlyn teased, running her fingers across the beaded bodice of the deerskin dress and kicking her legs out slightly to make the fringe dance. "It sure is purty, though, and reckon Silas'll be glad to get his britches back."

"Pretty, not purty. We got the moccasins, too," Jon reminded her, "even if you won't wear them. And all I gave her was my old possibles bag and my knife and sheath. I've still got the knife I won from Tall Man."

"Pretty," Caitlyn repeated agreeably. "Oh, I'm so full. I couldn't eat another bite. We keep eatin'—eating like this, you'll be right about me needing a bigger belt. That there roasted corn sure was good, though. And fresh buffalo steak. First I've had this summer. You and Silas figure on going on a buffalo hunt before we head back up into the mountains?"

"What would we do with all the meat? Among the three of us, we probably couldn't eat more than one haunch before it spoiled."

"Why, dry it and pickle it. Salt it down," Caitlyn said

in astonishment. "There's lot's you can do with it, or at least I can. I wouldn't expect you and Silas to do that part. You just need to bring it to me. Have you ever eaten jellied buffalo tongue?"

"Can't say as I have," Jon said with a grimace.

"You simmer the tongue in a pot with some wild onions, mint and a little coltsfoot salt and Indian vinegar. After it cools and the sauce jellies, you slice it up and there's not a better tasting dish on earth. Ummmm."

She ran her tongue around her lips and Jon watched the movement, fascinated by the two different shades of pink.

"How—what's the difference between regular vinegar and Indian vinegar?" he asked.

"Indian vinegar's made out of sap from the birch tree," Caitlyn explained. "Or maple, if you can find it. Maple's scarce out here, though, and most of the time people use its sap for syrup or candy, if they do run across a tree. Look, Jon. She's making *Wagmiza Wasna* over there!"

"What in the world's that?" he asked as he obeyed the tug on his arm and followed Caitlyn to a wigwam he recognized as Sioux. He should recognize it. Caitlyn had explained the different signs painted on the buffalo-skin structures over and over to him all morning.

"Pemmican!"

"Pemmican? We've got pemmican back at camp. And you just said you were so full you couldn't eat another bite."

"Not like this pemmican. Just wait. Here. Hold this stuff."

Caitlyn piled Jon's arms full of the treasures she had gathered over the morning, keeping only the basket to take with her to the wigwam.

"Took the ol' woman shoppin' this mornin', huh?"

Jon swiveled around to meet a pair of laughing eyes in the bearded face of a grizzled old trapper. He felt his face flush hotly. What a picture he must make, standing there with Caitlyn's purchases dangling from his arms!

"Here, Jon." Caitlyn stopped beside him and held out a deerskin pouch.

"Hell," Jon heard the trapper mutter. "Find me one like that there 'un, guess I'd buy out the whole dern rendezvous for her myself."

Jon's face darkened and the look he gave the trapper told the old man exactly who would be doing any buying for Caitlyn, but the old man just touched his forehead in greeting and ambled away.

"Is he someone you know, Jon?" Caitlyn asked.

"No. He was just admiring you—our *purchases*."

"Don't you want to try the pemmican? It's good for dessert. Oh. Your hands are full. Here."

Jon stood helplessly as Caitlyn reached into the pouch and pulled her fingers out, filled with lumps of the mixture. She raised her arm, and he opened his mouth so she could push the pemmican inside, her finger accidentally touching his tongue.

"Good, isn't it?" she demanded when he slowly began chewing.

Jon nodded his head in surprise. It wasn't the flat-tasting pemmican he was used to. His teeth clamped down on something, and sweetness filled his mouth.

"It's made from cornmeal and dried currants and sugar," Caitlyn said. " 'Course, this is maple sugar. I'll have to remind Silas we'll need to trade for our sugar. Only time you get maple sap is in the spring, but reckon Silas knows that."

A high yelp split the air and Caitlyn swung around. Before Jon could unload his arms and grab her, she let out a scream of dismay and ran toward the next wigwam.

"You quit that!" Caitlyn flew into the Indian man and pounded on his back just as the man swung his leg again, his kick aimed at the half-grown dog cringing at his feet. The shock of Caitlyn's weight against his back sent the Indian sprawling in the dirt. The dog crawled a few feet away on its belly, whimpering in fear but eyeing some scraps of bone on the ground.

Jon grabbed Caitlyn before she could launch herself at the Indian again and captured her wildly swinging fists in his hands.

"Caitlyn. Stop it!"

"Let go of me, dash nab it! He don't feed his animal, he ain't got no right to mistreat it when it's only trying to clean up what he don't want himself! Let the hell go of me!"

Jon wrapped his arms around Caitlyn and held her tightly against his chest. He looked down at the Indian man still sprawled on the ground.

"She's been under a strain," he said in an apologetic voice. "Too much shopping."

Caitlyn let out a giggle and collapsed in Jon's arms. Her giggles quickly escalated into laughter, and then full-fledged guffaws. She braced her legs under her and tried to stand, but her knees gave way and she had to depend on the support of Jon's arms to keep from falling beside the Indian man in the dirt.

"Caitlyn, hush," Jon said around his own laughter. "He'll think we're crazy."

"I'm sorry," Caitlyn gasped. "But you sounded just like we'd been prancing up and down one of those streets back where you come from, instead of wandering among almost every kind of Indian a person could name!"

Caitlyn finally managed to control her legs and stood, flashing Jon a look from eyes brimming with merriment and tears of laughter. "You did, you know." She lifted a hand and cocked her little finger. "Maybe I ought to have drank my coffee like this at dinner. Pa told me once that's how those eastern women drink their tea."

Jon's smile split his face and he threw back his head as the laughter roared from between his even, white teeth. His arms tightened around Caitlyn and she laid her forehead on his chest, giggling merrily and clenching one small fist around the fringes on his shirt.

The Indian man stared at them for a long moment. Then his own face creased in understanding, and he rose to his feet. He grabbed a piece of rope from beside the wigwam and held his hand out to the dog. It whimpered and crawled forward, and the man looped the rope around its neck.

The Sioux waited until the laughter subsided, then approached Jon and Caitlyn. Pushing the rope into Caitlyn's hand, he spoke a few words.

"Oh!" Caitlyn gasped. "No." She dropped her head to hide her flushed cheeks, but held onto the rope.

"What did he say?" Jon asked.

Caitlyn shook her head, and a wisp of hair loosened from her braid fell across her face.

"Caitlyn." Jon tipped her face up and studied the bright flush on her cheeks. "What did he say? Why's he giving you the dog?"

"He—" Caitlyn took a deep breath. "He says it's for our wedding present. He thinks we've just got married and he wants us to have—"

Caitlyn shrugged and eyed Jon warily. "We can't give it back."

"Ask him why he thinks we're married," Jon demanded.

"Jon, no—"

"Ask him, Caitlyn, or I'll give the dog back, no matter what the consequences."

"You wouldn't, would you?" she pleaded.

"No," Jon said with a sigh. She was getting to know him too well and it hadn't even been a full day yet. "But I want to know why he thought what he did. Please ask him, Caitlyn."

The please did it. She couldn't deny him when he asked so sweetly. Caitlyn turned to the Indian man and spoke a few words, the blush heightening on her face when he replied.

"Caitlyn," Jon prodded after the Indian man fell silent.

"He . . . he said only the young and in . . . in . . . well, there isn't a word for it in Sioux, but he means in love. He said only those in love enjoy feelings like we share."

"Did you tell him we weren't married?"

"No."

"Tell him."

Caitlyn spoke again and the man replied with a smile on his face, speaking far more words than he had in his previous comments.

Caitlyn knew it wouldn't be any use trying to avoid telling Jon what the Sioux had said, so she took a deep breath.

"He says if we aren't married now, we soon should be," she translated, the thought of lying to Jon never once crossing her mind. "He said we shouldn't ignore what we got—that it's rare to find it and he's only had it once, with his first wife. She died two years ago, and all he's got left now's his twelve-year-old daughter from her. He was remembering his wife when the dog tried to grab the scraps, and he kicked it without thinking. He's sorry now that he did it, and he wants me to have the dog to remind me that lo . . . love has . . . has many faces."

"Wonder what he means by that?"

"Jon, boyo! I been lookin' all over rendezvous for you and Cat! What you doin' standin' there talkin' to Reach for the Moon? And look what I found over there. Someone dropped a whole pile of stuff."

Jon groaned and turned toward Silas, somewhat disappointed at the interruption. He heard Caitlyn give a relieved sigh beside him and knew her own feelings were just the opposite.

"That's Caitlyn's stuff," Jon told Silas. "I laid it down while we came over here to get this dog."

"Dog, huh?" Silas mused. "Good idear, Jon, my boyo. We can build a sled and the dog can help us haul in the furs this winter when the snow's too deep for our horses. Soon's that there dog grows a bit, that is."

Silas knelt and reached out a hand to the dog, but it curled itself against Caitlyn's leg and drew back its lips. When Jon dropped down and held his hand out, the dog actually snapped at it.

"Now, look here, damn it . . . !"

"Leave him alone, Jon," Caitlyn said as she joined them on the ground and wrapped her arms around the dog. It stuck out its tongue and licked her slurpily on the face.

"You be careful of that animal, Caitlyn," Jon growled. "Maybe we should give it back."

"You already promised you wouldn't, Jon," Caitlyn said as she rose to her feet and took a firm grip on the rope.

The dog cast a worshipful glance at her and lifted a paw.

As Caitlyn gripped the dog's paw, then patted it on the head, Silas walked over and clapped Reach for the Moon on the back.

"What you been up to, you old varmint?" he asked in English.

"Same as always," the Sioux replied quietly in the same language, his voice pitched too low to reach Caitlyn and Jon. "You know, fussing and fighting with my daughter. Searching for another woman just maybe half as good as Spring Breeze. Thought I might have found one for a second." He cast a sly glance at Caitlyn. "Just like always, though, the ones worth anything are already taken."

" 'Pears that way, don't it?" Silas agreed.

"We need to talk, Swift Feet," Reach for the Moon said even more softly. "Come. We will smoke in my wigwam."

They both glanced over to see Caitlyn and Jon wandering away, the dog happily trotting at Caitlyn's side and Jon's arms again filled.

"Reckon we might's well," Silas said with a snicker. "Those two don't look like they'd 'preciate any company right now." Silas stepped aside and allowed Reach for the Moon to enter the wigwam first, ducking to follow him inside.

They settled on each side of the smoldering fire, and Reach for the Moon lit a long-stemmed pipe with an ember from the fire. He puffed until the makings in the pipe glowed, then blew smoke in each of the four directions before handing the pipe to Silas.

Silas's eyes narrowed as he realized the Indian man had gone through the more formal ceremony of appeasing the spirits, rather than just the normal lighting of the pipe and smoking between old friends. Blowing the smoke to the four winds meant Reach for the Moon had something mighty important to discuss, but Silas held his tongue while he took his own puff from the pipe, politely waiting until the Sioux opened the conversation.

They passed the pipe back and forth two more times before Reach for the Moon spoke.

"There is one here who seeks someone else, a woman

he is searching for. It is not our way, or the way of the white mountain men, to seek knowledge of another's past. This man acts like his questions have no reason, yet different ears think this is not so.''

"What sort of feller is this man?'' Silas asked.

"He is one who speaks from two sides of his mouth. He wears clothes like yours, chews and spits his tobacco instead of smoking it. He drinks the whiskey, but pays for it in coin, not furs. He eats what we do, but uses not his knife and fingers. He has a strange thing with prongs that he carries his food to his mouth with after he cuts it.''

"Sounds like some sort of fancy pants casterner.''

"He speaks that different way sometimes. But other times, when he drinks, he sounds like the one the grizzly bear killed in the last season of the shining leaves—Mad Mick.''

"Irish, huh? Ol' Mick was Irish. Well, there's a couple Irish clerks with the British companies at rendezvous. Couldn't really stop the British comin' down from Canada when they found out what ol' Ashley had it in his mind to do. And helps keep the prices down a little bit, them competin' with the Americans. Ol' Mick wasn't the only Irish mountain man out here, neither. But why's it matter to this other feller whether people thinks he's Irish or American?''

"It should not,'' Reach for the Moon agreed. "Unless his reason for being among us has to do with where he comes from. If he thinks that to seem American will place more secret about him. But even the white mountain men know our ways—that it is not done to ask what a man has been before. Or a woman.''

"What's his name? And has anyone figured out who the woman is he's lookin' for?''

"He answers to William Hogan, not Bill, as a mountain man would call himself. He likes to talk of the Blackfeet and how fierce they are—how they are a tribe that will never lay down their weapons for even long enough to trade with the whites a month in the summer. Many times he repeats a story to different people of an attack the Blackfeet made on a post far north of here—how the people were tortured to death. And that he has heard there was a small child there, whose body was never found.''

"Cat," Silas said angrily. "He's lookin' for Cat. What the hell's he want with her?''

"A man such as this Hogan could not have something honorable in mind," Reach for the Moon said. "Or he would be truthful about his reasons for seeking her.''

The Sioux knocked the pipe against a stone ringing the fire, dislodging the tobacco ashes. "The one called Mad Mick saved my daughter's life many summers ago," he said. "She wandered from the wigwam and found a puma's den. The young ones were to her playthings, but the mother returned. The shot Mick made across the valley did not seem thinkable, yet it killed the puma. I would protect the daughter Mick loved, as he did mine.''

Silas nodded his head and stood. "I understand. And Ol' Mick was a good pard to me, too. I spent a Christmas or two with them, when Cat was younger.''

"You should not seek this man out here, Swift Feet. If he does not find Mick's daughter, perhaps he will leave.''

"Yeah, no sense causin' a ruckus at rendezvous. Somebody's liable to get hurt. I think we better get our tradin' done and head on back into the mountains before this year's rendezvous is over. We can get an early start on scoutin' out where we want our lines to run. Seems a shame to miss all the fun, but there'll be another rendezvous next year.''

"You take her with you, then?''

"Yep. Maybe we'll head up to Mick's old cabin. Since he didn't trap there last year, should be good pickin's. And Cat said somethin' herself 'bout wishin' she could go back there.''

Silas paused at the flap in the wigwam. "Thanks, Reach for the Moon. I wish you favorable winds for huntin' and warm moccasins in the winter.''

"You are welcome to share my cooking pot when you like, Swift Feet. That is," he added with a laugh, "if you are not afraid my daughter's food will sit hard on your stomach. She is not the cook her mother was.''

"You'll find someone to replace Spring Breeze some day, ol' pard. Well, maybe not replace her, but you're too good a man for these women to let run loose for long. Bet you're beatin' them off with a stick at times."

"It is my daughter who carries the stick," Reach for the Moon said, a wry twist to his mouth. "She does not feel the coldness of the blankets at night yet."

" 'Round twelve, ain't she, if I 'member right. She looks anythin' like her ma, you're gonna need more than your own stick soon. Probably a club, or more likely that there butt'ler gun you skinned me out of a while back."

Reach for the Moon threw back his head and laughed. "You should not try to show how you earned your name with a belly full of whiskey, Swift Feet. Or perhaps it takes a pack of howling Blackfeet at your heels to make your feet fly."

Silas scratched his beard and chuckled. "Don't reckon I wanna find out which one it is," he admitted. "You take care of yourself 'til we run across one another again."

"And you, my friend."

Chapter Seven

"Where's Cat?" Silas demanded.

Jon lowered his tin cup. One more draught of doctored whiskey would surely dull his senses enough to search out some feminine companionship—physical, naturally. Drinking first always worked back in Richmond, and it was getting close enough to dark that the women should be open for business—not that daylight really seemed to matter, from what he'd seen so far of rendezvous.

"She's back at camp," he told Silas. "I left her sorting through all that stuff she got this morning and told her that she better not step one foot away from our lean-to."

"Gol'damn it, Jon! Sometimes I swear your brains have all leaked down into your big toe! Come on!"

One of the pack mules tethered near camp let out a bray and the dog stood up with a growl, eyes trained on the brush and hackles on his neck erect. Caitlyn sprang to her feet, the wicked-looking knife Jon had won from Tall Man in her hand. She curled her other fingers around the whetstone.

"Who's there?" she demanded.

The rustling in the brush escalated, followed by a thud and grunt of pain—a human grunt. Someone spat an angry oath and a dull thunk sounded. A second later, footsteps pounded away from the campsite, branches crackling and bush tops quivering along the path of escape.

But she still wasn't alone. The dog remained at her side, lips drawn back in a snarl and nose quivering. Pa had taught Caitlyn to do the same—use not only her ears and eyes, but also her nose, as the dog was doing, to protect herself from danger. Always be alert, he counseled, even when enjoying yourself. And she had seen that man in the vicinity of too many wigwams when she had stopped to examine the trade goods.

Caitlyn lifted the knife and clenched her fingers tighter as she sniffed the air. Tanned leather and smoke could mean the man was either white or Indian. Bear grease probably meant the latter, since usually only Indians used it on their hair. The man she had seen was white.

"Come on out of there and show yourself, or else get the hell away from here like that other one did," she snarled in an attempt to cover her fright. "This knife will gut a human just as easy as an animal!"

The brush didn't even rustle this time as the tall, well-proportioned young Indian warrior stepped into camp. A wry smile quirked lips set in a darkly handsome face, and he slipped his tomahawk into the leather band holding his loincloth against a flat stomach. Instead of leaping at the warrior, the dog wagged its tail.

"I am not so foolish that I would match weapons against you, Little Wind. Even my tongue is no match for yours."

"Spirit Eagle! What are you doing here?" Caitlyn dropped the knife to her side and and hurried over to the warrior. "Tall Man's here. If he finds out you're at rendezvous. . . ."

"No one else has seen me, Little Wind. I only came because I heard of your father's death. I felt a need to tell you how my heart bleeds for you and see for myself that you are all right. But the one in the brush there, he did not have concern for you in his heart.''

"Who was it? Did you know him? There's been a man following me. I guess it was me, anyway. Thought it might be Jon that he was interested in at first, but since he showed up here when I was alone, I figure that settles it.''

"I did not know him. He is not a man who has been among us before. And he would not have been any longer, had not my tomahawk brushed a dead limb when I raised it. He was a white man, and he had strength in his body and evil in his eyes.''

"You're hurt. Sit down and let me put a cold cloth on that bruise on your face.''

"I cannot stay, Little Wind.''

"Just for another second. Sit.''

Caitlyn tucked the whetstone into the dress pocket and took Spirit Eagle's arm to lead him over to the fallen log. She pushed against his broad, bare chest, and Spirit Eagle gave a sigh and sat. After laying the knife beside him, Caitlyn grabbed the bath sheet she had washed out earlier and hung on a nearby limb to dry. She carried it over to one of the water buckets and dunked it in.

"This ain't . . . isn't as cold as it was when Jon brought it in a while ago,'' Caitlyn said as she folded the wet corner of the bath sheet and held it against Spirit Eagle's face. "But maybe it'll help the swelling. Any of your teeth feel loose?''

"No. His blow glanced off.''

"Left a darned deep bruise for glancing off. Color skin you got, it takes a mighty powerful punch from a man's fist to leave a bruise this dark.''

"It was not his fist. He kicked, and he wore white man's boots.''

"Kicked?'' Caitlyn held the cloth in place and shook her head. "Dirty fighter, huh?''

"You must be careful of this one, Little Wind, if indeed it was you he was after and not just an unprotected woman to vent his lust on. How is it you come to be here alone?''

Caitlyn bristled and dropped her hand from the bath

sheet. Spirit Eagle watched Caitlyn prop her hands on her hips and glare at him.

"I can take care of myself! Darn it, I can ride just as well as you and throw a knife better! I haven't shot a rifle since Pa died—that awful grizzly broke his—but I'm just as good a shot as he was!"

"Sometimes evil cannot be fought with weapons, Little Wind," Spirit Eagle told her as he rose from the log. "You. . . ."

Spirit Eagle's head came up and he stared over Caitlyn's head. "Someone comes. I must go."

"Wait!" Caitlyn grabbed his arm. "Don't leave mad at me. We've been friends too long. I'm sorry I mouthed off like that."

Spirit Eagle stroked her cheek tenderly and his brown eyes softened. "We will always be friends, Little Wind. We have fought with our tongues before."

"Yeah, and more than that at times," Caitlyn said with a small laugh. She stood on tiptoe and kissed his cheek just as two figures topped the rise beyond the campsite. "You take care of that there bruise, and the rest of yourself, too."

Spirit Eagle wrapped the bath sheet around Caitlyn's neck and gave her a brief hug. He silently melded into the brush, but Jon's charge down the rise toward the camp was anything but quiet. The dog leapt up again, barking furiously.

"Oh, lordy, now what?" Caitlyn grabbed the rope and raced over to loop it around the dog's neck. She gripped the rope tightly as she unconsciously braced herself for another confrontation with Jon.

Jon passed Caitlyn with a roar of rage and barely a glance. The look, though, however brief, fired Caitlyn's anger, causing Silas to skid to a stop and raise his hand in a peaceful gesture when she turned on him.

"Whoa, Cat. Man wouldn't need a flint to start a fire right now. All he'd have to do is hold a piece of kindlin' in front of your eyes."

"What the hell are the two of you doing, busting in here like something's on fire!? Scaring off my friend! Hush now!'' Caitlyn dropped a hand to the dog's head, and the animal immediately quieted and curled at her feet.

"Hell, Cat, I tried to stop Jon when I saw it was Spirit Eagle with you. Was like tryin' to stop a wounded buff'ler bull. Guess it was partly my fault for lambastin' Jon for leavin' you alone all the way back here."

"Serves both of you right, you were worried a bit. Going off to enjoy yourselves and expecting me to stay here and do all the work. It'll be another year before I get a chance to see anyone again, and you promised I could go see Sky Woman."

Silas sat down on the upturned log and shook his head. "She's gone, Cat. Her and Tall Man both. Seems funny, 'cause all the rest of the Nez Perce are still here. Cat, was there anyone else came by here while we was gone?"

Caitlyn stared at him for a brief second, then shuttered her eyes and shrugged her shoulders. "No one I saw," she said truthfully.

Silas's face told her that he didn't really believe her, but Caitlyn bit back any further explanation. Lordy, they were already smothering her. What if she told them about the man following her—probably the same one Spirit Eagle ran off? They'd even start escorting her to relieve herself. And she'd be darned if she'd hang her bare backside over a log while Jon stood nearby!

"I couldn't find him," Jon said angrily as he strode over to Caitlyn. "Who the hell was he? And what the hell are you doing, entertaining men here in camp while we're gone?"

Caitlyn's head snapped up and she faced him defiantly. "He was a friend of mine, and you darned sure *wouldn't* have been able to find him, if he didn't want to be found! You've got a long ways to go before you can track a man smart as him!"

"I asked you who he was, damn it!"

"Forget it, Jon," Silas growled. "I know who he was, and Cat wasn't in any danger from him."

Jon whirled on Silas. "And is there some damned reason neither one of you wants to tell me his name?"

"Yes," Silas said as he stood. "Now, we got some plans to make. I want to get our tradin' done and leave day after tomorrow."

"Day after tomorrow?"

Jon and Caitlyn spoke simultaneously, both with shock on their faces. Caitlyn won the battle for speech when she plunged ahead with her words.

"You can't possibly get everythin' done by then. Why, we've got to get some meat in and you said you need new clothes. They can't be made in just a day. And it'll take you more than a day just to dicker with the traders and get a good price for your furs. You got the best bunch of furs I've seen in ages. You can't just take the first offer they make."

"Day after tomorrow," Silas said in a grim voice. "Anythin' not done by then can be done in the mountains. And we can stop on our way to hunt. There's buff'ler northwest of us—heard it from the Nez Perce. Figured we'd head up to your old cabin, Cat, and winter there."

"Oh. Well, if that's where we're headed, then I don't mind getting an early start," Caitlyn said with a nod of agreement. "I've got everything I need there to fix you both up with whatever you'll need this winter. Pa and I even left a few deer hides there to use when we got back. They ought to be cured right soft by now."

"Wait a minute. Don't I have anything to say about this?" Jon put in.

"If you do, say it," Silas replied. "Any reason you can think of we should hang around rendezvous any longer?"

None, except it means I'll be out there a good month longer, with no distraction except Silas from that luscious little package of curves. Jon shook his head in defeat. He wasn't about to voice that reason, and if he refused to go when Silas was ready, he'd have to follow through on the vague notion of striking out on his own.

And he owed Silas. Owed him for all the wilderness lessons the old man had taught him last winter: Showing him how the traps worked, the scent used to attract the beaver, the proper way to walk across the snow with the snowshoes Silas had helped him make. Hell, even where to place the traps, not only for beaver, but mink and ermine, fox and an occasional wolf. Jon wouldn't even have had enough furs to buy shot for his rifle this summer, if not for Silas.

And his blond scalp might be decorating a lodge pole right now if Silas hadn't passed on at least part of his vast store of Indian knowledge. Even at that, Silas had gotten him out of a couple jams when Jon unintentionally insulted an Indian leader. Too, there was that time a chief's daughter had matrimony on her mind. . . .

"Day after's fine with me," Jon gave in. "But it's your turn to stay in camp this evening, Silas. I've got a couple things to do."

"Suit's me," Silas agreed. "Me and Cat'll get somethin' to eat at one of the tents, then come back here and sort the furs, so's we won't have to do it in the morning."

Jon propped his rifle against a tree. "Where's the knife I got from Tall Man? I left it there by the fire."

Caitlyn walked over to the downed log. "I was sharpening it for you," she said as she picked up the knife and returned to the fire. "Got a good edge on it now."

"Thank you," Jon said gruffly. "You didn't have to do that."

"I told you I pay back." She reached down for the knife's sheath on a small rock by her feet and handed it to him. "I washed out that shirt you loaned me, too. It's clean, when you want to wear it again."

Jon tucked the knife into the sheath and fastened it to his belt without responding. He didn't care if he never saw that damned shirt again. It carried memories of his home in Richmond, and his ex-fiancee, Roxie, now his brother's wife. It even reminded him of Charlie, whom he had once thought of not only as his brother, but his best friend.

Jon swung around and strode from camp. "I'll be back in the morning in plenty of time to help with the furs, Silas," he called over his shoulder.

Caitlyn stared after him, an unexpected pain stabbing through her. She was pretty darned sure Jon didn't know anyone else in camp well enough to share their fire all night. He hadn't spoken to any of the people they met that morning as if they were friends. He had to sleep somewhere and, if not in their camp, only one other place came to mind.

It wasn't any of her business, she reminded herself. So what if one of those women for hire spent the night curled up in Jon's strong arms—like she had done almost the entire night before? So what if the woman did more than curl up with him? So what if Jon undressed the woman and himself by the light of a fire inside a wigwam, stroked her body, kissed her. . . .

Caitlyn unconsciously pursed her lips and a yearning need filled her. Her hands clenched and her nails bit into her palms. Her breasts grew heavy, the nipples puckering and scraping against her deerskin bodice when her breathing quickened.

"You ready to go eat, Cat?"

"Yes!" she snapped.

So what if he snuffed and snorted over that poor woman's body? That sort of thing got a woman with child, trapped her, lost her forever the freedom Caitlyn valued so highly. She had always avoided the young children in the Indian camps—never cooed over the babies, never chucked them under the chin or offered to watch them while their mothers did chores.

Thank goodness Sky Woman had never had a child with Pa. Caitlyn would have been hard pressed to show any interest in the new baby. Sky Woman was wrong when she told Caitlyn the day would come when she'd want to show her beauty to a man and share his life.

Marriage meant babies, unless she was lucky enough to find a man who didn't seem able to make them, like her Pa must have been after all the years he spent with Sky Woman.

She couldn't imagine a man like Jon not dropping babies behind him, though.

Somewhere in the restricted portion of Caitlyn's mind a baby cried, the sound cut off abruptly. She firmly clamped the door shut on the memory as she followed Silas from camp.

Jon paused a few feet from one of the liquor tents, his stomach roiling at the thought of forcing down any more of that rotgut. Why the hell had he been stupid enough to let slip that he didn't intend to return to camp that night, he chastised himself. He might as well have admitted to Silas and Caitlyn that he intended to find a whore to spend the night with.

Well, he might as well get his itch scratched and get it over with. Twelve more lonely months stretched out ahead of him, and a man's body needed surcease to keep it going. He'd barely been 14 when the young widow on the next plantation introduced him to the pleasures he'd only fantasized about until then. And he'd never lacked for sex after that, although he had steered clear of virgins, until Roxie.

Virgins were for marriage and families. At least, he'd always told himself they were. Once again he wondered what had gone through his brother Charlie's mind on his and Roxie's wedding night, but he brushed the thought aside.

Jon turned away from the liquor tent without ordering a drink. His steps were strangely reluctant as he headed for the edge of the huge campsite where the wigwams he sought were placed, affording those who had a desire for it a measure of privacy. Plenty of other men didn't give a darn, he realized as a high-pitched peal of laughter split the air, followed by a bass rumble.

Jon glanced at the camp fire as he passed. The woman sat in the bearded trapper's lap, her dress hanging around her waist and the man's lips slobbering over her bare breasts. The woman met Jon's glance with a sly look and dropped one eyelid.

"Plenty more here after he's done, honey," she called in a drunken voice. "It don't wear out—just gets juicier!"

Jon shook his head and his steps faltered, but not before

he was well past the scene. Get it over with, his mind repeated.

Get it over with?

Jon came to a complete halt and stared ahead of him at the circle of wigwams. Was he really that desperate? Even at the whorehouses he had visited in Richmond, the women washed between men. And even there a man could close his eyes and make believe he hadn't paid for the pleasure. Woo her with a few well-placed caresses and soft words. Pretend it wasn't just straight-out sex—lust to be relieved.

How many of those men he passed all day had already visited those wigwams—left behind their seed to mix with the next man's in line?

And lines there were, some short, others longer. As Jon watched, a man emerged from a wigwam, adjusting himself under his loincloth. His words carried on the air as he spoke to the next man in line and told him just what tricks the woman waiting inside knew. Two of the men in front of the next wigwam left their line and joined the other one.

Revulsed, Jon snorted and turned away, heading back for the liquor tent. His mind was filled with the images of the wigwams, and his heart with a new pity for the women inside.

Men had stood at the door of each wigwam—both white and Indian—directing the men in and out and collecting the furs.

It wasn't really much different back in Richmond. Almost all the houses were run by men, who raked in most of the money and paid a couple bouncers to control the rowdy men waiting their turn. Occasionally, the bouncers even sprinted up the stairs to one of the rooms, if the noises inside grew too violent. They weren't really protecting the women, though, but the merchandise the house sold—the women's bodies. A beaten woman had to rest a day or two—couldn't serve the customers.

"Clay! Hey, Jon Clay, over here!"

Jon turned toward the voice and saw Pete Smith motioning him to his tent. As Jon approached, Pete dug into his pocket and pulled out a stained envelope.

"Got to talking to a man from one of the other companies," Pete said. "Told me someone back in St. Louis asked him to bring this with him, in case he ran across you. I told him you'd be coming back for the music box, and he gave me this to pass on to you."

Jon reluctantly accepted the letter and held it beneath a lantern to read the scrawl on the envelope. He should have known Charlie wouldn't let him go so easily. Hell, his half-brother had talked himself blue in the face, demanding to know why Jon refused to stay for the wedding—assuring Jon that nothing would change, even though the will left by Charlie's father had specifically disinherited Jon and left the plantation to Charlie.

Maybe that would have worked. There had never been any problem between him and Charlie—just Jon and his stepfather. But not with Roxie in the picture. Not with the master bedroom, which Charlie had moved into after his father's death, only two doors down. Not after Charlie announced Roxie had accepted his marriage proposal.

"You want a little privacy to read that," Pete said, "you can go on over there."

"Thanks."

Jon walked over to the far end of the tent and settled on the bench beneath another lantern. He stared down at Charlie's scrawl another moment, remembering how their tutors despaired of ever teaching him and Charlie both to take their time and learn to put the stylish flourishes on their letters and words. Too many other things had demanded their attention during their lessons—tales of ferocious battles and conquering heroes, descriptions of lands and people they couldn't wait to visit.

And always, the plantation fields beckoned. Shoes and shirts came off immediately after the noon meal, tossed onto a hay bale in the barn. Barefoot and tanned, Jon and Charlie trudged the plowed fields in the summer, learning every step of the tobacco-growing process. By the time they were ten, they were both experts at sorting the cured leaves into piles by quality.

"Lord, Charlie, but I miss you," Jon murmured as he ran a finger beneath the envelope flap.

Chapter Eight

One Week Later

Jon lay on his stomach on top of the ridge and lined up the sights on his rifle before he gently squeezed the trigger. The buffalo dropped without a quiver, killed instantly by the bullet through its brain.

"Good shot," Caitlyn whispered beside him, a slightly amazed look on her face.

As he reloaded his rifle, Jon shot her a wry grin. "You sound like you thought I'd miss. I've been handling guns since I could walk."

Caitlyn giggled under her breath. "Stay out here much longer, and you can enter the liar's contest at rendezvous next summer. Rules there say you have to take a tale with a smidgen of truth and see how far you can stretch it. I reckon that one you just told would earn you a spot in line, especially if you hunker down like you're two years old and carry that buffalo gun on your shoulder."

"Hum," Jon mused as he lined up his sights again. "Seems like I'm remembering it a little better now. I was actually only crawling the first time. Had to brace the butt of the gun against my crib slat, and Nanny stuck her head in the nursery door just about the time I figured out where the trigger was. Poor Nanny. We had to retire her on a pension, since she couldn't even change a nappy after that, her hands shook so bad.''

Caitlyn's burst of laughter was drowned by the boom from the rifle. She shook her head, and her blue eyes sparkled merrily as she glanced from Jon toward the other shaggy brown body lying in the little valley.

''That's enough meat for now,'' she told Jon. ''Time I get all that fixed for us, we'll have a load on the horses.''

''You sure two tongues will be enough?'' Jon quirked an eyebrow at her. ''For you and Silas, I mean. I'll leave that delicacy to you two.''

''You just wait 'til you taste it,'' Caitlyn said with a pat on his arm. ''You didn't think you'd like *Wagmiza Wasna*, either, until you tasted it. You thought it'd be like regular pemmican.''

For the life of him, Jon couldn't remember the *Wagmiza Wasna* on his tongue, but he had an untarnished recall of the taste of Caitlyn's finger. He supposed he might sample a piece of buffalo tongue, if she offered it to him the same way. Jerking his eyes away from Caitlyn's slender fingers on his arm, Jon stared back down into the valley.

''First,'' he said in a gruff voice, ''we have to get down there and clean those animals. Why isn't the rest of the herd running off after those shots?''

''Buffalos are stupid critters,'' Caitlyn explained. ''Sometimes they'll stand there milling 'round for hours while a person's shooting them. Other times one of them'll spook at a shadow when a cloud covers the sun, and the whole herd'll take off and run 'til they drop. That's why Silas didn't want you picking off our meat out of that big herd yesterday. You never know which direction them skittish things will run, so we needed to wait 'til we found a small bunch off by itself.''

''Those skittish things,'' Jon corrected her.

''Those skittish things,'' Caitlyn repeated agreeably.

"Anyway, we'll have to go down there and chase them off soon as Silas gets here. He's heard your shots back where he's fixing up our camp, and he ought to be here with the packhorses in a while."

Caitlyn tossed her long, ebony braid back over her shoulder and sat up to stretch. She reached for the back of her neck to massage a small ache in her muscles, and her breasts strained against her doeskin dress bodice. Glancing down, she brushed at the dry grass clinging to the doeskin, and pulled out a long piece of dried weed that had somehow worked its way inside her neckline when she and Jon belly-crawled up to the ridge top.

Unaware of Jon's hungry gaze, she slipped a finger beneath her neckline and scratched a nail over the tickle left behind when she withdrew the weed, while she stuck the weed in her mouth to chew on it. Jon give a hiss as he scrambled to his feet, and the weed fell unnoticed to the ground when Caitlyn stared at him in astonishment.

"Where you going?" she demanded.

"Down there and chase off those buffalo so I can start butchering the dead ones," he tossed over his shoulder as he strode down the hillside toward where they had left their horses.

Caitlyn shrugged her shoulders and rose to follow him. They could probably handle the two hundred or so animals down there by themselves, she guessed. And the sooner they got the meat back to camp, the sooner she could start smoking and pickling it. The cabin she and Pa had built was still another week's journey away, and it would take her at least three days to cure the buffalo meat. They had already been traveling a week, and if her calculations were right, August was already upon them. She had seen snow as early as the end of August in these mountains.

Jon passed her without a glance as he rode toward the ridge top, and Caitlyn hurried over to the pinto Silas had traded several ermine furs for and given her to ride. Good grief, she hoped Jon at least had enough sense to wait for her before he rode down into that valley. She checked the noose around her pup's neck—she didn't need to be wor-

ried about him following them down there and spooking
the herd. Then she grabbed a handful of mane and leapt
onto the pinto's bare back. Her dress skirt barely covered
her thighs, but she ignored the cool breeze on her legs as
she urged the pinto up the hillside.

"Wait!" Caitlyn called, but Jon disappeared over the
ridge top. Caitlyn swiveled around to glance behind her,
but she saw no sign of Silas coming to help. Thinning her
lips in a gesture of both worry and displeasure at Jon's
foolishness, she kicked the pinto into a canter up the hill.

When he reached the valley floor, Jon reined his horse
in a sweep around the buffalo herd. Several shaggy heads,
topped by sharp horns, rose to watch his approach, but not
one of the animals moved away.

"Get!" Jon shouted. "Get out of here!"

Jon's horse balked when one huge bull lowered its head
and pawed the ground. Tightening the reins in one hand,
Jon picked up his rifle in the other. He kicked the horse in
the flanks, but it sidled sideways instead of ahead.

The breeze blew the herd's scent to him, and Jon opened
his mouth, trying not to breathe through his nose. God, they
stank. But stink or not, he had to get them moving—and
to do that he needed to get closer.

"Darn it, Jon," Caitlyn said as she rode up beside him.
"You're going about this the wrong way."

"Get your ass back up that hill," Jon growled, never
once taking his eyes from the bull buffalo, which snorted
and raised its head to glare at them with red eyes. "It's too
dangerous down here for you."

Caitlyn let out an exasperated whuff of air. "It's gonna
be danged dangerous for you here in a minute, you don't
listen to what I tell you. Even your horse has got more
sense than you do!"

By now the entire herd had turned their heads in the
direction of the two riders. Several cows snorted to call
their calves to their sides, and Jon's horse began backing
away.

Caitlyn reached over and grabbed the bridle of Jon's

horse. "Don't let him move," she ordered. "Keep him still."

"Why the hell should I do that?" Jon shot back. "Let's get out of here and back up the hill. I'll get them moving by shooting at them."

"Look," Caitlyn said. "They really can't see us. Buffalo have got poor eyesight, and the wind's blowing our way, so they can't smell us. That old feller there just senses there's something nearby he ought to be worried about— mostly because he can probably smell the blood on those two animals you shot."

Confirming Caitlyn's words, the huge bull lowered its head again and walked over to sniff at one of the dead buffalos. It nudged the carcass once, then lifted its head and let out a bellow. Several of the cows raised their tails and started trotting away, their calves following them, but the bull turned its head back toward Jon and Caitlyn.

"Why isn't that horse of yours acting skittish?" Jon asked.

"He's an Indian pony. He's hunted buffalo before."

"Well, how the hell long do we have to sit here?"

"Reckon that's gonna be up to that bull over there."

"If he can't see us, why don't we just ride away?"

" 'Cause he can hear," Caitlyn said with a look that told Jon just how stupid she thought that remark was. "And he can feel—he'll feel the ground shaking under our horses' feet and then know just where the heck we're at."

Suddenly a small buffalo calf stumbled out of the brush a few dozen yards from Caitlyn and Jon, bawling loudly for its missing mother. The bull charged with a bellow of rage.

Caitlyn gasped and dropped the bridle of Jon's horse, then slashed her own reins on its rump when it lunged away. Kneeing her pinto in the opposite direction of the one Jon's horse took, she bent low and craned her head over her shoulder to see which set of pounding hooves the enraged buffalo would follow.

It came after her—but so did the entire herd. The calf's mother paused only long enough to shove the calf once before she trailed through the choking dust after the stampede.

The rumbling roar behind her grew louder as Caitlyn's pony raced across the valley floor. She hoped like hell that Jon had enough sense buried somewhere in that greenhorn mind of his to get back up on the ridge and stay the heck out of the way. Glancing behind her again to gauge the distance separating her from the buffalo, she pulled the pony's head around and sent him flying across the path of the stampede, rather than in the same direction.

Horror crawled into her chest as Caitlyn realized she had misjudged the speed of the herd. They would be on her before she could get out of the way. One huge bull on the edge of the stampede was only ten feet away.

The bull crumbled to the ground, and the buffalo behind it crashed into the body and went down in a tumbling heap. The next huge body swung past the downed bodies, brushing the tip of the pinto's tail as it passed.

Caitlyn clenched her knees and sawed on the pinto's reins until it came to a halt. She turned the horse and watched the rest of the herd stream on by, gulping in draughts of air and trying to calm the frantic beat of her heart. Lordy, that had been close. If that bull hadn't stumbled. . . .

She glanced at the other end of the valley and saw Jon standing on the hillside, his rifle still against his shoulder as though he were frozen in place. The last of the stampede streamed past, and Caitlyn looked back at the buffalo that had almost run her down. The second buffalo got to its feet and raced after the herd, but the first one lay unmoving—obviously dead. Had it broken its neck in the fall, or—no, even her Pa would've had trouble picking off a moving buffalo in the middle of a stampede.

Caitlyn rode over to the dead buffalo and slid to the ground. After watching the animal for a few seconds to assure herself that it was indeed dead, she walked over and stared down at the body. Behind the horns, fresh blood seeped from a bullet wound.

Caitlyn turned to stare back at the hillside again. Now

Jon stood beside his upright rifle, the barrel of the gun topping even his tall frame, and his blond hair shining in the sunlight. She measured the distance between Jon and the buffalo bull with her eyes, shaking her head in denial, but knowing Jon had somehow actually made that impossible shot.

She knew those buffalo guns could shoot a fair distance—she had watched the matches at rendezvous and seen men hit targets a half-mile away. Stationary targets, though, not a moving buffalo bull that could almost outrun a horse when it was spooked.

Her respect for Jon went up a notch, but almost immediately she cringed inside at the thought of facing those icy blue eyes when she saw Jon move over and grab his horse's reins. Thank goodness—there came Silas over the ridge. Surely Silas would back her up and tell Jon it was his own darned fault Caitlyn had to lead the herd away to keep them both from being trampled.

She waited by the dead buffalo while Jon and Silas rode down the hillside and across the valley. Her chin tilted up and her shoulders stiffened as they came near, and she could hear the murmur of their voices, though she couldn't make out their words yet. They both fell silent when they came near.

Silas dismounted and looped the lead ropes of the two pack horses over his saddlehorn.

"You all right, Cat?" he asked in an anxious voice.

Caitlyn kept her eyes trained on Jon, who still sat on his horse. "Yeah. Thanks to Jon, there. I expect he told you that he shot that bull before it could run me down."

Jon ordered his body off the horse, but he couldn't seem to drop his reins. His clasp on them kept his fingers from trembling, and his knees were pressed against the horse's sides for the same reason. A picture of Caitlyn crouched over her wildly-galloping pinto's mane and the bull closing the gap between them kept flashing in and out of his mind, and he could still feel the imprint of his rifle butt against his shoulder.

The bull's head had kept bobbing up and down, and his

rifle sight had wavered in time as he instinctively tried to judge the rhythm of the bull's stride and calculate the drop of his bullet. He didn't even remember pulling the trigger— just the deadly fear in his heart for the everlasting seconds it took the smoke to clear the end of his barrel.

He scanned her as she stood there with a look of half trepidation and half defiance on her face. Although he knew in one corner of his mind that she hadn't been hurt, he couldn't make the other corner accept it.

Finally he forced himself to dismount and walk over to her.

"Don't you ever, ever pull a stupid stunt like that again," he growled in a voice rusty with suppressed emotion. "Jesus, you could've been killed."

Caitlyn inched her chin up, then dropped it when she read not anger but anxiety in his blue eyes. She toed at a rock and took a deep breath.

"Th . . . thank you for what you did. I wouldn't have been able to help you if those critters had come after you instead. I didn't have no gun with me."

"Any gun," Jon murmured.

Caitlyn lifted her face. "Any gun," she repeated. Then she swayed toward him and Jon caught her in his arms.

"Damn it, Caitlyn," Jon said as he buried his face in her hair, "you scared the living hell out of me."

Silas remounted and rode back toward the first two buffalo Jon had shot in the other end of the valley. Guess he could get started on them, and leave that one there to Cat and Jon. Hopefully, they'd get around to butchering it after a bit.

Chapter Nine

The little log cabin sat halfway up the mountainside, near the shore of an azure lake, which reflected the snowy clouds drifting overhead. Towering pines and birch surrounded it, except for an area behind and off to the right, where trees had been cut for logs and wood, allowing some underbrush to spring up. Jon glanced at Caitlyn as they rode into the clearing, watching her face brighten with delight.

"Home," she whispered loud enough for Jon to catch the word.

He studied the small structure as they approached. Home, she called it in that reverent voice. Home to him had been a huge, white-pillared mansion outside Richmond, with so many rooms he had never bothered to count them. He didn't recall ever having felt even a slight stirring when he returned from a trip and saw the house.

Guess that's the difference between a house and a home, Jon mused silently.

Suddenly the pup took off toward the cabin, barking furiously. An answering roar sounded behind the partially open door.

"Gol'darn it," Silas said as he pulled his horse to a halt. "There's a critter in there."

"Get back here, Dog!" Caitlyn yelled at the same moment Silas spoke. She wisely didn't follow the pup, but sat watching it ignore her and streak through the doorway.

A second later, the pup kie-yied and yelped, then raced back through the door with its tail between its legs. A yearling black bear cub was hot on the pup's rear, growling and snorting as it chased the pup in a circle.

Jon glanced back and forth from Silas to Caitlyn to see them both with hands folded on their mounts' necks, shaking their heads.

"Uh . . . you want me to try to shoot that bear?" he asked.

"Naw," Silas replied. "He ain't got enough fat on him this time of year to make him worth killin'."

"Dog's gonna have to learn," Caitlyn said, keeping her eyes on the fracas in the yard.

The bear cub reared on its hind legs and swatted at the dog, which dodged the deadly claws and then circled the cub and bit its rump. The cub whirled and slashed again. It threw its head back and roared, flashing white fangs. The dog backed away, barking wildly.

The bear charged. The dog ran. They both disappeared around the side of the cabin.

"Uh oh," Caitlyn said. "You might want to get that rifle ready now, Jon."

Jon shot her a quizzical look, but he lifted the rifle to his shoulder. Barely 30 seconds later, the pup flew back around the side of the cabin, with a much larger, louder snarling bear at its heels. The sow skidded to a stop when she caught sight of the humans, but the pup came barreling past the horses, and crouched behind them with a whimper.

"Wait, Jon," Caitlyn said. "Don't shoot just yet."

The sow stood up on her hind legs and roared.

"Now?" Jon asked.

"Huh uh. She's just warning us that she's protecting her cub," Caitlyn said. "Maybe she'll go back to take care of it and not bother us."

The sow dropped to the ground and lifted her nose, sniffing the air. She took a step forward, then halted and glanced over her shoulder. The yearling's head poked around the side of the cabin, and the sow whirled with a growl and headed for her cub.

The yearling's head disappeared with a snap, and Caitlyn giggled as the sow lumbered after it. A moment later, she caught sight of the cub running across an opening in the brush behind the cabin, with its mother close behind. The cub glanced back at its mother, missing a step and tumbling end over end. It regained its feet with the help of a swat from the sow, and both animals vanished in the underbrush.

"Young'uns," Silas said with a smile. "They ain't got a lick of sense sometimes."

"More trouble than they're worth," Caitlyn agreed, and Jon shot her a puzzled glance at the pointed tone of her voice.

Jon eased the rifle hammer back in place and picked up his reins to follow Caitlyn and Silas toward the cabin. They tied the horses to a hitching post, and Caitlyn propped her hands on her slender hips as she stared at the door.

"Probably gonna be a mess in there," she said. "I told Pa to put a lock on before we left, but he said a cabin ought to be left so's any mountain man who needed shelter or a meal could use it."

"That there's the code of the mountains," Silas said. "Nobody never takes more than they need—leastways, nobody who can call hisself a proper mountain man."

"Might's well go see," Caitlyn said with a shrug.

"Here," Jon said as he grabbed her arm. "I'll go in first. There may be another animal of some kind in there."

Caitlyn frowned at him for a second. That protective streak of his was getting a bit out of hand. Or was it? She sort of enjoyed the idea of him checking out the cabin first—poking around to make sure it was safe for her to go inside. It made her feel sort of—safe.

"All right," she said with a smile that almost knocked Jon's breath from his chest. "You want Dog to go with you?"

"Nope." Jon managed to return her smile somehow—he could see the reflection of his face in those lake-blue eyes. "You keep that animal out here. I'd probably be in more jeopardy from him inside than another bear cub."

"There won't be another bear in there, Jon," Caitlyn told him teasingly. "That old sow wouldn't have left it behind."

Jon glanced down at his fingers, which were stroking the silky skin on the underside of Caitlyn's forearm. Reluctantly, he drew his hand back and turned to the cabin door.

Inside, he shook his head in disgust. A clay pot lay shattered on the floor, honey oozing into the cracks between the pine boards. He stepped over a chair with a broken leg and eased between it and the table, which wobbled and crashed to the floor when he brushed against it. Another missing leg, he saw.

A shredded blanket hung down on his right, and Jon pushed it aside with his rifle barrel to find a cot built against the wall. The covers were in disarray, and pillow feathers lay scattered all around. After bending to glance under the cot, he dropped the blanket and turned to study the rest of the room.

Pots and pans hung on hooks beside the fireplace, which took up most of the back wall. No stove. Heck, he couldn't even begin to imagine what a job it would be to get a stove out to one of these isolated mountain cabins. A barrel that must have contained flour lay on its side, white piles of snowy drifts cascading across the floor. Here and there, Jon saw white bear paw prints on the pine boards.

The shelves along the other wall were empty—a jumble of the goods they had contained was piled beneath them. Jon shook his head. Salt, pepper, lard and other unrecognizable matter covered the mess.

He turned toward the back of the cabin again. Beside the fireplace, he noticed another door, also covered by a blanket. Bypassing a second chair, he carefully lifted the blanket to peer inside.

The cub evidently hadn't bothered this room. On the right, another neatly made up cot was built beneath a window with ruffled blue curtains covering the pane. Caitlyn's room. A rag rug lay beside the cot and an ermine fur stretched on the back wall for decoration, above a shelf holding some clothing. The side wall of the fireplace made up the left wall, assuring heat during the frigid winter.

"Jon?"

At the sound of Caitlyn's voice, Jon quickly left the room. "Just a second. . . ."

But she had already entered the cabin. Jon's heart melted when he saw the woebegone look on Caitlyn's face as she stared around the room.

"Don't worry, Caitlyn," he said as he hurried to her side. "I'll help you clean up the mess. It's really not as bad as it looks, and the cub never touched your room."

Caitlyn swiped at a stray tear on her cheek. "Pa worked awful hard building that there table and them chairs. Lots of trappers just haul in a cut log to set on, but Pa said he wanted us to have a nice place to live. He . . . he. . . ."

She broke off with a sob, and Jon pulled her into his arms, stroking her hair when she buried her face against his shoulder.

"Shhhh, honey," he murmured. "I'll fix them for you, I promise. Charlie and I used to help out the carpenter now and then, and I'm sure I can figure out how to mend them. Maybe even make a couple more chairs for around the table."

Caitlyn drew back and wiped the heels of her hands beneath her eyes. "Who . . . who's Charlie?"

"My brother," Jon told her.

"I didn't know you had a brother. You never mentioned him."

Refusing to relinquish his hold when she tried to pull away, Jon replied, "I'll tell you about him someday, Caitlyn. Are you feeling a little better now?"

She hiccuped a sob, but nodded her head, gazing up into his face. Her blue eyes were still tear-sparkled, shimmering in the dimness inside the cabin, and her lower lip was caught between her teeth as though to keep her sobs trapped. Jon lifted his hand and ran his thumb across her mouth—that mouth that was only a scant inch or two below his own lips.

He lowered his head. Her mouth opened slightly, freeing her lip. He cupped her cheek, tracing his thumb along the softness.

"Caitlyn?" he whispered.

"Yes?" Her breath mingled with his, and she tilted her head a little.

"I think I'm going to kiss you," Jon murmured.

"I sure hope so," Caitlyn breathed.

With a muffled groan, Jon caught her lips with his own and gathered her back into his arms. She tasted a little salty from the tear that had escaped her eye—but sweet, so sweet and so soft. Soft, yet firm. She stiffened just barely, as though she wasn't quite sure how he expected her to respond, and he coaxed—nibbled and coaxed some more, until she melted and wrapped her arms around his neck.

Jon buried his fingers in her hair to hold her near and keep those salty-wine tasting lips available at just the right angle for another kiss, as soon as he caught his breath.

Caitlyn smiled dreamily and barely opened her eyes. "Was . . . was it all right? I . . . I never kissed anyone before."

"It was perfect. Absolutely, utterly perfect. And you?"

"I've sort of forgot already," Caitlyn teased. "Maybe you could show me again how it feels."

Jon complied. This time he made sure she would have no failing of memory. He kissed her until he was afraid he would bruise her—kissed her eyes shut when she tried to open them—kissed her lips again, nuzzled her ears and left each one wet from his tongue. Kissed the delectably soft neck—ran his tongue along that pretty little chin bone. Captured that delicious mouth again until Caitlyn was forced to pull away with a gasp for air.

"Oh!" she said when she exhaled. Her knees wobbled and she tightened her hold on his neck. Her body sang to her with ripples of pleasure and flushes of warmth. Her neck wouldn't hold up her heavy head, and she laid her cheek against Jon's shoulder.

"Oh."

Jon cradled her against him, fitting each soft curve into a special place on his own body made for it. He laid his cheek on her hair, breathing in deeply and running his hands up and down her back.

"You want another reminder?" he whispered.

"I don't think I could stand one right now. I. . . . "

"Well, here now, Cat," Silas said as he came through the door. "Don't be crying like that. Me and Jon'll help you clean up this mess."

Immediately Silas realized his mistake when Jon glared at him and Caitlyn turned around to face him, her eyes danged sure not sparkling with tears.

"Oh, it'll be all right, Silas," Caitlyn said in a dreamy voice. "It can all be fixed, like Jon said."

Silas backed out of the room, almost tripping when his heel hit the chair inside the door. "Uh . . . you and Jon go ahead and see what needs to be done. I'll check around outside."

Caitlyn blinked, then slowly looked around the room again. Suddenly she whirled on Jon, her eyes narrowing dangerously.

"This has got to stop."

Jon splayed his hands wide in feigned ignorance. "What?"

"This . . . this huggin'. And k . . . kissin'," Caitlyn said, too flustered to notice she was dropping the "g's" on her words again. "This cabin's not big enough for us to move around real well in as it is. And I don't expect to have to worry about you pawin' me every time I get close to you."

"Me *pawing* you?" Jon shot back. "You were snuggling up to me just fine, and enjoying that *pawing* every damned bit as much as I was!"

Caitlyn took a deep breath. She was too honest to call him a liar, especially when he was definitely only speaking truthfully. Yet she couldn't bring herself to candidly admit how deeply his kisses and caresses had affected her.

"Well, it still has to stop," she insisted. "The first thing you know, you'll be waiting until Silas starts snoring and come sneaking into my bedroom. You just better remember that I sleep with a skinning knife Pa gave me under my piller!''

Jon leaned toward her, his fists clenched at his sides. ''I don't need to *sneak* into any woman's bedroom! I've never had to *sneak* into any woman's bedroom and force myself on her in my life! Any woman's bedroom I've ever gone into, I've been *invited* to enter!''

Caitlyn backed away a step before she could stop herself. ''Don't hold your breath waiting for an invite into mine,'' she said with a half-hearted smirk, which was all she could muster when faced with the furious blue iciness of Jon's eyes. ''Hell will freeze over before that happens.''

''Think so, huh?'' Jon advanced a step and Caitlyn wobbled another step backwards.

''Y . . . yes,'' she said.

''How many degrees will hell have to drop before you want me to kiss you again?''

After a second's hesitation, ''The s . . . same amount.''

''Wanna bet?''

''No!'' Caitlyn said with a little screech as she ran for the door.

Jon's laughter followed her, and she whirled around outside the door to glare back. Indignantly, she stamped her foot. How dare he laugh about what had just happened between them? How dare he make fun of her attempt to explain to him that she had no desire to let this—temptation, her mind finally supplied as she groped for the right word—this temptation get out of hand and saddle them both with a loss of freedom.

She started to march back inside and tell him exactly that—in clearer words this time—but she heard Jon's clumping, booted footsteps cross the floor. She grabbed a bucket hanging on a nail beside the door and fled to the lake. It was going to take a lot of water to clean up that mess inside.

For some silly reason, Caitlyn leaned over to peer into the smooth lake surface before she disturbed it by dipping in the bucket. Her face looked back at her, and she studied it closely.

Wisps of dark, ebony hair, tinged with reddish highlights from the sun, curled around her forehead and cheeks. The reflection wasn't mirror clear, but she could make out a faint flush on her cheeks. She had always admired the Indian women's high cheekbones, but her own face was more oval. Her nose was in pretty good proportion to the rest of her features, but her lips looked a little too large today.

She reached up and touched her mouth, probing a finger tenderly around it. Kiss-swollen, maybe? She stared into her own eyes, unable to tell if the color came from them or the lake water. It was so blue today—as blue as Jon's eyes.

She leaned over a little further, and her braid fell across her breast. She fingered it, comparing the silkiness of her own hair to the feel of Jon's blond locks, and deciding that the texture was awfully similar.

Caitlyn flipped her braid over her shoulder. She didn't need this, darn it. All she wanted was to have a good trapping season, so she could earn enough money from her own share of the furs to come back again next winter to her cabin.

She didn't need anything else. She didn't need a man to snuggle up to at night—she could add a bearskin to her bed if it got too cold. She didn't need kisses—she had gotten along right well all these years without them. She sure as hell didn't need to find herself swelling up with a babe—knowing that in nine months she would be stuck changing nappies and suckling a little figure that depended totally upon her for its very existence—an existence that would tie her down and cause her to lose the freedom she valued so highly.

Hugging and kissing led to that—hugging to kissing, and kissing to petting and pawing. Then to that final act Sky Woman and Pa had always tried to keep quiet, never knowing that she sometimes lay awake listening.

And that act led to babies. She knew that, although she

had avoided any attempt Sky Woman made to talk about it with her.

Somewhere in her memory that little cry started up again, cut off abruptly as always. She felt the shaking start, but she could control it in the daylight. It was only at night—dark and lonely when she sat up with a start in bed, swallowing screams she knew would lead to her own death if she voiced them—that restraint failed her and she cuddled under her blankets, shivering violently.

Caitlyn swiped the bucket through the water to fill it, then stood and turned. Her eyes unerringly went to the cabin, and she saw Jon standing in the doorway, one shoulder leaning against the jamb and hands tucked into his pockets. Despite the distance separating them, she could feel his gaze on her. It should have felt as cold as the lake water behind her, but for some reason a hot flush stole over her cheeks, down her neck, and even across her breasts. Even lower.

With a determined slant to her chin, she gripped the bucket and headed for the cabin.

Chapter Ten

Caitlyn laid her finger down so the black and orange woolly bear could crawl onto it. It tickled a little as it crept up her finger and onto the back of her hand, and she giggled as she carried it outside. After carefully lifting the woolly bear to a red sumac leaf, she noted how fat it was, then looked around her.

Barely a month after their arrival at the cabin, the signs were all there—the bushy coat of the caterpillar, early tinges of fall color on the leaves, squirrels continuing to gather nuts to store long past their usual morning hours. Today, with Jon and Silas already gone, she'd decided to take her own tour through the wilderness.

When she bridled her horse, she noticed her pinto's sleek coat beginning to lengthen. Every animal she saw as she rode appeared to be in a hurry, racing against the time when food would be hard to come by. The two bucks she scared from the brush were long out of velvet, their color muted from the brighter bronze of summer. She ran across several scrapes—trees with ragged bark where the bucks rubbed away the antler velvet, the ground beneath the trees torn

115

up from their hooves. Marking their territory in preparation for rut, she knew from Pa's lessons.

The male deer urinated, too, Pa had said, their scent also a warning. And the height of the chipped and scarred tree bark served as evidence of the stature and strength of the buck claiming that certain territory. Any other buck was free to challenge that buck's control, if it measured itself against the other buck's signs and thought it had a chance to defeat him.

Survival of the strongest and best of the breed, Cat. Pa's voice echoed in Caitlyn's mind, and she smiled to herself.

It was early for rut to begin, but also a little early for the huge flights of wild geese and ducks to be winging southward overhead. However, almost every night the haunting cries had followed her into sleep.

"Going to be a hard winter," Caitlyn told the dog trotting beside her pinto. "It'll make the furs good, if we're able to get out to run our trap lines."

She'd taken to talking to Dog a lot. Silas—fairly glib at rendezvous—had retreated by degrees into the silence he claimed to enjoy, which matched the peaceful solitude he loved in the wilderness. Jon—well, Jon talked a little more, but not a lot. Mostly he discussed with Silas what all needed to be done before winter set in.

Near the top of the mountain, at that special spot she always enjoyed no matter how many times she visited it, Caitlyn slid from the pinto. Other mountaintops stretched away in the distance, until only faint, purplish shadows outlined their sawtoothed peaks. The bright sun hovered in the brilliant blue, nearly cloudless sky, but still a tinge of chill shaded the air. Almost a mile below her, the trees and brush in the valley looked like she imagined the plush carpet Pa had told her some houses back east had covering their floors.

She still missed him—darn it, would it ever get any easier? As though sensing her misery, Dog belly-crawled up to her with a whimper, and she wrapped an arm around his neck.

"It's probably because it's getting nigh on a year now,"

she whispered to Dog in a clogged voice. "Next month was when it happened, you know."

Absently, Caitlyn ran her hand down Dog's side, where a new layer of fat covered his formerly protruding ribs.

"No," she acknowledged, "you can't know. You weren't here then."

She sighed and drew a leg up to prop her chin on her knee. Instead of focusing on the view before her, scenes from her and Pa's life ran through her mind. After a while, she realized it was the happy times she recalled—Pa's deep laugh and teasing voice when she determinedly floundered behind him in the snow, refusing to spend another lonely day in the cabin while he ran his lines. Her first attempt at tanning a beaver hide, which Pa solemnly assured her might make a good snowshoe, if she could do another one just like it.

Christmases together, and even a day set aside as her birthday—the day Pa had found her. Those two days each year were her very own, when she spent every minute with Pa. No matter how outrageous her request, Pa would try to fulfill it.

Her very own room had taken the two of them almost a month to build one fall. Pa had asked Sky Woman to sew the curtains for the window for her Christmas present that year. She got her own set of six traps a couple years ago, though he never would let her run her line on her own.

"Guess I miss our talks the most, Dog," Caitlyn mused. "Pa had been all over before he decided to be a mountain man—seen lots of things, lots of places. He'd tell me about them in the evenings, while he worked on the hides."

She gave Dog a stern look. "Not that I ever wanted to go see them myself. Pa always said there wasn't any place as beautiful as our mountains."

The pinto threw up its head and snorted. Dog leapt from Caitlyn's grasp, hackles bristling on his neck and a low rumble in his throat. She instinctively curled her fingers around the skinning knife at her waist, which she carried whenever she left the cabin.

"It's probably just an animal," she murmured to Dog,

but she pulled the knife from its sheath, eyes searching the underbrush around her.

For several long seconds, Caitlyn held her breath and listened, senses attuned for any wayward sound. A deer wouldn't have bothered the dog and horse. Bears usually favored slightly lower elevations, but wolves and pumas roamed even mountaintops. As the seconds lengthened into a minute, Caitlyn slowly let out her breath. Whatever it had been, it must have decided against attacking, because the pinto dropped its head to graze again and Dog sniffed the air a final time, then sat on his haunches.

Funny, though, she hadn't heard anything leave. Must have been a timber wolf, since even a puma would probably have dislodged at least a stone or two when it scrambled away.

She shrugged her shoulders and slipped the knife back into the sheath. The day darkened, and she glanced overhead to see a bank of clouds crawling toward the sun. Snow clouds, already this early in the season. She shivered in the increasing chill and hurried over to the pinto. A snowstorm might send Jon and Silas back in early from their scouting trip, and they'd have a conniption fit if they found her gone.

Shoot. Caitlyn swung onto the pinto and urged him down the mountain trail. They still acted like there was an imaginary fence around the cabin that she was forbidden to cross. She could go to the lake and back, but no farther. If they found out she'd dared ride out alone, they'd probably take the pinto with them from now on when they left.

Caitlyn shrugged and giggled to herself. Danged if that would stop her. Pa always said God gave men legs to walk on before he ever showed them horses were good to ride.

Huge, down-soft flakes began falling as Caitlyn rode into the clearing around the cabin. She hurriedly unbridled the pinto and shooed it into the corral Jon and Silas had repaired. At least there wasn't enough snow yet for the pinto to leave tracks through, and Jon and Silas's horses were still gone.

Worriedly, she watched a few more heavily falling flakes hit the pinto and melt in the steam from its back. No help for it if the men noticed the horse had been ridden when they returned. Maybe they'd listen to her the next time she asked to accompany them.

When Caitlyn threw aside the moccasin she was lining with rabbit fur and stomped over to look out the cabin door two hours later, several inches of snow covered the ground. Where the heck were they? The men hadn't taken overnight supplies this morning, as they had a few times before.

Silas, at least, had to know she would be worried about them. Despite the deceptive beauty of the new snow, it could prove treacherous. The temperature had continued to fall all day, and neither Jon nor Silas had taken the heavy, buffalo-skin coats she had made for them from the hides of the buffalo Jon shot.

A watery yellow sun struggled to peep through the cloud cover for a second, but retreated behind a new bank of roiling, indigo clouds. A frigid gust of wind sent Caitlyn back inside, and she slammed the door. Dog stretched awake from his coil in front of the fire, cocking his ears and whining at her.

"They ought to've been back by now," Caitlyn told him. "Silas knows better than to get caught out in a blizzard when he's got a shelter to go to. Soon's the snow started, they should've come on back and waited it out."

She started to pick up the moccasin again, then threw it aside and went into her room. After pulling her doeskin dress over her head, she hung it on a hook and grabbed a pair of buckskin trousers and shirt from the shelf holding her few articles of clothing. She shimmied into the trousers and shirt, then jerked her wolfskin jacket from its hook.

"Come on," she ordered Dog as she strode toward the door again. She paused to take down the two buffalo-skin coats hanging there, struggling beneath the weight of them but managing to fling them over her shoulder before she went outside.

Dog raced over to the corral, with Caitlyn following more slowly beneath the weight of the coats. She flung them over the rail until she bridled the pinto, then draped them across the horse's back and mounted. Thank goodness Silas had enough sense to always inform Caitlyn which area he intended to scout each trip.

She found them barely a half hour later, after peering through the blowing and gusting snow when she caught sight of a spark of light up ahead. Without Dog, though, she probably would have missed them. For the past ten minutes she had followed him, after it became obvious his sensitive nose had picked up something amid the wind gusts.

Dog must have smelled the fire smoke, she realized as the spark that had caught her attention glowed more brightly, finally shaping itself into the flames of a fire. Jon lay on the ground beside it, with Silas crouched over his legs.

Silas barely glanced at her as she rode in. "Damn glad to see you, Cat," he growled, and Jon's head swiveled toward her. "You bring us something warmer to wear? We had to stop here for a bit to thaw out afore we could ride any further."

Caitlyn slid to the ground and pulled the coats from the pinto. "What happened?" she asked as she hurried over to Silas. Her eyes worriedly scanned Jon, and she handed Silas one coat, then knelt to place the other one around Jon's shoulders.

"Danged fool wouldn't listen when I told him he better start wearin' moccasins, 'stead of them boots with worn-out soles. Slid on some ice on a rock and almost broke his damn fool leg. 'Pears like maybe he only twisted his knee, tho'."

Jon tore his gaze away from Caitlyn's face, but not before he saw her frown of worry give way to exasperation. He shrugged irritably when she tried to snug the coat across his chest and brushed her hands away. Shifting his body, he stuffed his arms into the coat sleeves.

Caitlyn sat back on her heels and clamped her lips into a thin line. The firelight outlined Jon's profile, his mouth set just as stubbornly as her own as he gazed past Silas's shoulder. No sense telling him that he should have listened to Silas about the boots—looked like Silas had, as usual, made his opinion real clear to Jon already.

A snowflake landed on Jon's eyelash, and she instinctively reached out to brush it away, her hand meeting Jon's finger when he reached up. She jerked her arm back, then scrambled to her feet.

"This weather ain't gonna let up," she said. "Looks like it's settled in for a while. We better get on back, if you two are warm enough to ride now."

"Isn't," Jon murmured. He turned his head toward her when Caitlyn agreeably echoed the word, and his eyes narrowed. "What the hell are you wearing?"

Caitlyn looked down at her legs, encased in skin-tight buckskin, and shrugged. "Same thing as you and Silas. Why? Wind starts blowing in the winter, them skirts don't protect a person's legs much."

"Jesus," Jon muttered as he dragged his eyes away.

"Don't appreciate you swearing at me," Caitlyn said with a stamp of her moccasin-clad foot.

"I'll do more than swear at you if you wear those things again. Looks like you outgrew them two years ago!"

"Well, I like that," Caitlyn fumed, plopping her hands on her hips. "If I hadn't been spending all my time sewing up stuff for you and Silas to wear, I might've had time to make me a new pair of britches!"

Jon clenched his fists and held his neck rigid—so he thought. How the hell, then, did his head swivel back around to stare at her? Her blue eyes sparkled with both firelight and indignation, and snowflakes dotted her raven hair, the white emphasizing the silky blackness. Her hands were splayed on trim hips, one index finger tapping out her irritation on a buckskin-covered thigh.

He groaned and pulled his uninjured leg under him, managing to gain his feet. When he swayed dangerously and touched his other foot to the ground with a grimace of pain, Caitlyn and Silas both hurried forward.

"Dang it, boyo," Silas growled. "You keep it up and you're gonna be laid up all winter with that knee."

"Like hell," Jon gritted through clenched teeth. He

shoved Caitlyn away and leaned on Silas. "Go get my horse," he ordered Caitlyn.

"Yes, sir!" she snapped sarcastically.

She flounced over to the horses, her hips twitching beneath the short wolfskin jacket, and Jon's eyes unerringly following her path. Silas bit off a chuckle, and Jon tore his gaze away to glare down at the shorter man.

"What's so damn funny?"

"Nothin', boyo. Nothin' a 'tall."

Chapter Eleven

"Ungrateful jackanapes," Caitlyn muttered two days later as she stomped out of the cabin, the water bucket dangling from her hand. She slammed the door behind her with a satisfying *thunk*, then paused to take a deep breath, squinting her eyes in the snowy whiteness reflected by the brilliant sun's rays.

Lordy, lordy, Jon was a danged trying patient. Wouldn't let her help prop his injured knee on a pillow. Wouldn't let her check the bandage. Wouldn't hardly even eat, unless she left his plate on the floor by the new bunk he and Silas had built along the cabin wall and retreated to the far side of the room.

That first evening, she had broken off a few of the icicles forming beneath the eaves and carried them inside, wrapped in a linen towel. His knee had appeared grossly swollen in the brief glimpse she'd had of it before Jon caught her looking after Silas removed Jon's britches.

Jon's roar of rage had set the tone for his attitude over the next two days. He'd grabbed the towel-wrapped ice from her hands without even a 'thank you kindly, ma'am,' then slapped it on his knee—after he insisted she turn her back, of course.

He was as snarly as a bear just out of its winter den in the springtime. Well, she'd had all she could take. From the looks of things, it would be another two or three days or so before Jon could even start limping around, and she danged sure wasn't going to spend that long cooped up with him in that small cabin. Silas could take his turn caring for his partner tomorrow. Caitlyn intended to find something else to do.

She'd seen a hickory tree the other day on the mountain slope. If the snow kept melting this fast, she might be able to gather the nuts the squirrels had missed.

A drip of icy water slithered down Caitlyn's neck, and she jumped away from the overhanging eaves. The icicle broke loose and fell into the snow with a soft plop, confirming the rising temperatures.

Snow didn't usually last long in early September. Heck, they should still have at least a week or two of warm, Indian Summer days before the first snowfall that would cover the ground until spring. New snow layers would pile one on top of another after that, until they had to cut steps up from the cabin door to reach the top of the drifts. She guessed she'd better take a look at the snowshoes stored under her bed to see if they needed any repairs.

When she reached the lake, Caitlyn knelt and cracked the thin ice near the shore with the bucket, then dipped out a pail full. Cupping her hand, she scooped up a palm of water and sipped. The cold trickled down her throat, and she repeated the motion several times until she satisfied her thirst. Probably that ache in her throat came from holding back the words to tell Jon just what sort of an ass he was being.

After she got to her feet, Caitlyn lifted her face to the sun for a second and closed her eyes. Hopefully it would warm up enough for her to at least get a few more baths before winter set in. She didn't really like confronting the frigid water each fall, but it was preferable to carrying a dozen buckets of water up to heat three or four times a week, so she could wash her hair.

As Caitlyn started to reach for the water bucket, she stopped and frowned at a mark on the ground. A moccasin print. Lots larger than her own feet, too. Silas never came down here to get water—figured that was her job, she guessed. Besides, that print was even larger than Silas would have left.

That did it. Someone was prowling around here. Probably what she'd thought was an animal on the mountain the other day could have been a human, too. She sighed in resignation. She wasn't stupid—she knew better than to keep something like this to herself. Whoever it was could be a danger to either her or the men.

If the man was honorable, he'd have made his presence known, instead of skulking around and trying to hide. She studied the print, but the sun had already begun to melt it, and she didn't see anything distinctive about the track. Most men's footprints had something a little different from the next man's—Pa had taught her that. Some leaned one way or the other when they walked. Some were pigeon-toed, some flat-footed. All she could determine from this half-melted print was that the man was large and heavy, probably near Jon's height and weight.

Caitlyn nervously scanned the area around her. She didn't have a sense that anyone was watching her, and the horses in the corral didn't appear alert. Nevertheless, she grabbed the water bucket and headed for the cabin. She'd just have to put up with Jon's surliness until Silas got home. She wasn't about to tell Jon about the footprint first. He'd probably try to hobble over in front of the door and plant himself, so she couldn't even go to the outhouse until Silas got home.

Caitlyn's hand went to her belt, but she hadn't attached the skinning knife that morning. And she'd left Dog inside, instead of calling him with her when she went to the lake. Darn that Jon, anyway. It was his fault her thoughts were too muddled to recall the cautions Pa had drilled into her over the years. Instead of remembering the rules for survival that morning, her mind had been gearing up to face

Jon's unrelenting sullenness over his injured knee.

Even through her pique at her carelessness, Caitlyn sensed a different atmosphere when she reentered the cabin. She glanced at Jon on her way across the room and saw him sitting up on his bunk, a somewhat less threatening look on his face. He had managed to get his trousers on, though Silas had cut the tight buckskin away from his swollen knee and Caitlyn hadn't yet sewn up the rip.

"Should have told me you wanted to get dressed," Caitlyn said as she hefted the bucket onto a hook in the fireplace to warm. "I made you another pair of britches, along with a shirt."

"Thank you, Caitlyn," Jon said so softly she had to strain for the words. "And thank you for taking care of me the past couple days. I've been pretty much of a bastard, haven't I?"

Caitlyn swung around in amazement. Was this the same patient she'd left in the bunk a few minutes ago? Had to be. It sure looked like Jon—same blond hair and blue eyes. Shadow of a beard on his face, though it was just a shade darker than his hair and didn't stand out too much.

"Uh . . . well, guess you've been in pain," she said. "Some folks don't tolerate pain as well as other do."

"I feel like a clumsy fool lately," Jon admitted. "First that knock on the head, then my knee. I'm not used to laying around."

"You want me to fetch one of those books you've got with you, so you can read?"

"I've been thinking about the books, but not to read to myself. I seem to recall promising to teach you to read. Since I can't do anything else, maybe this would be a good time to get started."

"Really?" Caitlyn questioned in awe. "I'd be right proud to give it a try. Of course, maybe I ain't . . . I'm not smart enough to learn. I figure reading must take a long time for a person to learn. Pa said people go to school for years and years."

Jon laughed quietly. "Caitlyn, if anyone can learn to read, you can. You're one of the smartest women I've ever met. And learning to read isn't the reason people go to school for so long. It's all the things they can study after they do learn to read that keeps them in school.''

Caitlyn preened just a little under Jon's unexpected praise. ''Oh. You mean they keep going there so they'll have peace and quiet to read more books?''

''Sort of. But when a person can read, a whole lot of other areas of study open up to him—arithmetic, history, geography. Philosophy and languages.''

''Well, I know what most of those things are, and I can do arithmetic, because Pa could do it. He called it ciphering sometimes, and he taught me so we wouldn't be cheated on our furs. But what's this philosophy thing?''

''I guess the simplest way to explain that is to say it's the study of knowledge down through the years.''

Caitlyn frowned and bit the inside of her cheek as she chewed over that sentence. ''I see,'' she finally said. ''If people study what others have learned before them, they don't waste time relearning it all over. Then they have time to learn more new things themselves.''

''Didn't I tell you that you were smart?''

''There's plenty of room in my mind to get smarter,'' she said with a smirk of satisfaction. ''Let's get to work. Then, I'll be able to read my. . . . ''

Journal, her mind said, but she caught the word before it escaped. ''I mean, *your* books.''

Long hours later, Jon glanced up from the table in surprise. He winced and massaged the small of his back while he looked around to see where Caitlyn had left the lanterns. Evening shadows were crawling through the door Caitlyn had opened to the afternoon sun a while ago, but Caitlyn still bent over the slate Jon had found at one of the trading tents at rendezvous.

She had soaked up knowledge like a flower opening to the sun all day, amazing even Jon with her quick capacity to learn. The abc's were a snap, and Jon recalled the wonder on her face when he told her that learning to write went hand in hand with learning to read. She rapidly tired of blocking out her letters and demanded that Jon show her how to do that other pretty writing she had seen in the rare letters some mountain men had to have read to them.

Now she looked at Jon with her tongue still unconsciously caught between her teeth and held the slate up for him to read.

"The mountains are beautiful," Jon read. "I love living in the mountains. Caitlyn O'Shaunessy." He leaned back in his chair and carefully stretched out his leg. "Great, Caitlyn. And every word is spelled right."

Caitlyn's tongue disappeared back into her mouth. "Well, you didn't tell me there were all these other different parts to reading."

"Like what?" Jon said, though his mind remained on that pink tongue tip, missing it already.

"Like spelling the words right, too."

"Think for a minute, Caitlyn. If words weren't spelled the same, how would anyone else read another person's writing? The words have to be spelled consistently to be understood by everyone."

"Doesn't make sense sometimes, though," Caitlyn mused. "If I have a certain ways to go, it's w-a-y-s. But if I want to know how much a fur weighs, it's w-e-i-g-h-s. Same sounding word, but spelled different."

"That's because the meanings are different. Think about that for a minute, too."

"Yeah, I guess," Caitlyn said fairly quickly. "Like too and two."

"Makes four?" Jon asked.

"Nope," Caitlyn said in a saucy voice. "Like two for me, and two for me, too, and none for you."

Jon threw back his head and laughed, his chuckles continuing when he glanced back at Caitlyn. "I think we've studied enough for one day. You're already getting smarter than your teacher. Besides, no sense straining your eyes in this dim light. We ought to light the lanterns."

Caitlyn jumped to her feet. "Oh, lordy. Look how late it is, and I haven't even got supper started. Silas will be starved when he gets back, and nothing ready to eat. Wonder where he is? He's not usually so late."

Silas stuck his head around the door jamb. "Been here for over an hour," he said. "You two was so busy you didn't even hear me come home. And I already took care of supper. Got a couple rabbits cooking over the fire I built outside here."

"Good," Caitlyn said. "This learning business sure takes it out of a person. I feel as tired as if I'd spent the day hauling water and washing dirty clothes."

"Awful pretty sunset out here," Silas said. "Why don't you two come on out and enjoy it with me?"

"Sure," Jon growled. "Just let me tell my leg to carry me out there."

Silas came on into the cabin. "I can take care of that, too, boyo. Whittled this out for you today. Let's see if it'll fit."

Silas held out the sturdy sapling crutch to Jon. It was fairly straight, and he'd wound the rabbit furs around the fork at the top.

"We'll have to replace them hides with something else tomorrow," Silas said. "I scraped them pretty well, but they ain't tanned. They shouldn't start smelling this soon, tho'."

"Thanks, Silas," Jon said with a grateful smile. "This will be great. I can probably even get out to the horses and at least be able to ride."

"Let's don't hurry it none, Jon. I'll fetch one of these chairs out for you to set on for right now."

Jon fit the crutch under his arm and hobbled outside. He took a deep breath of air and let it out.

"I feel like I've been cooped up in that cabin for a month instead of just two days. Damn, it feels good to be out here."

Caitlyn stopped beside him. "Felt like at least a month to me, too," she agreed.

Jon looked down into the twinkling blueness of her eyes. Her full lips were pursed into a kissable pout, the lower one stuck out just a hair past the upper one. Feathers of black silk surrounded her face, and her long braid hung over her shoulder, draping across one breast. His fingers itched to stroke that hair—maybe something else along with it.

He caught his breath and resolutely pulled his gaze away, his mind warring with the newfound easiness he and Caitlyn had shared today. Faced with being penned up with her tantalizing presence in the small cabin for days on end, he had snapped at her every chance he got. At least that had made her keep her distance, such as it was in that small confine.

"I told you I was sorry," he grumbled.

And he had been. When she disappeared out the door that morning, her back rigid with suppressed anger, he had chastised himself royally. A grown man ought to be able to handle his sexual urges, he'd told himself, without acting like an ungentlemanly asshole. At least, he always had been able to handle them with every other woman—even Roxie. But Caitlyn's closeness had him panting like a stallion scenting a mare in heat.

Just like right now. "Uh . . . I thought Silas was bringing me out a chair," Jon said.

"It's right over there, boyo," Silas said with a gesture of his head. "Put it down there a couple minutes ago. You need some help settin' in it?"

"I can help him."

Caitlyn laid a hand on Jon's arms and his muscles tightened in protest. He managed to shake his head, instead of shaking off her arm, though it took a lot of willpower to ignore the light but insistent curl of her fingers and intimacy of her presence along the lean lines of his own body. Her clean scent drifting up to his nose reminded him of his own inability to walk to the lake and bathe the last few days.

"I can do it myself," he said firmly. "I have to learn to manage this crutch."

"All right." Caitlyn dropped her hand. "I'll follow, just in case you run across a piece of soft ground that won't handle your weight."

"Thanks." Then under his breath, "I think."

He hobbled over and lowered himself into the chair. Caitlyn, thankfully, walked over to Silas as soon as he was settled. Searching for a different focus for his thoughts, Jon stared up at the sunset-lit sky.

Fingers of violet, orange and saffron were outlined by scattered clouds. Even as he watched, the colors faded, the spires shortening, following the sun's retreating path. Further down the mountainside, golden aspen were interspersed with emerald pines, and here and there a glowing red-orange maple. The brilliance of the trees dimmed as the light began to fade.

"Looks like we might get some more snow tonight."

When no one commented on his observation, Jon glanced over at the fire. Caitlyn and Silas had their heads together, Caitlyn murmuring words he couldn't make out and Silas with a grim look on his face. Silas chomped once, then spit a wad of tobacco into the fire.

Jon frowned in annoyance as he watched them. Their tense stances and abruptly halted glances in his direction told him they were discussing something he should be hearing.

"You two get over here," he called loudly. "Or I'm coming over there."

He started to rise, but Caitlyn hurried over, with Silas following her.

"We were going to tell you, Jon," she said, shoving gently against his shoulder to push him back into the chair. "You just stay setting there."

"Sitting," Jon corrected. "A hen sets. People sit. Or a better way to put it would be for me to stay seated."

"Whatever," Caitlyn said, the vagueness in her voice giving Jon pause.

Usually Caitlyn eagerly accepted any correction of her grammar, rarely making the same mistake again. She did, however, still like to use 'ain't' from time to time. What the hell had she and Silas been discussing that had put that worried look on her face?

"It's just. . . . " Caitlyn bit her lip and cast Silas an anxious look.

"Boyo," Silas said. " 'Pears we've got some problems here. Cat rode up the side of the mountain the same day she had to come out there after us. The day you hurt your knee. She thinks there might've been someone else up there, tho' she didn't get a look at him. Could've just been an animal, too.''

Caitlyn shifted uneasily when Jon glared at her. ''You're supposed to stay near the cabin.''

''Well, you both might have froze to death if I had done that,'' she countered, lifting her chin in defiance. ''And I can't stay *inside* that cabin all day long.''

''There's been someone prowling 'round here, too,'' Silas put in. ''Cat saw a footprint down by the lake this mornin'.''

Jon's growing anger overrode any pretense of treating Caitlyn as anything but the foolish woman her actions had proven her to be in his mind.

''You mean to tell me that you rode out of here the other day alone—strictly against our orders?'' he roared. ''And you never told us there might have been someone following you?''

Before Caitlyn could defend herself, he continued, ''And you knew this morning that someone had been snooping around this cabin and you never told me? Goddamn it, Caitlyn. . . .''

''Goddamn it, Jon, shut up!'' Silas snapped. ''This is just why Cat didn't say nothin' to you. Maybe if you'd act like you had as many brains above your belt as you seem to have below it, Cat wouldn't be a'feared to talk to you!''

''What the hell's that supposed to mean?'' Jon snarled as he surged to his feet, wobbling precariously until he got the crutch under his arm.

Silas refused to back down from Jon, who was at least a foot taller and 50 pounds heavier, let alone being half his age.

''You think on it, boyo!'' he ground out between clenched teeth. ''I'm sure a man smart's you think yourself to be can figure it out! I'll give you one hint. A man ain't clear growed 'til he comes to terms with that itch he gets— learns when it's just a urge and when it's got some meanin' behind it. Learns when to quit snarlin' and snappin' and think with what's a'tween his ears instead of. . . . ''

With a brief look at Caitlyn, Silas clamped his mouth shut. She giggled, then quickly clasped a hand over her mouth and widened her eyes in feigned innocence when Jon glared at her.

Dropping her hand, Caitlyn batted her eyelashes once. ''I think I smell the rabbit burning.'' Spinning on her heels, she hurried toward the fire.

Chapter Twelve

Well, what do you know about that?

Lingering in bed the next morning, Caitlyn stretched, then clasped her hands behind her head and stared at her small window. It was still pitch black outside, but she really should be up and about. It took a while for the sun to climb over the mountaintops this time of year, even though it was probably already at least five o'clock.

But she'd much rather lay here and contemplate whether she had correctly reasoned out the meaning of Silas's words yesterday evening. She'd planned on thinking about it when she went to bed. Instead, she'd nodded off too quickly. Rested now, with her mind fresh, she could muse on it to her heart's content.

Jon was attracted to her, at least in one way. Of course that way was what she had absolutely no intentions of allowing. Pa had been honest enough with her whenever he tried to answer her innocent questions over the years. She knew darned well what rut meant when talking about the deer. Without that pull between the does and bucks, Pa had explained, the species would die off. And she had reasoned out on her own that something sort of like that must happen with the other animals.

The problem was, though the baby fawns, skunks and bears each spring were cute, the mother animals spent months teaching their offspring how to survive on their own. Then they started all over again with a new batch of young ones the next year.

Shoot, what kind of a life was that? And human babies took a heck of a lot longer than a few months to raise. They took years and years.

Suddenly Caitlyn frowned into the darkness. Where would she have been if Pa hadn't taken over her care when he found her half-starved late that summer? What if he had looked ahead over the years and decided it would have been easier to let nature take its course—leave her to survive or die on her own?

And he'd raised her with love, not just tolerance for her weaker state. Pa would have given up his life for her. Indeed, he had, when he shoved her up that tree, assuring her own safety before he turned too late to confront that grizzly.

Caitlyn shuddered, hearing again in her mind the crunch of breaking bones and Pa's screams of agony; feeling again her own frustration and helpless love when the bear dragged Pa's lifeless body away, covered it with underbrush and strolled off. She knew enough about bear kills to understand that the grizzly would return later, when it was a little hungrier, to enjoy its kill.

Caitlyn blinked back a quick sheen of tears. Well, that damned bear hadn't eaten Pa. As soon as it disappeared, she had slid down and found their frightened pack horse. She'd ridden back and dug with their shovel until her arms gave out, then dug some more. She'd wrapped him in a blanket, then rolled Pa's body into the grave and shoveled the dirt back over him.

By the time she had carried enough rocks to cover the grave, her hands were cracked and bleeding. Still, she found the strength to fashion a wooden cross. She didn't have enough courage to stay any longer—evening was falling and every crackle of brush had her heart jumping in her throat as she imagined the bear creeping back up on her.

Someone shoved the blanket covering her door back and Caitlyn's eyes flew to the opening.

"Caitlyn?" Jon whispered. "Are you all right?"

Caitlyn bit back another sob. "N . . . no," she croaked out, instead of the "yes" she had meant to say. A tentative lightening at the window showed Jon limping toward her bed, though she would have known his voice anyway.

He hobbled to her bed and hesitantly lowered himself. "What is it, Caitlyn? I heard you sobbing."

Caitlyn stared at the window. "I didn't mean to wake you up."

"I wasn't sleeping. I haven't slept much all night."

"Oh." Caitlyn turned her head and peered at him through the dim light. "Is your knee hurting that bad? Sky Woman showed me how to make some pain liniment out of wintergreen. I could see if I have any of it left on the shelf. I had to make some once when Pa hurt his . . . oh . . . his . . ."

When she broke off into sobs, hands covering her face, Jon muttered a tender oath and reached for her. Pulling her into his arms, he held her against his chest, stroking her hair away from her face. She gasped out a louder, more wretched sob and flung her arms around his neck, burying her face and crying, her small shoulders shaking in a heart-breaking rhythm.

"Caitlyn." Jon held her tighter and laid his cheek on her head. "Honey, shhhh, don't cry. Ah, Caitlyn, don't. Tell me what's bothering you."

She shook her head against his neck, and Jon held her, letting her cry. Her tears trickled down his bare chest, searing a path of misery into his own soul. She had cried the day they arrived at the cabin, upset over the destruction of the furnishings, but she'd quickly controlled it. Now she sobbed as though she would never stop—couldn't stop—as though each inch of her ached with misery.

Jon cradled her, murmuring any soothing phrase that

came to mind, though he knew she couldn't possibly hear even one word. He glanced at the window after a few minutes, when he realized the room was somewhat lighter. He could make out the outline of the ruffled curtains.

Ruffled curtains and an ermine skin on the wall. A feisty, blue-eyed minx who loved to shop, and a fiercely loyal woman who risked her own safety to ride through a blizzard to rescue him and Silas. What a contradiction his little Caitlyn was.

Images of her flashed through Jon's mind as he held her. The tattered, foul-smelling ragamuffin Tall Man had dragged from the wigwam, and the concerned woman who had knelt over him in the soaked white shirt, worry on her face because he had been injured when he shot that puma. Until he spat at her and ordered her away.

Even then, she had swallowed what had to have been resentment at his mistreatment and cared for his head wound.

Caitlyn crouched low over the pinto's neck, hair flying and a herd of half-ton buffalo on the pinto's heels, because Jon had been stupid enough to ignore her wiser advice. The heart-stopping fear he had felt when he aimed the rifle at the lead buffalo.

Caitlyn facing the mother bear, when the only father she had ever known had been killed by a grizzly, yet allowing the sow to go free because she had only been protecting her cub.

Caitlyn in the snow, white flakes highlighting her raven hair and worry on her face for him and Silas. Instead of thanking her, he had snapped at her for wearing a pair of pants to keep herself warm while she came to help them.

Caitlyn in a blue gown that matched those beautiful eyes, swirling in his arms around the polished dance floor of the plantation mansion, staring up at him with love on her face. Jon glanced up at the first floor railing on the staircase and saw two blue-eyed, raven-curled imps staring through the rails, wide-eyed wonder on their faces. He couldn't quite tell if they were boys or girls. . . .

"I'm. . . . " Caitlyn sniffed and pushed at his chest. "I'm all right now."

Jon loosened his arms, but kept them around her. She sniffed again and swiped at her nose, and he grabbed the pillow, shaking the cotton case free and handing it to her.

"Sorry," he murmured. "I'm fresh out of handkerchiefs right now."

"This'll do." Head still lowered, Caitlyn wiped her face, then blew her nose on the end of the case. Crumbling the cotton material in her fists, she turned her head toward the window.

"It's . . . it's getting late. I better go get you and Silas some breakfast started."

A tear-soaked tress of hair lay across her cheek, and Jon brushed it back. "Caitlyn, won't you tell me why you were crying?"

She sat quietly for several long seconds, eyes on the window and her bottom lip caught between her teeth to hold back new sobs. Finally, she took a deep breath.

"I . . . I haven't even went out to Pa's grave to make sure it's all right since I got back. When I rode out the other day, I'd been thinking of heading up that way. But instead I went to the other side of the mountain. Folks . . . folks shouldn't let the graves of the people they love go uncared for."

"I'll take you there, if you want me to."

"I'd . . . I'd like that." She finally tore her gaze from the window. "But you can't go. Your knee. . . . "

"I've got the crutch Silas made. We can go today, if you want."

Caitlyn shyly nodded her head, and a final silver sparkle wobbled past her lashes and down her flushed cheek. She wiped it away with the pillowcase, then glanced at Jon's chest and frowned.

"Look, I've gone and got you all wet."

"Don't worry about it, Caitlyn."

But she was already brushing at the matted tendrils of hair beneath his neck with the clean end of the pillowcase. She unaffectedly rubbed the material over the damp curls, even the brown nipples on his chest. Jon clenched his jaw and closed his eyes, determined that this time he wouldn't give in to that base nature that made him want to kiss and caress her until she purred beneath him with her own awakening passion.

Or snarl at her until she scampered away from him like a frightened fawn.

How the hell could he go so fast from only wanting to comfort her to only wanting her? Obviously, he didn't affect her the same way. She just sat there, drying his chest . . . no, as still as a mouse.

His eyes opened, but Caitlyn's were closed. Her lips were slightly parted, tiny little gasps of air feathering between them, skittering across his chest and drying it much more effectively than the cotton case.

"Jon?"

"What, Caitlyn?" he whispered.

"I think you better leave now."

"Yeah, I think I better."

Reluctantly he dropped his arms and reached for the crutch, which had fallen on the floor. When he looked back at her, Caitlyn was staring at him, slowly shaking her head.

"I can't let these things happen, you know," she replied to his questioning look.

"What?" he repeated.

"You know. These. . . ." She tore her gaze away and shrugged. "These feelings I have around you."

"Can you at least tell me what kind of feelings they are?"

"I think you know what they are—the same sort of feelings Silas accused you of having about me last night." A turn of her head and she faced him again. "I guess maybe women have them too, and, like Silas said, a person's got to learn when there's no meaning behind it. So we have to quit having those feelings. Both of us."

When Jon didn't respond, she dropped her chin onto her chest. He reached over and tipped it back up with one finger, his blue eyes scanning the shadows in her azure depths.

"Maybe some day you'll tell me why you feel like that,

too, Caitlyn, like you managed to tell me why you were crying alone in the dark this morning. In the meantime, I'll try to do what you want. But I seem to remember Silas saying that a person needs to learn when there *is* some meaning behind those feelings, not just when there *isn't*. And since you've been honest with me, I'll tell you this. The feelings I'm beginning to have for you go a hell of a lot farther than just wanting to make love to you.''

Caitlyn tried to jerk her head aside, but Jon curled his fingers around her chin.

''I've been trying to take Silas's advice and decide what's going on, at least in my end of this. That's one reason I didn't sleep much last night. We don't have a whole lot in common, do we?''

''I guess not,'' she admitted grudgingly, ''what with me being raised out here and you having your fine education back east.'' He allowed Caitlyn to brush his hand aside this time, and she tilted her chin up an inch. ''Of course there's a few other things about you a woman could admire. Silas said you kept a clean camp and didn't kill anything you didn't need to eat. And the times you're not snarling at me, you're sort of pleasant to be with.''

''The snarling comes from fighting the urge to kiss you,'' Jon admitted, quirking his mouth into a wry grin when Caitlyn's hand flew up to cover her lips. ''And when you're not looking down that cute little nose of yours and shaking your head at me for being a clumsy fool, you're right pleasant to be with, too, Caitlyn, honey.''

Her hand crawled up over her nose, and Jon laughed aloud. ''That won't do any good. I've already memorized every inch of your face.''

Her hand dropped, landing clenched on her hip. ''Well, unmemorize it. And quit calling me 'honey.' And quit thinking about kissing me; then you won't be snarling like a wounded puma cat all the time.''

''Quit thinking about it? Good idea,'' Jon murmured.

He slipped a hand around her neck and bent his head slowly, giving her time to react if that was what she wanted to do. Her eyes widened like a startled fawn's and her lips parted, but she didn't pull away. Capturing her lips with his own, he gently kissed her, struggling with all his might not to give in to the raging desire the feel of her lips immediately touched off in him.

He sensed rather than heard the soft hint of a whimper in her throat. Only then did he deepen the kiss, and she leaned into it with him, wrapping her arms around his waist and clinging to him. Her response cracked his self-control, and he buried his hands in that lovely, silky hair and tasted inside her mouth.

At first his sweeping tongue startled her, and he groaned, forcing himself to loosen his hands and try to draw back. But at her shy flick of tongue against his, he gathered her close again. Her simultaneous rejoinder thrilled him beyond anything he had ever experienced. The small rational part of his mind not clouded with his growing craving to take advantage of the bed told him these feelings were for Caitlyn, not just any female.

And it being Caitlyn gave him the strength to rein in his passion—think with his head, instead of his aching need. She was special—very, very special. As he ever so yearningly released this special woman from his embrace, he realized another part of him was resisting his disengagement with her—his heart.

He stared into her flushed face and eyes dark with flaring passion for a few long seconds, long enough to garner his shreds of composure. Wisps of ebony hair curled becomingly around her face, and his fingers had tumbled the longer tresses into charming disarray. Finally, he chanced one last brief touch of his lips to that delicate nose, then grabbed his crutch from the floor and stood.

"Tell you what," he said. "You see what you can do about your feelings for me, and I'll do the same." When Caitlyn nodded a vague agreement, as though still distracted, he turned and limped to the doorway. "But," he said over his shoulder, "I don't think you're going to have any more luck than me at putting a lid on whatever's going on between us."

Shoving the blanket aside, he hobbled through the doorway, then stuck his head back into her room. "At least, I'm beginning to hope not, Caitlyn, *honey*."

Caitlyn threw the pillowcase at him, but without the weight of the pillow inside, it fluttered ineffectively to the floor. She glared at the white cotton, a mutinous frown crawling over her face while she tried to make sense of her jumbled emotions as she listened to Jon hobble across the cabin floor. When she heard the front door close behind him, she scrambled out of bed and grabbed the pillowcase, twisting and squeezing it viciously in her hands.

Suddenly she broke into giggles. She was wringing that case like she wanted to wring Jon's neck. She gave the case another experimental squeeze, then fell back onto the bed, giggling and winding the material in her hands.

Yes, she wanted to wring his neck, but not because he had kissed her. She was mad because he'd stopped kissing her, just when she was starting to figure out for herself what Silas had meant about the meaning behind this pull between her and Jon.

Honey. Huh. She sort of preferred sweetheart herself. And right pleasant to be with, was she? She might have to talk to Jon about how it appeared his speech was worsening out here in the mountains.

When she imagined how Jon would slip a teasing look at her out of the corner of his eye if she had the audacity to correct *his* grammar, she broke out into renewed laughter. It slowly stilled, and she tossed the pillowcase aside.

No. She'd almost forgotten. She couldn't allow herself to start dwelling on how much she enjoyed being with Jon sometimes. Her freedom meant too much to her, and he threatened that freedom with every inch of that masculinity she responded to. When she added to that the rare times they actually seemed to communicate and share their thoughts, it doubled the threat.

She had to remember where things like getting hung up on some man could lead—remember her own interpretation of Silas's words. A woman could just have an itch to be scratched, too, with no special meaning behind it. But it was the woman who would be left with the consequences, should she give in, while the man walked away unfettered. And, if by some miracle the man didn't wander off, the woman might spend the rest of her life catering not only to him, but also a passel of young ones he kept giving her.

She had come to only one firm conclusion from that horrible nightmare that plagued her. Caitlyn O'Shaunessy had no business even thinking about having babies of her own.

Chapter Thirteen

As they rode into the small clearing where Caitlyn had buried Mick on the mountainside, Jon saw her hands tighten on the reins. But when she glanced over and met his concerned gaze, she relaxed a little. Hopefully, his presence at her side was making this first journey to the grave site a lot easier than she had anticipated.

"Thanks for coming with me," she said quietly.

"Do you want me to ride in first and make sure everything's all right?" he asked.

"I need to see for myself. I did all I could, but if that grizzly did . . . come back. . . . "

Jon reached for the pinto's bridle and pulled her horse to a halt. "Let me do this for you, Caitlyn." A stab of displeasure stung him when Caitlyn glanced at him, obviously unsure how to interpret the solicitude in his voice. He supposed he couldn't blame her for that, given his usual testiness.

"Please," he told her in a gruff voice. "I'll come back and get you as soon as I can."

"All right," Caitlyn agreed after a second. "Thanks. Thanks again, I mean."

"Where is the grave site?"

Caitlyn tilted her head a little to the right. "Just across the clearing there, behind that big maple tree. Pa always said the maples were the prettiest in the fall."

Jon handed her his rifle. "You keep this here. And remember, there's someone prowling around. If you spot someone and think you're in danger, shoot."

As soon as she nodded, Jon nudged his horse forward and rode slowly across the clearing, keeping a wary eye out for any intruder—human or animal. Two dozen yards from the maple, he saw the huge pine Mick must have pushed Caitlyn up when the bear attacked. The dead, lower branches were broken off, but standing on another person's shoulders, Caitlyn could have reached the higher branches and climbed to safety.

She had explained what had happened in the clearing last fall while they rode, seeming to need to talk about it. Lightning had struck an old tree—he saw that one split in two over there—and the fire had burned off some of the underbrush. Blueberry plants had grown up, and each year Caitlyn had gathered the berries to preserve for the winter.

The problem they had encountered—not unusual in the mountains, but always deadly—was a bear in the blueberry patch. Neither she nor Pa had seen the bear on the far edge of the patch when they rode up. It evidently hadn't noticed them, either, what with the wind blowing down the mountain toward her and Pa.

She should have heard it, though, Caitlyn said more than once. The patch wasn't that large, and something as huge as a grizzly would have darn well made enough noise for a person to hear, especially a person taught to listen for bears around berry patches.

"Have you ever thought that maybe that bear wasn't there at first?" Jon had finally asked. "Maybe he came up on you two after you were already at the patch. I've heard that grizzlies can move pretty quietly through the brush, despite their size. Or maybe he was a rogue bear—those type don't need a motivation to attack, especially if the reason they turned rogue was a run-in with a human. Sometimes a wounded bear gets away, and the wound heals but leaves the bear in pain. It'll attack anything that moves.''

They'd ridden for several minutes, with Jon hoping that Caitlyn was thinking over his explanation, before she told him about the rest of the attack.

"He reared up not more than fifty feet from me," she had said. "He roared, and I felt like I was looking straight down his throat. Pa, he was sitting over under the maple, about half asleep, but I heard him yell just about the time the bear roared.

"I knew I didn't have much time—couldn't run nearly as fast as that bear could. I threw the berry bucket at him and he dropped down just as Pa shot. Pa probably would have hit him if I hadn't thrown that bucket, because the bear might have still been standing when he pulled the trigger.''

"You can't know that, Caitlyn," Jon said.

"No, I guess not," she had continued. "I ran for the pine and so did Pa. He was trying to reload his rifle as he ran—I'd seen him be able to do that during buffalo hunts— but we got to the tree before he rammed the ball home. Grizzlies can't climb, you know, and if you get high enough in a good, strong tree, they can't get you down if you get a tight hold while they shake the tree.''

When she fell silent again, Jon prodded her on. "I guess the bear got to the tree about the same time you did.''

"Just long enough afterwards for Pa to shove me up. The first branch I grabbed broke, and Pa shoved me higher. I think I even remember climbing on his shoulders. Then he tried to get the tree between him and that bear, but the bear swiped right around it and broke his gun. Pa never had a chance to get up the tree, because the bear's claws caught him in the arm and knocked him down.''

She hadn't told him about anything else except burying Mick afterwards, but Jon could imagine it. As he neared the maple tree, he kept his gaze fixed on the pine. She would have heard it all—seen it all. Mick's screams of pain, mixed with the bear's roars of rage. Probably even bones breaking when the bear bit down. The bear dragging the body off, with Caitlyn maybe thinking it was going to eat parts of its kill within her hearing.

Thank God it didn't, Jon thought, finally tearing his gaze from the pine as he rode around the maple. *And thank God it didn't come back—or at least, if it did, it was too confused to realize the body was buried under those rocks.*

He slid from his horse, wobbling on one leg until he settled the crutch under his arm, then limped over to the grave.

The cairn was undisturbed, mounded almost as high as his waist and at least six feet long. How much time had it taken Caitlyn to dig the grave, then carry all those rocks? She'd even taken time to fashion a wooden cross, all the while waiting for the bear to return, without even having a rifle to protect her. He remembered her telling him that her own gun had been lost in a rock slide earlier that fall.

The cross was leaning to one side, and Jon limped over to straighten it. Shifting one of the stones, he planted it firmly at the base of the wood to hold it upright. Then he went back around the maple and waved at Caitlyn to ride on in. As soon as she arrived, he awkwardly remounted and took the rifle from her.

"I'll wait just over there for you, all right? If you need me, call out."

When Caitlyn didn't answer, Jon hesitated, watching her gaze at the grave. She walked over and placed her hand on the wooden cross, bowing her head. He turned his horse as quietly as he could and left her to grieve in privacy.

Some of it she had cried out that morning on his chest—knowing her, possibly even the first time she had allowed her grief full rein. He wouldn't ride too far away. If she needed someone to help bear the pain this time, he'd be there again.

A while later, Caitlyn stepped from behind the maple and called to Jon, "Are you ready to go?"

"Stay as long as you like, Caitlyn," he replied. "I'm in no hurry."

She walked on out into the clearing and stopped, gazing at the pine tree—the berry patch. Then she looked back at Jon.

"I'd like to stay here awhile. Maybe gather some fall leaves for the grave, seeing as how the flowers are all gone. But. . . . " She turned her face back toward the berry patch, and Jon rode his horse forward and dismounted.

"You stay as long as you want, sweetheart. I won't let anything bother you."

Caitlyn turned a grateful face up to him. The breeze blew a strand of hair across her cheek, and she brushed it back with a half-hearted gesture.

"I should've braided my hair this morning, but Pa always liked to see me with it loose. And you really shouldn't be calling me that, either."

"Sweetheart?" Jon asked with a quirked eyebrow.

"Yes. You know what we agreed."

"We just agreed to try, Caitlyn, sweetheart. But I'll try a little harder, at least right now. I really don't think that same bear could be around a year later, but you never know. You go ahead and gather your leaves, while I keep an eye out."

After Jon swung into the saddle again, Caitlyn smiled up at him. "I think Pa would've liked you, Jon Clay. But I don't think he would've let you call me those sweet names."

Jon bent from the saddle and cupped her chin. "Think he would've shot me for thinking about kissing those sweet lips, too?"

Caitlyn giggled and swatted his hand away. "Probably."

"That's sort of a contradiction, isn't it?" Jon asked as he leaned on the saddlehorn. "You just said your pa would have liked me. And every man knows that when he has a daughter, he'll lose her one day to another man—someone who will take care of her for the rest of her life. Don't you think your pa might have been glad the man in your life was someone he liked?"

"But . . . you're not . . . I mean, we haven't talked about nothing like that. We said we'd forget about this thing between us."

"Caitlyn, darling, I can see that we've got some more studying to do. You're not understanding what we've been saying to each other at all." He reined his horse a step away. "Now, you go on and get your leaves while I keep an eye out for any danger. When you're finished, we'll eat the lunch we packed, and do a little more studying."

Jon rode to the edge of the clearing and turned his horse. Laying his rifle across the saddle in front of him, he gazed around, carefully ignoring Caitlyn's still figure, standing where he had left her. Finally, from the corner of his eye, he saw her move over to the maple and begin breaking off some of the lower-hanging branches, which were covered with bright, vermilion leaves. She disappeared around the tree, returning after a moment leading her pinto.

Jon kneed his horse forward, but Caitlyn swung into her saddle before he reached her.

"I think we better head on back," she said as she rode toward him. "I decided I really don't want to stay here and eat. We can eat back at the cabin."

"And be cooped up for the rest of the day back there?" Jon asked. "I thought you'd enjoy spending the day outside. If you don't want to stay here, we can find another place for a picnic, Caitlyn."

She shrugged her shoulders and rode on past him. "It's sort of chilly yet, after that snow. And the ground's too mushy to set on."

"Sit," Jon corrected as he urged his horse up beside Caitlyn's. "Remember. . . ."

"I know," she interrupted. "Hens set. People sit."

"Right. Well, if you insist on going back, I guess we can talk and study while we ride."

"I don't feel like it today."

"Which one? Studying—or talking?"

"Neither," Caitlyn said in a flat voice.

"Then I guess you don't want to learn as badly as I thought you did. Right now, what with being laid up with my knee, I've got time to teach you. But as soon as I'm able, I'll be going back out every day with Silas, getting our trap line routes figured out. There won't be much time then, and you'll probably forget everything you've learned.''

"No I won't.''

"Caitlyn,'' Jon said in exasperation. "When students go to school, they go every day during the school term. They don't just pick a day now and then when they *feel* like learning.''

Suddenly he reached over and grabbed the pinto's bridle, then began leading it off the trail.

"Stop that,'' Caitlyn insisted. "Where are you going?''

"I heard a stream running down the mountain over here when we rode by,'' Jon replied. "You might not be hungry—although I doubt it, since you only picked at your breakfast—but I am. And you can sit on a rock, if you don't want to get your dress wet on the *mushy* ground.''

Caitlyn attempted to jerk her pinto's head around, but Jon had a firm grip on the bridle. Rather than injure the pony's mouth, Caitlyn shrugged in surrender and loosened her reins.

Maybe Jon could make her go with him, but he couldn't force her to eat—or force her to study, if she didn't want to.

Or talk.

Immediately she thought of the leather-bound journal, now hidden under her mattress. What if Jon grew impatient with her and refused to teach her anymore? She had enjoyed every minute of yesterday, especially after she realized that the letters had sounds, and strung together, they made up words. Words that could be written down to preserve a person's feelings and thoughts.

Words that could be left behind after a person died, so people reading them would know about the person who had lived before.

Could there be something in that journal to explain her past—maybe fill in the blanks in her memory?

But maybe the journal would also tell her things she

didn't want to know. Caitlyn shivered, and a film of goose-bumps crawled over her bare arms. Maybe that was why she had buried those memories so deep inside her—so they wouldn't cause her pain or bring on the nightmare that surfaced from time to time.

Then she remembered the deep satisfaction she'd felt when she wrote just those two simple sentences on the slate and signed her name. And Jon had promised at the beginning of the lessons to let her start reading one of those books just as soon as he thought she could understand it. In fact, at one point yesterday afternoon, he'd told her that she might even be learning fast enough to study a book within a day or so.

"Caitlyn?"

Caitlyn blinked and stared around her. She'd been concentrating so hard on her thoughts that she hadn't even realized she was sitting on her pinto beside the bubbling creek. Sunlight dappled the clear water, bouncing around like skittering diamonds on the rippling surface. The creek wasn't very wide—maybe a couple dozen feet. The opposite shoreline was a riot of fall colors: bright yellow aspen leaves, red maple and orange oak, green pine and straight black and gray tree trunks interspersed with white birch. A beautiful place to stop for awhile.

She glanced toward Jon's voice and saw him beside a flat rock, where he had spread out the food from his saddle-bags on a piece of linen cloth. The new buckskins she had sewn for him fit perfectly, even though she hadn't fitted him while making them. Even Jon had expressed surprise that morning when he realized she had cut and sewn the shirt and pants just from observation.

'Course, she had told herself that she just mentally measured Jon's garments against the many shirts and pants she had made for Mick over the years. She'd had to add a couple inches in the shoulders, though, and taper the shirt in a little more toward the waist. The soft tan color was a shade lighter than Jon's blond hair, and it set off his tanned face, making those deep blue eyes even more striking.

His eyes were much bluer than the creek water. They

were more like the patches of sky showing through the towering trees overhead.

"Are you going to get down, or should I go ahead and eat by myself?" Jon asked.

Caitlyn's stomach gave a tiny growl, and she frowned down at the betraying sound. Giving a sigh of capitulation, she slid down and dropped her reins to ground-tie the pinto. She walked to the rock and picked up a cold buffalo roast sandwich, then stared down at it while she spoke.

"I do want to study, Jon," she said quietly. "I'm feeling more like it now."

"All right. In a minute. But first I want to talk."

Caitlyn shrugged in irritation. "Talking, I still don't feel like doing. Leastways, nothing beyond just what needs to be said while we study." She took a huge bite of her sandwich and chewed.

"Too bad then." Jon reached into his saddlebags and pulled out one of his books. "Guess I'll just read while we eat." He flipped open the book and settled back against the rock behind him, taking a huge bite of his own sandwich while he scanned the first page.

Caitlyn choked down her bite of sandwich, which had suddenly turned dry in her mouth, then flounced over to the other side of the rock. Brushing off some dead leaves from a smaller rock, she sat down with her back toward Jon. Still she heard him turn a page, and his low, almost whispered voice.

"Always liked this story," he murmured. "Old Bill Shakespeare really knew how to tame his women."

"Harumph!"

"Got a good title, too. *Taming of the Shrew.*"

Jon read a few lines from the book, which immediately elicited a response from Caitlyn.

"People don't talk like that," she said around a mouthful of meat. "That sounds more like song words, sort of rhyming like that."

"His writing is a sort of poetry," Jon admitted. "And it's written in a way to make whoever reads it stop and think about his meaning. Here, listen to this."

For the next half hour, Jon leafed through the book and read a passage here and there aloud. Caitlyn had unconsciously turned around just after he read the first passage, so she could explain her own interpretation of the words to Jon. She finished two of the sandwiches while they talked, and split the half dozen molasses cookies she had baked between them, quickly polishing off her three while Jon read.

She finally allowed herself a tiny smirk, trying to hide it from Jon, but he looked up before she could wipe it off her face.

"What's that look all about?" Jon asked. "Never mind, I know," he continued before Caitlyn could form a plausible excuse. "You think I've forgotten that I said I wouldn't study with you until we talked. Well, I haven't. I just wanted you to remember how much fun it is to learn. And now, if you want to go on, we'll get that talk over with first."

Caitlyn set her lips stubbornly. "You tricked me."

"Sure did," Jon admitted. "Now, I want you to tell me just what you have against allowing yourself to care for a man. Or is it just me, not all men?"

"I never had any trouble with any other men." Caitlyn lifted her chin an inch. "Never had any desire to kiss any of them—or let any of them hold onto me."

"But you do have that desire with me, don't you?"

"Oh, all right! I do!"

"Then," Jon said softly, "why are you fighting it so hard? Why do you want me to fight it, too, when we both know how wonderful it feels when we're close? Even when we're not close—just near each other."

"Because I don't ever aim to give up my freedom and let some man boss me around for the rest of my life! Getting married *ain't* in my plans for myself."

"Married?" Jon said with a gulp. "Now, Caitlyn, I didn't say anything about marriage. I just. . . . "

Caitlyn's eyes narrowed and she fixed Jon with a furious glare. "You just want to play around with me, huh? Like some of the mountain men do with the Indian women, then go back where they came from and leave those poor women to raise a passel of kids!''

"Well, no. I didn't . . . I mean. . . . ''

"Just what the blue blazes *do* you mean, Jon Clay? You know as well as I do what kissing and hugging around can lead to. And reckon you've felt it between us just like I have. You think you can do that with me—that making love you were talking about—then run back to your fancy women back east and maybe leave me tied down out here with a babe to raise? Do you?''

"Uh . . . well, no. But. . . . ''

"Ain't no 'buts' about it, Jon Clay. Since you don't have marriage in m . . . mind. . . . '' A surprising stab of hurt pierced Caitlyn at her words, but she forced herself to continue. "And since I sure don't have it in my own mind to up and marry any man, then we just better forget about this whole business of kissing and hugging. That way, when we get this trapping season over with, we can each go on with our lives!''

Jon groaned under his breath and shook his head. "Well,'' he said, "I asked you, and you told me. We better start back. It's getting late.''

"Didn't want to stop in the first place,'' Caitlyn muttered. "Now he's acting like it'll be my fault that it'll be close to dark when we get back.''

Chapter Fourteen

The tall Indian man waited in front of the log cabin. Jon raised his rifle, but Caitlyn stopped him with a gesture of annoyance.

"That's a friend of mine," she bit off, her irritated voice telling Jon that she was still peeved.

Jon swung his horse across the trail, blocking her path. "Friend or not, someone's been prowling around here. And you're not riding in there until I know it's safe." He kept his rifle barrel pointed at the cabin, his thumb near the hammer. "Who is that down there?"

Caitlyn blew out an exasperated breath, lifting a fringe of curls from her forehead. "You haven't met him, but you saw him back at rendezvous. Now, get out of my way!"

Ignoring her demand, Jon studied the man in front of the cabin. A scowl crawled across his features when a flicker of recognition dawned.

"He looks like that damned Indian you were kissing in camp," he growled. "Thought you said back on the creek bank that you hadn't ever wanted to kiss any other man."

"Oh, for pity's sake!" Caitlyn reined her horse around

155

a tree beside the trail and trotted it in front of Jon. "You got some studying to do yourself," she said over her shoulder when Jon urged his horse after her pinto. "There's kissing, and then there's kissing. Sounds like the same word, but different meanings!"

Jon grumbled a faint sound of displeasure, but he refused to answer her comment. Instead, he rode behind her, eyeing the Indian warily as they approached the cabin. His discontent grew rapidly when Caitlyn slid down from her pinto and ran to the Indian, flinging herself into his arms.

"It's good to see you, my friend," he heard her say in a soft, breathless voice. "I hope you've come to stay for a while."

Spirit Eagle hugged her close, then pushed her away. "I saw you at your father's grave, Little Wind, but I did not want to intrude. Have the days been good to you?"

Jon's finger tightened near the rifle trigger. He sure as hell hadn't known that Indian was around. How long had he been watching them? And how many times had he followed them?

"Pretty good," Caitlyn told him. "But there's been someone snooping around here. Did you run across anyone?"

"It was Tall Man," Spirit Eagle told her. "And he did not want you to know he was here. He has gone back to his winter camp now. I saw him leave as I came."

Jon snorted and swung down from his horse. "Well, I haven't seen anyone—just you! How the hell do I know it hasn't been you prowling around?"

"Because I have said so," Spirit Eagle said calmly as he turned to face Jon.

His voice belied the tenseness in his body, though, and Jon's eyes narrowed. This man could be dangerous. Jon sensed that as surely as he had the few times before in his life when he'd encountered men he respected. This man wouldn't back-shoot you—he'd face you down in a fair fight, then lift your hair and howl in victory if he won.

But this man also still had his arm around Caitlyn.

"Stop it! Both of you!" Caitlyn stepped between the

men. "My friend came here to see me, Jon, and he's welcome in my home. I'll take care of the horses, if you want to go on in and rest your knee."

"Has *your friend* got a name, Little Wind?" Jon asked, barely concealing the snarl in his voice.

"Most people do." Caitlyn started to reach for the reins of Jon's horse, but he jerked them back.

"I'll take care of my own damned horse." He turned to untie his crutch from the saddle, tensing once again when he sensed the Indian man moving over to him, though he couldn't hear the hushed footsteps of his moccasined feet.

"I am called Spirit Eagle," the Indian said.

Jon glanced down in surprise to see Spirit Eagle's hand extended in friendship. Honor-bound to accept, Jon grasped the other man's palm.

"Jon Clay," he said. "From Virginia."

"I have known Little Wind since she first came to this land with her father," Spirit Eagle explained after he shook Jon's hand. "I call her this because even on still days a little wind blows in the mountains."

Jon chuckled under his breath. "Yeah, I can understand that. Caitlyn's never still."

"You two quit talking about me like I can't hear every word you say!" Caitlyn demanded. When the men grinned at each other, she stamped her foot and crossed her arms beneath her breasts. "You can fix your own darned supper, you keep this up!"

Full-fledged laughter was her answer, and she grabbed her pinto's reins and stormed toward the corral. Maybe she *would* fix supper after all. Just to see their faces when they tried to eat it!

"I will care for your horse, if you wish," Spirit Eagle said when his laughter abated. "I will not be staying long enough for this meal Little Wind may change her mind and cook for you. When we meet the next time, you can tell me how it tasted."

"Thanks," Jon said as he handed the Indian the reins. "My knee is paining me pretty bad, but don't tell Caitlyn that. And there's some leftover stew from last night inside.

Figure I'll eat some of it now, so I won't be so hungry later on.'' Jon reached out his hand again. ''Good to meet you, Spirit Eagle.''

Spirit Eagle nodded as he grasped Jon's hand. ''Little Wind is a fine woman, now at last grown,'' he said. ''You are lucky she has chosen you.''

''Well, I don't know about that,'' Jon said as his face flushed. ''Caitlyn's determined not to get tied up with any man.''

''Even the little wind finds a home at night,'' Spirit Eagle said. ''I must talk to her now.''

Jon nodded agreeably and tucked his crutch under his arm to limp into the cabin. Just inside the door, he stopped abruptly and stared at what was laying on his bunk.

Uh oh. What was Caitlyn going to think about this? He glanced at the overhead shelf to see a few new articles there, already unpacked and looking like they were there to stay: a pile of clean cloths, a couple small, brightly-colored blankets, and a tiny drinking cup. Grinning to himself, he reached across Dog, who was lying on the edge of the bunk, and pulled his blanket up a little higher. Dog whined and brushed his tail back and forth, but remained in his protective position.

After Spirit Eagle unsaddled Jon's horse, he spoke quietly to Caitlyn. ''There is something I must ask you, Little Wind. It is something very important to me.''

Caitlyn dumped a pail of grain into the feed trough. ''Well, you got a funny way of asking a favor, Spirit Eagle. Do you laugh at Morning Star when you want her to do something for you?''

Spirit Eagle's face broke into pain, and Caitlyn quickly reached out a hand to him. ''What is it? No! Oh, Spirit Eagle, what's happened to Morning Star?''

Spirit Eagle clenched his fists at his sides, trying desperately to control his emotions. For a long, strained moment he stood rigid, unable to look into Caitlyn's worried face. Finally he whirled toward the corral fence and gripped the top railing, staring off at the mountain.

"Spirit Eagle?" Caitlyn whispered.

"In a few days the ghost month will be on us," Spirit Eagle said in a tight voice. "The weeks the whites call Indian Summer. It is said that the spirits of our ancestors come back with the morning mists we see on those days. I want to try to see her once more—to tell her that I will not forget her, and that our son will know her through me."

"My God," Caitlyn breathed. Her eyes filled with tears, both for the suffering she knew Spirit Eagle had to be experiencing and her own feeling of loss for the beautiful Indian woman she had also called friend.

"Oh, Spirit Eagle. I'm sorry."

"As I am," Spirit Eagle replied in a tortured voice. He glanced down at Caitlyn at last. "Will you do this for me then? You have already done much for Morning Star and me. You helped her escape Tall Man and run to me, even though Tall Man had already paid a bride's price for her. We were happy together, even if we could not return to the Nez Perce and visit our families."

Spirit Eagle drew in a deep breath. "I do not like to ask this of you, because I owe you my thanks for the two years of happiness I had with my loved one. But there is no one else."

"You haven't asked anything yet, Spirit Eagle." Caitlyn swiped at a tear running down her cheek, and suddenly her eyes widened. "Little Sun! Spirit Eagle, where's yours and Morning Star's son?"

Spirit Eagle smiled through his pain. "He is a fine son. There is much of Morning Star in him, but much of me, also. He will grow into a fine warrior."

"Spirit Eagle, I just can't! I mean, he's only about a year old. I don't know a thing about taking care of a young'un! Why, we don't even have any milk here. Babies need milk, don't they?"

"Little Sun is one season and three months," Spirit Eagle told her. "He has been eating out of the cooking pot for a long while."

Caitlyn glanced worriedly at the cabin, unconsciously chewing on the inside of her cheek. She'd visited Spirit

Eagle and his wife twice after they were banned from the Nez Perce—once when Morning Star was large with child and once when Little Sun was just four months old.

If any baby had ever threatened to break through her reserve around those tiny creatures, it had been Little Sun. She recalled his dark, inquisitive eyes on her face, and the smile he had directed at her, lifting his arms and begging for her to pick him up as he chortled senseless babbles. Morning Star had swept her baby up with a laugh, then placed him trustingly into Caitlyn's arms.

Her arms grew heavy with the remembered weight, and she could feel the silkiness of the baby's hair against her palm as though she had only touched him yesterday. But she slowly shook her head. The nightmare had returned that night when she camped with Pa on the mountainside. She'd awakened screaming in fear, and sobbed in Pa's arms for a long time.

She'd thought she'd conquered the nightmare—it had been years since she experienced it. But it returned almost nightly after Pa's death, until it had finally tapered off again.

"Spirit Eagle, you don't understand. I think I'm one of those women that doesn't have the nurturing feelings most females have. I'm just not cut out to be a mother."

"Morning Star will always be his mother," Spirit Eagle said in a quiet voice. "I am only asking you to care for him while I make my journey to seek my wife for one last time in the mists. I will return for him. He is my son."

"How . . . ?" Caitlyn steadied her voice with a gulp. "How long do you think you might be gone?"

Spirit Eagle shrugged. "That will depend on how long it will take me to talk to her. And on the snows. Sometimes the snows come early, shortening the warm weeks. If they catch me deep in the mountains, I cannot travel back right away."

Caitlyn crossed her arms and held herself again while her mind whirled. Friendships. How many times had Pa told her that nothing was more important than friendships in a person's life?

How many times had Spirit Eagle kept her out of trouble during her and Pa's visits to the Nez Perce? There was that time she followed after him, insisting she was old enough to go hunting with the Indian boys. Spirit Eagle had stood between her and the other young boys' taunts, then grudgingly took her back to Pa to ask his permission for her to go with them.

Spirit Eagle had taught her to swim—after he rescued her that summer she fell in the river. He'd taught her to shoot a bow and arrow—throw a knife so well she smirked in satisfaction when the Indian boys refused to compete against her any longer.

He'd come to see her, to make sure she was all right after Pa's death—run off whoever was skulking in the bushes near the camp, getting injured himself in return.

He'd never asked her for anything before.

"I . . ." Caitlyn began.

"I know I can never repay you for bringing Morning Star to me, Little Wind. And now I am asking more of you."

"You never asked me to help Morning Star," Caitlyn denied stoutly. "That was all my idea and hers. I couldn't have done anything else, being she was my friend and knowing how much she loved you."

"But it made an enemy for you. Tall Man believes it was you who helped Morning Star escape."

"He doesn't know for sure. And Sky Woman won't let him hurt me. Spirit Eagle, what happened to Morning Star? You never said."

"She was sick when I returned after seeing you," Spirit Eagle admitted in a ravaged voice. "She had a cough. She had this at other times, but would not let me try to return to the Nez Perce and ask for medicine. She knew I would be killed if someone saw me, because we were banned after I stole Tall Man's bride, breaking an honored custom. She was with child again, and I think it was too hard on her body."

"Why didn't you come back and get me? I would've tried to help."

"There was not time. She asked about you, Little Wind. She said to tell you she would carry with her always the thought of your friendship and the happiness you helped her have."

Caitlyn's heart twisted, and she bit back a moan. While Spirit Eagle had been checking on her, Morning Star had fallen ill. Yet even on her death bed, her friend had asked about her. How could she do any less than care for Little Sun, the baby of her dear friend, so Spirit Eagle could seek his final peace over her death?

"There's things you'll have to tell me," she informed Spirit Eagle as she straightened her shoulders. "Like I said, I don't know much about caring for a young'un. You'll have to tell me what he likes to eat—what he likes to play with. I suppose he's at least got a mouthful of teeth by now, since he's been eating out of the cooking pot."

"Thank you, Little Wind," Spirit Eagle whispered.

A few minutes later, Caitlyn watched the Indian ride away, her head whirling again, this time with thoughts of baby care. Thank goodness she had insisted that Silas also trade with the few Plains Indians who had wandered into rendezvous. Maybe Silas and Jon thought nothing of living out the winter on meat and fat, but she knew from Pa that a diet like that left a person weak and ill in the spring. After all, a person had to take care of a person's body.

The Sioux women had brought in wild rice to trade, and even some corn, plus maple syrup and sugar. But the Plains Indians had potatoes and squash—various types of beans and even herbs the women grew for their own cooking pots.

Berries had still hung on the bushes when she returned this summer with Jon and Silas. And she'd gathered wild grapes from the arbor near the cabin. No wild strawberries—they had ripened and gone—but she'd found plenty of dewberries, blackberries and even some blueberries in a small patch down by the lake.

Jon appeared in the cabin doorway and slouched against the jamb, cocking his fingers into his buckskin pockets. Well, by diddly darn, he better not say a word! And if she caught even a hint of a smirk on his face, why, she'd wipe it off real quick!

Caitlyn slid through the corral fence and started toward the cabin. But instead of a smirk, she saw concern on Jon's face as she approached. He straightened, placing a hand on the door jamb to steady himself, and smiled at her.

"I'll help you with him, sweetheart. He's sure a cute little fellow. And I imagine Spirit Eagle wouldn't have left him unless it was because of something important."

Caitlyn nodded and brushed by him, for some reason anxious to see Little Sun. After all, she told herself, she was responsible for him now.

Dog glanced up as Caitlyn approached, but when she didn't order him down, he curled his nose back beneath his tail. Caitlyn stood by the bunk and stared down at the tiny boy. He lay on his back, one hand resting on his cheek and his small lips pursed. A fringe of black silkiness fell over his forehead, and she reached down to brush it back.

"His mother died," Caitlyn told Jon in a whisper.

"You knew her, too?"

"Uh huh. Her name was Morning Star, and she was a real close friend. This is Little Sun."

Jon stepped forward and slid one arm around her waist while he held onto his crutch with the other. Forgetting their earlier disagreement, Caitlyn leaned back into the comfort he offered as she mourned her lost friend.

"I promised him I'd look after the babe while he was gone. He wants to try to talk to her one more time."

"I guess I don't understand how he can do that," Jon said, covering one of her bare arms with his palm and rubbing it gently. "Is he going back to her grave site?"

Caitlyn briefly explained the Indians' belief in the Indian Summer mists to Jon, and he nodded his head against the top of hers. Little Sun's eyes opened and he blinked, then looked up at Caitlyn and stretched out his arms with a laugh of glee.

"Oh, Jon, I think he remembers me!"

Caitlyn brushed Jon's arm aside and reached down for the baby. She shifted him to her shoulder, and Jon tweaked

Little Sun's nose. Another gleeful laugh sounded, and the little boy held out his arms to Jon.

Caitlyn willingly turned around and handed the boy to Jon, then surreptitiously lifted the wet buckskin dress away from her breast while she watched Jon hold the boy in a cocked arm and sit down on the bunk. After he laid his crutch aside, Jon wiggled his free fingers on Little Sun's stomach. Little Sun giggled wildly, but suddenly Jon's face lost its smile.

"Uh . . . here." He held the child out to Caitlyn, but she shook her head and tucked her arms behind her back.

"You promised to help with him. I think there's some nappies up on that shelf there. Spirit Eagle said he left some. I'll get supper started."

Jon gave a groan of frustration as Caitlyn walked away, but quickly changed his attitude when Little Sun's face puckered.

"Huh," he told the tiny boy with another tickle on the stomach. "She thinks I don't know how to change a nappy. Well, we'll show her, won't we?"

He stood on his good leg and grabbed a nappy from the shelf, then sat back on the bunk beside Little Sun. It took an inordinately long time, since Jon insisted on playing with the child in between removing the soiled nappy, cleaning him from the water basin and cloth Caitlyn brought him, then pinning on a clean cloth. But finally the job was done.

"We'll go outside and see the horsies while Caitlyn does women's work in here," he told Little Sun in a loud enough voice for Caitlyn to hear. "She can call us when the food's done."

He stood and fixed the crutch under one arm before he picked up the little boy and shifted him to his hip, calling over his shoulder as he went through the door, "Don't forget. This little fellow has to eat what you cook, too."

Caitlyn shook her head and laughed. But after Jon closed the door, leaving her alone in the quiet cabin, her smile faltered. A tiny voice tried to creep into her mind, but she determinedly shook her head and turned back to the fireplace.

Chapter Fifteen

Even Silas was taken by Little Sun and, at least for the first week, Caitlyn found the responsibility of caring for the boy caused barely a ripple in her daily chores. Silas left later and came in earlier, rather grumpily explaining when asked that there were chores that needed to be done around the cabin before winter.

Jon, determined to exercise his knee back to health, found Little Sun toddling after him when, aided by his crutch, he limped across the yard. The tiny boy wobbled now and then, plopping down onto his padded bottom, then scrambling to his feet with a laugh and toddling off again.

Jon and Silas took turns feeding Little Sun, good-naturedly arguing over whose turn it was at each meal. Caitlyn only had to cut the meat into tiny bites and mash the vegetables into a mush. And clean up the mess on the floor after each meal. Neither Jon nor Silas ever took note of that chore.

Jon became an expert on changing nappies, and even carried them to the lake to wash. He built a small tripod over a stone-ringed fire to heat water, carefully explaining

to Little Sun the danger of straying too near the flames.
However, the little boy already appeared to be aware of
that. He carefully kept his distance while Jon worked,
quickly learning that as soon as the cloth nappies were
done, Jon would heat more water for them both to bathe.
He thoroughly enjoyed splashing his hands in the warm
water while Jon ran a cloth over his body beneath the small
buckskin tunic.

One morning Caitlyn came out of the cabin to see Dog
lying in front of the outhouse, which was set off to a side
in the clearing. No doubt about where Little Sun was. Dog
had appointed himself the tiny child's protector the day
Spirit Eagle's son arrived.

A moment later, Jon and Little Sun emerged from the
outhouse. Jon had a slight grimace on his face, and when
Little Sun caught sight of Caitlyn, he toddled toward her,
babbling nonsense and stopping once to point back at Jon.

Caitlyn bent down and lifted the boy into her arms as
soon as he reached her, trying to make sense of his words.
Feeling his bare bottom beneath the buckskin tunic, she
glanced questioningly at Jon as he approached.

"Where's his nappy?" she asked.

"Right here." Jon held it up with two fingers. "But you
don't have to worry about him getting you wet. He's probably good for at least a little while yet."

"Why are *your* britches all wet?"

"I . . . uh . . . well, I figured it was time for him to learn
what the outhouse was for. But I'm going to have to build
a stool for him. And teach him to aim a little better."

Caitlyn giggled and Little Sun pushed against her, indicating for her to put him down. He ran over to Jon, then
lifted his small tunic. One tiny finger pointed up at Jon,
directly between his legs, as he turned his little face toward
Caitlyn.

This time Caitlyn could make sense of at least two of
his words. "Big" obviously referred to Jon, and "little"
to the boy's own anatomy. Caitlyn blushed furiously, but
the heat in Jon's cheeks matched her own.

"What have you been teaching him?" Caitlyn demanded through her embarrassment.

"N . . . nothing. I mean . . . ah, hell," Jon said. "I'm going down to the lake and clean my britches."

Jon limped away, and Little Sun turned a questioning gaze on Caitlyn as he dropped his tunic. "Hell?" he said clearly.

Caitlyn saw Jon falter a step when he heard Little Sun's voice, then duck his head and limp a little faster toward the lake.

"We're going to have a talk about your language, Jon Clay," she called after him. "Before we have my lessons this afternoon while Little Sun naps!"

"Shit," Jon muttered under his breath. "She sounds just like a nagging wife."

At the lakeshore, he turned and looked back at the cabin. Caitlyn again had Little Sun in her arms, evidently talking to him. Her index finger stroked the boy's plump cheek and that beautiful mouth was saying something, though he couldn't hear her words from down by the lake.

A shaft of sunlight filtered through a huge pine beside the cabin, striking reddish highlights from both Caitlyn's and Little Sun's raven hair. Caitlyn hadn't yet braided her hair this morning, and the luxurious mass fell over one shoulder, nearly to her knees, curling and waving its way downward. It contrasted with Little Sun's straight strands, but Jon knew both sets of locks were silky beneath his palms—and cheek.

Suddenly Caitlyn glanced toward him and their gazes met. Recalling the vision he'd had of Caitlyn in the blue gown, with the two curly-topped kids peeking through the banister, Jon held her gaze for a long second.

Caitlyn broke the contact first and shifted Little Sun to her hip as she walked back into the cabin. But Jon continued to stare at the cabin for several minutes after she disappeared, his thoughts swirling in his head and a contemplative frown on his face.

Why had he ever thought that he could build a life with a shallow woman like Roxie? Granted, Roxie had seemed the epitome of the woman that any Southern gentleman would give his eyeteeth to have for a wife—soft-spoken, ladylike, perfect manners and huge eyes batting at him over her fan as she hung onto his every word. But he'd soon found out that her apparent innocence covered up a calculating mind, which had its own idea about the type of life Roxie had been born and bred for.

The sex—allowed only after he had indeed proposed to Roxie—had been great at first. Now he wondered whether the clandestine meetings hadn't spiced it up somewhat. After they established a pattern of Jon sneaking into her bedroom twice a week, he'd at one point found himself just a little reluctant to make the ride to her plantation in the late night.

He hadn't even bedded Caitlyn yet, but something told him that their joining would be pure bliss—much more than just a physical act. He'd only seen one marriage in his life that appeared to be based on love instead of the result of careful plotting of bloodlines and fortunes. His uncle Jonathan, for whom he had been named, and his wife, Amanda—Aunt Mandy—had made no secret of the fact that their union was a love match. At balls their eyes would meet even while they were dancing with other partners, and Jon had never seen them within a foot of each other that Uncle Jonathan didn't have his arm around Mandy.

Hell, that was what love was all about. Jon knew it as surely as he knew that it was more than physical lust he felt for Caitlyn.

He didn't have a huge plantation to offer Caitlyn, where she could float around a polished ballroom in French gowns. His stepfather had made sure of that, when he deeded the plantation to Charlie. But, thanks in part to Silas, he had a start on a life for himself—and Caitlyn. He'd sent a large share of the money from his furs back with Pete Smith to bank in St. Louis. And he still had that small legacy from his grandfather—neither his mother nor his stepfather had been able to touch that.

Besides, the lure of Richmond and the plantation had faded somewhat, along with his anger towards his brother.

Life on the plantation had at one time been easy and satisfying, but his father and stepfather had created that existence. What he had a chance to do now was build something totally his own; and the more he thought about it, the more he realized he wanted the mountains and the fulfillment he had found out here to be part of his future.

As for Charlie, he had at least been honest with Jon. Roxie had been the deceitful one, using her fraudulent affection and sexual favors for her own gain. He really did feel sorry for Charlie. Even the total break in their relationship couldn't make him forget all the good times they had shared while growing up—couldn't completely override his love for his brother. What sort of family life would Charlie have now, with a woman like Roxie?

And what sort of family life did he want for himself? When he had ridden out of Richmond, the furthest thing from his mind had been planning a life that included a family—a wife and children. He had thought that desire was totally exterminated.

The breeze blew across his legs, and Jon chuckled as he plucked the damp material away from the chill on his left leg. And he was quickly gaining experience about teaching outhouse etiquette to any son he had. He just had to remember to remain behind the young one, instead of at his side, while he explained the rules. Recalling Little Sun's wide-eyed innocence at the outhouse seat when he swiveled around to watch Jon, his small stream spattering Jon's leg, he shook his head and laughed aloud.

Right now, he better get these britches off and rub some damp sand into them to clean the buckskin before the stain set, along with the smell. He headed for a huge boulder up the shore, where he could remove his britches without being seen from the cabin.

"So what you gonna do about it, boyo?" Silas asked a couple weeks later when they stopped for their noon meal.

"Huh?" Jon asked. "About what?"

"You and Cat, a'course. You've been more mooney-eyed than ever over her the last few weeks. You thinkin' about somethin' permanent here, or just some wintertime keepin' the cold off? She's under my pertection, don't forget.''

''You believe what you want, Silas,'' Jon said with a wry chuckle. ''But I've never met a woman in my life who's less needing of a man's protection than Caitlyn O'Shaunessy. Hell, she can ride as well as—better than most men. Probably shoot and hunt, too, if she needs to. I've never eaten this well in my life, and every meal's made up of stuff Caitlyn's gathered in the wild and prepared for us.''

Jon leaned his elbows on his knees and hunched over the fire, holding his tin cup in a spread palm. ''She makes her own clothing—ours, too. She's smart as a whip. You're enjoying her reading to us in the evenings every bit as much as I am.''

''She's still a woman, Jon.''

''A hell of a woman,'' Jon admitted with a reluctant sigh. ''But Caitlyn's made for life in these mountains, Silas. Out here, she's wild and free—like . . . like the eagles.'' He flicked the dregs from his coffee cup into the fire. ''Can you imagine what she'd be like back east? All those restrictions that are placed on a woman? Hell, she'd wither and die.''

''Them's your plans then, huh? To make you a pile of money from these furs we've been trappin', then go back and wave it under the noses of them there relatives you left behind? 'Specially under the nose of that there woman who sent you riding out here to the mountains like a dog that'd lost its prize bone to another dog? Show her what she missed?''

''I don't remember ever mentioning Roxie to you.''

''Hell, you didn't have to. I ain't so old that I don't remember how a woman can tie a man up in knots 'til he don't know which way's up. Just when you think you've got a handle on them, they bat those eyes a couple times and some woman you've never seen before looks up at you.''

''Man, you've got that right. Caitlyn's not like that, though, Silas. She's not contrived or dishonest. What you see with Caitlyn is who she is.''

Silas shook his head sadly. ''Boyo, you've still got a lot to learn. And what you're gonna learn some day is that there's not a woman on earth that any man will ever know completely—no matter if he lives with her fifty years. She's still gonna surprise you more often than not—and that's part of the wonder of lovin' a woman, boyo. It's all those there contradictions tied up in one beautiful package. And when she loves you back, it's like the best of both worlds. You ain't just tied to one woman—she's a bunch of different women in one, and each day's a whole new world.''

''So you've been in love, too, huh?'' Jon asked wryly.

''Naw,'' Silas denied with a laugh. ''Just observed over the years. Ain't never had no hankering for that sort of up and down life. Me, I like my peace and quiet too much. And I got itchy feet. Wouldn't've been right to 'spect some woman to trudge after me, and if we'd've had kids . . . well, I'd've wanted something more for them than a life like I've had.''

A sudden gust of wind blew a scattering of embers from the fire, and both Silas and Jon jumped to their feet to stamp out wisps of smoke in the dry grass near their camp fire. By the time Jon had shoveled dirt on the camp fire and then drowned the lingering embers with a bucket of water, fat snowflakes were lazily drifting around the men. After a brief consultation, they agreed to head on back to the cabin for the rest of the day.

''We've got our lines laid out in our minds, Jon,'' Silas said as they mounted their horses. ''We know where the best furs are gonna be this winter, and now all we have to do is get our traps set out. We'll see what this here weather's gonna do. If there's gonna be a storm, we'll ride it out and then get out there and see which way the animals are moving around. Track them in the snow, so we'll be sure we're settin' our traps in the right spots.''

Jon nodded his head indifferently. As far as he was concerned, it could snow for a week of days. It would be a week spent in the cabin with Caitlyn.

Chapter Sixteen

Caitlyn held the skinning knife balanced to throw, and Dog stood beside her, hackles raised and ears laid back, lips drawn away from viciously bared teeth. His snarls blended with her voice.

"You can take yourself right back the way you came, Tall Man," she snapped. "If I feel like visiting Sky Woman, I'll get Jon or Silas to take me. I'm not going anywhere with you!"

"My sister will be unhappy that you will not come." Tall Man urged his pony a step forward, ignoring the dog's increasing warning growl, but keeping a firm grip on his own knife in the hand hidden by his leg. "I promised her I would bring you."

"I don't believe you," Caitlyn said. "Sky Woman knows how late in the season it's getting. She wouldn't ask me to try to come to her camp now, with the snows fixing to set in and a chance of getting caught in a blizzard."

Tall Man's eyes narrowed dangerously. "Do you call me a liar, Smelly Woman?"

"Take it any way you want," Caitlyn spat, though a

slow fear began crawling around in her stomach. "You might have thought you were being real sneaky, but we knew you were around here. If you had a message for me from Sky Woman, why didn't you come in and tell me three weeks ago, when you first started hanging around my cabin?"

Tall Man's fingers tightened on his knife. Someone may have seen him, but it wasn't this woman or those two poor-eyed white men. He had been close to the men several times—close enough to have sent his knife whispering through the air to end their lives.

But the terms of the bargain had been laid out clearly. Only the woman was to be brought to the man, alive, with no one else knowing what had happened to her. Despite the huge area and few people, word spread quickly in the mountains, through a grapevine of contacts between both whites and Indians. The death of anyone connected to her would cause an uproar—make it less believable that the woman had tired of her life and returned to be with her own people.

With an effort, Tall Man controlled his anger. "The weather is turning now. I will stay here for a while and eat at your camp. You can give me food to last while I travel back to my own wigwam."

"Reckon I owe you some food," Caitlyn agreed cautiously, "since I ate at your wigwam last winter. But I don't want you here. You take your food and ride out and find your own camp."

"I could have told you the same thing when you came to my wigwam in the last season of the colored leaves," Tall Man spat. "But you were made welcome!"

"Not by you," Caitlyn denied. "And if my recollection is right, you're living with Sky Woman, not the other way around. Pa always made sure Sky Woman had everything she needed, and she lived alone when Pa wasn't with her. You moved in with her that summer before Pa died because you were tired of not having a woman around to cook for you. If Pa had've come back with me. . . ."

Caitlyn heard the door creak behind her. Darn it, she

should have hooked the latch, but she'd wanted to hear Little Sun if he woke. Before she could make a grab for him, Little Sun toddled around her, stopping abruptly when he saw the Indian on his pony.

Caitlyn snatched Little Sun into her arms, and his face immediately puckered into a scowl in preparation of a cry. "Hush," she ordered in a stern voice. "Quiet," she repeated in Nez Perce, which she knew the boy understood better.

Little Sun widened his eyes at the unaccustomed tone from what he usually expected of Caitlyn, but he stuck his thumb into his mouth and laid his head on her shoulder.

Still gripping her skinning knife, Caitlyn glanced at Tall Man. If she'd thought he looked dangerous before, she now saw a man whose entire being radiated a desire for vengeance—a hatred raging to be satisfied. Cold terror crawled up her spine.

"Spirit Eagle's son," Tall Man whispered in a deadly voice. "You are caring for my enemy's son—a man who has been banned from his own people. It could be no one else, or I would not have heard of it. We do not pass on to others tales of the shunned."

Tall Man hawked and spit a gob on the ground. "Waugh! You are as dead to the Nez Perce. Sky Woman will never welcome you again when she learns of this."

Caitlyn took an unconscious step backwards. "Your customs aren't mine," she managed to say in a calm voice. "You don't tell me what I can do—who I can or can't welcome into my own home."

"My *customs*," Tall Man whispered in warning, "say I may kill the spawn of my enemies."

His hand came up and Dog sprang. The pony reared in panic, and Tall Man's knife landed in the cabin wall, a bare inch from Caitlyn's shoulder.

She screamed and dodged inside the door, slamming it behind her and pushing the bar into place. Outside she could hear Dog's snarls and the pony's terrified neighs, interspersed with shouts of rage from Tall Man.

She dropped Little Sun onto the bunk. "Stay there," she ordered.

Racing back to the door, she hesitated only a second before she threw back the bar and opened it. After a brief glance at Tall Man trying to gain control of his frantic pony, she tugged the knife from the cabin wall, then pulled the door firmly closed behind her.

Shaking in fear, Caitlyn clutched a knife in each hand. *I might have to kill him.* The thought streaked through her head. Could she?

Little Sun's tiny, frightened face when she dropped him onto the bunk flashed in her mind. Tall Man wanted Little Sun dead. Whatever enigmatic reason had sent him here to try to trick her into returning to the Nez Perce camp had been wiped away as soon as he laid eyes on Spirit Eagle's son.

Dog flashed in and out between the pony's wildly dancing legs, barking furiously and nipping at whatever portion of the horse he could reach. Only the rigorous training gleaned from a lifetime spent on horseback kept Tall Man in place. Through the dust, Caitlyn caught sight of one of Tall Man's legs, his buckskin trousers shredded and ribbons of blood pouring down his leg.

Dog hadn't only been attacking the pony.

Suddenly Tall Man jerked cruelly on the pony's reins and turned it toward the far side of the clearing. It slashed out once more with its hind legs, catching Dog on his shoulder and spinning him through the air. He landed with a thump, but sprang immediately to his feet.

"Dog!" Caitlyn shouted. "No!"

With a whine, Dog looked at her, then back toward Tall Man. He made one, limping lunge, but Caitlyn sharply shouted at him again. Curling back his lips, Dog sank to the ground.

Tall Man viciously slapped his reins across the pony's nose, then jerked its head against its chest. The pony stood with chest heaving, flecks of foam spattering its muzzle.

Tall Man didn't speak. He didn't have to. Caitlyn clearly read every thought he had in the menace emanating from his tightly coiled body and hard, flinty eyes.

He flicked a glance at the knives held in her hands, then lifted his lips in a snarl that communicated to Caitlyn his lack of fear for her weapons. He slowly loosened his pony's reins, and the horse took a step forward.

Dog jumped to his feet again, pricking his ears and looking into the underbrush. Caitlyn glanced briefly away from Tall Man, and when she hurriedly drew her attention back, she saw only the white rump of Tall Man's pony, disappearing from sight.

Her shoulders slumped and she leaned back against the door, fingers still gripping the knives tightly. She couldn't seem to force her hold loose. When Jon and Silas rode into the clearing a moment later, they pulled their horses to an abrupt halt.

Tensing in their saddles, both men scanned the scene. Jon's urgent instinct was to go to Caitlyn, but he took rigid control of his emotions.

"Which way do you want me to go, Silas?" he asked in a quiet, deadly tone.

Silas raised his voice, so Caitlyn could hear across the clearing. "Which way did he go, Cat?"

Somehow Caitlyn managed to lift a hand and point. The snow, which had seemed to follow Jon and Silas on their ride back to the cabin, began falling, the soft flakes settling the churned up dust in the clearing.

"Where's the boy?" Silas called.

"In . . . inside," Caitlyn answered.

Jon glanced at Silas, and Silas nodded.

"Take care of Caitlyn," Jon said.

"I will, boyo."

Jon reined his horse around and kicked it into a gallop. With a half-whine of apology at Caitlyn, the dog took off in a limping run after Jon.

Jon followed the trail easily enough for the first mile or so, since Dog quickly took over the lead, nose to the ground. But as the snow fell more heavily, it began obliterating the signs, and even Dog slowed. He sniffed in one place, then cast in a circle.

Jon glanced ahead of them and saw a freshly-broken twig on a bush. Whistling to Dog, Jon pointed and urged his horse forward. A wind-swept portion of bare ground lay ahead of them, and Dog caught the scent again.

Jon scanned the mountainside ahead as he rode. The traces of hoofprints he followed indicated that the horse was still running full tilt, but there were any number of ambush spots around.

Whoever had attacked Caitlyn didn't have a real good start on Jon and the dog. He had the advantage, though, of not worrying about someone waiting ahead of him. The necessity of assuring himself the man he trailed wasn't hidden in a crevice waiting for him—or didn't circle back like a wounded grizzly on the prowl—slowed Jon's pace.

And the snow fell more thickly, fat flakes as large as silver dollars drifting earthward in a deceptively lazy spiral. Piling on one another in soft silence, they layered over the leaves and pine needles, covering the trail ahead and behind. They melted on exposed rocks and boulders, which still held remnants of sun rays, but the falling temperature would soon assure a blanket of snow even on those outcroppings.

When Jon found himself straining his eyes as he tried to peer through the snow-streaked openness ahead of him, he reluctantly pulled his horse to a halt. Dog was casting circles across the trail, having lost the scent again.

Jon didn't know who he was following, or what weapons the attacker might have. His fury and determination to wreak his anger on whoever had left Caitlyn in that stunned, fearful state had carried him this far, but he'd be no use to Caitlyn if he got killed out here. And if he let something happen to that crazy pup she adored. . . .

Jon dismounted and called to the dog. Tongue lolling, the animal limped toward him, favoring one hind leg even more than Jon had noticed before. He knelt and picked Dog up, prepared to drop him in an instant if he snapped at him as he had on occasion.

But Jon got a slurpy tongue on his face. He laid Dog across the saddle and climbed on behind him.

"No, fella," he said, laying a firm hand on the animal when Dog tried to jump down. "We'll go back and find out if Caitlyn knows who the son of a bitch was. If she does, there won't be a place in heaven or hell where he can hide from me."

Tall Man's exhausted pony stumbled once again, but he whipped it mercilessly across the rump and jerked its head up. At any time he could have turned to confront his pursuer—his bow and arrow quiver were strapped securely on the pony's rump. But still he rode on, chasing the face of the white-eyes woman called Caitlyn by her people. No matter how fast his pony ran, the face hovered just out of reach in his mind.

Shreds of sanity scattered on the wind rushing past him, replaced by the humiliation he had suffered from his tribal members when word of Morning Star's betrayal and disappearance had spread through the camp. The woman he had just left had aided in that humiliation. Though he had no proof, he knew that as surely as he knew he would have his vengeance on her.

Angrily he had turned his back on the offer to return his prize stallion and mares when Morning Star's uncle had extended the lead ropes. Proudly he had endured the council meeting, which had culminated in the treacherous bitch and her lover being designated as shunned—their names never to be spoken again by the Nez Perce.

They had done nothing to the white-eyes woman. He could have ordered her forth—demanded she answer his accusations against her. But it would only have furthered his humiliation, should she have admitted to outfoxing him.

The pony stumbled a final time and went down. Tall Man leapt from its back as it fell and, ignoring the poor beast's rasping gasps for breath, shook his fist into the falling snow.

"By the spirits of all who have gone before me," he shouted, "I vow vengeance on that white-eyes woman! And the cur dog she helped deceive me! They will die, or

I will never again walk in oneness with your spirits! The shadow on my name will be gone before I leave this world! This I say! This I swear! This I *vow*!''

Over the next few days, whenever she wasn't busy cooking or cleaning, Caitlyn alternately paced the cabin floor and stared out the lone window in the front of the small structure. Once when she reached out to scrub at a film of frost, she remembered how proud Pa had been when he presented her with those two precious panes of glass one Christmas morning. He would never tell her how he'd managed to come by that glass—probably ordered it at one rendezvous and had a friend pick it up for him the next summer and spirit it out to the cabin to hide until Christmas.

The snow had finally stopped today. The storm never did turn into a full-blown blizzard, merely minuscule white slices gathering into ever deepening, feathery layers. Silvery moonlight bathed the clearing this evening in an eerie light, the shadows of tree trunks flickering as the night breeze blew the towering tops of the pines back and forth.

Little Sun stirred and stretched in his crib in front of the fireplace, and Caitlyn instinctively tensed. But she heard him murmur quietly, then turn over to a more comfortable position.

Jon and Silas had built the crib the evening after Little Sun arrived, lining it with a portion of a buffalo hide. At first, Caitlyn had been tempted to place the crib in her own room. It crowded the small front room of the cabin, but placing it by the fireplace assured Little Sun of being warm while he slept. Jon and Silas fed the fire at intervals during the night, though her own room still grew chilly now and then.

She hadn't been sleeping at all well herself, so she heard any sound the little boy made during the night. Just last night he had whimpered the Nez Perce words for mother and father in his sleep, and Caitlyn had padded out to hold him until the dream passed.

Caitlyn watched a snowshoe rabbit hop into the clearing, then turn in a flurry of snow and race back into the underbrush. The owl glided after the rabbit on silent wings, but missed its prey by several inches. Its talons dragged the snow, and it swerved back upwards, into the treetops.

She barely took note of the life and death confrontation. Behind her, she could hear Silas scraping the tobacco dregs from the pipe he had taken to smoking in the evenings, and Jon's barely audible humming as he worked on a pair of snowshoes Silas was teaching him to make.

That darned nightmare was back. She rigidly fought sleep each night, knowing that soon after she fell into the darkness it would wake her in soundless, screaming fright.

She thought she knew what had brought it on. Any time she had been close to a small child in earlier years it had returned. But why, then, hadn't it started as soon as Spirit Eagle left his son with her? Why hadn't it begun until after Tall Man showed up, leaving behind a large chink in her self-assurance?

She'd never been so afraid in her life as when Tall Man glared at her from across the clearing. She looked at the spot where he had sat on his horse and shivered slightly. Could it have been the thought of not only having to protect herself, but also the small, defenseless child in the cabin?

Caitlyn closed her eyes for a brief second, fighting once more the growing resentment she felt against Little Sun. She thought she had covered it up fairly well. She still cared for him, made sure he was clean and well fed. But last night, when she had picked him up to comfort him, the little boy must have felt the stiffness in her arms and lack of conviction in her voice.

He had stared up at her, his small face outlined in the dancing firelight, whimpering and struggling to be laid back down. After she placed him in the crib again, he turned and curled away from her. With a sigh, she had covered him once more and returned to bed, wondering what she would do when Silas and Jon left for the trap lines, leaving her solely in charge of Little Sun once more.

Lying wide-eyed in the darkness, she had resisted the exhaustion with every fiber of her being. She realized she had succumbed to sleep only when she sat up in bed, beads of sweat covering her forehead and her mouth straining in aching openness.

"Cat," Silas said. "Where'd you hide the tobacco?"

Caitlyn turned from the window. "Right where I always hide it," she said with an attempt at a smile. "Beside the coffee."

"That there's almost gone. I know I bought some more at rendezvous this past summer."

Caitlyn walked over to the lower shelf beside the fireplace, where she had stored some of the extra supplies. "Well, I'd hope you bought another supply for yourself. You never smoked this much before."

"Don't smoke when I'm out huntin'—scares off the animals. But there ain't much to do around here right now. And when my feet get itchy, smokin' calms them down."

With a tolerant smile, Caitlyn handed Silas a parcel wrapped in brown paper. "This is yours. It felt like tobacco when I put it away."

The fire flared up, and Jon studied Caitlyn's face. Dark shadows lay under those beautiful eyes, highlighting their blueness, and her cheekbones stood out. He could almost swear she had lost weight in the past three days.

She had brushed him off whenever he tried to talk to her, though. As small as the cabin was, Jon wouldn't have believed it possible for Caitlyn to avoid him, but she did. She carried an impenetrable armor around with her, appearing pleasant enough on the surface—but any time he or Silas got within a foot or two of her, she found something to do on the other side of the room.

She refused to discuss what had happened to her beyond informing them that it had been Tall Man who had been there. Maybe she had told Silas a little more before Jon returned after losing the Indian's trail—there hadn't been any privacy for him to talk to the old man yet.

Some decisions had to be made. They couldn't leave Caitlyn and Little Sun alone here at the cabin while they set out and ran the trap lines. There were only two rifles for the three of them, and neither he nor Silas would feel comfortable out in the wilderness without a gun. Who knew whether Tall Man had left, or was still skulking around?

Little Sun let out a brief howl, and Jon saw Caitlyn grow rigid. That had changed, too, the last three days. She also avoided the little boy whenever possible.

"Take care of him, will you please, Silas?" Caitlyn said as she headed toward the door to grab her wolfskin jacket. "I need to go to the outhouse."

Jon threw aside the snowshoe and stood, reaching for the rifle propped in the corner by his bunk. He didn't forbid Caitlyn to go out alone, but as soon as the door closed behind her, he opened it and stepped halfway out to watch her. He heard Silas at the crib, cooing and nudging it to rock it, and opened the door a little farther when Dog bumped at his leg.

"Is he going back to sleep?" Jon asked over his shoulder.

"Yeah, he always does," Silas replied.

Jon waited until Caitlyn closed the outhouse door and Dog laid down in the snow in front of the building before he spoke again. "What are we going to do, Silas?"

Silas gave a deep sigh. "Reckon I'm as worried about her as you are, boyo. One thing for sure, we can't leave her here while we run our lines. She'll have to come along with us."

"A few days ago, I'd have said that Caitlyn would throw a fit if we tried to keep her with one or the other of us all the time. But she's scared, Silas. What the hell did that bastard do to her? She won't talk to me."

"Me neither. I been trying to piece it together in my mind, but there's a piece here and there missin'. You heard the story of Spirit Eagle and Morning Star yet?"

"Not all of it," Jon admitted.

Silas briefly related the tale to Jon—a story that had spread through the mountains with the speed of wildfire as soon as it happened. Anger slowly seeped through Jon's mind, and not just at Caitlyn's foolishness in making an enemy of Tall Man.

She must have some awfully strong feelings for Spirit Eagle to take a chance like that. Though Silas said that

Caitlyn's involvement with Morning Star's escape from marriage to a man she didn't love had never been proven, what else could explain the mess they found themselves in now?

Shunned by his own people, Spirit Eagle had brought his son to a woman he knew would care for the boy—Caitlyn, who had shared his childhood. What else had been between the Indian man and Caitlyn? Had she maybe chosen him for her own, then stepped aside in the name of love when her friend, Morning Star, fell in love with the warrior?

Caitlyn emerged from the small building, but instead of returning to the cabin, she walked several yards away and stared across the clearing. She crossed her arms in front of her, her head leaning slightly toward one shoulder as though she were contemplating her thoughts—or missing someone.

Missing Spirit Eagle? Had her withdrawal from Little Sun the last few days been due to her distaste at handling the son of the other woman her Indian love had married? Had she vowed not to marry because she knew no one could ever take his place?

Now that he was free, did she plan to make another attempt to win his love?

"Jon . . . ah. . . ." Silas stopped beside Jon and took a drag on his pipe. He glanced out the doorway, a worried frown on his face.

"What is it, Silas?"

"Maybe you ought to shut that door. Don't want it to get chilled in here."

Jon swung the door to, but left a crack through which he could peer out at Caitlyn.

"That better, Silas?"

"Yeah. Listen, boyo, I. . . ."

"Spit it out, Silas. What's on your mind?"

Silas bit his pipe stem for a moment, then pulled the pipe from his mouth. "Look, Jon, I've told you time and again how much I like to be by myself in these here mountains. But we gotta run them trap lines every day, or ain't no use even settin' them out. Wolverines and wolves'll tear up our pelts, we don't get to them right away.''

"Get to the point, Silas. I know all that.''

"One of us is gonna have to take Cat and the boy along,'' Silas finally grumbled.

"And you'd rather it be me than you that they go with?''

"Well, yeah, boyo. I know I'm the one who took Cat on. And she's under my pertection. But. . . . ''

A smile crawled over Jon's face. "You owe me for this, Silas.''

Silas chuckled under his breath. *Oh no, Jon, my boy. This is one you owe me.*

Chapter Seventeen

Little Sun chortled and clapped his mittened hands as the sled bounced along behind Dog. As soon as he laid eyes on the sled several mornings ago, he exhibited a stubborn streak that seldom surfaced. Twisting and squirming in Caitlyn's arms, where she held him on the pinto's back, he had made it clear that the sled would be what he rode on—pulled by his friend, Dog, of course.

Dog padded tolerantly in the harness, following the trail broken by Jon's horse, and Caitlyn's heart melted as she looked at the little boy's bundled-up body, tucked into the buffalo robe.

She'd made him a pair of rabbit-fur-lined moccasins, wolfskin leggings and a small wolfskin jacket to match her own. She'd unraveled one of Jon's red knit hats, studying the stitches as she went so she could refashion it into a smaller version for Little Sun.

But that had been a waste of time. She laughed silently to herself. Dressed in his new togs, Little Sun had seemed to realize just what they were for. He'd toddled over to where Silas hung his wolfskin hat and pointed up at it in a determined manner. Then he'd pulled the knit hat from his head and dropped it on the floor.

"Hat," he'd said clearly. "My hat."

Silas had given in graciously and a smaller hat, made from Silas's extra hat in his pack, now perched on Little Sun's head, the shortened tail bouncing in rhythm with the sled.

The nightmares had finally fled. Shoot, who could dream when she fell into bed each night happily tired from days spent out in the wilderness she loved?

She and Jon ran the two shorter trap lines, varying their path each day. They arrived back at the cabin in late afternoon, spending the evenings curing the furs. Now and then they had to devote an entire day at the cabin to tanning, if Silas brought in an especially large load of furs, but even those days were a welcome break in their daily lives.

She'd pushed Tall Man into the back of her mind, telling herself he wouldn't be foolish enough to attempt anything with Jon always near. He was probably back at his winter camp. Surely he wouldn't be stupid enough to try to winter out here on his own.

The nagging thought that kept her from complete contentment was her knowledge of an Indian's patience. After living among them all her life, she knew a warrior would wait months, even years, to avenge himself.

Jon led the way to a sheltered nook, where he had stored dry wood inside a small cave in the mountainside. They usually stopped here for their noon meal, and remnants of previous fires lay inside a stone ring.

As usual, too, Jon swung down and came over to help Caitlyn from her pinto. She gave in with a sigh. No matter how many times she told him she could get off that darned horse on her own, he ignored her. And no matter how many times she decided that she wasn't going to react this time, she slid down against his body and allowed him to hold her for that extra-long second.

"Cold?" he murmured, his palms rubbing up and down the back of her jacket.

Cold? How could she be cold standing this close to him? She shook her head slightly, hands still on his shoulders and head tilted back. His face was always so close to her own when he held her like this, and he usually. . . .

She parted her lips and sighed as Jon bent his head. His lips met hers gently, but briefly, before he stepped away.

"Let me know if you get cold, honey," he said, then walked over to the fire site.

Caitlyn glared at him. He must have kissed her three dozen times like that since they started running the lines—not that she was keeping count.

The first time he took her by surprise. He hadn't pressed the matter then, either, just slipped a kiss, then gone on about the fire building business. And despite her wariness from then on, he wouldn't turn her loose until he got his kiss.

He never demanded it in words—instead, he waited patiently until Caitlyn gave in and tilted her head up. Darn it, why didn't he just take one good long kiss and make it last all day?

And touching her. He sat down right next to her while they ate. If she tried to move an inch or so away, he draped a casual arm around her waist and pulled her back. Whenever she had Little Sun on her lap, Jon curled an arm around Caitlyn's shoulders and bent his head toward the little boy. They would discuss the day's happenings, and Little Sun's vocabulary was growing quickly.

Mindful of Little Sun's heritage, Caitlyn also taught him the Nez Perce words for the English words he was picking up. Jon solemnly repeated them also, and sometimes their conversations were a funny mixture of both languages.

Jon soon had the fire blazing and clean snow melting in the fire-blackened coffeepot.

"You want tea or coffee today, sweetheart?" he called to Caitlyn.

A mischievous gleam lit Caitlyn's eyes. "Tea, darling," she called back, a satisfied grin curving her lips when Jon glanced over at her in surprise. "With honey in it, honey."

Jon bit back his own smile and nodded. "Whatever you want, sweetie pie."

Sweetie pie? Huh, that was a new one.

Jon dug into his pack and pulled out the tea canister. "And what would my angel like to eat today?" he asked. "Let's see. We've got moose steaks, or moose steaks. Or how about moose steaks? Would those satisfy the beautiful lady's hunger?"

Caitlyn tapped a finger beside her mouth. "I do believe that I'll have the moose steaks today, love." She batted her eyes as Jon watched her. "This restaurant does have such wonderful moose steaks, don't you agree?"

"My own opinion is that it's the company that makes the meal so wonderful," he growled in a low voice. He turned back to the pack and pulled out a skillet, leaving Caitlyn standing there with a flush on her cheeks.

But she wasn't about to let him think he had bested her. A few minutes later, when he handed a plate over to where she sat on a fallen log with Little Sun, Caitlyn looked at him with a glorious smile. As soon as he sat down, she snuggled a little closer to him. She cut her steak up into various-sized bites, then fed a small one to Little Sun, popped one into her own mouth, and picked up a third piece on the end of her knife to offer it to Jon.

Jon gently nipped the piece of steak from the knife point, and Caitlyn turned back to Little Sun as nonchalantly as she could when Jon murmured, "Ummmm. Yours is better than mine."

"How do you know that?" Caitlyn managed in a saucy voice. "You haven't even tasted yours yet."

Jon chuckled and slipped his steak back into the frying pan to keep it warm, adding the beans beside it.

"I just know it is," he replied. He picked up his wooden spoon and scooped it full of the beans on Caitlyn's plate. "Here. We better not let these get cold."

He held the spoonful of beans by her mouth, and Caitlyn agreeably accepted them. Then she mashed up a few beans with her own spoon and gave Little Sun a bite.

The meal continued until all the food had disappeared.

Jon refused to use his own plate, refilling Caitlyn's from the skillet after it was empty.

"The food tastes better off your plate, honey," he said with a laugh. "Sweeter and juicier somehow."

At one point, Caitlyn realized she was in over her depth. But she couldn't back down now. She'd intended to show Jon that she could banter back at him just as unaffectedly as he seemed to be able to use those sweet words on her and go on about his business.

But their teasing, low-murmured conversation was wrapping her in a cocoon of coziness. When they couldn't eat another bite, Little Sun slipped to the ground and picked up Dog's bowl. Jon agreeably scraped the scraps of their meal into it and forked in the third steak from the iron frying pan.

After Little Sun set the bowl in front of Dog, he crawled onto the sled by himself and snuggled under the buffalo robe. Caitlyn started to rise, but Jon captured her in both arms.

"He's all right, sweetheart," he said as he nuzzled her ear. "He's covered up fine."

A languid contentment stole over Caitlyn, and she leaned against his chest. The fire, burning down to embers, snapped and popped a couple times, and she frowned at it She ought to be getting chilly without its heat, but warmth suffused her. Her eyes drooped and she stifled a yawn.

But she wasn't sleepy. She was all too aware of every sense. She could feel the rise and fall of Jon's chest beneath her ear and hear his breath whisper in and out. The smell of wood smoke rose from his coat, mingled with the spicy scent of his aftershave. In her mind, his face floated, blue eyes twinkling with mischief, then darkening as he bent his head toward her, lips separating slightly as his mouth neared hers.

Caitlyn's lips parted in answer to the soft, gentle caress on her mouth. When Jon started to pull back, she cupped his head and twisted in his arms to stand. Wrapping one arm around his neck, she kissed him—once, twice, then again.

Jon pulled her onto his lap. Kneading her slim hip with one hand, he swept his tongue around her lips, then tasted inside her mouth, savoring the silkiness and the gentle rasping of his tongue against the even teeth. At her almost inaudible moan of surrender, he slipped his hand under her jacket, stroking the slender back before he almost urgently traced a path around her ribs to cup her breast.

Caitlyn's arm tightened on his neck and her head fell against his shoulder. Jon kissed her cheek, nuzzled the hair away from her ear and breathed her name. He licked at the delicate earlobe, then circled his tongue on the satiny skin of her neck before he gently nipped a path downward. Beneath her jacket, he ran his thumb over her nipple, which surged against the callused pad.

Neglecting the breast a necessary second, he reached beneath her buckskin blouse and teasingly danced his fingers across bare skin, back toward her breast. When he cupped it again, Caitlyn choked out a gasp and tightened her fingers in his hair.

"Jon," she said with an aching sob of need. "I didn't mean . . . oh, God, Jon."

"What, darlin'?" he whispered, pulling his hand free and unbuttoning the wolfskin jacket with no resistance from Caitlyn. "What did you mean?"

He unlaced the front of her blouse as he kissed a path along her collarbone.

"I only thought . . . the little kisses," Caitlyn admitted in a forced voice, "weren't long enough."

Jon pushed the buckskin blouse from her shoulder and found her breast again. "You only had to ask, sweetheart. I've got all the kisses for you that you could ever want."

"I didn't *want* to want them!"

Jon looked into Caitlyn's half-open eyes, now a deep, aquamarine pool of desire. "Neither did I at first," he said in a rueful voice. "But you've crept into my heart, darlin'. And I want more than kisses from you. I want all of you— now and forever, Caitlyn."

The aching need swept through Caitlyn when he kissed her again, whispering over her body at first, then flaming into a yearning want that swept away any.thought of not yielding to his caresses. She gasped with loss when he broke the kiss, only to emit little whimpers when he closed soft, wet lips over her breast. A trail of wanting followed his fingers across her flat stomach, bursting into demand when he slid his hand beneath the thongs holding the front of her buckskin trousers.

He cupped and massaged her, gently at first, then more firmly swirling his palm against her. When he reached inside to touch her, a blazing shiver of heat ran over her, crescendoing into a shatter that swept her entire body. She swirled with the feeling, glorying in the wondrous fulfillment and crying his name over and over.

When she could think again, it was only thoughts of Jon. Jon's kisses—Jon's hands. Jon whispering her name again, his own aching need echoing in the word.

He pushed the hair away from her face. "God, Caitlyn, darling, I want you. Let me love you. Please don't stop me now."

"Little Sun," she murmured.

Jon turned her to look at the sled. All they could see were Little Sun's closed eyes and tiny nose, peeking out from between his hat and the buffalo robe. Dog curled protectively at the little boy's back.

"Caitlyn?" Jon whispered.

She kissed him for her answer, and Jon swept her into his arms to carry her over to where the low-hung boughs of a huge pine made a sheltering nest. Snow showered them both as he ducked through the branches, but it failed utterly to cool the demands of their bodies. He only released her long enough to shrug out of his heavy buffalo-skin coat and toss it down for them to lie on.

Lips greedily transmitting his need, Jon pushed Caitlyn's jacket from her shoulders and tossed it aside. He cupped her hips and pulled her against his throbbing want, moaning deep in his throat when she didn't pull away, and sinking down onto his robe.

Caitlyn tugged against his shirt, and Jon rose above her briefly to pull it off. He reached down and pushed her blouse from her shoulders, unable to stifle a gasp of enjoyment when she pulled her arms free, baring both her breasts to him. He'd neglected one and he immediately lowered his head.

Caitlyn instinctively wrapped her arms and legs around him. Her hands stroked his back, and she tossed her head, tendrils of hair escaping from her now useless braid.

"Jon?" she murmured. "How can it feel like this?"

"Like what?" he asked with a groan as he raised himself to gaze down at her.

"Like . . . like I want something—something I don't even know what it is I want—and the wanting almost hurts."

Jon knelt over her and slowly began slipping her buckskin pants downward. "Me, too, sweetheart. But it's more than want—or need. It's wanting to love you—and to have you love me back."

He slipped her moccasins off along with the pants, then removed his own pants as he stared at her wonderful nakedness. Caitlyn stared at him in return, her eyes stroking over his body, with Jon feeling every sweep of her gaze.

"This is a part of love, then," she murmured in a throaty voice. "This need I feel for you."

Jon leaned over her on one arm, cupping himself and nudging against the heat between her legs. "It's a wonderful part of love, Caitlyn, darlin'. Let me show you even how much more pleasurable it can be."

She opened her legs wider to him and Jon settled against her, prepared to make her his own.

But before he made that final thrust, he kissed her, then looked into her eyes. "I love you, Caitlyn. Do you think you can ever love me back?"

"Yes," she replied in a breathless voice. "I already do."

Her gasp of pain was swept away at once in the rapture that came when Jon filled her. As much as she gloried in her own feelings, Jon's desire for her needs to be met, as well as his evident enjoyment of her, completed more than just her physical wanting. A sense of her own womanhood shadowed her thoughts.

She was giving this man—this wonderful man who loved her—every bit as much pleasure as he gave her in return. And he told her so with murmured, nonsense words of love—words that took wing in her heart and echoed in the beautiful wilderness around her.

"I love you, Jon!" she cried at the moment of their simultaneous final fulfillment.

Chapter Eighteen

Jon carefully rolled aside and wrapped them both in his buffalo-skin robe. When Caitlyn shivered, he cuddled her even closer, and Caitlyn snuggled a flushed cheek against his chest as her breathing calmed. She wrapped an arm around his waist, and her slender fingers traced a path back and forth, tantalizing Jon with the gentle pressure.

As she tried to sort through her feelings, Caitlyn remained aware of every masculine inch of the body lying entwined with her own. She loved him. All right, darn it, she did. No sense even thinking about hiding that now, when she'd cried it out for the entire wilderness to hear.

Why didn't he say something? He'd definitely had plenty to say up until now.

Love. Huh, love and lust. There really was a difference, like Sky Woman had tried to tell her. And the best thing she could see about this love business was having it returned by the person you picked to love.

Well, this other part was real nice, too. But enjoying it so much must have something to do with love. Otherwise, why had she taken such pains to keep Tall Man away, as well as any other man who looked on her with a leer?

Little Sun!

Caitlyn pushed urgently on Jon's chest. "Jon, let me go. I have to check on Little Sun!"

"Shhhh, darlin'. I can see him through the branches, and he's fine. Dog's curled up beside him."

"He's not Dog's responsibility," Caitlyn said with another push. "He's mine."

Jon captured her hands and dropped a kiss on her nose. "All right, settle down. I'll go. Just let me get my clothes back on."

Caitlyn stared up into his face, so near her own and so dear to her. Sweat-dried wisps of blond curls layered his forehead, and his blue eyes gazed at her tenderly. He dropped her hands and reached out to brush back a tendril of hair from her face.

"Are you all right?" he asked softly.

"Yes," Caitlyn replied. "I. . . ."

When Jon quirked an eyebrow at her, she gave a languid sigh. "I don't think I've ever been more all right in my entire life," she admitted.

Jon gave a low growl and buried his face on her neck, his hand curling in her raven hair. He held her tightly for a long instant, then drew back to gaze at her again.

"I. . . ." When Caitlyn pursed her lips and lifted an eyebrow he chuckled softly and continued, "I feel like I've just been given the world on a silver platter. And it's all wrapped up in a beautiful package named Caitlyn."

A flush climbed Caitlyn's cheeks. "Took you long enough to say anything," she grumbled.

"I was trying to think of words strong enough to say it, darlin'. But I guess I love you is about the best I can do."

He ran his index finger down her cheek and around her mouth before he kissed her, gently nibbling at first. In answer to Caitlyn's tug on his shoulder, he deepened the pressure, kissing her as though he could linger forever.

But the world outside their pine bough–sheltered nest kept turning—the responsibilities waited. He lifted his head and covered Caitlyn's hand with his own when she touched his cheek.

"I've got to get dressed," he murmured.

"I love you," Caitlyn breathed.

"Took you long enough to realize it," Jon whispered.

"Yeah, I guess it did."

Jon kissed her again briefly, then slid free of the robe. Shivering violently, he hurried into his clothing while Caitlyn cuddled down into the warmth from their bodies.

"You're going to need your coat," she said when he sat back down near her feet to pull on his moccasins.

"Keep it until you get dressed. I'll build up the fire."

Rising, Jon ducked out of the sheltering pines, hurried to the fire and threw on some dry wood. He rubbed his hands together as the flames flickered into new life, standing as close as he dared without taking a chance of catching his buckskin fringe on fire. As soon as he soaked up a little heat, he walked over to the sled to check on the little boy.

After Jon moved away from the fire, Caitlyn reluctantly sat up, keeping the buffalo robe firmly around her body. She glanced around for her clothing and reached out to snag her buckskin blouse in her fingers first. Giggling at her predicament, she shook her head and tried to decide whether to face the cold and drop the robe, or pull the blouse inside and somehow struggle into it.

She glanced back at the fire to see Jon again standing by it, rubbing his hands up and down his arms. With swift movements, she dropped the robe and slipped into the buckskin blouse. Missing Jon's warmth more each second, she scurried into the rest of her clothing and shrugged into her jacket. Once outside the pine boughs, she shook Jon's buffalo robe free of pine needles and carried it over to the fire.

"Here," she said as she held the robe up. "Put this on before you catch a cold."

Jon slipped his arms in, turning immediately and capturing Caitlyn before she could move away. He whirled her around once, and Caitlyn grasped his shoulders and threw back her head, her silky hair swirling. A throaty laugh echoed in Jon's ears. Instead of setting her back on her feet, he carried Caitlyn over to the fallen log and sat down with her on his lap.

"Do you want us to talk about this now, darlin'?" he asked. "Or would you rather think about it for a while?"

"Guess we've already been thinking about it for a few months," Caitlyn said with a sigh. "And even if we talk until we're both blue in the face, it's not going to change things much."

"What's that supposed to mean?" When Caitlyn ducked her head, Jon tipped her face up, forcing her to meet his frown. "I told you. This is a forever thing—at least as far as I'm concerned."

"Forever in whose world?" Caitlyn asked softly. "Jon, I love you, but I love living here in the mountains, too. I've been reading about how things are back where you come from. Fancy manners—fancy meals. Fancy dances and big houses it takes a whole mess of people to keep running smoothly. I'd feel like a fish flopping around in the desert back there."

"So, we'll live out here," Jon said with a shrug.

"And just how long do you think it'd be before you got to yearning for better clothes than the buckskins I can sew up for you? To talk to your kinfolks? Get a new bunch of books to read?"

"Caitlyn, there's times I wish I'd never even thought about teaching you to read." When Caitlyn shot him a disgruntled glance, Jon's eyes softened and he tightened his grasp. "I didn't really mean that, darlin'. Look, you can learn all you need to know for when we visit back east. I'll teach you that, too, along with anything else you think you might like to learn. And who knows? You might decide someday that you want our children to have an eastern education. That way, they can choose where they want to live. . . ."

Caitlyn struggled wildly in his arms and Jon had all he could do to hold her. "Caitlyn, stop it," he demanded. "What the hell's wrong with you?"

"Let me up, dash nab it!"

Jon released her with a muffled oath and rose to his feet when Caitlyn began backing away from him, her blue eyes wide and her arms clasped across her stomach.

"Now you listen here, Caitlyn," he growled. "I intend to have children—several of them. Don't you want babies someday?"

"No," Caitlyn breathed in a barely audible whisper. "I can't."

"You don't know that you can't have children, Caitlyn. And look at how well you take care of Little Sun—how much you love him. Your own children. . . . "

"No!" Caitlyn frantically shook her head. "It's different with him. Spirit Eagle will be back to get him. I can't . . . oh, God! I can't!"

The nightmare had never intruded in the daylight—only in the darkest night. But now she heard the baby whimper again, upset by the tension he sensed in the woman who held him. The mother's worried shush—the whimpers growing louder.

Caitlyn clapped her hands over her ears and gazed frenziedly around her, seeing things now that she had buried in her mind years ago. Painted faces and bronze bodies, mouths opened in shrieked shouts of triumph and blood-stained hatchets and war clubs raised high in their hands. Agonized screams echoed in her head.

Before Jon could react, she ran for the pine tree and dove underneath. She wrapped her arms around her head and buried her face on her knees. Still the screams echoed, and now the baby screeched, an ear-splitting sound that tore at her heart.

She had to go to him!

But the pine branches shivered overhead. Someone was there! Caitlyn dove for deeper shelter. Arms captured her legs and dragged her backwards.

"No!" She twisted and fought, terror crowding her mind and her own screams joining the echoes in her mind. Behind her closed eyelids, pictures flashed. Blood dripping down an upraised bronze arm; a glimpse of a crumpled woman's body in the underbrush—another tiny body also lying there.

The smashing sound that preceded the baby's shrieks being cut off abruptly.

"No." Caitlyn's voice fell to a whimper. A heavy body covered hers now and she gave up fighting. "No," she whimpered again, shaking her head in the pine needles. Then a welcome blackness stole over her and she drifted gratefully into it, lying as still as death.

Jon rose over her. "Caitlyn?" She lay with arms outflung, her fingers curled into a grasping reach. But her head was pillowed on her shoulder and her eyes closed.

Frantically Jon grabbed her and shook her. "Caitlyn! Damn it, wake up!"

Her arms flopped uselessly and her head wobbled on her slender neck. Almost flinging her back down, Jon ripped open her jacket and laid his ear on her chest. His own loud gasps for breath were all he could hear.

"Caitlyn!"

Sobbing with frustration, Jon pushed up her jacket sleeve and held his fingers on her pulse. A steady beat feathered against his touch, but Caitlyn never moved.

Gathering her into his arms, Jon ducked out of pine branches and carried her to the fire. Her head lolled against him, her arms and legs hanging from her body as though she were entirely paralyzed and had no control over them. He hesitated, undecided whether to try to bring her back to consciousness here or take her to the cabin.

She could lie on the sled with Little Sun, but Dog would never be able to pull the sled with the extra weight. Or could he?

If Dog couldn't, he didn't have any way to attach the sled to one of the horses.

The hell with it. He'd pull that damned sled himself!

Little Sun barely woke as Jon ordered Dog to move, laid Caitlyn beside the boy, then rearranged the furs covering them both. He quickly scooped snow over the fire to smother it, then tied the horses' lead ropes to the back of the sled.

For a long moment, Jon stared down at Caitlyn's still figure, hands clenched at his sides and his lips moving soundlessly. Finally he grabbed the harness and slipped it over his shoulders, moving off back down the trail they had broken that morning.

Barely halfway back to the cabin, the damned snow began falling. Jon ignored it at first, concentrating on the trail before him, counting off each traveled foot in his mind and judging how far yet he had to go. Periodically he stopped and checked to make sure Caitlyn and Little Sun were still covered—usually at the top of each particularly high rise, so he could also ease his straining muscles.

He pulled up, gasping, wishing like hell there was some way to have either Dog or one of the horses share the load. Either he or Caitlyn always climbed down and pushed when Dog had an especially hard pull to make. He lifted his bowed head, at last realizing just how thick the falling snow had become.

Shrugging the harness off, Jon plowed through a drift beside the trail and checked Caitlyn and Little Sun. Caitlyn lay in the same position—eyes closed and the rise and fall of her chest nearly imperceptible.

But Little Sun opened his eyes and pulled his arms free of the covering robe.

"Up!" he said with a chortle.

"No, son," Jon murmured. "You have to ride back here for now."

Little Sun stuck out his bottom lip in a protesting pout, but he obeyed the pressure of Jon's hands when Jon tucked his arms back into the warmth. Glancing overhead, Jon pulled the buffalo skin up to cover both his passengers' heads. When he straightened, he reached around to massage his aching back for a few seconds, then took a deep breath and waded through the snow toward the harness.

After a while, no matter how hard he squinted, Jon had problems following the trail. More and more often he stumbled into a high drift, and spent precious seconds finding the path again. But it couldn't be much farther. By his reckoning of passing time, the cabin should be less than a half-mile ahead.

Dog appeared out of the snow and grabbed at Jon's leg with his teeth.

"Get away," Jon said wearily. "Get."

Dog trotted off a few steps, and Jon bent into the harness. The dog leapt forward again and grabbed his leg.

"Damn it, Dog. . . ."

Dog trotted away, at an angle to the direction Jon had been heading. As soon as Jon took another step, Dog raced back and blocked the trail.

"Move, Dog!" Jon ordered.

Dog cocked his head away from Jon and whined.

"What the hell is it?" Suddenly Jon realized he'd been breaking new trail for the last hundred feet. Somehow he had lost the path again. Dog was trying to get that through his head.

"All right, boy," Jon said. "We'll go your way."

Dog headed out again, but he stayed within Jon's sight. Almost at once the trail became easier as Jon walked along their previous path. A short while later, a large shadow loomed out of the swirling whiteness and Jon knew they had found the cabin. If not for that darned dog that Caitlyn loved to distraction. . . .

He shoved open the door and hauled the sled right up to the opening. There was still a measure of warmth left in the cabin, and he hastened to carry both Caitlyn and Little Sun inside, so he could shut the door and rebuild the fire. The horses could wait a few minutes, but he made sure Dog came in.

Caitlyn lay unstirring on Jon's bunk, but when Jon closed the door, Little Sun sat up in his crib. He stood and grabbed the side, rocking it back and forth. Jon hurried over and pushed him back down, shaking a warning finger at him.

"You stay there a minute until I get the fire going, Little Sun."

The little lip came out again, but the boy sat still.

Jon went to the fireplace and raked back the covering of ashes he had used to bank the fire that morning. Quickly he added small pieces of kindling, then a few larger ones. Flames burst forth and he reached for a somewhat larger piece of wood just as the crib squeaked again.

Little Sun climbed over the railing and hung precariously for a second before dropping to the floor. Without a glance at Jon, he toddled toward Caitlyn. Scrambling up onto Jon's bunk, he squatted beside Caitlyn and reached out a pudgy hand.

"Cat?" He patted her on the cheek again, repeating her name in a cadence. "Cat? Cat . . . Cat . . . Cat."

Caitlyn's eyes flew open. "Reggie?" she whispered in an awestruck voice. "Reggie?"

Suddenly she sat up and grabbed Little Sun in her arms.

"Oh, God, Reggie," Jon heard her say. "They didn't kill you. I didn't let you die! Reggie!"

Chapter Nineteen

"Caitlyn?"

Jon approached cautiously, pausing when Caitlyn's head whipped up and she stared first at him, then around the cabin. Her arms tightened on Little Sun, and he squirmed to be let down, twisting and kicking his legs as he pushed against Caitlyn's chest. She glanced down at him, a frown creasing her face.

"Reggie?" she whispered.

"Down, Cat," the little boy insisted.

Caitlyn stroked his cheek once, then allowed him to climb from the bunk. She watched him toddle over to Jon and wrap his arms around Jon's leg.

"Eat," Little Sun said.

Jon chuckled softly and picked him up. After returning the small body to the crib, he gave Little Sun a piece of maple syrup candy to chew on.

"He won't eat his supper," Caitlyn said from the bunk.

Jon slowly walked towards her. "Are you all right, Caitlyn? Do you remember what happened?"

"How did you get us back here?" Caitlyn asked instead of answering Jon's questions.

"On the sled." Jon sat down on the edge of the bunk. "You know, you don't look that heavy. But if I have to pull you that far again, I'm gonna insist you go on a diet first."

A sad hint of a smile curved Caitlyn's lips, and when Jon tentatively reached for her hand, she clenched her fingers around his. But she kept her eyes on the crib.

"I thought he was Reggie," she said softly. "I called him Reggie, didn't I?"

"Who is Reggie, darlin'?"

"He *was* my little brother—half-brother, anyway. They . . . they killed all of them. Except for me. M . . . Mama hid with us, and when Reggie started to cry . . . She couldn't get him to stop, and she moved to a different place."

"Ah, Caitlyn. Honey." She had to be talking about the Indian massacre that Silas had told Jon of, after which Silas's old friend Mick had found Caitlyn, the only survivor. Something had triggered those buried memories.

"Caitlyn. . . . "

"When they found Mama and Reggie," Caitlyn interrupted, "I kept telling myself I had to go help her protect Reggie." Her nails dug into Jon's palm, but he ignored the pain. "But I knew they couldn't see me. And Mama had told me that whatever happened, I wasn't to move."

Caitlyn finally glanced at Jon, her eyes haunted with uncertain questions. "I had to obey Mama, didn't I?"

"Yes, darlin'," Jon said with conviction. "You had to." Recalling the story that Silas had confided to him, Jon continued, "Lord, Caitlyn, you were only around five. There wasn't anything you could do. Your mother did what she thought was right."

"But she left me," Caitlyn said with a whimper. She dropped Jon's hand and threw herself against his chest. "She left me." She pounded one small fist against his shoulder. "I should have been with them. I should have helped take care of Reggie. I *always* helped take care of Reggie. Oh, Mama!''

Jon held her tightly, waiting for the rain of grief. God, how much she had already gone through in her short life. The Indian attack that had wiped out her family. And then her adopted father and that damned grizzly.

Caitlyn shuddered in his arms. But just as he thought she might allow her tears to fall, she pushed against him and shook her head.

''It was a long time ago. But how could I have forgotten it all like that? When Pa came by a few days later, I couldn't even tell him my last name. I still can't remember anything that happened before . . . before the Blackfeet attacked. Pa said they were Blackfeet, anyway. He could read the sign.''

Suddenly Caitlyn stared across the cabin at the blanket covering the door to her room. *The journal.* She could read it now, maybe find out something of her background.

Jon can help me.

''No,'' Caitlyn said aloud, surprising herself with the vehemence of the word. Immediately she caught herself wondering what secrets the journal held that she didn't want revealed to anyone else.

''Caitlyn? What's wrong?'' Jon stared at her profile, seeing the slight lift of her chin and the barely perceptible thinning of her lips before she looked back at him.

''What do you mean, 'no'?'' he asked. ''What don't you want to tell me?''

''I . . . I'm not sure,'' Caitlyn replied honestly. She shuddered slightly, trying to ignore the pictures swirling faintly in the memory mists. ''Jon, I really don't want to talk about this anymore right now. Maybe later. Please?''

''Just so you promise me that you'll remember I'm always here for you, darlin'. Will you remember that?''

Caitlyn reluctantly nodded her head. Probably Jon thought he meant it, but 'always' wasn't a word she could make herself believe about their relationship right now—or any other relationship, for that matter. People left her all the time.

Little Sun would go with his father one day. Spirit Eagle would teach his son the Nez Perce ways—maybe find another woman to love and be a mother to his son.

Her father had died in the raid on the trading post, along with her mother and Reggie. *No, stepfather,* she reminded herself. That much she could recall, but no amount of searching in her mind dredged up any remembrance of her real father.

The memory was there, though—lurking just beneath the surface of those mists. But there was another man, too—a memory she couldn't bring herself to examine, even now. He overshadowed the brighter, more loving reminiscences, muddying them into a mixture of dark and light.

And Jon. She slipped a sideways glance at him, still sitting beside her with that tender look of concern on his face. But she remembered the words he had spoken after their wonderful lovemaking.

You might decide someday that you want our children to have an eastern education.

Children. Oh, God, she couldn't deal with that right now. That was what had caused her to lose all shred of control and crawl into the welcome blackness.

Desperately she tried to focus on something else. She felt an urgent need to get some space between her and Jon, to give herself a little time to think. Their differences might do—her referring to his eastern ways usually got him a little riled. Maybe he would leave her alone for a while if she could turn their conversation around.

Feeling somewhat guilty, she still gratefully grabbed hold of the turn her thoughts were taking, away from those other shadowy memories.

"Uh . . . look, don't get so persnickety. I'm not one of those eastern women like you're used to. I don't need you hovering over me. And about what you were saying back there where we camped. I don't see where *your* eastern education does you much good out here. What makes you think just because I don't have as much schooling as I could have gotten if I'd been raised where you were, those people are better than me?"

"Whoa, Caitlyn," Jon said as he spread his hands wide. "I think I missed something here. What's my offer of always being there for you got to do with me being persnickety? And when did I ever mention that you weren't as good as anyone else?"

Fighting her guilt and her escalating need to be alone, Caitlyn glared at him without answering.

Jon glared back at her, recalling Silas's words about all the different women wrapped up inside what looked like just one woman.

He thought he'd done pretty well so far recognizing Caitlyn's different personalities. Her tender mothering of Little Sun. Her pride in keeping the cabin clean, and fixing meals that he and Silas praised. Her love of the wilderness—she changed from his little homemaker into a cute little tomboy outdoors-woman as soon as she slipped into that wolfskin jacket.

And the woman he had made love to had been someone he'd thought he would find only in his dreams.

But this supercilious woman, glaring at him with a mixture of exasperation and disgust, hadn't appeared before.

Yes, she has, he reminded himself, remembering how Caitlyn had barely concealed her disdain for his awkwardness when he injured his knee, and the inept shot that had landed the puma on him.

Well, that woman could go back into hiding anytime, as far as he was concerned.

"Men," Caitlyn said, her tone of voice confirming Jon's analysis of this revived personality. "A person would think that there's just empty space up there between your ears at times. Can't you ever remember what you've said before?"

"Now just a damn minute, Caitlyn. . . . "

Caitlyn slid past him and stood. "I don't guess you can remember what I've said before, either," she told him as she slipped out of her jacket and walked toward the hooks beside the door. "You watch your language around Little Sun. I don't want Spirit Eagle coming back here and finding his son talking dirty. Why, most of the Indian languages don't even have any curse words in them."

"So now I'm a bad influence on your friend's son, huh?" Jon rose to his feet, his face darkening in anger when Caitlyn tossed him an if-the-shoe-fits look. "Just what the hell else do I have wrong with me?"

"Hell," Little Sun said clearly.

Jon swung toward the crib, black thunder still clouding his face. When Little Sun looked at Jon, his face puckered up immediately, and he dropped his piece of maple candy. His howl quickly escalated into a shriek.

"Now look what you've done!" Caitlyn spat as she hurried to the crib. "Shhhh. Shhhh, baby," she soothed as she reached into the crib. "The nasty man didn't mean to make you cry."

Jon's mouth dropped open. He clamped it shut with an audible snap when Caitlyn turned around with Little Sun in her arms. Caitlyn's lips were pursed in disapproval, her blue eyes flashing a warning. Little Sun glanced at him, then hurriedly stuck his thumb in his mouth and buried his head on Caitlyn's shoulder.

"I'm going out to take care of the horses!" Jon almost shouted.

"You do that," Caitlyn said to his back. "And don't be mean to them, either!"

The door slammed against the wall with a thud, and swirling snow swept past Jon into the cabin. At his smothered "Shi . . . shoot" as he reached for the doorknob again, Caitlyn's lips quirked into a sad smile. As soon as the door closed behind him, she sniffed back a contrite sob, although she did feel a certain relief at having Jon gone. Little Sun raised his head from her shoulder and patted a pudgy hand on her check. His face showed his concern.

"Men," Caitlyn said in an attempted cheerful voice. She couldn't let the little boy suffer from her disquietude.

"M'n," Little Sun obediently repeated.

"Uh oh," Caitlyn chastised herself. "Guess I better watch what I say around you, too, little one. You're going to grow up into one of those dumb men someday."

"Dum' m'n?" Little Sun asked.

Caitlyn groaned under her breath. "Uh . . . nice men, Little Sun. Nice."

"'Ice."

"Right." She carried him over to the window and rubbed a spot free of covering frost. Outside, Jon was walking toward the lean-to.

She shook her head at herself. What on earth was wrong with her? Jon had been the epitome of kindness to her, and she sure hadn't acted like she appreciated his concern. Instead, she had forced herself to drive him away.

Epitome. Huh. She must have picked up that word somewhere in her new reading skills—skills Jon had taught her.

"Jon." Little Sun pointed a finger. His excitement indicated that he'd already forgotten Jon's glowering face. "Jon, 'ice."

"Yes," Caitlyn said with a tolerant smile through the glass. "Jon's very nice."

Just then Jon glanced over his shoulder at the window. He stopped walking when he caught sight of Caitlyn, and the horses docilely dropped their heads.

Stifling a sigh of frustration at herself for her idiotic actions of a few moments ago, Caitlyn lifted her free hand and wiggled her fingers at him in an attempt to make peace. Jon's mouth dropped open for the second time and he shook his head. She really couldn't fault him for his amazement, she guessed. After all, a minute ago she'd been more or less rebuking him for his language, and now she was standing there waving at him.

A teasing glint entered her eyes, and Caitlyn lifted a finger to her lips, kissed it and blew the kiss to Jon. She couldn't hear him, of course, but she could lip-read his response: "Women!"

Jon took a step, then stopped again. Turning back toward the window, he lifted one hand in a wave before he led the horses off again.

Humming to herself in relief, Caitlyn turned away from the window to see what she could fix for supper. After consigning Little Sun to the crib again, where he happily picked up his maple candy once more, she laid a couple more logs on the fire.

As she started supper preparations, she tried to sort through her thoughts, focusing on today's happenings, rather than those long-ago memories. She could dust them off and examine them later.

She'd become a woman today—and she had no regrets about that. She couldn't find one iota of guilt anywhere about making love with Jon. In fact, given the chance, she didn't think she would be able to resist him again.

But she darned well knew where things like that led. Sky Woman had never told her the details of the act, but she'd overheard Sky Woman and another woman discussing things one day. Lore passed down woman-to-woman through the years said that a woman couldn't get with child while she was nursing her current baby.

Well, that didn't apply to Caitlyn, but Sky Woman had also said that if a couple decided they didn't want another child immediately after weaning one, the couple would avoid. . . .

Caitlyn frowned as she poured flour into a bowl for biscuits. What was the Nez Perce word for it? Well, never mind, it still meant lovemaking. They avoided lovemaking during the middle days between a woman's monthly courses. How on earth the women had figured this out down through time she had no idea. Perhaps they'd noticed that if their men were off on a hunting or raiding trip during this time, they received their flow as usual that month.

That should make her safe, if it were true, since her next flow was due to start any day.

Despite her resolve to keep her other thoughts at bay until she had some privacy that evening, flashes of memory intruded again. Perhaps because of her longing for another woman to talk to about today, the memories were mostly of her mother—and Reggie. But a tall, salt-and-pepper haired man was there, too. Someone she had idolized with every fiber of her being, who treated her with love in return.

Was that why she had buried the attack in her mind? Was it too painful for her to remember how much love had been torn from her young life on that day, which had started out so peacefully?

Jon came through the door and shut it quickly. He glanced briefly at her, then shrugged out of his buffalo-skin robe and hung it up.

"Silas is back," he said without looking at her. "He's putting up his horse. I was starting to think I might have to go out and try to find him."

"Silas is smart enough to know he needs to get back here when a storm blows in."

"I'm glad you think at least some men have a few brains left," Jon grumbled as he walked over and sat down on his bunk. He leaned down and pulled out the mate to the snowshoe he had already finished. Toying with the still unstrung rawhide lacing, he ignored Caitlyn's approach.

"I'm sorry, Jon," she murmured, and Jon finally glanced up. "I don't know what got into me. You were being so nice to me, and I acted like that shrew in the story we were discussing, didn't I?"

"Well, I guess you were still kind of upset," Jon said a little less grumpily. "I should have realized that."

" 'Ice," Little Sun called, pushing himself to his feet and rocking the crib. "Jon, 'ice!"

"Nice," Caitlyn corrected him. "Jon's very nice."

"Ver' 'ice," Little Sun said with a chortle.

"Aw, who's been teaching him that?" Jon asked needlessly.

Caitlyn bent her head and kissed him softly. "Ver' 'ice," she whispered before she turned back toward the table to finish the biscuits.

Silas slammed the door behind him, but Little Sun and Dog appeared to be the only ones who noticed his entry. Dog crawled out from under Silas's bunk, and Little Sun held the now almost nonexistent piece of maple candy out to him.

Caitlyn looked up from cutting out biscuits on the table, but her eyes centered on Jon. And Jon sat there on the bunk with a silly grin on his face, not even attempting to work on the snowshoe in his hand.

"Hey, boyo," Silas called, finally getting Jon's attention. "What's all that white stuff on your face? You been helping Cat make biscuits?"

Jon reached up and brushed at his face, his hand coming away with a glob of dough.

"Nope, not biscuits, Silas. Not biscuits at all."

But though Silas waited for him to continue, Jon only chuckled to himself and rolled the piece of dough between his fingers. Not biscuits. No, not biscuit making, but lovemaking crowded his mind.

Chapter Twenty

Caitlyn gently laid the leather-bound journal against her propped-up legs and ran her fingertips across the cover. The flame on the candle in the brass holder sitting on her bedside table glowed steadily, enclosing her in a cocoon of light, though shadows lingered in the deeper recesses of her room.

Other shadows lingered, also—memory shadows, still caught in the mists of her mind. The clearer images—at least some of them—were probably waiting for her on the journal pages. But first she had to deal with the memories that she could now recall.

It had truly been a beautiful day. Late September, perhaps, or maybe even early October. The tree leaves had already changed, and her stepfather, James, the manager of the trading post, expected his men back any day from their trip to sell the furs and bring in new supplies for the winter trading. Until that group of almost a dozen men returned, there were only seven people at the post.

She remembered all their names now. There was her stepfather, James, of course, and her mother, Maureen. Little Reggie, her baby brother, was not even walking yet, though he scooted and crawled so fast Caitlyn could barely take her eyes off him whenever her mother was busy.

The Indian woman cook, Yellow Wing, had been kept on through the summer, even though Caitlyn's mother could have handled cooking for so few people. The men thoroughly enjoyed the meals the cook prepared, and well-fed men worked harder, her stepfather had insisted. It would be too hard to replace Yellow Wing after the men returned, if she moved somewhere else with her people over the summer. Better to keep her with them.

A couple other men had also stayed to help her stepfather with the summer chores—stockpiling enough wood for the long winter; recaulking the spaces between the logs that had settled since the post and men's quarters were built the previous summer.

Her mother and Yellow Wing gathered and dried berries over the summer, and her mother even tended a small vegetable garden she had planted with seeds she brought with her. Caitlyn recalled her stepfather chuckling tolerantly when her mother demanded that he spade up the earth for her. So what if she had never planted a garden before in her life, her mother had said in a haughty voice. She had bought a book on gardening before they came out here. And she read and planted, read some more and planted some more. Her stepfather was voracious in his praise when the garden started bearing and fresh vegetables appeared at their meals.

But he did bemoan the calluses on Maureen's formerly soft hands, and she had to assure him more than once that she didn't give a diddly darn about her skin now being a golden tan, rather than milky white. Nevertheless, her stepfather told her mother that he had ordered his men to bring back a dozen pair of gardening gloves, and several wide-brimmed straw hats.

Caitlyn frowned in concentration at the nagging thought that gave way to flashes of pictures of her mother: Giggling when she lifted her long skirts and stared at the moccasins on her feet; daintily stepping into a canoe, which wobbled wildly, and her stepfather grabbing her mother just as the canoe tipped over; her mother staring in dismay at Yellow Wing, who was plucking feathers from the wild turkeys the men brought into camp, then bravely reaching out to help.

But now Caitlyn recalled that every one of her own dresses had been decorated with fine embroidery. And Reggie's gowns, though dirt-stained at the end of the day, had all been hand-sewn by her mother.

The seeming contradiction cleared in Caitlyn's mind. Her mother had come from a lady's background. She could sew and embroider, and Caitlyn now remembered some other little touches in the log post. Beautiful wildflowers were arranged on the table and countertop, and the Indians who came to trade stared at them in amazement. The place settings were grouped just so for their evening meals. She recalled her mother's voice explaining to her when she was reluctant to sit still and quiet after her active day, that they wouldn't always live so far from civilization. She wanted Caitlyn and Reggie to fit in properly back in polite society.

Her stepfather, too, made a ceremony of supper each evening. The family ate separately from the men, who more often than not just filled their plates and carried them to their quarters or, weather permitting, plopped down under a nearby tree. But Yellow Wing good-naturedly served that one meal course-by-course to the family she had come to love.

From reading Jon's books, Caitlyn knew her mother had insisted on retaining at least that semblance of her former life. To know these genteel manners, she had to have been taught herself. Her stepfather, too, evidently had a similar background, since he seemed completely at ease each evening, though during the day he could curse and back-slap with the best of his men, and even the Indians who came to trade.

Why then, with backgrounds that obviously included servants and refinement, had they come so far out into the wilderness to live? And where had they lived these lives of a lady and gentleman?

Try as she would, Caitlyn couldn't penetrate the darker

memory mists. She could, however, now remember in acute detail that last day.

She had been playing in the yard with Reggie late that afternoon, one ear cocked toward the cabin, since she knew her mother would call her in any minute to clean up before the evening meal. The lone man to escape the attack on the supply caravan had stumbled into the yard, bleeding and babbling incoherently. Caitlyn had screamed in fright, and her mother and stepfather both raced out of the cabin, with Yellow Wing close behind. The two other men emerged from their quarters, rifles in hand.

James ran over to the wounded man, who had collapsed in the yard. "What happened, man? Who did this?" he demanded as he knelt and slipped a hand under the man's head.

Maureen grabbed Reggie into her arms, and Caitlyn buried her face in her mother's skirts. But she could hear the wounded man's gasping voice.

"We . . . we had no warning. They . . . they came from nowhere!"

"Who, man?" James demanded again.

"I . . . Indians. Painted devils. All . . . all are dead."

"When?" James insisted.

"This . . . this   morning—just   after   dawn.   So many . . . too many to fight."

"Jesus," James breathed. "Where are they now? How did you get away?"

"I swam," the man said. "The others . . . they could not. I . . . I know we were to protect your supplies. But there were too many!"

Despite the man's injuries, James shook him roughly. "Are you sure they didn't follow you? Tell me!"

He groaned and a bubble of blood escaped his mouth. James tore open the man's shirt, his mouth thinning into a grim line when he saw the shaft of an arrow protruding from beneath the man's rib cage.

"My God," James muttered with a glance at the other two men, who stood on the opposite side of the wounded man's body. "He couldn't have traveled far with that wound, and his progress would have been extremely slow. He was probably in too much pain to try to hide his trail, and left blood spots and crushed underbrush, easy for them to follow. The bastards are close, you can bet."

He swung his head to Maureen. "Get the children inside the post!" he shouted. As his wife ran toward the cabin, pulling Caitlyn along by her hand, James waved the other two men to his side.

"Get him into the cabin," he ordered. "I'll get the other rifles ready."

But even inside the cabin Caitlyn could hear the war whoops and shouts of defiance from out in the yard. Maureen choked out a scream of fright and tried to hand Reggie to Yellow Wing and turn back to the doorway. The Indian woman grabbed Maureen by the shoulders and hissed at her to be quiet. Shoving Maureen and the children ahead of her, she pushed them out the rear doorway.

They ran through the underbrush until Caitlyn was gasping for breath, stumbling more than running. Yellow Wing took Reggie, and Maureen picked Caitlyn up, then they ran some more.

"James," Maureen sobbed over and over. "Oh, God, James, my darling!"

When even the women could run no more, they staggered to a stop. Maureen sank to the ground, pulling Caitlyn onto her lap and burying her face in Caitlyn's small neck. Clutching Reggie tightly, Yellow Wing gazed wildly around her.

Yellow Wing reached down and grabbed Maureen's shoulder. "Up," she ordered.

"I . . . can't!" Maureen said with a sob. "I can't go any farther!"

"You can," Yellow Wing replied. "Over there. It will be safe."

Maureen lifted her head and her gaze followed Yellow Wing's pointing finger. The Indian woman was indicating a huge dead tree, the upper portion of which had toppled from the trunk.

"Come!" Yellow Wing commanded.

Maureen somehow managed to stumble to her feet and follow Yellow Wing. The Indian woman led them around the tree and showed them a large split on the other side. The tree was dead because lightning had split it at some time, and the charred interior of the trunk would hold all of them.

Her mother scrambled inside with Caitlyn, and Yellow Wing handed Reggie to her.

"You get in here, too, Yellow Wing," Maureen insisted.

"No. I will go on. With their blood lust high, they may not think to check if they still follow two women's tracks. You will be safe. And the children."

"You can't sacrifice yourself for us," Maureen said with a gasp of dismay.

"I can run fast. And, if I can, I will return for you. I will take you to my people."

"James," Maureen said with a whimper as she understood Yellow Wing's meaning. "He's dead, isn't he?"

"They will leave no one alive," Yellow Wing informed her in a flat voice. "It is their way."

Tears streamed from Maureen's eyes, and she laid her head back against the charred tree trunk. Tears clouding her own eyes, Caitlyn peered past her mother and watched Yellow Wing race lightly away. Just before the Indian woman disappeared once more, she broke off a small branch, so the attackers would see it and follow her trail.

Reggie, overcome by the tension in the air and his mother's sobbing, started whimpering. Maureen jerked her head upright and tried to soothe him.

"Hush. Oh darling Reggie, please hush."

But her own voice broke, and Reggie whimpered louder. In a moment, he would be crying loudly.

Maureen grabbed Caitlyn and shoved her deeper into the tree trunk. Caitlyn's eyes widened in terror, but Maureen laid a hand on her shoulder and squeezed it tightly.

"Whatever happens, you stay here and don't move," she ordered. "I'm just going to take Reggie over to a new hiding place until I get him quiet."

"I want to go with you!" Caitlyn said.

"You obey me, Caitlyn Maureen O'Neal. Do you hear me?"

"Yes, Mama," Caitlyn whispered.

Maureen pulled Caitlyn against her breast and kissed her hair. After she released her, she cupped Caitlyn's cheek in her palm. "I love you, Caitlyn," she said in a quiet voice. "I'll always love you."

"I love you, too, Mama. Please, let me go. . . ."

"No! Promise me, Caitlyn. Whatever happens—whatever you see, you stay here in hiding. Promise me!"

"I . . . I promise, Mama," Caitlyn choked out.

Maureen tenderly stroked Caitlyn's cheek, then resolutely gathered Reggie into her arms. Slipping outside the tree trunk, she stood for a moment, studying the area around her. Reggie continued whimpering, and she walked away from the tree trunk. Suddenly her head whipped around and she stared back the way they had come.

With a sob, Maureen clapped a hand over Reggie's mouth and ran. Caitlyn watched her disappear, her hands covering her own mouth to stifle her sobs. Then she heard a guttural cry and shrank back into the tree trunk.

Feet whispered by her hiding place and a second later Caitlyn heard a ki-yi-yip of victory—and her mother's scream. She buried her face on her raised knees, her arms clenching her legs tightly. But still she could hear.

Reggie's cries joined her mother's. Then she heard a thud, and the baby's cries were cut off. Maureen's screams grew higher, her shrieks of despair ending in a keening sound of complete madness.

A second later, near silence reigned. The underbrush rustled faintly, but no other sounds broke the quiet until one loud whoop. The sounds of feet returning were pounding now, and try as she might to keep her head buried, Caitlyn couldn't. She lifted her head and, despite being so far back in the huge tree trunk, found that she could see out through the split.

The Indian stopped nearby, dancing in a circle and blood streaming down his upraised arm. He finally stopped and threw back his head, his scream echoing as he shook his arm at the heavens and raised his other arm in accompaniment.

As soon as his cry died out, two more Indian men joined the first one and the three of them disappeared back down the trail.

Caitlyn raised her head from where she had buried it on her knees, as she had that long-ago evening. Candlelight still illuminated the room, but she stared unseeingly ahead of her, still living that day over in her mind.

She had stayed in the tree trunk all night. She could still remember the lingering smell of charred wood that surrounded her. As young as she was, she knew her mother was dead, even though she hadn't seen what happened. But she remained obedient to her mother's last command. What else could she do?

The men back at the post were dead, too, including her stepfather. She had clearly understood Yellow Wing's words to her mother. And Yellow Wing had promised to return. She could only wait for her.

She'd woken the next morning, somehow having fallen asleep despite the ravaged sobs she couldn't hold back any longer. Hunger pangs stabbed her stomach, but still she lay curled up in the tree trunk. Her mouth was dry with thirst, but her bladder was bursting. She could still recall her shame when her bladder finally gave way, leaving her sitting there in a damp puddle.

Animals wandered by. Each time Caitlyn heard a faint sound, she shrank back into the trunk, but strained her eyes to see if it could be Yellow Wing. But only a deer passed, then a moose cow and calf. Later a bear with two half-grown cubs walked by her hiding place, seemingly unaware of the huddled human figure inside the tree trunk.

As evening fell, Caitlyn gave up hope of Yellow Wing returning that day. She fell into another exhausted sleep. When she woke the next morning, she knew she had to at least find water. But outside her safe haven lay horror. Her mother and Reggie's bodies were close. And back the other way . . . at the post. . . .

She had to wait for Yellow Wing. But what if the Indians had found her, too? She didn't know how many Indians had come after them from the post. What if there had been more than the three she saw—others, who had gone on after Yellow Wing?

Caitlyn finally tried to leave the tree trunk, but her legs wouldn't support her when she attempted to stand. Sobbing at the aches and cramps in her muscles, she got to her knees and crawled toward the entrance of her hiding place. She managed to creep outside before her filthy, urine-soaked body collapsed.

Several long moments passed before she tried to stand again. Bracing her small hands against the tree trunk, she levered herself to her feet and stood swaying when she pushed away from the rough bark.

Though she willed herself not to, her small head swung toward where her mother had gone with Reggie.

"Mama," she whispered in agony.

Her first stumbling steps led her resolutely toward her mother. But as soon as she glimpsed the bodies through the underbrush, she backed away in horror.

At least they didn't rape her, Caitlyn thought to herself now in her room. There hadn't been time for them to do that before they left. But no wonder her mother had screamed that horrible, keening sound. She had watched them kill her baby.

Caitlyn shifted on her bunk, shamefully remembering her thoughts on that horrible day. She had blamed her small brother. If he'd only been quiet, they could have all been saved. Reggie had forced her mother to choose between her children—choose who would live and who would die.

And Caitlyn should have gone to her mother—tried to help her fight them off—instead of staying safe in her hiding place while they died out there. Her mother had told her over and over how much she depended on Caitlyn to help her with Reggie. She couldn't get along without Caitlyn's help. . . .

No, Caitlyn finally accepted. She couldn't have done anything—not at age five. She had done as her mother wished—had ordered. But she had carried her resentment with her all these years, a resentment that had probably helped force those terrible memories into a corner of her mind and close the door on them.

Her resentment, however, had probably been the reason she would ignore the Indian babies—why she wanted no children herself. Guiltily, she realized that her mother might have escaped with Yellow Wing if not for her children. But of course a mother would not leave her young. She would die trying to protect them, as her mother had done, and as Pa had done to save her from the grizzly.

Caitlyn took a deep breath and forced herself to continue allowing the memories to roll from her subconscious into her consciousness.

She had stumbled back down the trail toward the trading post. It had taken her all day to find her way back, since she wandered off the trail time after time, and stopped once at a stream crossing to drink, twice to eat her fill of some hickory nuts she found beneath the trees, cracking the shells open between two rocks.

She had little hope that Yellow Wing would return for her now, but she didn't know where else to go. At least at the cabin there might be some food. She remembered wishing fervently there would at least be some food.

The red oak leaves shone brightly in the evening sun's rays when Caitlyn stumbled into the cabin yard. She shut her eyes against the sight. They reminded her too much of the color of blood. Cautiously she slit her eyes to look around the yard.

The man who had warned them of the attack still lay where he had fallen, his scalp, of course, gone. Three charred tree trunks stood in the ground in the middle of the clearing, with unrecognizable masses crumpled at their bases in beds of dead ashes. She knew now that the masses were what was left of her stepfather's body, along with the other two men. They must have died in horrible agony.

And she would have to pass the stakes to get into the cabin.

No, she had thought to herself in relief. She could go in the back door.

And she had. In an almost catatonic state, she had walked to the rear of the cabin.

Not a whole lot remained inside, but she managed to find some dried berries scattered in the mess on the floor. What the Indians didn't want to carry with them, they had tried to destroy. To this day Caitlyn didn't know why they hadn't just burned the cabin, but perhaps they'd been afraid the fire would draw attention to their raid. Warriors from other tribes might decide to come after them and steal back the goods they would have had to trade for that winter.

As the days passed, Caitlyn was forced to resort to scooping the mess on the floor—a mixture of flour, sugar and wild rice—into a cup and adding some water. She stirred and drank it whenever she felt hunger pangs.

On one of her forages through the cabin for food, she had found her mother's journal. New sobs had torn her small body when she pulled it from under a pile of clothing the Indians had tossed into a corner. She could remember her mother sitting in the firelight each evening, writing in the journal.

As her body grew weaker, Caitlyn recalled her mind clouding over. She remembered looking at the front cabin door from time to time, but never going out that way. The bodies in the yard had to have been decaying, she knew now, but she gratefully could only vaguely remember smelling them. And she hadn't seen them again.

She left the cabin by the rear when she needed water—slept in her parents' bed at night, the journal clasped in her arms, but not recalling any longer whose journal it was. She filled her cup less and less often from the pile on the floor.

One day faded into another, and she had no idea even today how long she had been alone at the cabin. Maybe a week—even two or three. But she clearly recalled the day the gentle giant of a man had come into the cabin and found her huddled on her mother's bed, a blanket around her shoulders as she shivered with cold.

"Me poor little darlin'," Mick O'Shaunessy had said. "Never you mind now, darlin'. Old Mick'll take care of ye."

Caitlyn had trustingly held up skeleton-thin arms to him and he had picked her up, soiled and stinking though she was.

Those strong, corded arms had held her tenderly against his chest, and Caitlyn had stared at him in wide-eyed wonder.

"You've got hair on your face," she'd croaked in a long-unused voice.

"Keeps me warm, sweetheart," Mick had said with a chuckle. "How 'bout I start a fire so ye can get warm, too?"

"Please. I'm pretty cold."

"Ye'll not be cold again, me little darlin'," Mick had promised. "Nor hungry, neither."

And she hadn't been, Caitlyn remembered as she blew the candle out and laid down, snuggling against the pillow. Pa had kept his promises to her. He had treated her as though she were a precious gift from God through the years.

Caitlyn slipped the journal under her pillow as her eyes closed drowsily. She could read it later. Right now, after dealing with all those other horrible memories, she wanted to savor the wonderful memories she had of Pa over the years.

His laughing face when he teased her. The wonderful Christmas gifts. His patience with her questions. His strong arms and soothing murmurs when the nightmares woke her. . . .

Chapter Twenty-one

The bitter cold after the snowstorm appeared to have set in for the balance of the winter, Silas and Jon waited one day, then another after the four days of furious winds and blowing snow abated.

The first day they dug out from the cabin, clearing paths to the lake and outhouse. The lake still held a thin space of clear water near the center, but the ice out there wouldn't bear their weight. They chopped a hole nearer the shore, marking it with a tall sapling so they could find it each morning and clear the thinner ice to draw water.

At least twice a day, they checked the platform in the tree holding the meat they had stored so far for the winter. The smoked venison, moose and buffalo haunches were frozen solid now, and they deliberately brushed their hands over them and the platform, leaving behind a human scent to warn any marauding animal away.

"We need to get a couple more deer and maybe another moose up there," Silas said to Jon the second day as he climbed down the wooden steps nailed to the oak tree. "It's cold enough now that it'll keep without bein' smoked."

"We need to get back out and run those lines, too, Silas. Aren't we missing the easiest part of the beaver season? After those lakes and ponds freeze over solid, it's gonna take a hell of a lot more work to cut through the ice and get our traps out, then reset them."

"Yeah, I know, boyo. Them beavers just go back and forth from their huts to the tree limbs and saplings they got stored under water for winter food when it freezes over. We'll still get a few, tho' mostly we'll get fox and wolf then. But I found me a good place to trap some ermine and mink, too, and they'll bring us almost as much as beaver."

"You leave them in the traps too long," Jon reminded Silas, "a wolverine will find them. Then we might as well forget having a line in that territory. He'll run our lines before we can get there, and destroy everything he finds."

Silas walked over to the path between the cabin and the lake, but instead of turning to go inside, he stopped and stared toward the lake.

"It ain't a simple situation, is it, Jon?" he asked. "We can't take Cat and the boy out in this cold. Cat, she'd probably enjoy it, but the little one might catch his death. And it needs both of us to run those lines, if we're gonna have a decent season."

"When do you think Spirit Eagle will be back?" Jon asked.

"I doubt it'll be before spring," Silas replied. "He ain't got no woman to watch the boy for him, and it'd be pretty rough on him trying to take care of him by himself."

Unless he figures he can stay here with us, Jon thought, though he didn't voice the words aloud. *Caitlyn would probably welcome him with open arms. Then she and that damned Indian could visit all day while Silas and I are gone.*

Caitlyn had told him she loved him, but what if her words had just been a reaction to her passion? Plenty of his men friends had wooed women's legs open with 'I love you, too's' in reply to the women's words spoken first. Women seemed to expect love to go hand in hand with lovemaking, and maybe Caitlyn was justifying giving him her virginity by telling herself it was in the name of love.

It was—at least on his part. They hadn't had a minute's privacy, though, to talk about that day. Would her love for him dissipate as soon as Spirit Eagle returned?

She and the Indian sure had a lot more in common. They loved this life out here. Caitlyn had pointed out the differences between herself and Jon more than once.

"Sure would make it easier if he showed up," Silas mused.

"Who?" Jon demanded.

"Who we been talkin' about?" Silas said. "Spirit Eagle, 'course."

"Like hell!" Jon spat. "We don't have room in that cabin for another body!"

Silas glanced at Jon, his beard hiding the slight grin on his lips. Things appeared to be going just like he'd predicted to himself at rendezvous. Hopefully, he could hand his protection of Cat over to Jon when this season was done. His word as a mountain man, along with the vow he had made to Cat, bound him to her for now. But he reckoned that Jon would gladly accept the burden pretty soon.

And maybe when he finally quit these mountains because of old age, he'd have a warm fireplace to sit in front of. Maybe a couple little rug rats to call him Uncle Silas.

"Well," Silas said into the stillness, feeling that he covered up his laughter pretty good. "Well," he repeated, "you know Cat. We better discuss things with her. I aim to get back on them lines in the morning, one way or another."

Inside the cabin, Caitlyn kneaded bread dough at the table, while Little Sun took his morning nap. Every few seconds, she glanced over her shoulder at the blanketed door to her bedroom.

Why on earth couldn't she bring herself to open that journal? Each night since her memory had begun to return, she had left the candle burning until Jon and Silas's snores told her they were asleep. But she'd only gone as far as opening the leather cover the third night.

Maureen O'Neal. The inscription was written in a neat

hand inside the cover. Nothing else. Not even a date to indicate the period the journal covered.

At least she knew her last name now. She supposed she had the right to use O'Neal, even though her mother had been married to another man at her birth. She vaguely recalled one lesson time with her mother, when she was teaching her letters. Her mother had traced out words she said spelled Caitlyn's name, and the spoken explanation had been Caitlyn O'Neal.

Somehow she knew that name was Irish, also. Funny how a fellow Irishman had found her after the massacre—raised her as his own. Pa had been proud of his Irish heritage, now and then telling her tales of the beautiful land for a bedtime story.

Little people, fairies and leprechauns. Caitlyn smiled to herself, thinking how much Silas reminded her of how she had imagined the leprechauns—though Silas was lots larger.

At that moment Silas came through the door, and she lifted her head, the smile growing. But it grew into full brilliance when Jon followed Silas into the cabin.

Lordy, how she loved that man. One reason the journal had gone unread was that her nights were spent thinking about Jon. Recalling every word they spoke to each other each day—every time they had touched.

Her smile dimmed just a little as she recalled every reason on earth they could never have a future together—and tried to figure some way to overcome their obvious differences.

Jon turned from hanging up his robe to face Caitlyn's gaze. God, he loved her. Wisps of raven curls clung to her forehead, above the deep blue eyes that were shining with the love she had told him of in words. The strawberry-sweet lips tilted up just a little at the corners, looking so damned kissable, and a spot of flour dotted the end of her nose. Another white spot streaked one flushed cheek.

If only Silas wasn't in the room, he could carry Caitlyn to her bedroom and wash her face with his tongue. Jon muffled a groan when he felt himself harden and tore his eyes from Caitlyn's face to glare at Silas when the old man chuckled and whistled a tune under his breath.

Silas ignored him and walked over to Caitlyn. "Monday," he said as he approached the table. "Gotta be Monday if you're makin' bread, Cat. Figure you can make me an extra loaf to take with me in the mornin'?"

"We're going to start running the lines again tomorrow?" Caitlyn asked.

"Well, now, Cat." Silas pulled out a chair and sat down. "We gotta talk about that. You know me and Jon has got to get back out there. We don't want to leave you here alone, but it's too derned cold out there for us to drag the boy out."

"I know," Caitlyn agreed, surprising Jon, who took the chair across from Silas. "And I realize Little Sun's care is in my hands. I'm the one who agreed to let Spirit Eagle leave him here."

Jon's heart caught at the yearning he heard in her voice. He knew her so well. She thoroughly enjoyed traipsing through the snow with him and, no matter how tired she was in the evenings, she did her share tanning the hides. It would bore her to tears to be confined to the cabin day in and night out.

"Look," he said when Silas opened his mouth to speak. "How about you and I take turns?"

Caitlyn stared at him, just a tiny bit of hope shining in her eyes. "I . . . I can't ask you to stay with Little Sun," she said. "That's my job."

"Caitlyn, you know you're going to have to stay strictly inside every time Silas and I are gone, don't you? We've only got two rifles, and we'll have to leave one with you. Whoever's running lines will have to go as a pair, so they'll have the gun with them."

Silas nodded in agreement. "He's right, Cat. Don't neither one of us want to be caught out there without a gun. But we can't leave you unpertected, neither."

Caitlyn stared back and forth between the two men. "So?" she questioned. "I really don't think Tall Man—or anyone else for that matter—will try to come here in this snow. But I'm not about to take a chance that I'm wrong. I'll keep the door locked while you're both gone. I can tan the hides during the day, and you can rest evenings.''

''And just how long will it be before you fade away and get sick, without being out in the daylight now and then?'' Jon asked. ''It's a long time until spring. No, we'll take turns going with Silas. Days it warms up enough, I'll take you and the boy with me.''

''You . . . you'd really do that for me, Jon?'' Caitlyn asked with soft wonder in her voice.

''Sure,'' Jon replied in a gruff voice. ''We don't want you getting sick, do we, Silas?''

''Nope,'' Silas agreed. ''Gotta keep our bodies well. Minds, too.''

Bodies, Jon's mind repeated. If Silas weren't here, he could show Caitlyn another way they could keep their bodies healthy. Did Caitlyn remember the wonderful feeling of satiation after they made love? Did she toss and turn at night, yearning to be in his arms—aching with frustration?

That damned blanket in her doorway, thin enough so he could see her shadow in the evenings when she prepared for bed, might as well have been a double-bricked wall. But Silas's presence kept them apart.

If only Silas weren't there. . . .

''Well.'' Silas slapped his palms on the table, then rose. ''Well, I'm glad that's settled. Look, Cat, my feet's so dad-blamed itchy I gotta get out for a while. Me and Jon was just talkin' about how we needed some fresh meat to go 'long with that smoked stuff on our storage platform. And I thought I heard a moose bellowin' up the mountain a few minutes ago.''

''Some fresh meat would be good,'' Caitlyn agreed. ''But you better take Dog with you, and the sled.''

''Yep, I'll do that. That critter's runnin' around outside somewhere. I'll whistle him up.''

Silas headed for his robe by the door, and Caitlyn shaped the final bread loaf, rinsing and wiping her hands as Silas went out the door. As soon as the door closed, Jon scooted his chair back from the table and held out his arms.

"Come here," Jon said softly. "I've been aching to hold you, darlin'."

"Oh, Jon." Caitlyn tossed the linen hand towel on the table and hurried to him.

He pulled her onto his lap and his lips immediately found hers. He kissed her hungrily, greedily, his arms tightening around her until she could hardly catch her breath, and Caitlyn kissed him back just as hungrily. It was impossible to make up for all the so-close, yet so-far-away frustration they had experienced in the small cabin these past few days with just one kiss, but hopefully Silas would be gone for a while. A damned long while.

Silas turned from the window and rubbed his hands together, chuckling under his breath. Almost tiptoeing, he walked a few paces away from the cabin and whistled quietly for Dog. The animal bounded from the trees and raced up to him, tail wagging, and Silas cautiously held a finger to his lips.

"Let's don't make a whole lot of noise out here, critter," he whispered, and Dog sat down in front of him, cocking his head to the side.

"I don't want that little one inside to hear you barking and wake up," Silas explained to Dog's questioning gaze. "Little Sun oughta sleep for at least another hour, lessen he hears you and wants to play with you. We'll just sneak off, and you and me'll have us a nice little huntin' trip."

Inside the cabin, Jon finally released Caitlyn, cupping her face as he gazed down into her eyes.

"God, I love you," he whispered. "I've missed you."

"Missed me?" Caitlyn teased. "We haven't been more than a few feet from each other all week."

"It might as well have been a mile," Jon responded. "Do you realize how beautiful you are in the evenings when you're sitting there reading to us? How the firelight shines in those pretty eyes? How luscious those lips of yours look when you're puzzling out a new word? Hell, I haven't even heard one word you read all week. I've been too occupied with watching you, remembering how it felt when we made love." ·

Caitlyn traced a finger around his lips. "I love you," she said. "And I wasn't having trouble with any words. Every time I stumbled over my reading, it was because I couldn't concentrate with you staring at me."

Jon captured her hand and gently nipped her finger, then sucked it into his mouth, caressing it with his tongue. At her intake of breath, he released her finger and buried his hands in her hair, seeking her mouth again. Her lips opened willingly to his and he caressed inside her mouth as he had her finger, tasting her, claiming her for his own.

Smoothing his hands down her braid, he untied the ribbon on the end and worked his hands back upward, freeing the glossy strands and spreading them across her back like a raven cape. When he slipped an arm beneath her legs and stood, Caitlyn's hair hung down almost to the floor.

"I want you, darlin'," Jon said, scarcely lifting his mouth from hers to speak. "I need you. Only you, Caitlyn, sweetheart. Caitlyn, my love."

She kissed him for her answer and Jon carried her into her bedroom. Sliding her down his body, he cupped her hips as soon as her feet touched the floor, drawing her against his need, grinding against her stomach. Caitlyn's arms clenched around his neck and pulled at him. Jon bent to slip his hands under her buckskin dress to her hips, lifting her a few inches from the floor and settling himself between her legs.

Caitlyn whimpered in want, instinctively clasping her legs around him. The twin flames of passion and need raced through her, and she rocked with him, all too aware that the buckskin of his trousers kept them from the final joining her body cried for.

Her head fell back, and Caitlyn closed her eyes in frustration. "Please," she cried, sobbing out her yearning. "Please, Jon."

Splaying one hand to hold her, Jon jerked his trousers down and slid into her. She was wet—wet and wanting and wonderfully tight. Her nails bit into his back even through his shirt and she reached fulfillment immediately, biting her lips to hold back her cries of completion. Sweat beaded

Jon's face as he watched her, and his legs trembled with the effort not to join her.

As soon as the quivers of Caitlyn's fulfillment slowed, Jon sat down on her bed, keeping himself joined to her and pulling her dress over her head.

Caitlyn lazily gazed up at him. "I love you," she whispered. Her blue eyes were drugged with receding passion—passion Jon knew exactly how to restore.

He dipped his head and found a turgid nipple. While he sucked, he ran his hands down her legs and pulled her moccasins from her feet. As he kicked his own moccasins and trousers free, his movements drove him deeper inside her. Caitlyn gasped and the silkiness of her surrounding him clasped him tighter, nearly driving him over the edge.

Somehow he held back yet again.

When Jon licked a path to her other nipple and ran his tongue around it, Caitlyn smoothed her hands down the back of his shirt and bunched the fringe in her fingers. She tugged, thrusting her breast deeper into the welcoming mouth. Their bodies pinned the shirt between them, and she opened her eyes to try to find a better hold.

Jon's eyes were closed in ecstasy when she gazed down at him, suckling her breast, one callused palm holding and kneading it. She threaded her fingers in his blond hair, then ran her hand up and down his corded neck. His skin was sweat-slick and hot to her touch, and she groaned and tightened her legs around his waist when he sucked her breast deeper into his mouth.

"Your . . . your shirt," she managed to gasp. "Not fair."

Slowly Jon raised his head, giving a final flick of his tongue on her nipple, which began aching at once with loss.

"My shirt?" he whispered. "You want me naked, too?"

"Yes," Caitlyn admitted with a lazy smile. "I need to touch you—feel you wanting me."

Jon pushed upward. "Feel me?" he whispered when Caitlyn clenched his shoulders. "Can you feel how bad I want you?"

She couldn't answer him this time, and Jon released her to roughly jerk his shirt over his head. Tossing it aside, he placed his hands beside her breasts and pulled her closer. Her nipples touched him, and he rubbed his chest back and forth across them, the pebbled tips tangling with the kinky hair, now curled from the sweat on his body.

One nipple tip brushed Jon's chest, and he groaned a choked sound. Cupping his palm around Caitlyn's breast, he guided her nipple back to his own and rubbed them together, back and forth, then in a circular motion. The pleasurable feeling rushed to his groin, and he hardened even larger inside her.

"Caitlyn. Oh, God, Caitlyn, sweetheart. I can't hold back any longer," he muttered, voice deep and guttural with need.

In one swift motion he laid her on the bed. The little whimpers from her throat told him how badly she wanted him, too. Teeth grinding with his effort, he raised himself and stared down at their joined bodies long enough to watch himself pull free, then re-enter her—once, then again.

Caitlyn gasped his name and wrapped her legs around his back, and he couldn't see anymore. But it didn't matter. He could feel—and he could find her mouth, even with his eyes closed. With a moan of surrender, Jon kissed her, thrusting his tongue inside in time to the dance of their joined bodies.

His release shattered him into pieces, mingled with pieces of Caitlyn—separate, yet the same—made all the more intoxicating by Caitlyn's fall into rapture with him. He carried them both into that culmination of pleasure that swirled around them both for hours—for never-ending days, all the while mumbling love words he didn't know if she could even hear.

He had just enough strength left to gather Caitlyn's limp body into his arms and roll to his side. Holding every delicious inch of her against him, he waited for his heart to cease thundering and the pieces of their bodies to merge back into place.

Several long moments later, Caitlyn's indolent giggle prodded Jon back to consciousness. He slit his eyes and gazed down at her as she patted her hand up his arm, then leaned back an inch or two and smoothed her palm across his chest.

"I just wanted to see if you were all there," she said with a quirk of her kiss-swollen lips. "A minute ago, I could have sworn we were both all broken apart."

Jon chuckled quietly and propped his head on his hand. "That's amazing," he murmured. "I felt exactly the same. I better feel you, too, and make sure you got back together all right. I wouldn't want even one tiny part of you out of place."

"Hummm," Caitlyn responded. "Make sure you go over me completely, then. I want all of me to be just right for you."

"Let's see." Jon touched each eye as Caitlyn closed her lids. "Those pretty eyes are there, right where they should be. And your nose." He gently tapped it, then bent his head to kiss her. "Lips are in place, too," he murmured.

When he remained quiet for quite a while, Caitlyn opened her eyes with a sigh to see what he was doing. Her face flushed when she saw his hand lying idle between them, while Jon scanned his eyes over her body.

Biting her lip to control her embarrassment, she propped her head up in imitation of Jon's and began studying every inch of his body in return. The silence in the room lengthened as Caitlyn became caught up in her own examination of what there was about his body—so different from her own—that gave her such unparalleled pleasure.

His blond hair felt just as silky to her as her own black locks did when she brushed them out at night. She liked the longer length of his hair—her fingers had more to play with. Dark blond lashes outlined his blue eyes, a near match to her own. Their color changed with his moods, darkening with passion, sparkling lighter when he teased her.

She liked his nose. Those lips fit exactly right over her own, his mouth not too wide, but wide enough for part of her breast to fit inside. She couldn't see his tongue now, but she didn't need to. It was just the right size to pleasure her.

Below his corded neck, his shoulders widened to just the proper width to balance the rest of his body, at least twice the breadth of her own slender shoulders. The blond mat of hair on his chest rolled over and around firm muscles that begged her fingers to trace them. But she controlled the urge and studied his arms.

The bicep on the arm holding his head up bulged with strength, and even the arm lying free from strain had cords of power showing, veins running over the muscles. His hand flexed slightly when her eyes fell on it, his long fingers casual now. But they could play over her body in a dance of pleasure, the rough calluses counteracting the softness of her skin in a decidedly enjoyable way.

A trim waist sat above his hips, and the path of blond chest hair narrowed on his flat stomach. It bushed out once again in a swath, though, a slight shade darker down there. Caitlyn avoided lingering her gaze on that point for the time being, and studied the muscled thighs, on down his legs.

Teasingly, she measured her small toes against his larger ones, then giggled under her breath.

"What's so funny?" Jon demanded.

"Uh . . . nothing," Caitlyn denied, the blush renewing on her cheeks. "Nothing."

With a quick movement, Jon pushed her back onto the bed and covered her body with his. "Tell me what's so funny about my toes," he said. "Or else. . . . "

"Or else what?" Caitlyn said with another giggle.

"Are you ticklish?" Jon asked in an ominous voice, running a hand across her ribs.

"Uh uh," Caitlyn denied, but when he wiggled his fingers slightly, her giggle denied the lie.

He tickled her mercilessly for several seconds, and Caitlyn bucked under his body, her laughter flowing unchecked until tears found their way past her tightly closed eyelids.

"Stop," she finally gasped. "Oh, Jon, stop. Please I . . . I'll tell you!"

Jon stilled his fingers, but kept them in place on her ribs. When she glanced up at him, a smile hovered on his full lips and his eyes twinkled merrily. He raised his eyebrows as he waited for her to speak.

"I . . . I heard . . . oh, Jon, I can't tell you!"

His fingers wiggled and Caitlyn grabbed his hands. "Stop! All right, just stop, please. I'll tell you."

"Well," Jon demanded when she opened her eyes again.

"I . . . I heard two young Indian girls talking to each other," Caitlyn choked out. "It was at a f . . . fertility dance one fall."

"What did they say? And what the heck's that got to do with my toes?"

"They . . . oh, darn. The men . . . the men danced barefoot, and we could see how long their toes were. The girls said you could measure some . . . some other part by how long their toes were. There!"

Jon broke up into laughter and buried his face on her neck. When he could speak again, he lifted his head and said, "So you were measuring my toes against my. . . . "

Caitlyn clapped a hand over his mouth. "Hush! I wasn't . . . I mean. . . . "

Jon pulled her hand away and nudged her legs open with his knee. "You don't have to imagine," he said with a chuckle. "I'll be real glad to show you how big. . . , "

A howl of displeasure sounded in the other room and Jon let out a sigh. "Guess that will have to wait," he growled. "Our other hindrance to making love is awake out there."

"Oh, Jon," Caitlyn said with a gasp. "Where's my dress? Hurry. Get up, before Little Sun crawls out of his bed and comes in here!"

Jon stepped from the bed and swept his trousers up. As he slipped his legs into them, they both heard the crib creak. Chuckling under his breath, Jon grabbed Caitlyn's dress and tossed it to her before he started out the bedroom door.

"I'll get him," he said over his shoulder. "He already knows how much bigger I am than he is."

"So do I," Caitlyn said to herself with a soft laugh as the blanket covering the door fell back into place. "And those girls must have been right."

Stifling her laughter, she pulled her dress over her head and shrugged into it. Rising from the rumpled bed, she pulled her hair free and reached for her brush on the bedside table. Instead of taking time to rebraid her hair, she brushed it back and tied it with a new ribbon. Maybe when Little Sun took his afternoon nap, Jon would take that ribbon out, too, and run his hands through her hair. She truly loved feeling his hands in her hair.

When Caitlyn came out into the main room, Jon caught her gaze, his look a promise that their interrupted interlude would continue later.

Chapter Twenty-two

Glancing over her shoulder to make sure Jon and Little Sun were still occupied, Caitlyn pulled the tray of cookies from the fireplace oven. Neither Jon nor the little boy had seemed aware of the molasses smell permeating the room after the bread had been baked, and she silently slipped the tray onto the table, smiling secretly as she looked forward to their surprise.

She and Pa had always made cookies for Christmas, with molasses his favorite, though she favored the sugar cookies herself. Pa carved that dough into animal shapes, wielding his huge knife with delicate strokes and poking a hole into every one, so they could hang it on the small pine tree he cut each season. Caitlyn sprinkled the cookies from the precious store of white sugar they saved for the occasion, and she loved watching the diamond-bright sugar sparkles in the evening candle and lantern light.

While the cookies cooled, she stood silently watching the scene across the room on Jon's bunk.

Little Sun sat on Jon's lap, his eyes bright and inquisitive as he watched the animal shape emerging from the piece of wood Jon held. As Jon carved, he told Little Sun the story of how Caitlyn had ended up with Dog. Neither one of them noticed the wood shavings littering the bunk and floor, Caitlyn realized with a sigh.

She wasn't sure how much Little Sun understood, but he appeared to be taking in Jon's every word. Just then Jon bent his head closer to Little Sun's, though his voice still carried across the room.

"He thought we were *married*," Jon told the little boy. "Can you imagine that? And do you know what he said then?"

Little Sun solemnly shook his head.

"He said we ought to be," Jon told him, lifting his head and staring across the room at Caitlyn as though fully aware all along that she, too, was listening to every word. "And you know what else?"

Caitlyn couldn't tear her eyes from Jon's and her breath caught in her throat. She let it out in an exasperated whoosh when Jon bent his head again and whispered in Little Sun's ear. Try as she might, she couldn't hear what he said.

When Jon looked back at her, Little Sun bounced around to see her, too. Clapping his pudgy hands together, he called, "Yite. Yite."

The question came out before Caitlyn could stop it. "What did you say to him?"

"It's a secret," Jon informed her with a saucy grin. "Couldn't you tell? I whispered it because it's a secret between Little Sun and me."

Caitlyn resisted the twinkling glint in Jon's eyes, which reminded her of sugar cookie sparkles, by dropping her own gaze to the tray on the table. "Well," she mused. "I think it's rude to whisper secrets in front of another person. And rude people sure don't deserve any of the molasses cookies I just baked."

She glanced up in time to see a hint of contriteness replace the teasing look on Jon's face.

"Aw, Caitlyn," he said.

But Little Sun, who had no idea what a cookie was—or a secret—reached for the figure in Jon's hand, and Jon had to quickly pull his knife out of the way.

"Dog," Little Sun said, clasping his fingers open and shut. "Dog. Dog."

"All right," Jon said. "Just let me finish his ears first."

He carved two small points on the figure's head, then handed it over. Little Sun chortled with laughter and slid from Jon's knee. He ran across the room and climbed onto a chair by the table, holding the figure out for Caitlyn to admire.

"Dog," he said again. "Jon, dog."

"Why, it looks just like him," Caitlyn said. "It's very nice."

" 'Ice," Little Sun said with a nod. "Jon, 'ice."

Jon rose from the bunk and brushed the wood shavings onto the floor. Walking over to where Caitlyn kept the broom beside the fireplace, he carried it and the dustpan back to the bunk. Though Caitlyn watched him closely, she didn't see him glance at the cookies.

But Little Sun had finally noticed them. He reached out a hand that Caitlyn quickly caught before it could touch the still hot tray.

"Hot," she told him sternly. "Here, you sit down and I'll give you one."

Little Sun obediently sat in the chair and Caitlyn pushed the tray to the far side of the table. She carefully removed one of the cookies and broke it into several pieces to cool, laying the pieces on her linen hand towel. A smile quirked her lips between blows of breath on the cookie to hurry the cooling. Jon kept his back to her while he swept the shavings into a neat pile.

"Ummmm, good," Caitlyn said as she laid the broken pieces in front of Little Sun. "Careful, now. It's still a little warm."

Little Sun picked up a piece and stared at it for a second, then popped it into his mouth. His small face split into a grin as he chewed, and Caitlyn laughed in response.

Jon passed the table again, the dustpan full of wood shavings. He threw them into the fireplace, then returned the broom and pan to their hooks on the wall. When he turned around, Caitlyn stood there.

She offered him the cookie. "Jon, 'ice," she said in a soft voice. "Jon cleaned up after himself. Jon ver' 'ice."

Smiling down at her, Jon covered her hand with his. He bent his head and bit off a chunk of cookie, his lips barely brushing her fingertips.

A shiver of pleasure ran up Caitlyn's arm and she almost dropped the cookie. Jon closed his hand more firmly around hers and bent his head again. He cupped her hand in his while he bit off piece after piece and chewed slowly, then bent a last time for the crumbs.

His soft tongue licked her palm slowly, caressingly. He probed it between each finger and cascades of delectable sensations crawled up her arm, spreading to other parts of her body. Caitlyn's legs trembled as she fought for control.

When her hand was at last clean, Jon raised his head. "Ver' 'ice," he said with a nod. "The cookie, too."

He kissed her parted lips gently, and Caitlyn blushed as she pushed him away.

"Jon . . . Little Sun," she said with a gasp.

"He better get used to it," Jon told her in a firm voice. "Silas, too. I'm tired of hiding my feelings for you. From now on, I'm going to touch you when I want to—kiss you when I want to. Tell you I love you whenever I feel like it, no matter who's listening."

Caitlyn tried to whirl away from him, but Jon caught her shoulders. "Scared?" he questioned when she glanced shyly up at him.

At her nod, he continued, "Yeah, me, too. I thought I cared for someone else once, but it was nothing like this."

"And just who was that?" Caitlyn spat around the pangs of jealously clouding her mind.

"Nobody important," Jon assured her. "Nobody the least bit important. But this *is* important—this feeling I have for you. And I'm not going to give it up without one hell of a fight."

"Hell," Little Sun said from the table.

Jon's face flushed and Caitlyn dissolved into laughter.

"You're just going to have to learn to watch your language," she said when she could speak. "He's picking up words right and left now."

"Yeah. Well, I'll try." Caitlyn pulled against his hold again, but Jon bent his head once more.

"Hey," he said quietly. "Wanna know a secret?"

She shrugged, and he nudged the hair away from her ear. "He was right," he whispered, then quickly walked over to the table to sit with Little Sun.

Caitlyn stared wide-eyed after him, her ear still tingling from the feel of his breath feathering across it and her mind whirling as she tried to make sense of his words. Suddenly she remembered what Jon had said just before he bent to whisper his secret to Little Sun.

He'd repeated the Sioux's words that she and Jon ought to be married, if they weren't then. She could hear Reach for the Moon's voice again in the Sioux language, which she had translated for Jon.

She glanced at the figure of Dog that Little Sun had discarded on the table in favor of the cookies. Reach for the Moon had given her Dog at first for a wedding present. When informed that they weren't married, the Sioux told her to keep the dog to remind herself that love had many faces.

But that wasn't what Jon had been referring to. She backed up her thoughts a little. "Yitc," Little Sun had said. Jon had told him that Reach for the Moon had been right in saying that she and Jon should be married.

Her frown of concentration deepened. Jon knew as well as she that they couldn't get married. Didn't he? Though he'd told her they could live in the mountains, he hadn't contradicted her when she reminded him that he would miss his life back east.

Well, she wouldn't really mind seeing a few of the places she'd read about in Jon's books, but none of them could possibly be as beautiful as her mountains.

And look at how attached Jon had grown to Little Sun. He'd definitely want sons of his own someday, and she had no intentions of ever having a baby.

Of course, it might not tie her down as much as she'd thought at first, if Jon helped with the children like he did with Little Sun.

Silas opened the door a crack and called, "Hey, Jon, I got us some meat, but I'm gonna need a little help."

Jon quickly rose and walked to the door, speaking to Silas through the slight crack so the frigid air outside would be kept at bay. "What's up, Silas?" he asked.

Caitlyn followed Jon to the door and clearly heard Silas's voice reply, "Shot me a moose, but the danged noise from my rifle started a slide. The moose ain't buried deep, seeing as how it's sort of early in the season for us to have any of them large avalanches we get later on. And it ain't very far away. But it'll take both of us to get it out of there."

"I'll be right out, Silas."

Jon closed the door and reached for his buffalo robe as Caitlyn hurried back to the table.

"I'll wrap up a few of the cookies for you to take," she said, picking up the linen towel and reaching for the tray. "Silas is probably hungry."

A few minutes later, the men were both gone, and Caitlyn busied herself straightening the cabin. Though she lingered over washing the few dirty dishes, and even heated water to scrub the pine-plank floor, at least another hour faced her before Jon and Silas could possibly return. Since the idea of fresh meat settled her plans for supper, she had no preparations to make for the evening meal.

Little Sun, enraptured with the figure of Dog, quietly amused himself on the newly-scrubbed floor, jabbering nonsense as he and Dog played out adventures in his mind. Caitlyn didn't even have the job of washing his nappies since Jon had taught the little boy to use either the outhouse or chamberpot Caitlyn kept in her room.

There had to be something else to do. Caitlyn paced restlessly around the room, pausing to straighten a pan on one of the hooks by the fireplace. Though she grumbled at them from time to time, Silas and Jon usually kept their corners of the room fairly neat. She noticed that Jon had even snugged the fur covers he and Little Sun had wrinkled over his bunk before he swept up the wood shavings.

As usual, he'd left his rifle propped in the corner for her, beside the pack filled with extra supplies he took when he ran the lines. On the shelf above his bunk, his belongings lay in orderly stacks—two more sets of long underwear, wool socks rolled together lying on top of the new moccasins she had made him, an extra set of buckskins.

Maybe she should work on those two shirts for Jon and Silas's Christmas presents. She still had to attach the sleeves and decorate Jon's with beading and dyed porcupine quills to match the possibles bag she got him at rendezvous.

She'd much rather sit and read, though. She studied the stack of Jon's books on the shelf. With a long winter ahead of them yet, they'd all agreed to carefully ration the books—just a chapter each evening. Tonight they would start a new book, since she had finished one while they were snowbound the last few days.

Noticing the quiet in the cabin, Caitlyn glanced around to see Little Sun stretched out on the floor, the figure of Dog clasped tightly in his small hand. With a smile of love on her face, she carefully lifted him into her arms. Holding him close for a moment, she stroked the raven hair back from his face, then kissed his cheek and laid him in his crib.

"Little boy," she whispered. "I'm going to have to watch out or I'll be as attached to you as Jon is. I have to keep reminding myself that you belong to Spirit Eagle."

With a sigh, she turned away. "All right, Caitlyn," she continued whispering. "You already are attached to him. And he's not near the trouble you tried to tell yourself babies would be. Shoot, Jon and Silas are a lot more trouble. They eat more—wear bigger clothes. Take up more space."

What the heck was wrong with her? Normally she enjoyed her time alone at the cabin—well, most of the time, as long as she had something to do to keep her hands busy. Now that big hole in the corner of the room, which Jon filled when he came in, mocked her. Darn it, she missed him, and he'd only been gone a couple hours.

What in the world will you do when he leaves for good?

Caitlyn shook her head to chase away that aching thought. Determinedly she walked over to the shelf and took down the book she'd decided to start reading tonight. She could read the first chapter now, and repeat it tonight for Jon and Silas.

Settling herself near the window at the foot of Jon's bunk for light, she propped the book on her upraised knees and opened the cover. An envelope slid onto her lap, followed by a thin piece of foolscap paper. She picked them up and started to lay them aside, and another, stiffer piece of paper fell from the folded foolscap.

Curious, Caitlyn picked it up. A tiny image of Jon as a baby stared back at her. Those same eyes, that determined chin with a slight cleft. Blond hair curling around the baby's ears, with the same little cowlick on his forehead. She couldn't mistake the baby's identity.

Caitlyn ran a fingertip across the slightly bumpy texture of the small painting, marveling at the resemblance to the grown man now a part of her life. It had to have been done 25 years ago or more, yet beneath the chubby face she could clearly make out the rugged features of the man to come—Jon today.

Caitlyn retrieved the foolscap paper to stuff it back into the envelope. She had no business prying into Jon's personal letters.

He came a little early, and Roxie would hardly even let me hold him until he grew some.

Huh. Though she still practiced whenever she could, her own handwriting already formed words much easier to read than these. You would think a person would be more careful doing something as important as writing, she mused as her eyes continued to skim the foolscap.

Remember cousin Ben and how he always fooled around drawing and sketching when we were kids? He just got back from Philadelphia, where he studied painting under Thomas Sully. Ben's practicing on any family member who catches his interest, with an eye toward suporting himself by doing portraits some day. Little Charles is one of his favorite subjects, and Ben's done several very good likenesses of the chap. Thought you might enjoy this one.

Caitlyn dropped the paper as though scalded, then grabbed it back up to look at the date on the other side. Last spring! Someone had written to Jon enclosing a small painting of a baby about three months old last spring, and sent the letter to him at rendezvous. Rendezvous could have been the only place for the letter to catch up to him.

And just who the hell was Roxie?

Without even a stab of guilt, Caitlyn picked up the foolscap again to read the entire letter. By the time she finished it, she was even more confused. Charles had to be the half-brother Jon had told her about, and this Roxie was Charles's wife. Charles begged Jon to come back to the plantation, offering him, obviously not for the first time, a share in the plantation.

You always were the brains behind our profits, Jon, and it's just not running the same without you. Roxie wanted to turn your room into little Charles's nursery, but that's one thing I stood up to her about. And you yourself know how hard it is to deny Roxie anything.

And just how the hell would Jon know that?

Jon's voice echoed in her head. *I thought I cared for someone else once, but it was nothing like this.*

Caitlyn grabbed the picture again. *He came a little early.* The pieces fell into place. Jon's baby. He'd left behind the woman he claimed to once care for—pregnant with his baby. His brother had married her instead. And his brother wanted Jon to come home.

Wouldn't that make a nice little threesome? No, foursome, with the baby.

Caitlyn snorted her disgust at Jon as she stuffed the letter and painting back into the envelope. Slamming the book cover back into place, she jumped from the bunk and thudded the book back onto the shelf.

Words! She wished she'd never learned to read them. The pain tore at her as she paced around the room.

Sweet words, like Jon whispered to her. False words, the

words in the letter confirming the lies.

Had he whispered promises of marriage to Roxie, too? Had the sincerity in his eyes appeared as genuine when he said I love you? What sort of a man could his brother be, to have taken Jon's leavings and even be raising Jon's son as his own?

How could she have even contemplated changing her mind about the life she wanted for herself—a life of peace and solitude in the mountains she loved. With no ties to anyone who could die and leave her again.

She'd only gone to Sky Woman after Pa's death because she realized there was no way she could prepare for the long winter to come without Pa's help. They hadn't even cut wood yet, a task that usually occupied Pa through the winter months.

Jon and Silas had seemed a godsend when they agreed to winter with her. She'd needed their help to get through this first winter, but with the proper planning she could make it on her own from now on. She'd just have to start her winter preparations as soon as spring broke each year.

She could do it—she knew she could. She could run her own lines, trade her own furs for supplies at rendezvous and visit with some of Pa's old mountain men friends each summer. The long winters alone wouldn't bother her that much.

If only Jon hadn't opened her eyes to the world outside her mountain paradise with those darned books he'd brought along.

She stared around the cabin, imagining it next winter without any companions to break the solitude. Now it appeared snug and homey, with the extra bunks and clothing on the shelves.

No, it's cramped, she told herself. Next winter she would have plenty of room to move around, without stumbling over other people.

Besides, it had to be better than living in a world with a man who nonchalantly walked away from his unborn baby and just as quickly started wheedling his way between the legs of the next woman he ran across. Lies, lies, lies. Silas lied, too. Jon would never make a mountain man, because mountain men stood by their word.

He's never come right out and asked you to marry him, Caitlyn's logical mind told her. *And you've been telling him all along that you absolutely had no plans to get tied down with a marriage and family.*

"And I'm sure as heck not going to!" Caitlyn answered her mind aloud. "I'm going to make sure that Silas and Jon both know that I'm coming back up here by myself after the next rendezvous. They can find their own danged territory to run lines in!"

As Caitlyn continued to fume, Jon shouldered the door open and dropped a hide-wrapped haunch of meat on the floor. "Silas is putting the rest of the meat up on our storage platform," he said to Caitlyn as he shrugged off his robe. "I thought you might like to slice some steaks off this for supper. . . ."

He turned into Caitlyn's blazing glare, his face creasing into a frown. "What's wrong?"

"Nothing *important*," Caitlyn spat at him. "Nothing *important* at all!"

Jon crossed the room in two strides and reached out for her. "Well, then, how about a welcome-home kiss?"

Caitlyn roughly shoved his arms away. "This isn't your home! It's mine, and I'll thank you to remember that from now on. If you want a kiss, go kiss that moose's cold nose, because you'll get about as much response out of that as you will from me from now on!"

Caitlyn whirled and ran into her room, wrenching the blanket across the door back into place before she threw herself onto her bed. She buried her face on her pillow, then quickly sat back up. The pillow still smelled of Jon.

Well, he damned well better not follow her in here! She glared at the doorway, but the blanket remained undisturbed. A long moment later, she heard the door open again and Dog's toenails clicking across the pine floor. The door slammed shut and Silas spoke.

"What you doin' standin' there like you got a stick up your butt, Jon? And where's Cat?"

"Resting, I guess," Jon muttered in reply.

"She's probably been busy," Silas said. "Look how nice and cheery everything is. Makes a man feel good, comin' home to a nice place like this."

"Home, hell," Jon snarled. "I'm gonna take my horse out for some exercise."

"Jon, it's almost dark. . . . "

Caitlyn heard the door slam once again on Silas's words.

Chapter Twenty-three

The days slowly crawled toward Christmas, and Caitlyn resented each passing week. The holiday should be celebrated with loved ones, and she struggled between the earlier, happy memories of Christmases with Pa and her certainty that this year the coming day would be flat and meaningless.

Jon kept his promise about alternating days with Silas, but Caitlyn found herself not enjoying the time in the wilderness nearly as much as she had with Jon—though she buried that thought each time it surfaced. Whenever they passed the huge pine where she and Jon had first made love, she resolutely turned her face away. Silas once or twice tried to probe into the reason for Caitlyn's surliness, but he was met with a blank stare and a change of subject.

She couldn't ignore Silas's hints about a nice Thanksgiving meal, however. The old man frequently mused on the memories he carried from his own childhood, and his yearning reminded Caitlyn so much of Pa's pleasure in their little celebrations that Caitlyn gave in. Since the day fell on one of her days at the cabin, she cooked and baked, and

251

even fashioned a small centerpiece for the table from acorns and pinecones.

The bad moment came when Silas insisted they clasp hands and say grace. Jon, as usual, sat beside her, and every second of that embrace lingered in her mind—especially since Jon unconsciously ran his thumb across her palm while Silas prayed.

She tried to come up with a reason to halt the evening readings, but Silas looked so hurt the first time she claimed tiredness and went on to bed that she couldn't bring herself to disappoint him again. If only Silas didn't remind her so much of Pa. They didn't look at all alike, but they had similar characteristics, and Silas's mountain man drawl tugged at her heart when he sat with Little Sun once in a while to tell him a tall tale for a bedtime story.

It wasn't fair for Silas to be caught in the middle of her and Jon's warring emotions, Caitlyn realized. Especially since Jon appeared to be ignoring the entire matter completely.

He didn't touch her anymore. He spoke to her when necessary, and always politely. He spent as much time as possible out of the cabin, replenishing the wood pile or exercising the horses.

The snow deepened to the point where they couldn't use the horses to run the lines any longer, and Dog pulled the sled while whoever ran the lines broke trail in snowshoes. Jon rode the horses beneath the trees, away from the deep drifts, insisting they would be too fat and lazy to carry them to rendezvous next summer if allowed to while away the winter without exercise.

One day she and Silas returned to find that Jon had made Little Sun another sled. An already well-worn path down the mountainside beside the cabin indicated what the two of them had done to while away at least part of the day.

Another afternoon when they came in somewhat earlier than usual, Jon and Little Sun were out on the lake, with a fire going on the shoreline. Silas led the way over to the fire, and Caitlyn stared out at the two figures on the ice in amazement.

As soon as Little Sun caught sight of her, he laughed gaily and pushed away from Jon's steadying hands. He fell once or twice, finally managing to gain the shore, and then sat down in the snow and lifted a small foot to Caitlyn.

" 'Kates," he cried. "Jon, 'kates for me! See, Cat?"

Caitlyn studied the contraption closely. Jon had carved two wooden blades, connected with another piece of wood. Leather straps held each skate in place over Little Sun's moccasin. She looked up at Jon as he approached, an instinctive smile of delight on her face.

"That's amazing, Jon," she said. "He'll have hours of fun on those."

"I started on a pair for you, too," Jon said with a shrug. "I'll finish them day after tomorrow, while I'm ho. . . . " He tore his eyes away from Caitlyn's. "While I'm at the cabin."

Not noticing the hesitation in Jon's voice, Caitlyn swooped Little Sun into her arms. "Well, little boy," she said. "Look how red your cheeks and nose are. We better get you inside to warm up."

She carried Little Sun with her, and Jon stared after them, a look of resentment on his face. "I haven't had him out very long," he told Silas. "And I built the fire, so we could warm up now and then."

"Oh, that's just her motherin' instinct," Silas said with a laugh. "She didn't mean nothin' by it."

"Yeah, sure," Jon said in a grudging voice.

He turned away from Silas to stare out over the lake. Just like she didn't mean anything when she informed him in that icy-hot voice of anger that the cabin was *her* home, not his.

Caitlyn couldn't have cut him any deeper if she'd told him that she despised him. Home—such a small word, with a meaning that transcended the insignificance of the few letters strung together.

At one time he had considered the plantation outside Richmond his home. All the wrenching pain he'd felt when he rode away just days before Roxie and Charlie's wedding had descended on him when Caitlyn spat those vicious words at him. In just one short month the summer before last, his entire world had been shattered.

Charlie had appeared as shocked as Jon when the attorney read the will that Charlie's father had left. Nothing would change, he assured Jon as soon as they were alone. He would speak to the attorney—have him draw up papers giving Jon his rightful half of the plantation.

But Roxie had moved into Charlie's life with a vengeance as soon as she realized the plantation had not gone to the older son, Jon. Instead, Charlie, the younger but natural son of Jon's stepfather, inherited it all. And Roxie had no intentions of giving up her plans to be mistress of that vast estate.

Jon vividly recalled Charlie's hesitant and embarrassed voice when his brother told him how sorry he was. He'd always been attracted to Roxie, he admitted, and she had visited him that day. Tearfully, she had confessed that she cared for Charlie, not Jon. Despite the fact that they should be in mourning, Roxie wanted the wedding to take place as soon as possible, within a month of the death of Charlie's father. It would be easier for Jon that way, Charlie insisted. Get it over with and on with their lives.

Charlie should have left it there. Jon's pride—and his disgust that he hadn't seen through Roxie before this— allowed him to shrug his shoulders and assure Charlie that there would be no hard feelings. He even deluded himself into believing they could still run the plantation together. However, Charlie kept pushing, insisting Jon be his best man, trying to maintain the same camaraderie they had shared while growing up. Even inviting Jon to accompany him and Roxie on a picnic or a buggy ride. Jon casually refused each invitation, but Charlie couldn't let it lie.

One rare evening when Roxie had other plans—another whirlwind session with her dressmaker, if Jon recalled right—he and Charlie shared a few drinks in the study. Charlie, his tongue loosened by liquor, chuckled as they reminisced about some of his and Jon's dalliances with other young southern belles as they went through their teen years.

"I swear, though, brother," Charlie said with a laugh. "I've never had as much trouble keeping my hands to myself with anyone as I do with Roxie. She'll be lucky if she's still a virgin this Sunday when we get married. Of course, I don't guess it will matter, since she seems as eager as me to jump into that wedding bed. Lucky, aren't I?"

As much as he loved his brother, Jon couldn't keep the biting sarcasm from his words when he snarled, "Yeah, she's a hot little piece, isn't she?"

Without warning, Charlie surged to his feet and swung. His fist connected with Jon's jaw, hurtling him from his chair to the floor. Jon leapt back to his feet with catlike grace, facing Charlie with his own fists clenched, ignoring the trickle of blood running from the side of his mouth.

"Goddamn you, Charlie," he snarled. "What the hell was that for?"

Charlie swung again, but Jon jumped out of the way, landing a punch in Charlie's stomach as he went by. He turned back to his brother's doubled-over figure, his anger leaving him as he listened to Charlie's tortured gasps for breath.

"Look, Charlie," he began as he laid a hand on Charlie's shoulder.

"Get the hell away from me!" Charlie gasped, shrugging off Jon's hand and managing to straighten. "You listen to me, Jon. Roxie's *my* fiancee now, and I won't have anyone else making snide remarks about her, not even you!"

"Hell, you were the one saying. . . . "

"She's going to be *my* wife!" Charlie shouted. "Mistress of *my* plantation, *my* home! What's past is past, and I'll hear nothing from your filthy damned mouth about your former relationship with her! You gave her up!"

Jon had stormed out of the room before their argument could escalate again into blows. Charlie had tried to apologize the next day, insisting the liquor had controlled his tongue. It didn't matter, though. After a day of turbulent reflections, Jon saddled his horse that night. He only took what he could stuff into his saddlebags, along with the pouch of poker winnings he kept in his room.

Jon heard Silas's snowshoes crunching away and realized he'd heard Silas speak to him at least twice, trying to get his attention. It was a long trip, though, from the Richmond memories to the mountainside lake where he stood, and it took him several seconds to return to the present. By then, he saw Silas at the cabin door.

My wife. Mistress of my plantation, my home. Charlie's words hurt as deeply in remembrance as they had when he'd shouted them at Jon.

This isn't your home. It's mine, and I'll thank you to remember that from now on. Hell, he'd be glad to remember Caitlyn's words. He was sick and tired of women who cared more about the four walls around them than they did a man they professed to love.

Sick and tired, too, of quixotic women who changed personalities and feelings as easily as they changed their dresses. Roxie loved him, then she loved Charlie. Caitlyn fell into his arms and relished his lovemaking, his caresses, then spat blue fire at him for no reason.

Home. Well, one day he would have a home of his own again—a home he built with his own money, which no one else could claim. Maybe he might even have a wife to share it with, but it damned sure wasn't going to be a woman who tore his soul out with a single, unexpected turn of her quicksilver personality.

And it sure as hell wouldn't be a woman he loved. He'd supposedly found love and lost it twice already. To hell with love and the horse it rode in on. His days with Little Sun reinforced his desire over and over to have sons of his own to carry on his name. He could father them just as well on a woman he didn't love. After all, it only took a few pokes between a woman's legs to spill his seed.

The pain he experienced when he thought of the rapture he'd found when he made love to Caitlyn would pass some day. All he had to do was get through the next few months until spring opened the land so he could travel away from here—journey away from her tantalizing presence.

Hopefully—God, he hoped desperately that spring would come early this time.

* * *

The nights tortured Caitlyn the worst. She lay in bed sleepless, hearing every faint snore from the next room, every shift of position on the bunks when Jon or Silas turned over. Little Sun never woke crying for his mother or father anymore—he seemed to have accepted his place in their small family.

Though she tried to deny it, her sensitivity to Jon's movements remained the strongest. Each time she drifted toward drowsiness, she found herself interrupting the cadence of her breath, holding it to see if she could determine whether it matched the rhythm of Jon's breathing. Her ear always tingled when she remembered Jon's breath feathering over it in passion or teasing, whispered secrets.

Turning onto her stomach and covering her head with her pillow didn't help at all. Though she couldn't hear, her mind could imagine.

Jon slept with at least the upper portion of his body naked—she'd seen that more than once when she still had to get up and comfort Little Sun at night. Usually he pillowed his head not only on a folded blanket, but also on his palm. His other hand lay outside the fur coverings, fingers curled in relaxation. His blond hair, tousled from sleep, curled around his face, across his forehead above the long, golden lashes tipping his eyelids.

She ached to touch those broad shoulders just once more—feel those long, callused fingers on her neck, her breasts—run her fingers just one more time through the blond curls, brushing them back from his face.

He shaved every morning, either before he left with Silas or after she and Silas had gone. Nothing ever marred the fullness of his mouth—a mouth that still sent shivers of pleasure over her whenever she unwillingly found her eyes drawn to it.

His blue eyes didn't twinkle anymore. Even when he played with Little Sun, Caitlyn could sense a tiny cloud of pain hanging over his voice—see a shadow intrude into the blueness of his eyes while he watched the little boy.

He deserved it, she kept telling herself, pounding on the

pillow night after night to try to make it more comfortable. Lies. She hated a liar. She hated Jon now that she had discovered the confirmation of his lies, shoving aside the thought that she had no business prying into that letter. She was damned glad she *had* read it.

Curiosity killed the cat, and ye're sure a curious little cat, Cat, me darlin'.

"Shut up, Pa," Caitlyn whispered weakly in reply to Pa's echoing voice in her mind late one night. "It's darned well killing me, but I can't forget it now that I know about it. I'll get over it. Soon as spring comes and Jon leaves. Soon as spring comes."

Finally, in desperation for a distraction from her racing thoughts one long, lingering night, Caitlyn sat up and struck the flint from her tinderbox to light the bedside candle. She drew her mother's journal from beneath the pillow and opened it. She traced a finger across the inscription, then resolutely turned to the first page and began to read.

March 15, 1814
This new journal will start with my new life and our new name. James O'Neal and I were married two weeks ago, on March 1, 1814. We are now on a ship bound for America, my new husband, my daughter, Caitlyn, and I. I hate to think that I will never see Ireland again, but my father made it very clear that he would never give his permission for or his blessing on my marriage to James. And I love James so dearly. I never thought I would love again after Edward died from the fever, while I was still carrying Caitlyn, but James has broken through the ice around my heart. I cannot give him up. Had I not found James, I might have married the man my father chose for me, to assure that Caitlyn had a secure future. I have complete faith in James, however. He will take care of us, even in this distant land we now travel to.

I thought my father loved me enough to want to see me happy, but it appears he did not. I thought he would at least want to be a part of his granddaughter's life, since he loved Caitlyn so very much. But he has turned against

*us all. His last words to me broke my heart almost as much
as when Edward died. He said he would rather see me dead
than married to James. I can only hope that down through
the years, he might soften.*

*It still hurts me very badly even to write about it, but I
have made my choice. I do not care that James is a second
son. I love him.*

The next few pages were mostly details of the journey,
made in what appeared to be weekly intervals. Caitlyn
smiled to herself as she read about some of her own es-
capades on the ship: her precocious chattering to the sailors;
her near fall over the side and subsequent banishment to
the cabin for an entire day; how she had befriended the
captain's parrot and cried when they left it behind after they
reached America.

Her mother touched briefly on how James had met with
a fur company and agreed to manage one of their far-flung
outposts. One page was devoted to her mother's stubborn
refusal to stay behind while James went into the wilderness.
Her place was with him, she wrote, and she would not be
separated from him. Besides, she still feared her father
might come after her, might drag her back to Ireland, separating her from James. She had unbent enough to write a
letter to her father, telling him that she and James were
now married and in America, but not giving him their lo-
cation.

On their journey west, her mother had realized she was
carrying another child. Her words on the pages reflected
her joy.

*I am feeling so wonderful! As with Caitlyn, I have none
of the morning sickness some of my friends experienced.
There is just this wonderful peace and expectation inside
me, knowing that a child will be born of the love between
James and me. He's a little worried about me giving birth
in such an isolated area, but I assured him that Caitlyn's
birth was without any problem. He tries to hide his pref-
erence for a son, assuring me that another daughter would
be fine. He does love Caitlyn so much, as though she were
truly his own.*

On the next page, Caitlyn gave a start and tears misted her eyes. Her mother had left a message for her.

Dear Caitlyn, it began: *With another child coming, it occurs to me that you, my dear first-born, may want answers someday on your background. You will realize that everyone around you has family, aunts, uncles and grandparents, while you have none. Hopefully, I will be around to tell you all this, and the day will have come and gone when we have discussed it. What I will tell you is this:*

Your family stretches far back into the annals of Irish history. It is a proud lineage, with ancestors who have always made good names for themselves. Perhaps, however, their pride in their ancestry has become a detriment, rather than a benefit. In my mind, they have concerned themselves too much with ever expanding their holdings, instead of focusing on the true meaning of happiness: love and family. Don't get me wrong, my dear. Security can mean an easier life, but without love, it can be an empty life.

In Ireland, you have a grandfather, Sean Keefe. He is a proud and stubborn man, with huge holdings that by right should be yours and my coming babe's inheritance. But there are, as I have said, more important things in life than material possessions. By now perhaps your grandfather is also a lonely man. Most of our family was wiped out in the plague of fever that took your father, Edward. There is one cousin left, Edward's sister Nan's son, who is called Patrick. I never knew him well.

I do not know what the future will bring—but whatever it is, know that I have made the choice my heart told me to make. I cannot say that I am proud of the scandal I left behind for my father to face or that he will ever forgive me for it. I am perhaps the first black sheep of our illustrious lineage, but it is a title I willingly accept because of the deep love I have for James. I hope one day you find as deep a love for yourself, my daughter.

After blinking away her tears, Caitlyn read the rest of the journal to the end. It gave weekly chronicles again of their life, Reggie's birth and his growth. It never mentioned her grandfather again, and ended on what must have been the week before the massacre. Through it all, her mother never indicated that she'd had any alteration in her feelings of having made the correct choice when she left her home and followed James.

The candle flickered and Caitlyn glanced over to see the wick sputtering in a pool of melted wax. Slipping the journal under her pillow, she blew out the flame and settled into sleep.

William Hogan threw down the piece of wood he'd been using to poke at the fire in the middle of the wigwam. "Damn it," he snarled. "I already sent a letter back, telling them I'd found the bitch. They're going to expect me at least on a ship arriving this coming spring. Why didn't ye just grab her, when ye had the chance?"

Tall Man stood up from the fire, towering over the other man. "I have told you that she saw through my story," he spat in a mixture of the English he was learning from the white man and the Nez Perce language, which Hogan was picking up. "It would have been easy to kill her, but you want her alive. And I will not return now—risk my own life in the winter snows. You can wait, or you can go yourself."

"Hell, I'd never find her, and ye know that. And she's got those men living with her. But I said I'd go with ye. We can each pick one of them off, then grab the woman."

"You white eyes should learn patience," Tall Man said. "They will not be moving over the coming months. They will be there when we are ready."

Sky Woman entered the wigwam, casting a disgruntled look at both men and effectively cutting off their conversation. She had made it clear to Tall Man that she wanted him to leave her wigwam—take his friend with him and find his own living quarters. But she was not strong enough to enforce her words. He would stay until spring, then she would get her wish. He would leave, but she would never know until too late that his path would take him on the trail of revenge.

* * *

Any feeble hope Caitlyn fostered that they could ignore Christmas this year disappeared the day before Christmas Eve. She and Silas ran the lines that day and, as they retraced their path and came near the cabin, Silas stopped by a small pine tree.

"Reckon this one'll do, Cat?" he asked. "I'd like to have a bigger tree, but it wouldn't fit inside, what with all of us needin' room to walk around."

"I suppose you mean for a Christmas tree, Silas," she replied with a sigh.

" 'Course I do. Why, one or two of us men always found each other for Christmas every year at somebody's cabin or the other. Always had us a tree, too. Ain't Christmas without a tree. 'Sides, all of us been sneakin' off alone and hidin' things 'round that cabin. Gotta have a tree to put them there presents under."

"I haven't noticed anyone sneaking around and hiding things," Caitlyn said in a grudging voice.

"Then you ain't been payin' no attention," Silas said with a smirk. "I guess you been too wrapped up in whatever's got you into a snit over Jon, but that don't mean we ain't gonna have a Christmas for that there little boy."

"Silas," Caitlyn warned.

"Don't worry, I ain't gonna pry into yours and Jon's business. Some things are better left alone. Curiosity killed the cat, you know. But me and Little Sun mean to celebrate Christmas, and it'd be right nice if you and Jon joined in with us. Sort of like us bein' a family."

"We're not a family, Silas," she told him in a flat voice, making an effort to overcome her pain at Silas's reference to the old adage Pa had also quoted to her. The adage, still close to the forefront of her mind, hit awfully near home.

"There's more than one kind of family, Cat. I figure what we've been through together makes us a family. 'Course," he continued in a hurt voice, "place belongs to you, and you've got the say-so over it. It ain't mine and Jon's home. Don't guess neither me nor Jon either one's got a home of our own right now."

"W . . . what did you say, Silas?" Caitlyn asked in a tormented voice.

"It's true as that there nose on your face," Silas replied. "Me and Jon's just squattin' with you this winter. We both know that. Jon's told me enough 'bout how much he lost back there in the east for me to know he'd sooner eat a pile of Dog's leavin's than ever swaller his pride and go back there to live. Reckon he'll just have to build his own place someday."

Caitlyn bowed her head and nudged her foot against a low-hanging branch on the small pine. A shower of snow covered her moccasin. "What . . . he didn't tell me exactly what happened," she halfway lied. He hadn't told her any of it—she only knew bits and pieces from the letter. "I thought his brother wanted him to come back and help run the place."

Silas shot her a crafty look, but his beard covered his grin, even if Caitlyn had been looking at him.

"Well, now, a man's got his pride, like I said. Reckon Jon put just as much sweat and blood into that land as his brother did, but his step-daddy's will cut Jon off without nothin'. Must've been a hell of a hurt on Jon, havin' his home took away from him after all those years of work—seein' everythin' he'd helped build go to his brother."

Caitlyn's head shot up, a faint misting of tears beginning in her eyes. "Oh, Silas, I said something awful to Jon. I told him my home wasn't his, either. I . . . I told him . . . Silas, I didn't mean it. I want you and Jon both to feel like the cabin's home to all of us. At least . . . at least until we have to split up after rendezvous next summer."

"Thought we'd sorta talked about having another season up here next year, Cat."

"We can't," Caitlyn said with a shake of her head. "I . . . you and Jon can find another place with just as many furs to trap. I've decided I want to have my privacy back next winter."

When Silas frowned at her, Caitlyn hurried on to say, "But that doesn't mean I want you to feel unwelcome this season. I mean it, Silas. I'm sorry if I've acted ungrateful to have you both around. I couldn't have come back up here at all this year without your help.''

Caitlyn stared over Silas's shoulder while he studied her. Or—or maybe, if she solidified the tentative plans she'd been making after reading her mother's journal, Silas and Jon could have the place to themselves—at least until she decided if she wanted to return or not.

''Well,'' Silas broke into her thoughts, ''the first thing we gotta do if we aim to have us a home-like, family Christmas and maybe forget the last few weeks of problems is get us a tree cut. How 'bout it, Cat? You never said if you liked this one or not. You got another one in mind?''

''As a matter of fact, I do,'' Caitlyn told him, giggling under her breath when Silas looked up at the sky with a groan. ''See? This tree's missing a limb on the side there. I saw another, beautiful one the other day, and it's only about a half mile from here. We better get started.''

But the next tree proved to be not to Caitlyn's satisfaction, either, after she shook the snow off and studied it. She led Silas from tree to tree, none of them reaching up to her measure.

Silas finally sat down on the sled with a thump. ''You go find your tree and I'll wait here, Cat,'' he said with a huff. ''Or maybe you and Jon could bring Little Sun out tomorrow and find one you like.''

''I just want it to be special, Silas,'' Caitlyn said. ''Sort of an apology to Jon, too. Please? Oh, look. That one over there. I'm sure it will be perfect.''

Silas shoved himself to his feet, but Dog refused to move. He laid his head on his paws and ignored Silas's tug on the rope.

''Don't blame you, critter,'' Silas said. ''This is her last chance. If she don't like this one, we'll haul her back and let Jon bring her out tomorrow.''

Dog wagged his tail in the snow, still refusing to rise to his feet.

''This one's the one I want, really it is,'' Caitlyn called. ''Would you please bring the ax and chop it down? Please, Silas?''

Dog glanced over at Caitlyn and finally rose to his feet. Silas could have sworn he heard the animal give a resentful sigh. They both plowed through the snow once more in Caitlyn's direction, and Silas untied the ax from the sled.

After he chopped the tree down, Caitlyn reached for the trunk. "It'll be too heavy a load for Dog to carry the tree, too," she told Silas. "I'll drag it with us."

"Suit yourself," Silas said with a nod. "Gets too heavy, I'll help you with it."

As they walked on toward the cabin, Caitlyn caught herself biting her lower lip to keep from asking Silas more questions about Jon. Curiosity, she kept telling herself.

"Uh . . . Silas, Jon's brother's raising his own family back on that plantation now, isn't he?"

Since Caitlyn dragged the pine tree behind the sled, through the easier trail, she couldn't see Silas slide another one of his crafty looks down at Dog.

"Yeah, I 'member Jon tellin' me his brother was married now. They got a young'un."

"Do . . . has Jon ever said if he and his brother look very much alike? I don't suppose they do, what with them having different fathers."

"Never mentioned it," Silas told her. "Happens at times, you know. 'Specially if the boys take after their mama, rather than their daddy."

Caitlyn stumbled on the trail, righting herself with a wrench before Silas noticed. Could she have possibly misjudged the letter's contents—the picture of the little boy who was the image of Jon?

Curiosity killed the cat.

Oh, God, had the dagger-like words she threw at Jon, without first admitting that she had pried into his letter and asking him for an explanation, killed his feelings for her? They had—she knew they had.

He'd kept his distance ever since that day. The pain shadowing his eyes was their love dying. Oh, God, what had she done?

Chapter Twenty-four

At least she hadn't let her anger keep her from finishing the shirts for Jon and Silas, Caitlyn told herself the next morning after breakfast. She'd completed the design on Jon's shirt during her days at the cabin, and even had enough beads and quills left to make a similar pattern on Silas's and a tiny shirt for Little Sun. She could hardly wait to see the looks on their faces when they saw the three matching shirts the next morning—Christmas Day.

Silas declared a two-day holiday, allowing that the lines would just have to take care of themselves until after Christmas. Truthfully, he and Jon were more trouble than they were worth all day, bumping into her as they tried to help Caitlyn cook and bake.

And each brush of her shoulder against Jon's—each inadvertent touch of their hands when she bent over the cookie dough rolled out on the table to trace an animal pattern with her fingernail so Jon could carve it out—sent a stab of longing and remorse through Caitlyn. More than once her heart caught in her throat, and she found herself on the verge of crying out to Jon to please forgive her—

or at least talk to her about it. But Silas and Little Sun, not to be left out of one moment of the preparations, remained inside the entire day.

Of course, they made a trip or two to the outhouse, but Little Sun stubbornly refused to let anyone except Jon accompany him there. The second time Jon walked out the door, with Little Sun's tiny hand clasped in his, Caitlyn stifled a sob of misery after the door closed.

"What's the matter, Cat?" Silas asked in a worried voice. "Don't you have no presents to put under the tree? Heck, Cat, it don't matter. You'll cook us a darn good meal—you always do. That can be your present to us."

"I . . . I've got presents," Caitlyn said with a sniff. "I've . . . even got something for Little Sun to give you and Jon. It's just . . . oh, Silas," she broke off with a wail. "I've made such a mess of things!"

Silas hurried over to take Caitlyn in his arms, patting her unsurely on the back and looking like he desperately wished he'd gone on out to run his lines today. "Aw, Cat, honey. Don't." Dang it, he didn't have any idea what to do with a crying woman in his arms. "Cat. Honey, it'll be all right."

"No, it won't," Caitlyn said with a louder sob. "And don't call me that. I don't ever want anyone to call me honey again!"

"All right. All right, Cat," Silas soothed, understanding dawning in the grin he hid under his beard. "But today's supposed to be a happy day—today and tomorrow. The happiest days of the year."

Caitlyn buried her face in his neck, her shoulders quaking and her tears running in rivulets. Silas pulled his handkerchief from his back pocket, then thought better of it when he remembered it was far from clean. He reached behind Caitlyn to the table and retrieved a linen hand towel.

"Here, Cat," he said, pushing her a little away from him. "Wipe your pretty eyes and hush up for a minute. Will you?"

Caitlyn grabbed the towel and nodded her head. "I'm . . . I'm sorry. I don't want to spoil things anymore, like I have the past few weeks.''

Silas led her over to his bunk and sat her down. He took the place beside her and waited for a few seconds, until she wiped her eyes and drew in a steadying breath.

"You know, Cat," he mused. "I been thinking that maybe *you* been thinking that you spoiled what you and Jon appeared to be having together. That right?''

Caitlyn nodded her head and wiped another stray tear.

"You and Mick ever have a fight?'' Silas asked.

"Of course," Caitlyn said. "Not often, but now and then.''

"Reckon you made up after them, didn't you?''

"Of course," Caitlyn repeated. "We couldn't have lived together if we hadn't.''

"How'd you make up?''

"It depended on who was wrong—Pa or me. Sometimes he. . . . '' Caitlyn stared up at Silas, a light dawning in her eyes. "But most of the time, me,'' she admitted. "I . . . I heard Pa and Sky Woman talking one day. She said Pa had sort of spoiled me, but Pa said, if so, the spoiling had been with love. Sky Woman agreed with him. We'd had a fight about me going with him to rendezvous of an evening, when Pa really wanted to be by himself. Sky Woman said I'd get over it and tell Pa that I was sorry when I realized that I'd been selfish. That Pa needed some time alone now and then.''

"You still haven't told me how you made up,'' Silas said with a grin that even split his beard. "I don't reckon you did it across a room. Figure you at least got close enough to talk without shouting at each other. Maybe reach out a hand and touch one another. Show each other you were sorry not just with words, but the way you acted, too.''

"I've been bumping into Jon all day,'' Caitlyn said in a forlorn voice. "He just moves away from me.''

"Bumpin' ain't the same as touchin' for a reason, Cat. And I'll tell you a secret that other men would consider me a traitor to our race for lettin' you in on. Ain't a man on earth that can stand up against a woman who tells him she's sorry. Who turns those big, soulful eyes on him and admits she might've misjudged him just a little.''

He slapped his hands on his knees. '' 'Course, it takes a little preparation at first afore she blurts that out. A little touch here and there, showin' him that she's missin' him, remindin' him just how good he used to feel when he kissed her.''

Caitlyn dropped her head and blushed, but Silas reached over and raised her face. ''She don't make them sort of apologetic gestures first, why, a man just might think she was only leadin' him on again. Seein' if she could wrap him 'round her finger again.''

''I wouldn't do that to Jon,'' Caitlyn whispered. ''Silas, I love him. I'm so afraid that I've killed his love for me. I don't blame him, because I've been awful to him. He's . . . so cold to me now.''

''Smart gal like you oughta be able to figure out a way to warm him back up, don't you think? Lessen you got too much pride yourself to admit you might've been wrong. Pride's a pretty cold bedfellow, Cat.''

''What if he hates me now?''

''Don't reckon you'll know that lessen you give makin' up a try,'' Silas told her. ''Don't you figure it's at least worth that? Shoot, I always thought you was a fighter. Appears to me you've dumped that gumption I always admired in you somewhere down there under that hurt pride.''

''Curiosity killed the cat,'' Caitlyn said with a smile of gratitude. ''And pride's a cold bedfellow. You're pretty smart sometimes, Silas.''

The door opened, admitting Jon and Little Sun into the room. Caitlyn tossed Silas a determined look and rose from the bunk. She caught Jon's buffalo robe as he shrugged it from his shoulders and pushed his hand away with a tender caress when he tried to reach for it.

''I'll hang it up for you, Jon,'' she said in a soft, breathless voice. ''I left a few of the cookies on the table for you and Little Sun to eat. We've got enough to decorate the tree this evening.''

''Thanks,'' Jon muttered, quickly turning away from her

to help Little Sun take off his wolfskin coat. When he stood to hang it on the hook beside his robe, he found Caitlyn still standing near—too near.

"Why are your eyes so red?" he asked before he could stop himself, Little Sun's coat dangling from one hand. "Have you been crying?"

"Oh, I was just remembering some things," Caitlyn admitted with a small shrug. "It's been . . . a lot of things have happened this past year or so."

"I imagine you miss your father around this time of year," Jon said quietly.

"I've been missing a lot of things here lately," Caitlyn told him. "Some things that I didn't have any control over losing from my life. Other things that I was foolish enough to throw away all on my own."

Jon snorted in disbelief, but Caitlyn grabbed his hand after he hung up Little Sun's coat and started to turn away.

"Hey, don't forget those cookies." She tugged him toward the table, grateful that Jon didn't jerk his hand free, since he was definitely strong enough to do that with little effort. She pushed him into a chair, then lifted Little Sun into the chair beside him.

"Cookies," she said as she handed one to Little Sun, who clapped his hands together before he reached for it. She picked up another one and handed it to Jon, staring down at her palm after he took it, carefully grasping the end farthest from her fingers. Seemingly unconscious of Jon's intent gaze, she touched her tongue to one crumb after the other until she cleaned her hand.

"Ummmm," she said with a nod. "I still like sugar cookies the best. Or at least, I think do. Molasses cookies just might take over being my favorite. Oh, Silas, do you want a cookie?"

"Surely do," Silas said as he came over to the table. "Say, Cat, what you planning for dinner tomorrow? You ain't never cooked nothin' we ain't liked, but that there meal you fixed us for Thanksgiving's gonna be hard to top."

"Well," Caitlyn mused as she propped her chin on her

hand. "There's one smoked turkey left from those you and Jon shot this fall. A duck or two, I think." She licked the tip of her finger and picked up a few more crumbs from the cookie tray, carrying them to her mouth and sliding them onto her tongue.

"We had turkey for Thanksgiving, though, and I fixed a duck last week. I know. Goose. Christmas goose, like we read about in that book. Is there a goose left, Silas?"

"Three of them," Silas said. "You gonna fix that stuffing, like you did in the turkey?"

"If you want," Caitlyn said. "What other side dishes would you both like?" She glanced at Jon, who still held his cookie uneaten in his hand.

"If you've got any berries left," Jon said at last when he realized it would be rude to let the silence linger any longer, "I sort of liked that blackberry cobbler we had before."

"I'll fix that for you, Jon," Caitlyn promised. "What about you, Little Sun? What do you want to eat tomorrow?"

"Dump'in's," Little Sun replied with a bob of his head as he reached for another cookie. "Cat, dump'in's. Good!"

"Dumplings it is," Caitlyn said with a laugh, tossing Jon a teasing grin. "Do you like my dumplings, Jon?"

"Whatever you cook is always delicious, Caitlyn," he replied. One of those damned cookie crumbs clung to the side of her lip, and he clamped his teeth firmly over his tongue before it could escape his mouth. "We better finish decorating the tree."

He shoved his chair back, and Caitlyn and Silas both rose. Stuffing a last bite of cookie into his mouth, Little Sun scrambled down and followed them as they all approached the tree. Caitlyn drew Jon's attention when she tapped a finger against her lips and cocked her head from side to side. Her braid bounced from her shoulder and brushed Jon's arm, and he moved a slight step away.

"You know," Caitlyn mused, not seeming to notice that Jon had put some distance between them, "I made an angel one Christmas. Pa and I fixed a paste out of flour and water, then tore up little bits of paper and mixed them up with the paste to form an angel. But that darn bear cub got hold of that when he tore up the cabin.''

''Angel,'' Little Sun said with a chortle. He grabbed Jon's hand and tugged him toward his bunk. ''Angel!''

''Look, son,'' Jon said in a reluctant voice. ''That was supposed to be a surprise. I was going to put the angel on the tree after everyone went to sleep tonight.''

Little Sun dropped to the floor and reached under Jon's bunk. He pulled out a small box and began unwrapping the brown paper from the figures inside. Finally he held up the figure of an angel.

''Angel,'' he said with satisfaction. He got to his feet and carried his prize over to Caitlyn. Changing his mind at the last second, he turned and held it out to Silas.

''Angel. Cat, angel.''

''Why, so it is, Little Sun,'' Silas agreed. He turned the figure over in his fingers, then studied the face again. ''It looks just like Cat, doesn't it? You sure do carve a good likeness, boyo.''

Caitlyn reached for the figure and ran her fingers over the face. ''Oh,'' she murmured with a blush. ''This isn't me. It's much too pretty.''

''Cat,'' Little Sun said with determination. ''Angel Cat.''

Jon grabbed the box and set it on his bunk. ''There's some figures for a crèche in here. I thought we'd put it under the tree, along with the presents.''

Caitlyn reached the bunk first, and sat down beside Jon as he removed the brown paper from the remaining figures. She took each one from him, oohing and aahing her admiration.

''They're beautiful, Jon. You must have spent hours carving these.''

''Not that many,'' Jon muttered as he jerked his arm away when her breast brushed it. He stood up and strode to the door. ''I'll get some dried hay from the stable to arrange around the crèche,'' he said as he shrugged again into his robe. ''You and Silas can look at the figures and see how you want to arrange them.''

"Jon," Caitlyn called before he could shut the door. When he looked back at her, she asked, "Do you think we might have a fire on the lake this evening and skate for a while? The wind always dies down in the evening, and it won't be that cold."

Jon nodded curtly in reply, then disappeared out the door. Caitlyn glanced at Silas, and he gave her a grin of satisfaction.

"Don't rush it, Cat," he said. "Took more than a day for those walls to build up a'tween you two. Might even take as long as two days to tear them down."

"Oh, Silas, I feel like I'm playing games with him. And I'm not at all sure that this is one game I'll win."

"Game brought you two together," Silas reminded her. "Game just might keep you that way."

"I'll try," she murmured. "With everything I have."

Jon knocked on the door and called through it without opening it, "The hay's outside here. I'm going down to brush the snow off the ice on the lake."

Caitlyn hurried over to open the door. "We can't decorate the tree until you get back, Jon," she reminded him before he was more than a few steps away. "We should all do it together."

Jon hesitated, then strode on. "I'll be back in a while."

As soon as he heard the door close behind him, he whirled and stared at the cabin. "What the hell's this all about, Caitlyn?" he muttered. "For weeks you've been just as happy as me to act like we'll catch a pox from each other if we get too close. Now you're practically crawling all over me."

He glared at the cabin, his fists clenched at his sides. "I guess this is just another one of your little personality turns that Silas warned me about. Well, it's not going to work on me. Not this time."

After he cleaned the ice with a broom he had made from some more of the dried hay and prepared a fire to light, Jon returned to the cabin. Silas and Caitlyn had arranged the crèche under the tree, and it didn't take long to hang the decorations in place. Little Sun took care of that, hang-

ing cookies willy-nilly on the branches, with Caitlyn surreptitiously moving them to a better position while Jon
occupied Little Sun with placing a new cookie. She grinned
and winked at Jon each time she successfully rehung a
cookie without Little Sun catching her, and each look thudded into Jon's heart like a pole-axe.

Caitlyn dished up a stew for supper, then went around
blowing out lanterns and candles before she sat at the table
with them. She left one candle burning on the table and a
lantern on the beam above the tree. The light twinkled on
the sugar-dotted cookies, shimmering them in sparkling
beams of brilliance.

"It's beautiful, isn't it?" Caitlyn said in a voice tinged
with wonder. "Each year I almost forget how pretty it is."

"Pretty," Little Sun said around a mouthful of stew,
dribbling a drop down his chin. "Tree, pretty."

Caitlyn laughed softly and wiped his chin. "Don't talk
with your mouth full," she reminded him.

"Won't," Little Sun agreed. He shoved in his last bite
of stew and swallowed it, then slid from his chair.
" 'Kate," he demanded as he ran over and pointed up at
his coat. " 'Kate, now."

"You have to wait until after I do the dishes," Caitlyn
said.

"No, you don't, Cat," Silas said, gathering up the dishes
into a pile in front of his plate. "I'll do these here dishes
this evenin'. You young'uns go on out and skate. I ain't
about to take a chance on falling on that ice, breakin' these
old bones."

"You'll do dishes?" Caitlyn said around a gasp of surprise. "Why, Silas. . . . "

"Get!" Silas insisted. "I've washed many a dish in my
day. I'll come down in a while and get Little Sun to put
him to bed. He's not gonna last too long out there tonight.
It's way past his bedtime already."

"As soon as he's asleep, we can put out the presents,"
Caitlyn whispered with a wink at Jon. "Come get us as
soon as he nods off, Silas."

In answer to Little Sun's urging, they hurried into their

coats and set off to the lake. Caitlyn threw her head back, breathing in the crisp air and slipping her hand into Jon's as they walked. Their mittens were a barrier to flesh meeting bare flesh, but she squeezed until she could feel the outline of Jon's fingers against her own. He didn't pull away, but neither did he respond to the pressure.

"Isn't it just wonderful out tonight?" Caitlyn asked. "See, the wind's died down."

"I still better light the fire." Jon removed his hand and knelt by his previously-prepared wood, while Caitlyn sat down on a nearby log placed there for that purpose and strapped hers and Little Sun's skates to their feet.

"Jon, 'kate," Little Sun said as he tromped over to Jon. "Jon, 'kate, too."

"I will, son," Jon promised with a smile. "I left my skates there on that tree limb the other day after we skated. You and Caitlyn go ahead while I get ready."

Little Sun toddled onto the ice, and Caitlyn quickly joined him, swooping his hands into hers and gliding them both across the frozen surface. She'd managed to get pretty good at this since Jon had given her a pair of skates for herself. She and the small boy skated hand in hand, their gleeful voices filling the night air with sounds of enjoyment.

Jon soon glided up beside them and reached for one of Little Sun's hands. They skated around in ever widening circles, until Jon called a halt after they all three nearly fell when they ran across an especially rough spot of ice.

"We better go back in and warm up by the fire," he said. Little Sun stifled a tired yawn, and Jon reached down to pick him up. "Come on." He took Caitlyn's hand in his own and she glided beside him toward the shoreline. They arrived just as Silas emerged from behind the fire.

"I'll carry the little fellow up to bed," Silas said, taking him from Jon's arms. "Looks like he's finally tuckered out."

Little Sun snuggled his head on Silas's shoulder. "Ti-'ed," he agreed around another yawn.

"You two go ahead and stay here," Silas said when Jon

sat down and began to unlace his skates. "Heck, it's early yet for young people. We can do those there . . . uh . . . hidden things after you come up."

Silas walked away, and Caitlyn turned her head up to the sky again. Silvery light from a full moon fell on her face, and the Christmas star hung low, its brilliance outshining the bright sparkles dusting the rest of the ebony sky. She closed her eyes briefly and made a wish, then shook her hood back and combed her fingers through her hair, which she had brushed out before supper and deliberately neglected to tie back into her usual braids. She lifted her hair free, allowing it to stream down her back.

"It's so beautiful tonight," she said with a sigh. "A perfect Christmas Eve. I'm not a bit cold. I think I'll skate some more."

Without waiting to see if Jon wanted to join her, she walked back onto the ice and pushed off again. She handled the double-bladed skates easily enough. She'd caught the smell of beeswax on them once in a while, and decided Jon must treat them with it now and then to make the wooden blades more slippery.

Jon watched her with a wrench in his gut, determined that hell would flare up beneath the ice and melt it before he would join Caitlyn in her carefree dance. She skated with abandon, her legs flashing in the tight, buckskin trousers she wore this evening beneath her wolfskin jacket. Her hair swung from side to side, beams of moonlight brushing it as it danced with her movements.

Without even realizing he had moved, Jon glided silently onto the ice and caught up with her. He wrapped an arm around her waist, and Caitlyn placed her other hand in his and laid her head on his shoulder. She hummed a few bars at first, then sang the words in a lilting voice.

"Oh, Holy Night. The stars are brightly shining. . . . "

Jon held her tighter, and his deeper, baritone voice blended with hers as they sang the rest of the beautiful Christmas carol together.

As the last note faded from both their lips, he whirled Caitlyn into his arms and crushed her mouth with his own.

When he could finally bring himself to break the kiss, he cupped her face between his palms and glared down at her.

"What the hell are you trying to do to me, Caitlyn?"

"Just wishing you a Merry Christmas, Jon," she said as she covered his hands with hers. "Just trying to say I'm sorry I've been such a fool. Christmas should be a time of soul-searching, truth and renewal, don't you think? We can't have peace in our lives if we don't come to terms with our past mistakes."

"You've never acted like you've ever made a mistake in your entire life."

"I have, though. Lots of them. And the one I made a while back was so terrible that it's threatening to destroy my entire life if I don't find some way to correct it."

Jon dropped his hands, but Caitlyn placed hers on his shoulders. He couldn't move away without shoving her aside.

"Can I ask for a present from you for Christmas, Jon?" she whispered. "Just one, though I know I don't deserve it."

"What?"

"Just a few minutes for us to talk together. That's all."

"It's too cold out here."

Jon grabbed her waist again and skated her toward the shore, and Caitlyn's heart collapsed in pain. She didn't resist when he led her to the log and pushed her down, then knelt to remove her skates. After handing them to her, he rose and sat beside her, taking off his own skates with a few sure movements.

He stood, pulling her up with him and slipping his arm around her waist as they started toward the cabin.

"Silas sleeps pretty soundly," he said after a few steps. "We can talk after we get the presents under the tree and he goes to sleep."

The moonlight illuminated Caitlyn's grateful gaze, and Jon paused to brush a perilous tear from her lower lash. "Just don't cry, all right? A person shouldn't cry at Christmastime."

"I won't," Caitlyn promised, hoping with all her might that she could keep that vow.

Chapter Twenty-five

"Don't you dare!"

Startled by Jon's sharp voice, Caitlyn whirled, her hair swirling around her and a wide-eyed, virtuous look on her face. "Don't what? I wasn't...."

"You were trying to see what was in your package," Jon teased. "You thought you'd distract me with cookies and sneak a peek."

"Well, you've got it in a box," Caitlyn said through lips pursed into a pout, but the firelit twinkle in her eyes belied her disgruntlement. "I can't tell what it is anyway."

Silas gave a huge snore from his bunk, smacked his lips and rolled over with his face to the wall. Jon and Caitlyn chuckled under their breaths, and Jon laid his cookie on the table. He walked over to Caitlyn and turned her to face the tree. Slipping his arms around her, he laid his head on her hair and snuggled her close.

"Pretty, isn't it?" he said.

"I always think every year that each tree is the prettiest," she said with a sigh, curling her hands around his and leaning back against his chest.

"Oh, yeah. The tree, too."

"I thought you *were* talking about the tree." She tried to twist in his arms to look up at him, but Jon held her tight, rubbing his chin on her hair.

"Maybe I should have said beautiful instead of pretty," he murmured. "Then you would've known I was referring to you, not the tree."

"Pa always told me that pretty is as pretty does. I haven't been acting very pretty lately."

"And what did your pa say about a man when he acted like a jackass?"

Caitlyn giggled and stroked the back of his hand with her fingers. "That he was a jackass," she admitted. "But. . . ." She managed to wiggle around in his arms and raised her hands to Jon's shoulders. "It hasn't been you, Jon. I . . . stuck my nose somewhere I had no business sticking it, and. . . ."

Jon dropped a kiss on her nose, and smoothed his hands up and down her back as he said, "It's a cute nose. A beautiful nose. God, I've missed you, darlin'."

He bent and touched her lips, sipped them gently, then once more. Caitlyn's lips parted and her breathing quickened when he gently moved his lips back and forth across hers, barely brushing them.

She clenched her fingers on his shoulders, and when Jon groaned and pulled her against him to claim her mouth fully, Caitlyn whimpered with both relief at being in his arms again, where she belonged, and the need to be even closer. Burying her fingers in his hair, she kissed him back with all the banked longing of the last few weeks.

Jon gradually released her mouth, as though he could barely bring himself to break the kiss. He leaned his forehead against hers, his breath panting and his heart thundering in his chest.

"God, Caitlyn. God, I can't believe you're really in my arms again."

Caitlyn buried her face in his neck with a shiver. "You . . . may not want me here, after I tell you how stupid I've been."

"I doubt that very damned much." Jon cupped her chin and tilted her face up for another kiss, then forced himself to release her. "Let's sit on the floor by the fire. I'll get a fur from my bunk for us."

"Silas already spread one out. Didn't you see it while we were putting the presents under the tree?"

"I guess I had my attention on something else," Jon said with a growl. "Come on." He led her over to the fireplace and sat down, pulling Caitlyn onto his lap. "Silas even moved Little Sun's bed so we'd have room to sit here," he mused, stroking the hair away from her face. "I think that old coot's giving us an early Christmas present."

"Not too early," Caitlyn said with a languid sigh, snuggling her head on his shoulder. "It's almost midnight."

Jon ran a finger down her cheek, continuing down her soft neck. "Hum. Then I guess it's not too early to give you a Christmas kiss."

His lips covered hers again and Caitlyn wrapped her arm around his neck, returning his kiss freely. The kiss deepened and Jon probed his tongue around her lips, between them, inside to sweep her mouth. Aching need raced through her, and her breasts surged against his chest. Jon pulled her hips closer to the strain between his legs, then laid back, carrying her with him until she lay on his stomach, cradled on his straining need. He ached for her—not just for any woman—for Caitlyn.

He buried one hand in her hair, clutched her hips and pulled her even tighter against him still. His tongue probed in and out of her mouth in time to the movements of their lower bodies. Suddenly Jon wrenched his mouth free with a gasp.

"Caitlyn! Oh, God, darlin', we have to stop. Otherwise, I'm going to take you right here."

When Caitlyn stared down at him with parted lips and eyes begging him for completion of their loving, Jon closed his eyes to block out her face. Holding her in his arms, he sat up and stared into the fire as their breathing lightened.

"I want you," he finally murmured. "I want you like hell. Every time I hold you like this, I want you more than

I did the last time. But there's no privacy here. Maybe tomorrow. Maybe Silas will take Little Sun . . . sledding . . . or something.''

Finally able to gain control over her own rebellious body, Caitlyn sighed deeply and turned on his lap to face him. "Jon?" she asked softly, continuing when he nodded at her, "Is this still more than wanting? I . . . please tell me I haven't made you quit loving me."

She dropped her eyes and toyed a finger in the rawhide laces on his shirt, unable to face her disappointment if she saw the wrong answer on his face.

"What do you think?" he whispered.

"I . . . think. . . . '' She wrapped the end of the lace around her finger. "I think . . . I *know* I still love you—I never stopped, though I kept lying to myself, saying I had."

Jon removed the lace from her finger and carried her hand to his mouth. "I love you, Caitlyn. I love you more than life. Are you going to tell me what's behind all this?"

"Yes," she murmured. "I said I was, didn't I? It's just . . . I . . . oh, Jon, I read the letter," she finally blurted. "And saw the little painting."

Jon nibbled her fingers for another second. "What letter?" he said, licking a crevice between two of her fingers. "Oh." He flicked his tongue across her palm. "You mean the letter from Charlie and that small painting of his little boy?"

"Jon, please," she begged as she pulled her hand away. "You're acting like it's not important at all."

"It's important," he said with a sigh of loss as he glanced at her hand. Finally he looked into her frowning face. "I guess it's damned important, if it made you want to stop loving me. But I still don't understand why."

"Did you look at that painting, Jon? And read the letter?"

"Yeah. So?"

"Men!" Caitlyn muttered. She straightened and folded her arms beneath her breasts. "Were you in love with your brother's wife before they got married?"

"No," Jon said, sending a quiver of hope through Caitlyn, but it slowly faded as he continued. "What I felt for Roxie wasn't love, though I might have thought so at the time. It wasn't until I fell in love with you that I knew what real love was."

"But . . . but the baby."

"People have babies after they get married," Jon informed her with a grin. "Sometimes before that."

"That's what I mean," Caitlyn insisted. "Jon, do you and your brother look like each other?"

"No, not really. He's one of those men you women call tall, dark and handsome."

Caitlyn shuttered her eyes in pain, and Jon ran his hands up and down her arms in comfort.

"Caitlyn? What is it? Why all these questions that don't make sense?"

"Did . . . did you make love to Roxie while you were courting her?"

"No," Jon denied. "That wasn't making love. Making love is what I do with you."

"But you did bed her?" Caitlyn demanded.

"Caitlyn. . . ."

"Jon, that letter says that the baby was born early. And that painting is not of a baby born to a tall, dark father."

Jon stiffened and his hands fell to his legs. "No. Christ, Caitlyn, he can't be. I mean. . . ."

"Did you or did you not bed her?" Caitlyn demanded again.

Jon refused to answer her, staring over her shoulder into the firelight. Caitlyn reached up to caress his cheek.

"That at least tells me something," she said softly. "You didn't know, did you? Would . . . would you have married her, if you had known?"

"Probably," Jon admitted in a dry voice. "Probably," he whispered.

"Jon, maybe . . . well, maybe she was also sleeping with your brother. Maybe she didn't know which. . . ."

"They hadn't slept together yet four days before their wedding," Jon told her in a quiet voice, flickering out that tiny flame of hope. "Charlie let me know that. He's mine.

He has to be. Damn her! Damn her to hell!''

Caitlyn sat unmoving, fighting her own hurt and the desire she felt to comfort Jon in his pain. Mouth tight with anger, he glared past her, reflected flames from the fire highlighting the fury in his eyes. The silent room mocked the raging emotions she could sense him trying to control.

She'd never been afraid of Jon before—not physically, though she had been deathly afraid of the emotional pain she would feel if he'd told her tonight that she had killed his love. Hesitantly, she reached her hand up to his cheek again.

"Jon?"

Jon grabbed her close and buried his face in her neck. "Damn, it hurts, Caitlyn. Almost as much as it did when I thought I'd lost you."

"Jon, talk to me about it. Please."

"Sure," he said with a fierce grunt of torment. He raised his head in order to see her face. "How the hell can I sit here with the woman I love in my arms and talk to her about a baby I had with another woman?"

"I'm not saying that it won't hurt me to hear about it, Jon. But it's real. It's happened. It's something we have to deal with."

Jon shook his head and a blond curl fell over his forehead, which Caitlyn tenderly pushed back into place.

"There isn't any way to deal with it," he muttered "Charlie's raising him as his own son. It'd tear him apart to know Roxie had tricked him—that the boy was mine."

"I agree," Caitlyn told him. "But I was talking about dealing with it between us—since, thank God, you told me there still is an us."

"You're damned right there is, and there's going to be forever. We're not going to let anything like this happen between us again, Caitlyn. When you've got something to ask me about, you ask it. Hear me, woman?"

"I hear you, man," she said with a soft chuckle. "And now you do the same to me. Talk to me. Tell me about it."

With a wry twist to his lips, Jon said, "Roxie was. . . . "

"No!" Caitlyn covered his mouth and shook her head. "Not that part. I don't think I want to hear that part."

Jon carefully removed her hand and held it in his. "She's part of it, darlin'. I can't tell you about any of it without including her. You have to understand what a deceitful, vicious bitch I finally realized she was."

A smile curved Caitlyn's lips. "Well, if that's how it is, I guess I can listen to that."

"I'll bet you can," Jon said with a disgruntled laugh. "And you can sit there and think to yourself what a stupid jackass I was, with me confirming that fact with every word I say."

"I'll try not to," Caitlyn said with a smirk. "But it's awfully hard for people to control their thoughts sometimes."

Jon growled and bit her on the neck, and Caitlyn smothered her laughter, so she wouldn't wake Silas. "Jon." She pushed on his shoulders, trying desperately to control her giggles. "Jon, stop it. You . . . can't talk . . . with my . . . neck in your mouth."

"Ummmm." He licked a path up to her ear. "I'd rather have your neck in my mouth than words admitting to you how dumb I used to be."

"You know," Caitlyn forced past a gasp of pleasure, "I think I'd rather that, too."

"Well, at least I'm glad to hear that. But. . . . " He kissed her briefly, then settled her more comfortably on his lap. "But you're right. I have to tell you about it."

Jon spoke in a low voice, also aware that Silas lay only a few feet away. He explained how he and most of his friends looked at their futures always with the idea in their minds that a woman who would be a good match for their own social status would one day be their wife. Once in a while they mused that it would be nice to fall in love, but that wasn't necessarily a requirement. Bloodlines and an equally large fortune rated highest on the list.

And evidently, Jon admitted, the women carried a similar list in their minds after they reached a marriageable age. Obviously, Roxie had. Luckily they hadn't announced a formal betrothal, the breaking of which would have been treated as a scandal when Roxie changed her mind and decided to marry Charlie.

"Silas told me some of it," Caitlyn admitted into the silence when Jon appeared to be trying to gather his thoughts to tell her the rest. "Your half-brother got the entire plantation, and you were cut completely out of the will. I guess Roxie wanted the brother with the money."

"Yeah," Jon said ruefully. "And she charmed Charlie into having the wedding within a month of his father's death, even though he was officially still in mourning. Now I know why. She was already carrying my baby."

"A seven- or eight-month baby is a lot easier to explain than one born in less time than that. Even if you were of a mind to do anything about it, it would be hard for you to prove the baby wasn't just early, like she told your brother."

"This changes everything, you know," Jon mused. "Charlie wrote that the plantation's in trouble. Hell, I didn't give a shit when I rode away from there if it went bankrupt within a year, and I was pretty sure that might happen. Charlie never could manage the money end of it. He was better with the crops."

Caitlyn stiffened in his arms. "What . . . what do you mean by that?"

"It's my son's heritage, Caitlyn. He's mine, but Charlie doesn't know that. He'll leave everything to his first born. I'll have to go back—see what I can do to make sure there's something for him to inherit someday."

"I . . . see."

"You better *see* this, too, Caitlyn. You're going with me. I want you to marry me, be my wife. You don't think I'm going to leave you behind, do you? Not after I've realized that all those friends of mine were wrong. You can find a wife you also love. I love you, Caitlyn. Marry me. Please."

Caitlyn wrung her hands together in her lap, biting her bottom lip until she thought it would tear in two, fighting against the 'yes' she wanted to scream loud enough to wake up Silas and everyone or everything else that heard. She couldn't. No matter how badly she wanted to be Jon's wife, she couldn't marry him.

"Caitlyn."

"I . . . can't," she whispered. "I can't."

Rather than throw her from his lap in disgust, as she expected Jon to do, he chuckled and shook his head tolerantly.

"Uh uh, Caitlyn, darlin'. You're not going to get by with that. I've bared my soul to you, and you're not clamming up on me without explaining why you're saying no to me, when I know damned well you want to say yes."

Caitlyn shot him a sideways glance from under her lashes. Her mouth moved into a mutinous pout. At least he could have looked a little disappointed. Instead, he stared at her with that darned smirk on his face, waiting with a self-assurance that pricked her temper. She turned her head away, refusing to speak.

"Caitlyn, didn't we just promise that we'd talk to each other about things? You're breaking your promise already."

"We didn't say that," she denied. "You ordered me to. I didn't agree."

"That's splitting hairs, darlin'." He picked up a handful of her raven hair and gently caressed it against his cheek. "And you've got such beautiful hair. I love your hair. Have I ever told you how much I love your hair?"

Caitlyn clenched her jaws, and Jon released her hair to run a fingertip across her lips.

"Talk to me, Caitlyn. Please, darlin'."

Caitlyn shook her head in defiance. She couldn't tell him. Her secret was much worse than Jon's. It went to the very core of her womanhood. No man would want a woman like her for a wife, especially Jon. Maybe a mistress, but never a wife.

"All right," Jon said with an exasperated sigh. "I guess I'll just have to try and figure it out on my own. Let's see."

He cocked his head to one side and studied her. "Surely you aren't thinking of what I said when I mentioned what I used to look for in a wife. Caitlyn, I don't give a damn about how you've been raised or the fact that you don't have a large dowry to offer. I'm far from rich myself, though I've got enough for us to get started with, or will have after this trapping season. And the only bloodline I'm interested in is the bloodline our children will have from the two of us.''

Caitlyn's gasp of anguish told Jon that he had finally hit close to the mark of whatever distressed her. He took her shoulders and turned her to face him, but she wouldn't meet his gaze, shuttering her eyes with her lashes.

''Caitlyn?''

Chapter Twenty-six

Caitlyn wrenched free and scrambled to her feet. Crossing her arms, she dug her fingers tight, trying to transfer the pain in her mind to her body. It didn't work. Her shattered thoughts swirled in her head, finally centering into a core of torment that nearly took her breath away.

"Caitlyn," Jon said quietly. "I'm not going away. And you don't have to talk to me, but you *will* marry me. I'll just tell the preacher that you're mute and have a stiff neck, so you can't nod your head. At least the stiff neck part won't be a lie."

A half sob of laughter escaped her, and Caitlyn lifted her chin. "It's not the bloodline part of it, Jon," she finally forced out. "I . . . I've been reading my mother's journal, and I want to give it to you to read, too. I guess I've got just as good a bloodline—probably better—than those silly southern belles you were trying to find a wife among back east."

"I told you that didn't matter, sweetheart. I've known since the first time I saw you that there was something special about you. We'll have plenty of time to talk about that, though. Right now, I want to. . . . ''

"Damn it, Jon," Caitlyn swore, facing him with her eyes flashing fury rather than firelight. "What's the whole point of what we've been talking about the last hour?"

"You and me. Us."

"No! We've talked about your son—a son that you love so much, even if you haven't seen him yet, that you're going back to make sure his heritage is safe for him. And look how much you love Little Sun! You even said that marriage was important to you because you wanted children of your own. They were even more important than the wife you chose!"

"Are you telling me that you can't have children, sweetheart?" Jon asked, unable to keep a tinge of disappointment from his voice.

Caitlyn bit her lip again and shook her head violently.

"It won't matter," Jon soothed, rising to his feet and trying to take her in his arms. "There's plenty of kids who need a home. . . . ''

Caitlyn swept his arms aside and turned her tearful face up to his. "You still don't understand. It's not that I can't. I mean, I don't really know if I can or can't. It's that I won't. You want a wife who'll bear your children, and I won't have a child." She collapsed against Jon's chest. "I won't, I won't!"

Jon rocked her against him, murmuring soothing sounds and dropping kisses on her hair. He held her until her shoulders stopped quaking, then drew her back down in front of the fire. Cuddling her close, he stroked her back.

"Does this have something to do with Reggie?" he asked, and Caitlyn nodded her head against his chest. "Can you tell me about it?"

She shook her head negatively.

"It's after midnight by now," Jon said, seeming to comply with Caitlyn's refusal to discuss her denial of childbearing with him. "Remember what day it is, Caitlyn?"

She raised her head and swiped at her cheek, glancing across the shadowy room to the pine tree in front of the window. The lantern hanging from the ceiling, turned low, cast a subdued light on the Caitlyn angel that Jon had carved, now gracing the top of the tree. Here and there a sugar sparkle gleamed on a cookie dangling from a branch.

Beneath the silent symbol of the season, the presents lay scattered—one from each of them to the other three. Though wrapped in brown paper, the only thing available, Caitlyn had tied a hair ribbon around each of her packages for decoration. Under the presents, she had spread the white fur from an albino wolf Pa had trapped one winter.

"It's Christmas Day," she murmured quietly.

"Yeah, Christ's birthday," Jon agreed. "You know, I've never been an overly religious man, though Charlie and I found our butts parked on a church pew practically every Sunday, and always on Christmas Day. I thought about something once, but the Sunday School teacher acted like I was blaspheming when I asked her about it."

"What was that?" Caitlyn asked with a sniff.

"I asked her if she didn't think Mary was awfully scared when she had her baby. I mean, Joseph evidently knew it wasn't his child, since I seemed to recall that Joseph knew about the Immaculate Conception end of it. And not only was Mary probably worrying that Joseph might leave her one day because of doubts about that, but she was in a stable. A cold stable, meant for animals to live in, without another woman around to help her in the birth."

"She . . . she was awfully brave," Caitlyn admitted.

"That wasn't all she was brave about, don't you think? The Sunday School teacher told me to shut up, but I thought about it several times. I'll bet Mary was frightened that she wouldn't be a good mother to that baby."

Caitlyn gasped softly, and Jon soothed her again with his hands.

"I mean, this was God's child. And Mary was only a mortal woman. She must have been scared to death that she'd fall short of the expectations God had of her in raising His child. Maybe not be a good influence on him. That she might let something happen to the baby."

"Oh, Jon."

"Is that what you're afraid of, Caitlyn? That you might

lose a child of ours, like you lost your brother Reggie? Do
you think you should have done something to keep him
from dying?''

"You . . . don't know . . . what happened.''

"Just some of it," Jon admitted. "Silas knows the story
that was told in the mountains when Mick showed up with
you. You can tell me all of it whenever you want to. But
you shouldn't be carrying that guilt with you now, sweetheart. Surely by now you realize there wasn't anything you
could do. You were only what? Five or so?''

Once again Caitlyn recalled how small she felt, curled
up in that huge tree trunk—how helpless. How huge the
warriors looked as they strode past her, toward her mother's
hiding place. The one who had reappeared to do his victory
dance towered skyward, to her young mind almost reaching
the treetops.

She remembered the smell of blood and quickly chased
it from her mind by breathing deeply of the pine scent
filling the cabin.

"I can't help it, Jon. I'm . . . not really afraid of *having*
a baby. Females have babies all the time—animals and humans.''

"It's the possibility of losing it after you have it, isn't
it?" Jon asked.

When Caitlyn nodded again, Jon went on, "There aren't
many promises in life, darlin'. But I will promise you this.
We'll wait until you're ready. There's ways we can. . . . ''
Jon frowned at her. "Caitlyn, you already know some way
to keep from having a baby, don't you? Otherwise, you
wouldn't have made love with me.''

Caitlyn quirked her lips at him and peeked from beneath
her lashes. "You mean you didn't just sweep me off my
feet and over beneath the pine tree that day with your masculine charm? Wipe everything from my mind except my
wanting you?''

Jon rolled her onto the floor and covered her with his
body. "I'll show you my masculine charm," he growled.

She giggled wildly and thrashed under him, forgetting

that Silas lay near. Jon kissed her neck while he wiggled his fingers on her ribs.

"Stop," she gasped. "Oh, Jon, don't. You know I'm ticklish!"

He kissed her ear, kissed her eyes closed, and moved his hands up to her breasts. But when she reached for his face to try to pull him close for a kiss on her lips, Jon shook his head.

"Uh uh." He moved his fingers back down to her ribs. "No more kisses until you say you'll marry me."

"Jon," she pleaded.

He wiggled his fingers just a tad. "Will you?"

Caitlyn grabbed his hands to still them, her eyes twinkling merrily up at him. "What was the question again? And why?"

"You little minx."

Jon pulled her up and left her in front of the fireplace for a second to carry one of the chairs over from the table. Setting it down, he gently pushed her into the seat, then stood studying her in the firelight.

Her hair fell gloriously down her back, raven black and shining even in the dim light. He hadn't even come close to capturing the beauty of her face when he carved the angel. It would take a master painter to portray those uniquely-Caitlyn features—satin curves of cheekbone and china-blue eyes large enough for a man to drown in, outlined by a thick fringe of ebony lashes.

A cute nose—he couldn't call it anything else, since it could wrinkle at him in mischief, or serve as a point for her to gaze across at him with haughty disdain. The lips, still pouting from her lost kiss, beckoned him almost beyond the bounds of his control.

Caitlyn wiggled on the chair. "Jon, quit staring at me," she whispered, a tinge of embarrassment in her voice.

"Hush, honey."

One day he would have her portrait painted just like this. In front of a fireplace at night, the flickering flames shadowing her face with a beauty that tore at his gut. She'd be dressed in buckskin, the soft leather caressing her skin like a glove—like his hands longed to do right now. And there had to be a Christmas tree in the painting—a reminder to them both of this sacred night.

He knelt on one knee.

"Jon!" Caitlyn bent forward and tugged on his shoulders, trying to get him back on his feet. "That's not necessary."

Jon took her hands and folded them onto her lap, covering them with his. "I love you, Caitlyn O'Shaunessy. . . ."

"O'Neal," Caitlyn interrupted. "I found out from my mother's journal that my real last name's O'Neal."

Jon raised his eyes to the ceiling in exasperation. "Damn it, Caitlyn. Will you shut up for a minute?"

"Well!" she said around pursed lips. "If you're so intent on doing this right, I want you to use my real name. And I'd prefer that you didn't curse at me."

Jon choked on a chuckle, then bowed his head for a moment. When he looked back at Caitlyn, she caught her breath at the depth of love shining from his blue eyes.

"I love you, Caitlyn O'Neal," Jon said sincerely. "Will you marry me?"

Caitlyn jerked her hands free and flung them around his neck. "Yes. Yes, Jon. I love you! Yes, I'll marry you!"

The force of her lunge threw them both back down onto the fur on the floor, and their muffled laughter skittered through the room as they tried to untangle themselves. When he at last freed himself, Jon quickly flipped Caitlyn beneath him. Hovering over her, he whispered, "I love you, Caitlyn, with all my heart," before he kissed her.

Silas opened his eyes for a brief second, then winked at the wall in front of him. "Merry Christmas, my old pard, Mick," he whispered gruffly.

Chapter Twenty-seven

As she had every morning for the past two and a half months, Caitlyn reached from beneath the covers and picked up the music box on the bedside table. She wound the key and set it back. Crawling out of bed, she scurried into her clothing as the strains of "Greensleeves" tinkled through her room.

And, as she did every morning, she recalled Jon's face on Christmas morning as he watched her tear eagerly at the brown paper around her present. Remembered her own joy and awe as she gingerly lifted out the music box, memories of the day she and Jon had found it crowding her mind.

But the most precious memory was the remembrance of the sense she'd had of Jon's own pleasure in giving her the gift—not only the music box, but also a keepsake of her time with Pa. Her grief had mellowed now—replaced in part with her love for Jon. Pa would always be there—after all, what she had become was a reflection of Pa's raising. And she had become the woman Jon loved.

She frowned and hesitated before pulling back the blanket over her doorway. She loved Jon—totally and completely. But he had his faults, that darn persistence of his being her main peeve.

Well, not the persistence he showed in managing to find a stolen hour here and there for them to make love. That took a measure of ingenuity she just had to admire, especially during the blustery January and February days just past. The frequent blizzards kept Silas at the cabin more often, and Little Sun napped shorter periods as he grew.

Silas didn't seem to see through the thin excuses Jon found to return to the cabin early—or to stay behind for a little while on his scheduled days to run the lines. Carrying water for her from the lake on wash day always worked, though that day sometimes fell during a time lovemaking had to be denied. A day she feared she might get with child—or a day during her monthly courses, which thankfully appeared each month.

But she wished he'd forget about that darned journal. She'd left that world behind—as had her mother. Maybe one day she would want to visit Ireland. If so, she would do it anonymously, only to have a first-hand look at the relatives her mother had fled.

Quietly, Caitlyn slipped into the main room of the cabin. She loved this time of morning, when she could look at her small family, still abed, to her heart's content.

Little Sun lay on his back, one arm upflung over his head. She padded over, her moccasins silent on the pine floor, and snugged his blanket up around his shoulders.

Silas always grumbled and snorted for several minutes before he came fully awake, and just then she heard the first preparatory snort as he rolled from his stomach to his back.

Jon. Jon came awake in an instant. She could sense the change in him even the mornings she worked across the room, busy at the fireplace, with her back to him.

Cheek pillowed on his palm, he lay still asleep right now. Lordy, she didn't know how it was possible, but each morning when she looked at him, she loved him more. His blond hair fell across his forehead, begging for her fingers to brush it back in place, **and his slight**ly parted lips invited her own for a kiss.

With the longer days of the approaching mountain spring, more light filtered into the cabin on these early mornings. She could see Jon's gold-tipped lashes against his cheeks. Suddenly he opened his eyes, focusing unerringly on her and sending a thrill of tenderness coursing through her.

"Morning, darlin'," he whispered just loud enough to reach her ears.

"Morning," Caitlyn breathed.

Jon sat up, reaching for his britches at the end of the bunk. He wore his two-piece longjohns—the ones she had washed for him yesterday on wash day—but she knew the feel of his skin beneath the material way too well for the wool to conceal the pleasure the layers of muscles and sinews gave her. She crossed the room as he stood and pulled on his britches, lifting her face for their private, morning kiss as she drew near.

Jon granted her silent request, drawing her close and threading his fingers through her still unbound hair.

"I love you, sweetheart," he said when he lifted his head.

Caitlyn wrapped her arms around his waist and snuggled against his chest. "Yes, I think I remember you saying that a time or two yesterday."

"And I believe you admitted it a time or two yourself," he growled in a low voice. "In between the times you begged me to make you my own."

She buried her nose deeper in his chest to hide her blushing cheeks. Jon's smothered laughter rumbled, the rhythm of it rippling against her forehead, and she bunched the hem of his longjohn shirt upward, then scraped a fingernail lightly against that ticklish spot she had found on his waist.

"Hey," Jon whispered with a chuckle as he caught her hand. "Quit that, or I'll start laughing loud enough to wake up Silas and the boy. And I wanted us to slip out and watch the sunrise together this morning."

Caitlyn stepped back and nodded her agreement, a smile

of contentment on her face. "Let's do. I'll just get the fire started while you finish dressing."

"Do it quietly," Jon ordered with a mock frown. "I'm not in the mood for company with us this morning."

Caitlyn mimicked a curtsey of compliance before she walked back to the fireplace. As fresh flames curled around her kindling a few minutes later, she glanced at the doorway in answer to Jon's hiss for her attention.

"I'll meet you outside," he mouthed as he pointed at the door.

Caitlyn nodded, and he opened the door, closing it softly behind him. She propped a few larger pieces of wood over the kindling, then rose and padded over to where her jacket hung beside the door. As noiselessly as Jon, she made her escape into the predawn wilderness.

As always, the lovely black and white world almost took her breath away. A few stars still glinted overhead, their normal glitter muted to a hazy glow. Shoulder-high banks of snow surrounded her, but she walked up the gradual rise in the path ahead of her until she stood above the drifts. Alternate freezes and thaws had settled the snow into a firm foundation to walk across, except for a few inches of new flakes that had fallen during the night.

Towering trees loomed way higher than the snowdrifts—pines sooty black instead of green without the sun to highlight their color where the snow had dropped from their branches. Birch, their black-veined trunks gray-white in contrast to the milky snow, grew in profusion. Stark, denuded oak and maple branches stretched leaflessly upward, forming helter-skelter jumbles against the sky.

Soaring mountains overrode it all, their tips almost kissing the fading stars. The icy clarity of the frigid air made everything appear close enough to touch, yet much too beautiful to make the attempt.

Caitlyn saw Jon waiting on the edge of the clearing. He opened his arms, and she raced across the newly fallen snow, scattering flakes that misted her feet the same way her puffs of breath floated around her face.

Instead of hugging her close, Jon grabbed her at the waist

and lifted her into the air. He whirled her around twice, kissing her into further dizziness after he lowered her body back toward earth.

Caitlyn broke the kiss first, with a gasp. "I thought we came out here to watch the sunrise!"

"That was just an excuse to get you alone so I could get my hands on you without four other eyes watching," Jon admitted around a satisfied grin. "But if you want, you can watch the sunrise and I'll watch you watching it. I don't want to overload myself with beauty this early in the morning. There's a plateful of it right here in my arms."

"Ummmm, how you do go on," Caitlyn said with a look that encouraged him to continue his wonderful flattery. "I suppose you think you can turn a girl's head with those pretty words and have your way with her."

"I can." Jon nuzzled her nose. "I don't have to think about it. I know I can."

Caitlyn swatted his shoulder, then turned in his arms to face the east, already tinged a faint pink. She heard Jon muffle a grunt of annoyance, but she reached back and pulled his arms around her.

"I can't see you as well this way," Jon grumbled.

Caitlyn patted his hands as though comforting Little Sun. "Watch the sunrise," she commanded.

Jon propped his chin on her head and obeyed for a while. The pink brightened to crimson, lightening the charcoal sky overhead until it shaded toward blue. The mountaintops sawtoothed through the blazing colors that foreshadowed the new day—colors that imperceptibly changed the clouds from blood-red to magenta, lightened them to lilac, then, as the blue of the sky deepened, allowed their true, storm-dark color to appear.

"Looks like more snow today," Jon murmured.

"Um hum. But it won't last too many more weeks—at least the hard storms won't. Spring will start breaking through in another month or so. After we sell the furs at rendezvous, we can go on to Richmond. I'm sure you'll be able to help your brother get everything straightened out."

"Yep. And maybe somewhere during our trip back into

civilization, we'll find a minister to marry us. We might have to wait until we get back to St. Louis, unless there's a minister with one of the rendezvous pack trains. One came out with them last summer—not that very many of the men paid much attention to him.''

"Mountain men are religious, Jon," Caitlyn said, tilting her head to look over her shoulder at him. "It's just that they've come out here to avoid those same restrictions ministers spout at times. They don't feel it's anybody's business but their own if they have a few drinks now and then—or even get drunk if they want to. They live by their own creed, and it says a man's loyalty to his friends is even more important than his own life. And they think living their lives being true to themselves and their friends is more important than paying some preacher to keep their souls out of a hell that may or may not be there.''

"Sounds like some Mick O'Shaunessy philosophy to me," Jon said, tapping her cute nose with a fingertip. "Did Mick run away from something back in Ireland, too?''

"Pa came out here from New York City," Caitlyn told him. "He was born in this country, not Ireland. But he said he couldn't stand the poverty the Irish were forced to live in back there—the low-life jobs his father had to take to support his mother and the other six children in their family. The children couldn't even go to school—they had to pick up rags almost as soon as they could walk. Then go to work in those factories when they were old enough, just so their family could have two meager meals a day!''

"I know, darlin'," Jon said. "Some of the slaveholders in Virginia don't treat their blacks much better than that.''

"Huh. Pa said in a way it was sometimes worse than that. The slaves at least usually got fed every day, so they could go out and work again. Every mouthful of food Pa and his family put in their stomachs, they had to scrape together the money to buy. And if they couldn't work, they didn't eat. Winters were especially rough, when the shipping and docks were slow.''

"I . . .'' Jon began.

"Where was all that religious love for their fellow man

while babies died of hunger and children turned old before they were in their teens, Jon? Pa ran away when he was barely eleven and worked his way west. He never went back. Never saw anyone in his family again.''

''Like your mother never went back to Ireland?''

''You read the journal. You know she didn't.''

''Caitlyn, there's something else in that journal about why she left. . . . ''

''Phooey. That's . . . what's that word I learned in one of your books? Archaic, that's it. Jon, I'm not about to worry over the fact that some man who calls himself my grandfather—who I can't even remember—is upset because my mother married a man he thought was beneath her. Mama didn't accept him trying to dictate how she should live her life—insisting she marry a man she didn't love after she was widowed. She married my stepfather, James, instead, and came to America with him.''

Jon studied her resolute face for a moment. This could quickly escalate into an argument, and that had definitely not been what he had in mind when they escaped the cabin to have a few minutes alone in the breaking morning. But his nagging suspicions just wouldn't quit.

''Caitlyn, there's a caste system in Ireland that's pretty rigid. Who a man's daughter marries reflects on hundreds of years of family history.''

''Mama evidently didn't agree with that. It's as archaic,'' Caitlyn repeated, liking the way the new word rolled from her tongue, ''to think you can force a woman into marriage these days as it is for you and your friends to think bloodlines are more important than love in a marriage. Morning Star left her family behind to be with Spirit Eagle because she loved him so much. She knew she would be banned and that she was breaking their customs. Besides, Mama defying my grandfather happened over fifteen years ago, Jon. It doesn't have anything to do with me now.''

Fifteen years against hundreds of years of family history. But Caitlyn probably couldn't even imagine that, since she had been raised among the mountain men. Those men, though loyal to one another, as Caitlyn said, still valued their freedom and independence above all else. They met once a year—visited and caroused—then slipped back into their mostly solitary lives for the rest of the year.

She'd even admitted to him once that she hadn't allowed herself to be close to any Indian family with small children, because her nightmares always returned.

He'd tried to discuss this with Caitlyn before, though, and he knew he had to handle her gently, as he had promised he would. He chuckled under his breath and dropped a kiss on her lips. "Reading your mother's journal was almost like reading about you, sweetheart. You're a lot like her."

"I hope so. I admire her almost as much as I love her. And from what I can remember, she loved Reggie and me an awful lot. She even gave up her life for me."

Dog loped toward them, barking a greeting and jumping at Caitlyn. She dropped her hands from Jon's shoulders and grabbed Dog's furry ruff.

"Good morning," she said as she dug her fingers into his fur. "I guess this means Silas is up, and probably Little Sun, too. You didn't get out of the cabin by yourself."

Dog slurped her cheek in answer, then dropped back to his feet and trotted off into the trees. A second later, a snowshoe rabbit bounded out into the clearing, with Dog howling gleefully at its heels. The two animals raced around the clearing before disappearing once again into the woods.

"Dog's just playing with it," Jon said in response to Caitlyn's worried look. "He won't kill it. He's too well fed to have to catch his food."

"I hope you're right. That's the rabbit that hops out here and lets Little Sun watch it mornings when we come outside to get some air. He's got that one black ear."

Dog ran out of the woods again. He hit a soft spot in the snow and floundered wildly until he crawled out of the hole. Shaking the snow from his coat, he stared at Jon and Caitlyn, a look on his furry face that could only be reproach for their laughter. They laughed harder, and Dog sat on his haunches, turning his face away.

"I swear," Jon said with a guffaw, "that animal acts human sometimes."

"What do you expect?" Caitlyn said around her giggles. "He doesn't have another dog around to show him any different."

"Look."

Jon pointed at the woods as the rabbit hopped a few steps into the clearing. It stopped, nose wiggling and its black ear standing at attention, the white one lying against its back. Dog caught sight of it, and the chase began again.

"They're just working off their high spirits," Jon said, wrapping an arm around Caitlyn's waist to walk her down the path. "Hope Dog doesn't get too tired to pull the sled for us today."

"Did Silas tell you how Dog laid down and refused to help us keep looking for a Christmas tree that day?"

"If I heard the story right," Jon teased, "Dog refused to help *you* keep looking for that tree."

"I wanted it to be the right one—for a special day."

At the cabin door, Jon pulled her into his arms. "It was a special day. It will always be one of the most special days in my life."

He kissed her lingeringly, tasting her mouth in that extraordinary way only Jon had. Caitlyn gave him back caress for caress, whimper for growl of flaring passion. With similar, reluctant sighs, they drew apart.

"I guess we should go in, darlin'."

"I guess so."

"Caitlyn. . . . "

"Hum?"

"About that stuff in the journal. . . . "

"Oh, for pity sakes, Jon. Look, all this bloodline business just isn't important to me. I've lived all this time without worrying about who my family was, what kind of people they were. Pa was my father, and I was perfectly happy to be with him."

"Caitlyn. . . . "

She softened her voice. "Jon, I know you were raised differently—you had family around you all the time. You had rules to go by—expectations they had of you. When I meet your family, I'll do my darndest to make you proud of me.''

''I already am proud of you, sweetheart. So damned proud I could bust. But you've got to realize that sometimes there's family obligations a person can't just walk away from. Things that are part of your life.''

Caitlyn patted his cheek. ''We already talked about that, Jon. I won't stand in your way of making sure your son's taken care of. Now.'' She reached to open the door. ''I better get in there and see about breakfast for everyone.''

Halfway through the door, she turned back to him. ''Are you coming?''

''I'll be there in a minute.''

Caitlyn blew him a surreptitious kiss, then closed the door, and Jon frowned at the wood barrier. After a second, he stuck his hands into the pockets of his robe and turned to walk back up the path.

Darn, he loved her, but sometimes the very same guilelessness and openness that had drawn him to Caitlyn in the beginning rankled him. She expected the world around her to abide by the same philosophy she practiced herself. Live and let live. Accept what you have, what you can do for yourself and your friends, and don't worry about what the rest of the world thinks.

It didn't work that way, as Jon well knew. The plantation and Clay fortune were a hell of a lot more important to Roxie than love in her marriage. Poor Charlie had a hefty measure of the same naivete as Caitlyn, and now he was probably paying the price. Jon would bet his entire small bank account to the last dime that part of the plantation's money problems came from the lavish lifestyle Roxie preferred.

Jon could have handled that in Roxie, but his much milder mannered brother wouldn't have a clue as to how to deny Roxie anything she set her mind to having. Charlie had a huge measure of the Clay family pride, too, and he wouldn't want his wife whining to her friends that her husband couldn't support her.

Family pride. That's what bothered Jon about the journal. Though society didn't place quite as stringent codes on women in this country, certain expectations remained. Had Roxie and he already formally announced their betrothal, the scandal when she recanted it and married Charlie— Jon's own brother—would have soured her reputation. And reputation meant almost as much to Roxie as money.

Roxie's father might even have put his foot down and demanded that the originally planned marriage take place to avoid a slur on their family name. How much more adamant in avoiding a family disgrace might Caitlyn's grandfather be? How far would he go to erase or correct that humiliation?

The fact that Caitlyn had escaped the Blackfoot massacre was common knowledge in the mountains. Had word of the rest of her family's fate traveled back to their homeland? Had it been one of Jon's family members, he knew the answer to that. When his Uncle Jonathan had been reported missing at sea, the ships that provided the fortune to that branch of the family had scoured the ocean until they found him.

But they had scoured the seas in the name of love, not revenge. Would Caitlyn's grandfather—from what Jon could tell from the journal, an evidently influential man from a well-placed Irish family—have been pursuing his daughter's betrayal in a misguided effort to clear his family name?

Caitlyn's recollection of Morning Star and Spirit Eagle's love was all one-sided. She deliberately refused to discuss the other side of the situation. Didn't she remember how frightened she had been when Tall Man found her caring for Little Sun—the child of the man who had caused him to lose face with his people? Did she really think Tall Man would forget his quest for vengeance while he and Spirit Eagle both walked this earth?

Family pride. When mixed with a desire for vengeance, Jon couldn't imagine a deadlier set of circumstances. Could the man trying to find Caitlyn at rendezvous last summer have been sent on a vengeance mission? His devious behavior seemed to indicate he meant Caitlyn no good if he found her.

He could do nothing right now, though. Snowed-in mountain passes precluded any travel at all until spring. Even then, if they started out too early, a deadly avalanche could end their journey with their deaths.

A feather-light breeze caressed Jon's face, and he opened his buffalo skin robe to cool the sweatiness on his body.

"Hurry up, Spring," he murmured before he shrugged out of his robe and headed back to the cabin.

Chapter Twenty-eight

"Damn boring, this time of year, ain't it, Jon?" Silas grumbled from his seat on a log beside the woodpile.

"Boring?" Jon split the piece of wood on the ground in front of him with a sure stroke. "Hell, there's plenty to do, if you'd help me do it. You want to winter up here next season, you're gonna need wood. You know that as well as I do. And you might want to clean and oil those traps before we store them away. Otherwise, they'll rust over the summer. A half-dozen or so of them need a chain or a spring fixed, too."

Jon leaned on his ax and wiped his forehead. Spring, long awaited, had finally made a tentative arrival.

"Aw, I ain't real sure I want to come up here alone, boyo. Depends on what furs are goin' for this summer. Get me a good enough bank roll, I might just set the next season out."

"Whatever you decide, I want you to stand up with me at our wedding."

"Figured you'd want your brother to do that," Silas said gruffly, but Jon caught the hint of pleasure in his voice.

"A fellow's best man should be his best friend, Silas," Jon said with a smile at the old man. "And I'm not waiting until we get back to Virginia to get married. The first minister we can find is going to get the privilege of marrying Caitlyn and me."

" 'Fraid she might change her mind?" Silas asked with a chuckle.

Jon winked at his partner, a broad grin on his face. "I'm not about to give her the chance."

"I wish you both the best, you know that, don't you, boyo? And I know you'll take care of Cat. Ol' Mad Mick, he'd've liked you, Jon."

"I appreciate hearing that, Silas. And you can damned well bet every fur you trapped this winter that Caitlyn will never want for anything if it's within my power to give her."

Silas slapped his knees and stood, though Jon saw a grimace of slight pain in his partner's narrowed eyes. He and Caitlyn had discussed the joint aches that had plagued Silas more and more over the winter, and both of them had tried to do the bulk of the labor when they ran lines with Silas. Once in a while they had even received his agreement to stay behind and care for Little Sun, while they checked the lines themselves.

Not that the effort paid off real well in the late winter months. The animals that weren't hibernating carried coats that showed signs of wear and the lack of winter forage. Still, the trips kept cabin fever at bay and, more importantly, kept them from getting on each other's nerves.

"Think I'll take my old pony out for some exercise," Silas mused. "Reckon Little Sun might like to go along?"

"I reckon he might, Silas. He sure does like to ride."

"Yeah, he does, don't he? I'll see you after a while. Those there traps ain't gonna go nowhere. They'll wait 'til I get ready to work on them."

Jon gestured Silas off and picked up his ax. A few minutes later, as he stacked slabs of newly cut logs onto the growing woodpile, he saw Silas riding out of the clearing, with Little Sun perched on the saddle in front of him. Dog trotted at the horse's heels. Jon returned Silas's wave before he rolled another log into place for splitting.

The sun climbed high while Jon worked, and once he stopped long enough to tie his hair back with a leather thong he carried in his pocket. Finally he even removed his shirt, his exertions keeping him warm enough, since the temperature rose with the sun's course. It would drop drastically as evening approached, but for now he enjoyed the heat.

Now and then a layer of snow slipped from a pine bough and plopped to the ground with a soft whoosh, and rivulets of water dripped over the cabin eaves from the snow melting on the roof. Dozens of birds hopped and twittered in the trees, and a black-capped chickadee flew back and forth from the trees to a bush by the cabin. Earlier, Caitlyn had draped the strands of hair she had saved over the winter on the bush. Each time the chickadee left, it carried a beak full of hair to thread into its new nest.

As Caitlyn emerged from the cabin, Jon's grumbling stomach reminded him that noon had come and gone.

"Hi," he said as she approached. "Saw my naked body from the window and couldn't keep your hands to yourself, huh?"

"Huh, to you," Caitlyn retorted. "I was watching the chickadee from the window and came out for a closer look."

"Little liar." Jon's grin grew wider when a hint of pink stole over Caitlyn's cheeks.

"Well, your naked body is working awfully close to that chickadee," she admitted. After returning his light kiss, she wrinkled her nose. "You need a bath, Jon."

"Think I could have something to eat first? I'll eat out here, if I'm too stinking to sit at the table."

When Caitlyn ignored his teasing jibe, he turned to follow her gaze toward the trail Silas had ridden down. "Something wrong, sweetheart?"

"I've had the stew ready for over half an hour, Jon. Silas said he'd be back in time to eat."

"Probably forgot the time. You know how he enjoys

taking Little Sun out to show him the mountains and the animals.''

''Maybe.''

''You want me to go look for him?''

''Would you?'' The face she tilted up to him showed Caitlyn's concern. ''I'll fix you a slice of meat and bread to eat while you ride. Probably I'm just being a fussbudget, but Pa and I always kept our promises to each other when we were supposed to meet somewhere. If one or the other of us was late, it meant something had happened.''

Jon swung his ax blade into a log and reached for his shirt. After he pulled it on, he kissed Caitlyn and shoved her toward the cabin.

''Go fix me that food,'' he said, ''while I saddle up. And don't worry, all right? Silas could've sent Dog back for us if they'd run into a problem.''

Despite Jon's request, Caitlyn worried. She worried while she sliced the leftover venison roast and layered it with bread to give to Jon. And she worried long after Jon rode out of the clearing, down the trail Silas had taken.

She couldn't put a finger on her uneasiness on this beautiful spring day. Still, she paced into the cabin, covered the roast again and moved the stew to the side of the coals to stay warm. Then paced back outside, eyes trained on the trail into the surrounding wilderness.

It couldn't be only Silas's lateness—the old mountain man could take care of himself, and he'd probably snort his displeasure over her concern when he returned. She hoped he would.

And she surely needn't worry over Silas caring for Little Sun. Silas would sooner die than allow Little Sun to even prick his finger on a briar.

The minutes passed into an hour and her concern leaned toward anger. Darn it, even Jon should have been back by now. What the blue blazes were they doing out there— watching the snow melt? Or an eagle build its nest? Shoot, she hadn't even seen an eagle yet this spring.

Caitlyn headed for the corral, calling her pinto to her as she walked. The horse met her at the fence, and she slipped between the rails and retrieved her bridle from the small shed that had sheltered the horses during the winter. With a reluctant sigh, she went back for her saddle. Jon had left the second rifle with her, and it would be easier to carry in the saddle scabbard.

She led the pinto through the gate and over to the cabin. Dropping the reins to ground tie the horse, she went in after the rifle. After reemerging from the cabin and dropping the bar into place across the door, she turned and gasped in terror.

Tall Man sat motionless on his horse, in the same spot where she had last seen him last fall. Even across the distance separating them, she could feel the hostility radiating from the Indian's narrowed eyes. Tall Man's horse shook its head and started walking toward the cabin.

Caitlyn fanatically stared at her pinto, then took a step toward it. Tall Man's knife landed in the ground in front of her feet, and Caitlyn swung around, bringing the rifle to her shoulder.

"You will not find the boy if you kill me," Tall Man snarled before she could steady the heavy gun.

The rifle fell from her nerveless hands. "Little Sun," she choked out. "Damn you, Tall Man! What have you done to him?"

"Nothing . . . yet," he replied, the menace of looming possibilities in his voice. "But no one will find him if I do not return for him. Or maybe the animals will find him first."

"Take me to him!"

"Yes," Tall Man hissed. "Yes, I do choose to take you to him. What happens after that will also be my choice. Give the rifle to me and get on your horse."

Caitlyn picked up the rifle and handed it to him, then ran to the pinto and lunged into the saddle. She lifted her reins, but Tall Man shook his head at her.

"No. I do not worry that you will try to run from me—not until at least after I take you to the boy. But you will go as my prisoner."

He kneed his horse closer and pulled a rope from his

belt. Leaning over, he bound Caitlyn's hands tightly to her saddlehorn. She grimaced in pain, but he only knotted the rope another loop.

Grabbing the pinto's reins, Tall Man led off across the clearing.

"Silas," Caitlyn called to him. "What's happened to Silas and J . . . Jon?"

Tall Man tossed one deadly glance over his shoulder and continued riding.

"Silas! Damn it, man, don't you give up on me now!"

Jon pulled Silas's slumped body closer against his chest. Blood had already soaked through the bandage over Silas's wound, saturating Jon's buckskin sleeve.

"T . . . told you to . . . leave me there," Silas whispered, his head falling forward again. "Go . . . after the . . . boy."

"I did," Jon gritted. "I couldn't find the trail. He must have left his horse somewhere while he followed you, then attacked you and grabbed Little Sun. I'm not a damned Indian, Silas. I can't trail a man who doesn't leave a track!"

"G . . . gotta . . . find him."

"I will. Soon as I get you back for Caitlyn to take care of. And if he's harmed one hair on that boy's head, I'll kill him so slowly that he'll have plenty of time to think about what he did."

Silas lapsed into unconsciousness, and Jon fought the urge to kick his horse into a faster gait. The jarring would make the blood flow even faster from Silas's shoulder wound, and the old man had already lost way too much.

Caitlyn would be frantic. He hoped like hell she had sense enough to wait at the cabin and not come out looking for them herself. He had no idea where that damned Indian had gone—Tall Man had proven he could stay nearly invisible in the wilderness when he took Silas unaware. Nobody was better in the mountains than Silas—except a damned Indian.

Somehow Tall Man got by Dog, too. At least, Jon hadn't found the animal, though he had discovered a spot of blood on the trail—right at the point where Silas had left their usually traveled path to take Little Sun down to the beaver pond to see if the beaver kits were out playing yet.

Jon heard a sound behind him and jerked his horse around in the trail. Even in his unconscious state, Silas groaned, and Jon dropped his reins to pull his knife from his belt. Silas's horse trotted out of the underbrush.

"Goddamn it, horse," Jon snarled. "You almost got your throat cut!"

The horse halted, and Jon saw Silas's rifle still in the scabbard, the long rifle almost the length of the horse.

"Shit, Silas," he muttered to the unconscious man. "So that's how Tall Man got you. How many times have you told me that one little stupid mistake can get you hurt in the mountains? You probably carried Little Sun to the pond, instead of your rifle."

Jon replaced his knife and grabbed the other horse's trailing reins, tying them to his saddlehorn before he turned back up the trail. A few minutes later, he rode into the clearing by the cabin.

"Caitlyn!" he called before noticing the bar across the cabin door. Heart starting to pound with tension, he swung his eyes to the corral. Her pinto was gone, and something told him it wasn't inside the shed.

Caitlyn! Oh, God, Caitlyn. No!

Jon unlooped the reins of Silas's horse from his saddlehorn and reached over to pull the rifle free. Silas's horse trotted across the clearing toward the corral, and Jon carefully watched for any other signs of movement. Everything remained silent—too silent.

He had to get Silas into the cabin. The old man's breathing grew shallower by the minute. But, God, he had to find Caitlyn and Little Sun, too.

Jon scanned the ground in the clearing and saw a trail of hoofprints that hadn't been there when he left earlier. With a suppressed groan for his aching arm, he pulled Silas up high enough to lay the rifle across the saddle in front of him and picked up his reins.

He reined his horse over to the hoofprints. Caitlyn rode her pinto unshod, but she kept her pony's hoofs neatly trimmed. The horse that made the other set of prints, which traveled toward the cabin and back again, had a nick in one hind hoof.

The trail told its own story. She had left with someone—or been forced to go.

Thoughts scrambled with fear and frustration, Jon got Silas into the cabin and rebandaged his wound. If Tall Man's knife had penetrated an inch to the right, he'd have been preparing Silas for burial, rather than trying to save his life. And he wasn't at all sure Silas would be alive when he returned. The old man never woke while Jon worked.

He managed to pour part of a cup of water down Silas's throat before the old man choked. He left the bucket and some food on a chair by the bunk—he couldn't do any more. He had to go after Caitlyn and Little Sun.

At the cabin door, Jon grabbed the door jamb on each side of him and squeezed until splinters pierced his palms as he stared out across the clearing. He bowed his head for a brief second, then glanced back over his shoulder at Silas.

Tall Man had planned it well by getting rid of both Dog and Silas. Jon's own tracking skills fell far short of Silas's, though he had learned a few things from the old mountain man. He straightened his shoulders and grabbed the rifle beside the door, closing the door behind him without another glance at Silas.

He led his horse into the corral. It was already tired from the double load it had carried back to the cabin. Silas's fresher pony would be better in the mountains anyway. He shoved the long rifle into the scabbard and swung into the saddle.

The deadly snow clouds started gathering before he had ridden a mile from the cabin. Jesus, could that goddamned Indian even predict the weather? Jon rode on relentlessly. The horses he followed galloped, but he had to follow more slowly while picking out their trail.

The temperature began dropping as the snowflakes feathered down. Jon cursed his foolishness in not grabbing his buffalo-skin robe before he left. But he damned sure wasn't going back for it now.

A rider rode out from between two pines trees ahead of Jon and blocked the trail. Silas's horse reared in shock at the unexpected obstacle, but Jon was already sliding from the horse's back, the rifle in his hand.

Chapter Twenty-nine

Drawn by Little Sun's weak sobs, Caitlyn raced across the cave floor, stumbling and falling in the darkness. She shoved herself to her feet, ignoring the stabbing pains in her palms and knees.

Finding Little Sun at last, she sat down and gathered him into her arms. He flinched away at first, then threw his arms around her neck when she murmured his name.

"Cat," the tiny boy sobbed. "Man. Bad man."

"Shush, darling," Caitlyn soothed. "Cat's here now. It's all right."

She tried to rise with him in her arms, but Little Sun choked and grabbed his throat. Caitlyn ran her hands over him. Feeling the rope tied around the small neck, she turned a furious gaze on Tall Man when she heard him strike a flint across the cave.

"You bastard!" she spat. "You tied him up like a dog!"

A flame flickered in the fire Tall Man had laid before he left the cave, outlining his lethal face.

"You would rather I left him to run away and die in the snow? I had no wish to go looking for him again, and his

315

usefulness to me is not finished yet.''

Caitlyn started to untie the rope, but Tall Man's sharp voice stilled her fingers.

"No! He stays on the rope until we leave!''

Little Sun began crying in earnest, tugging at the rope, and Tall Man snarled, "Shut him up! Now!''

Caitlyn gathered Little Sun onto her lap and moved closer to the wall, so the rope wouldn't strain the boy's neck. She rubbed his small back with one hand, while her other hand, hidden in the darkness, felt along the rope to determine how it had been tied. It looped through a crack in the rocks, emerging again lower down, where it had been knotted—knotted much too tightly to work loose with the fingers of one hand.

"He needs some food,'' she said to Tall Man as Little Sun snuggled against her breasts, his sobs quieting.

"I do not feed my enemies!''

"He's just a little boy. . . . ''

"He is my enemy's son!''

Tall Man rose to his feet, his eyes glittering hatred and his lips drawn back. Caitlyn shrank against the unyielding wall behind her.

"You will only have warmth in here because I have need of it myself,'' Tall Man continued in a vicious voice. "I do not give *comfort* to my enemies, either. And you have chosen the side of my enemy. You only live because I have bargained to bring you to the man who will pay for you alive.''

"Who?'' she whispered. "Why?''

"I did not ask his reason, and I do not know if the name he gave me was truth or a lie. You can ask him your questions. He waits not far from here.''

Tall Man squatted again by the fire and pulled some jerky from the rawhide bag on his belt. He ate slowly, tearing off chunks and chewing them completely before he swallowed. Caitlyn huddled against the cold wall, watching every move the Indian made as her mind frantically sought a way to escape.

She might have surprised him, had she been alone. But

she couldn't leave Little Sun. Before Tall Man had untied her outside the cave, he had removed the knife from her belt and searched her, even feeling inside her moccasins for a hidden weapon. He went through her saddlebags, tossing the pemmican she carried there into a snow bank and slipping her hatchet into his own belt.

All too soon, Tall Man stood and ordered Caitlyn to untie Little Sun. She reached for the knot at the boy's neck.

"Untie it at the other end," Tall Man barked.

Little Sun whimpered, and Caitlyn worriedly shushed him again. Using both hands, she loosened the other knot and pulled the rope free, then stood with Little Sun in her arms.

"He rides with me," Tall Man told her in an icy voice. "You will ride alone. I have no fear that you will run from me as long as I have him."

"Oh, God," Caitlyn pleaded. "At least let me give you my saddle blanket to wrap around him. And some pemmican for him to chew on. Otherwise, he'll be crying from hunger and cold."

"He could cry all he wants if I left him here," Tall Man mused with narrowed eyes.

"I'll fight you every damned step of the way if you leave him behind," Caitlyn warned. "You'll have to kill me, before I find some way to kill you!"

A growl of menacing laughter left Tall Man's throat, but he shrugged his shoulders. "I have no time to waste beating you and no wish to listen to a bawling child. Give him to me and go outside to get your blanket from your horse."

Caitlyn clutched Little Sun tighter. "I'll take him with me."

"I am not ready to kill him yet," Tall Man said as he took a threatening step toward her, reaching for Little Sun. "He will bring my enemy to me, then Spirit Eagle will watch this one die before him."

Caitlyn bit back a sob of terror and looked down at Little Sun to see if he understood Tall Man's words. He stared back at her with fear on his small face, his hand clenched in her buckskin blouse.

"It'll be all right, Little Sun." She lied the promise with all the fervency she could get into her voice, but Little Sun buried his face against her neck.

Tall Man laid his hand on the hilt of his knife. "He will do just as well for me only half alive."

Slowly, reluctantly, Caitlyn allowed him to take Little Sun from her arms. She didn't have a choice. The tiny boy, wide-eyed with panic, glanced briefly at the Indian's face, and wisely didn't struggle. As Caitlyn walked toward the cave's entrance, she glanced over her shoulder at Tall Man, who followed her. Little Sun's eyes were closed now, his figure rigid with fright and the rope dangling from his neck.

Caitlyn first ran over to the snowbank and dug out her bag of pemmican. She handed it up to Tall Man, already on his horse, and quickly unsaddled her pinto. Leaving the saddle on the ground, she carried her blanket over and reached up to wrap it around Little Sun.

The Indian sat stoically, gazing out through the falling snow with his face dead of emotion. She took a breath and removed the pemmican bag from Tall Man's grasp, reaching inside for a piece. Pushing the pemmican into Little Sun's unresponsive hand, she caressed his cheek briefly before she turned to mount her horse.

They rode for hours, even after darkness fell. Caitlyn shivered violently as the night deepened. Her long-sleeved buckskin dress and knee-high moccasins protected her somewhat at first, since even though snow fell, the temperatures remained mild until after the sun set. Then the cold pierced her clothing, penetrating her skin, icing her fingers blue. She wrapped her hair around her and kept working her fingers to try to bring some warmth back into them.

Tall Man stopped briefly once, pulled the blanket he rode upon free, and tossed it around his shoulders. He ignored the pitifully shivering figure on the pinto and rode on. Caitlyn finally laid down on the pinto's neck, burrowing into its warmth, trusting the pinto to follow Tall Man's horse on its own.

The cold seeped into her mind, almost dulling the pain of her thoughts.

Jon. He must be back at the cabin—warm. She started to slide from the pinto and grabbed its neck. No, Jon was . . . what? Hurt? Dead? Tall Man refused to tell her.

And Silas. Little Sun being with Tall Man told that tale. The old mountain man would have protected Little Sun with the last breath in his body.

At the moment she could care less who waited at the end of their ride for Tall Man to deliver her to. She only wanted to be warm again. The snow mounded on her hair and back, and Caitlyn suddenly felt warmer. She could go to sleep now—someone had built a fire.

Little Sun! No one remained now to care for him but her. Tall Man intended to kill the boy, as well as Spirit Eagle.

Caitlyn struggled against the lethargy and drowsiness drawing her toward unconsciousness. With a groan of misery, she pushed herself upright, shaking her head to dislodge the snow. Some of it slid down her back, and sodden tresses of hair hung around her face. She shoved them back with frozen fingers.

The pinto halted abruptly, and Caitlyn made a grab for its mane. Her unresponsive fingers refused to cling to the harsh strands of hair and she tried to grip the neck again, but her body slipped from the horse. She lay on the ground, trying to will herself to her feet, and blinked suddenly in a circle of lantern light.

"That her?" an unfamiliar voice snarled.

"She is the one the Blackfeet missed in their raid," Tall Man said. "You will have to decide if she is who you seek."

"Get her inside. Shit, man, what the hell are ye doing with a baby?"

"That is for me to know. I have brought you what you wanted—what we agreed on. He will go with me tomorrow, while you go wherever it is you want to go now."

Caitlyn struggled again to rise as Tall Man walked away. The lantern light blinded her as it came closer, and she turned her head aside. A rough hand reached out and gripped her chin, turning her face back into the light.

"Jesus," that voice said. "Ye're her, all right. Ye look just like Maureen. I tried to get close enough to make sure last summer, but ye had too many damned men protecting you—Indians and whites both."

Caitlyn mewed in protest as he dropped her chin and grabbed her arm to try to pull her to her feet.

"Goddamn it, get up and into the cabin, or I'll leave ye out here to die. Guess one ways just as good as another, long as I take back proof that ye're dead."

Little Sun. The boy's name in her mind did what the man's cruel grasp couldn't, and Caitlyn rose shakily to her feet. She had to go to the little boy. And, oh God, the man had said something about a cabin, where it would be warm.

Stumbling awkwardly in the direction the man shoved her, Caitlyn lifted her head and saw the dark shape of a cabin in front of her. No light beckoned from the windowless front wall, but the door was partially open. She half-walked, half-crawled forward, and tripped over her numb feet as she reached it.

She sprawled across the doorway, and heard the man behind her give a muffled snort of anger. He stepped over her and grabbed her by an arm to drag her on into the cabin, slamming the door behind them.

Caitlyn lay on the dirt floor for a long moment before the sounds of a crackling fire penetrated her dazed senses. Opening her eyes, she saw welcome flames flickering in the fireplace against the back wall. Little Sun sat huddled on her saddle blanket in front of the fire, and Caitlyn somehow tensed her arm muscles, raising herself a few inches above the floor.

She got to her hands and knees and began to crawl toward the fire. The cabin was tiny—barely a fourth the size of her own. But she could only move a foot or so at a time, willing a hand forward, a leg to follow. She heard a low voice mutter, a guffaw of menacing laughter, but she concentrated too hard on her movements to make any attempt to understand the words spoken with the laughter.

At last she collapsed by the fire. Little Sun whimpered, but she couldn't move her arms to reach for him. He scooted closer to her and patted her cheek.

"Cat? Cat a'right?"

"I'm . . . I'll be all right in a minute, Little Sun," she managed to whisper. "Just let me get warm."

He stood and picked up the blanket, then laid it over Caitlyn's shoulders. As soon as she realized what he had done, a sob escaped her lips. Still a month or so shy of two years old, Little Sun had tried to care for her. But, oh, God, she was supposed to be taking care of him.

Ever so slowly the warmth chased the icy depth of chill from her body. And, though her senses were slowly clearing, Caitlyn laid as though unresponsive in front of the fire, straining now to listen to what Tall Man and the other man were saying.

"Listen, goddamn it," the stranger said. He must be white from his speech, Caitlyn thought. "I need a guide back out of these damned mountains. If ye want to get paid, ye'll wait until we get back to where I can find my own way."

Suddenly Caitlyn heard the man gasp in fear. "All right," he said in a hurried voice. "Put that damned knife away. I'll give ye what I owe ye now. And I'll double that if ye take me to wherever rendezvous will be held this summer. I can wait there and go back with the pack trains."

"I have no need of more coins than what you owe me now," Tall Man said in a deadly voice, surprising Caitlyn when he spoke in English. "They will buy me all I wish from the traders. I have no woman to carry what I own and my sister has what I do not wish to burden myself with."

Caitlyn heard coins jingle. "There," the man said. "Look, I'll give ye two more or . . . or my extra rifle, if ye'll at least draw me a map. Or give me directions."

"It is a poor man who cannot find his way to where he wants to go," Tall Man muttered, this time in Nez Perce.

"I can't understand ye," the other man said. "Ye learned English faster than I did yer language while we waited out that damned long winter."

Returning sensation crawled through Caitlyn's veins with prickles of pain, and she couldn't hold back a groan. Knowing she had drawn the men's attention, she sat up, but kept her back to them while she gathered Little Sun onto her lap.

"What will you do with that one?" Tall Man asked.

"Not that it's any of yer business, just like ye told me the boy wasn't none of mine, but I've gotta figure out how I can take proof of her death back to Ireland. Her cousin will only pay me if he's damned sure she's dead. Her grandfather will want proof, too."

Caitlyn bent her head over Little Sun's. Oh, God, Jon had been right. Her past—the past she had declined to discuss with him—had followed her, even down through all these years. The freedom of her life with Pa had lulled her into a false sense that whatever her mother had run from would never affect her—that she could ignore any ties to a family she didn't even remember.

And now her refusal to face what could happen and take proper precautions would cost her—had already cost her. Jon, Silas and even her dog littered the trail of her blithe stupidity. She even had a hand in the danger that faced Little Sun.

Her shoulders bowed under the weight of her guilt and grief, but Little Sun shifted in her arms and she took a deep breath against the threatening tears. She still had a chance to protect him, though at the moment she had to admit that it was about as much of a chance as the snow had of melting from the mountains in one short day. In the morning, Tall Man and the stranger would separate—Tall Man to wreak his vengeance on Spirit Eagle through the tiny boy.

And her? She still had no clear idea why her family wanted her dead—why they had sent a man across the ocean and over halfway across this country to kill her. No wonder her mother had run from a man as vicious as her grandfather must be.

Caitlyn tried to remember if there had been any clue in her mother's journal as to why even her children would be in danger from their grandfather, but failed. Instead, she recalled a passage or two where her mother had written yearningly of her home.

"Here, Miss Keefe."

Caitlyn looked up at the stranger's face, not at all surprised to recognize the man who had followed her and Jon around at rendezvous. William Hogan, she remembered Jon and Silas telling her that Reach for the Moon had said the man's name was.

"My name's O'Neal," she said, sorry at once that she had confirmed her identity. The twist of the man's lips told her that his supposed mistake of her name had been a trick.

"Oh, yeah, I guess it would be," he said with a smirk. "Yer mother married that James O'Neal, all right. I found the record at that parish where they stopped to do it. Here." He pushed a plate at her again. "The boy's probably hungry."

Caitlyn took the plate and glanced over her shoulder at Tall Man. His stony face gave her no indication as to whether she would be allowed to feed Little Sun or not. Drawing in a breath of courage, she turned her back again and picked up the wooden spoon on the plate.

The stew meat—venison as best she could tell—was half raw, but she and Little Sun ate it anyway. She waited until he pushed the spoon away from his mouth before she finished the small portion left.

As she set the plate on the floor, Little Sun said with a whimper, "Pot, Cat. Me, pot."

Caitlyn rose to her feet and took his hand. "He has to got to the pot," she said, eyeing Tall Man warily.

"Send him here," the Indian ordered.

"No," Little Sun cried, tugging on Caitlyn's hand. "Jon. Jon me pot, Cat."

Caitlyn knelt and cupped his small face. "Listen to me, Little Sun. Jon isn't here. You have to go with him."

"Cat. Cat me pot," he replied with a mutinous pout.

"Take him the hell over in the corner," Hogan snarled. "We're leaving here in the morning anyway."

"No," Tall Man growled. "He will go outside. I do not plan to sleep in here with the stink of piss in my nose."

"Please, Little Sun," Caitlyn pleaded. When he shook his small head, she stood and faced Tall Man. "Look, I have to go too. . . . ''

Tall Man crossed the room in two strides and grabbed the rope still around Little Sun's neck. He pulled him behind him as he walked to the door and opened it, the rope choking off Little Sun's cries. Caitlyn started after them, but Hogan grabbed her hair and threw her to the floor.

"Ye can go next," he said with a rude laugh.

Tall Man picked Little Sun up by the back of his shirt and shoved him through the door. Caitlyn's nails bit into her palms until she felt her skin split, and she shot daggers of hatred at him. The Indian held the end of the rope and met her glare with icy disregard.

A moment later, Little Sun came back into the cabin, fumbling with his small britches to pull them up and sobs shaking his shoulders. Caitlyn scrambled to her feet as he started to run to her, but Tall Man jerked the rope, sending the tiny boy sprawling.

"You son of a bitch!" Caitlyn arched her nails and took a step. She halted instantly when Tall Man drew his knife.

Hogan grabbed her arm and shoved her forward. "Come on, if ye gotta go," he said. "I'll keep an eye on ye."

"I can go by myself," she spat at him.

Hogan backhanded her across the face and Caitlyn's head snapped on her neck. Swallowing her cry of pain, she lifted a hand to wipe at a trickle of blood from her nose as she glared at him with blue fury.

"Just because I fed ye," he warned, "don't start thinking that I'm gonna go easy on ye. Your being dead's the only way I'll get what's owed me."

"Why do you wait?" Tall Man asked with a shrug.

"I told ye," Hogan said. "I've gotta figure out what kind of proof I can take back with me. The man who hired me said something about her mother keeping journals all her life." He looked back at Caitlyn. "If ye've got something like that, my getting it might keep ye alive a little longer."

"Why should I . . . ?"

Hogan raised his hand again, and Caitlyn couldn't keep

from flinching. Hogan gave a sardonic chuckle and dropped his arm.

"Reckon that tells me what I want to know. And before I'm done with ye, ye'll tell me just where my proof is. Maybe not willingly, but ye'll tell me."

He shoved her toward the door again, and Caitlyn stumbled outside. She turned to see him leaning against the door, a rifle he must have picked up before he followed her in his arms. She'd noticed three rifles against the wall, one of them Jon's long rifle, but Tall Man had always remained between them and her.

"Don't try to run," Hogan snarled, "or I'll put a bullet in one of yer kneecaps. That Indian may be sure ye won't leave the boy until ye have to, but I won't take that chance."

He kept his eyes on her and Caitlyn thought briefly of asking him to turn his back. But she wouldn't give him the satisfaction of breaking her pride—making her beg. She lifted her dress and squatted, then wiped herself with a handful of snow. She rose and, head high, walked back into the cabin.

Chapter Thirty

Caitlyn's pride did her no good the next morning when Tall Man rode away from the cabin with Little Sun. She screamed the little boy's name over and over, fighting with all her strength to wrest free from Hogan's hold. Hogan finally landed a vicious blow on her jaw, and she crumbled into the snow.

"Ye damned bitch! What the hell . . . ?"

Caitlyn managed to lift her head just as Spirit Eagle landed behind Tall Man on his horse and pulled his son's kidnapper to the ground. The horse neighed in terror and whirled, sending Little Sun flying from its back. Caitlyn shoved herself upward with a sob, but Hogan kicked her in the stomach, and she rolled a few feet away, gasping for breath.

A second later, she heard a crunching thud, and Hogan's dead weight landed on her. Frantically, she shoved at his body, and an instant later it was jerked from her and thrown aside. Jon reached down and pulled her into his arms.

She sobbed and cried for only a second, then twisted in Jon's arms. "Little Sun! Jon, we have to. . . . "

Jon grabbed her and shook her shoulders. "Stay here, Caitlyn," he ordered. "That horse is going crazy over there!"

He shoved her behind him and lifted the rifle. Caitlyn stared wildly at the two struggling figures in the snow, Tall Man's horse dancing around them in terror. Why didn't the horse run? Then she caught a quick glimpse of the horse's lead rope, caught between two branches.

"Jon!" she gasped. "Where's Little Sun?"

"He's in a snowbank over there. I don't think he's hurt. Hush, now, Caitlyn, so I can get off a shot."

It was over in an instant. The horse reared yet again, his hoof landing with a thump on the head of one of the fighting figures. The other Indian jerked the lead rope loose and flung himself onto the horse.

Jon pulled the rifle hammer back, but just then Little Sun scrambled out of the snow bank and raced toward them. Distracted, Jon's rifle barrel wavered a scant fraction and his shot missed. Tall Man galloped away unscathed.

Little Sun ran to Caitlyn and she grabbed him up with arms trembling so hard she could barely hold him. Between her sobs, she kissed his face all over and hugged him until he gasped for breath. Jon ran a hand beneath her hair and stroked her neck. "Sweetheart, you're going to squeeze him to death if you don't let loose."

Lifting her head, Caitlyn tenderly wiped at a smudge of tear-streaked dirt on Little Sun's face. "Are you all right, darling?" she asked. "Are you hurt?"

"I a'right," Little Sun said, raising his tiny hand to Caitlyn's cheek. "Cat a'right?"

Gulping back new tears, Caitlyn nodded her head. "I . . . Cat's a'right, baby." With a muffled gasp, Caitlyn threw both herself and Little Sun into Jon's arms.

Jon held her for only a moment, then gently pushed her away. "I have to go check on Spirit Eagle, darlin'. Are you sure you're all right? They didn't hurt. . . . " His eyes narrowed when he saw the bruise on her jaw and her puffy nose. "Which one did that?" he growled.

Caitlyn looked down at Hogan.

''Well, he's dead,'' Jon said in a flat voice. The lifeless eyes staring skyward confirmed his words. ''I hit him hard enough to kill two men, and he's lucky I did. He would've died a lot slower, but I couldn't hold back when I saw him kick you.''

''Spirit Eagle,'' Caitlyn reminded him.

They heard a groan and Spirit Eagle stumbled to his feet. Leaving Caitlyn, Jon hurried over to help the Indian support himself. As they started back toward Caitlyn, with Jon's arm around Spirit Eagle's waist, a fierce scream split the air.

As one, they stared up the mountainside. Tall Man shook his rifle over his head, his fury at seeing his enemy still alive echoing in his insane cries. He had ridden farther up the mountain, where deep snow still lay on both the ground and in huge drifts on a boulder-strewn cliff face. He and his roan pony stood out starkly in the white surroundings.

Caitlyn knew what would happen, but she kept her eyes on Tall Man. The snow on the cliff to the Indian's right shifted in warning, disturbed by the rebounding echoes of Tall Man's howls of fury. The Indian cut off his last shout in mid-cry when he heard the muffled groan from the snow.

Too late, he turned his pony and whipped it with the lead rope. The snow came loose with a rumble, following Tall Man's path, irresolutely creeping closer. At one point, Caitlyn thought the snow almost seemed to toy with the Indian. Then it gathered force and swept over him.

They all stood silently until the last echo of thunder from the avalanche faded. Realizing that Little Sun had seen what happened, Caitlyn glanced down at him.

''Bad man dead,'' Little Sun said in reply to her worried face. ''Bad man dead. Good.''

''I see you have not weakened my son while he was in your care, Little Wind,'' Spirit Eagle said as he reached for his son. ''He still has an Indian's gladness at the defeat of his enemy.''

For a second, Little Sun stared at his father, then, with a glad cry, he sprang into his arms. Caitlyn saw a suspicious glint in Spirit Eagle's eyes, but when he noticed her watching him, he tried to deadpan his face. She wrinkled her nose at him as far as she could with the puffiness, and laughed aloud.

"And I see that you aren't any better at hiding your love like you think an Indian man's supposed to, my friend," she teased in a relieved voice.

Turning away so she wouldn't embarrass Spirit Eagle even more by watching his emotional reunion with his son, Caitlyn snuggled into Jon's arms.

Jon touched the bruise on her cheek and her slightly swollen lower lip. "Will it hurt you if I kiss you, darlin'?" he whispered.

"It'll hurt more if you don't," she breathed.

Jon gently kissed her, holding in reserve the fierce kiss he wanted to give her. Instead, he contented himself with running his hands over her, claiming her with his touch and fighting against the urge to crush her against him.

"Damn, I was scared," he said when he lifted his head.

"How did you find us?" she asked.

"Spirit Eagle knew where you'd been taken," Jon admitted. "He knows this country just as well as Tall Man does . . . did. He found me following you, and I almost shot the crazy fool when he appeared out of that snow."

"S . . . Silas?" Caitlyn asked more softly.

"I don't know. He was hurt pretty bad, and I had to leave him at the cabin. We've got to get back to him."

Caitlyn turned in his arms to look at Spirit Eagle again. "Are . . . are you le . . . leaving now? T . . . taking Little Sun?"

"I will come with you to thank Swift Feet for trying to protect my son," Spirit Eagle said with a smile. "If he lives, that is. You will have time to say your good-bye. And I will have time to tell you how great my thanks are for your care of him."

"Sure," Caitlyn said in a denigrating tone. "I even let Tall Man kidnap him."

She kicked at a clump of snow, and Spirit Eagle tipped her chin up with his finger, forcing her to meet his gaze.

"You would have given your life for him," he said quietly. "I know this. I heard your voice when you called after him. You cannot think that I would fault you—forget all the love and care you gave my son the many months I was gone, trying to find my own peace."

Caitlyn gulped a sigh filled with both relief and the beginning of the misery she knew she would feel when Spirit Eagle rode away with his son.

"He's . . . he's got some toys at the cabin," she said. "And we're going to be leaving soon. If you need a place to stay. . . ."

Spirit Eagle nodded at her. "A cabin would be warmer than a wigwam," he mused.

"Caitlyn," Jon said. "We have to get back and check on Silas."

"Oh, lord," Caitlyn said with a gasp. "Let's get going."

Jon made her wait until they retrieved some blankets from the cabin for warmth as they rode. Then, while Caitlyn waited on her pinto, he searched Hogan's body. Finding the bag of coins, he tossed them to Spirit Eagle.

"These are small enough payment for what Little Sun had to go through," he said. "You take his horse, too."

Spirit Eagle nodded and rode over to where Hogan's horse was still tied to a ring in the cabin wall.

"Are you going to bury him?" Caitlyn asked.

"We're going back to Silas," Jon said in a flat voice. "Let the buzzards have him."

Where the trail allowed, they galloped their horses, but stretches of it were too rugged to let them go faster than a walk. Jon questioned Caitlyn about Hogan when they could ride close enough to talk, but she could tell him little beyond the fact that Hogan had been supposed to take proof of her death back to Ireland.

"There must be something we're missing in that journal," Jon said at one point.

"Well, I've no idea what it is," Caitlyn said. "We can read it again and see if we can figure it out, I guess."

It didn't matter anyway, she told herself, though she wouldn't voice it yet to Jon. The journal meant that she had to cut Jon out of her life. At least for now, and maybe forever. She couldn't ask him to wait—and she definitely couldn't ask him to stay with her.

Love means doing what's best for another person, even when it hurts you, Cat. Pa's voice echoed in her head. He'd told her that during one of their rare arguments, when he had been determined to stand firm in a matter of discipline and she had been just as determined to flaunt his authority over her.

Pa had won—as usual. She couldn't even remember now what the fight had been about, but she remembered Pa telling her that just because he had never laid a hand on her didn't mean that he wouldn't turn her over his knee and tan her little behind good if she disobeyed him. The break in his voice when he said that had told her how badly it would hurt him to spank her, but the determination behind his words let her know that he would indeed handle his hurt and do what needed to be done.

Like she would have to handle her hurt at losing both Jon and Little Sun from her life.

They made the trip back to the cabin in less than half the time it had taken for Tall Man to get Caitlyn to the cabin where Hogan waited the night before. They galloped across the clearing and Caitlyn slid from her pony before it came to a complete halt. But at the cabin door, she stopped with a jerk, her hand a bare inch from the door.

"What . . . what if he's . . . !"

Jon gently shoved her aside. "Wait out here," he ordered.

He pushed the door open and stepped inside.

"Heard the bunch of you ride in, so I guess you got Cat and the boy," Caitlyn heard Silas say in a weak voice before Jon could shut the door. "Now go get me and this here dog some more dadblamed water."

With a cry of joy, Caitlyn ran across the threshold.

Jon gathered Caitlyn against his sweat-slick body and threw an arm across his face, protecting his eyes from the brilliant sun. His heart slowed its thundering to a dull throb as he gradually became aware of the world beyond the edges of the blanket, where they had just made love. Everything was finally falling into place in his life, and nothing was more right than this woman he loved, lying in his arms.

A few songbirds twittered, but not nearly as sweetly as Caitlyn did when she whimpered her need for him. A slight breeze blew over their bodies, but Caitlyn's breath feathered and puffed on his neck, caressing him in a much nicer way. She had seemed a little withdrawn while Silas recovered, though Jon put it down to her worry over the old man. But she definitely still lost herself in their lovemaking. He couldn't quite keep a smirk of masculine satisfaction from his lips as he ran his hand over her bare hip and remembered how she had called his name in joyous abandon a moment ago.

In another day or so, they could start out of the mountains. Silas had regained his strength over the last month. Despite his attempt at bravado the day they found him still alive at the cabin, it had been touch and go for the first week. He and Caitlyn had sat with him day and night, having to almost force-feed him at times. But Little Sun had done the most good—Silas just couldn't turn him down when he carried cups of broth over to his elderly friend.

Silas told them that Dog had arrived at the cabin an hour or so before the rest of them had returned. Probably he had lain unconscious wherever Tall Man had left him. Caitlyn had already promised to leave Dog with Little Sun when they left, since she knew she would be unable to bear Little Sun's tears if the animal left with them.

"Jon?"

"Hum, darlin'?"

Caitlyn sat up, swatting at Jon's hand with a subdued giggle when he tried to pull her back against him.

"We better get back to the cabin. I've still got some packing to do."

"Aw, honey. This will probably be the last time we have any privacy for the next month or so—maybe even until we get all the way back to St. Louis, and that might take two months. You know Silas has decided to go with us.

And he won't stand for us sharing our bedrolls right under his nose until after we find a minister. He still considers you under his 'pertection' until I get that ring on your finger.''

Tell him, Caitlyn's mind said. But she couldn't. Not just yet. Why spoil the few weeks they had left?

She pasted a smile on her face and tapped her finger on his nose. ''I'm sure you'll manage to figure out a way for us to get a few minutes alone now and then. You always do.''

''A few minutes! Hell, a few hours isn't enough.''

He rolled over and propped his head on his hand, reaching out to cup her bare breast and run a thumb back and forth across the nipple. When Caitlyn gasped his name and closed her eyes, he chuckled under his breath.

''Sure I can't talk you into staying here for a while longer?'' he murmured.

She slit her eyes and, catching sight of the smirk on his face, grabbed his hand and pushed it away.

''You behave yourself, Jon Clay! We have to think of our responsibilities first.''

Joan groaned and laid back down. ''Responsibilities? Caitlyn, you're already beginning to sound like a nagging wife.''

Tell him you're not going to marry him.

''No,'' Caitlyn said aloud.

''No, you're not sounding like a nagging wife?'' Jon asked with a quirked eyebrow. ''You mean, it can get worse?''

Caitlyn shook her head and looked around for her dress. She saw it snagged on the branch of a nearby bush and rose to her feet to get it. After she pulled it on, she picked up Jon's britches and shirt to toss to him, then stared down the trail they had ridden up earlier.

Jon caught his clothes, but held them on his lap. ''Caitlyn?'' he asked after a second. ''What's wrong? You're not yourself.''

''You're wrong, Jon. I'm very much myself. Now, come on and get dressed. I want to finish my packing.''

"Is it because you're already missing Little Sun?" Jon asked without moving. "I don't presume to think you'll ever forget that little tyke, but when you're ready, we'll have our own children. After we're married, we can. . . . "

Caitlyn whirled with her hands on her hips. "I'm not going to marry you, Jon!" She gasped and took a step backwards as a thunderous scowl crawled over his face and Jon rose slowly to his feet.

"What the hell did you say?" he snarled.

"You . . . you heard me. We're not going to get married."

"You just laid here with me and begged me to make love to you! You screamed my name and told me how much you loved me! And now—you're *not* going to marry me?"

"I didn't mean to tell you just yet," Caitlyn said, struggling to stand steady in the face of his anger, though she couldn't meet his gaze. "I was going to wait until we got back to St. Louis."

"And were you going to tell me *why* when we got to St. Louis, too? Let me ride all that damned way thinking everything was fine between us—that all I had to do was find a minister? Or were you going to wait until after I found the minister—then stand there and say 'no' instead of 'yes' when he asked you if you took me to be your husband!?"

"I would have let you know before that."

"Then maybe it's for the best," Jon spat, and Caitlyn's head jerked up to face him. "I'm tired of this, Caitlyn! One month you love me—the next one you don't! You want to marry me—you don't want to marry me! You hide your thoughts and won't be honest with me. I never know from one day to the next who I'll be in love with—the Caitlyn who loves me back or the Caitlyn who crawls off into her own little world and won't share it with me!"

He muttered a vile oath and turned his back on her. After pulling on his britches and shrugging into his shirt, he grabbed the blanket and strode over to his horse.

He swung into the saddle and reined his horse around to face her. "Get on your damned horse and come on. I'm not about to leave you up here alone where someone else can come along and carry you off again. I don't have time to come after you. I want to get the hell out of here as soon as I can.''

Caitlyn stiffened her shoulders and walked to her pinto. After mounting, she kneed the horse forward, passing Jon with her back straight and her head high.

''And don't worry about me trying to talk you out of it, Caitlyn,'' he snarled as she rode by. ''It's over this time. I'm leaving as soon as we get back to the cabin. You and Silas can do what you want!''

Over, over, her pinto's hooves pounded in cadence as she rode ahead of Jon. It's what she wanted. It's what had to be. She gritted her teeth against the cry of denial that tried to escape.

Over, over. At least no one else would be hurt protecting her. She would risk only herself as she faced the danger that had entered her life. She could not run from it forever, always wondering if someone else would attempt to get to her through the loved ones around her—her very existence bringing the threat of death to everyone her life touched.

Hogan would have killed her after torturing her until she revealed where to find the proof he needed to take back to Ireland and collect his pay for her death. Already Silas had nearly died, caught in the tentacles of some far-reaching effort at retaliation on her.

The words she had not really paid that much attention to when she first read the journal had echoed again and again in her thoughts ever since Tall Man had delivered her to Hogan.

I thought my father loved me. His last words to me broke my heart . . . he said he would rather see me dead than married to James.

Had her mother fled in fear of her life? Had James taken her from Ireland for her own safety? If so, they had met their deaths in the rugged wilderness because of her grandfather. They might still be alive and safe, and her little brother, too, if not for her grandfather's refusal to allow Maureen to marry the man she loved.

Her resolve firmed. Evidently, as her mother's daughter, her life hung under the threatening knife of some sort of vengeance. Any child she had herself would be in jeopardy, too—a potential victim. She would never be able to rest until she found some way to end the threat hanging over her life—her future, and the future of anyone who tried to share her life with her.

Jon deserved better. He deserved a life with a wife who could give him the children that he wanted. He deserved a life with a woman who wouldn't bring the danger hovering over her own life into his.

Love means doing what's best for another person, even when it hurts you, Cat.

"I know, Pa," she whispered low.

Over, over, pounded the pinto's hooves.

Chapter Thirty-one

Jon kept his vow. He left that evening, without speaking to her again. By the time she had unsaddled her pinto and put him in the corral, he was already throwing a pack behind the saddle of his horse. He mounted without looking at her and rode down toward the lake, where Silas, Spirit Eagle and Little Sun were fishing. She stood in the doorway, unable to force herself to forgo this one last sight of him.

She watched him dismount again, shake hands with Spirit Eagle, hug Little Sun, then walk off a ways with Silas. After a few minutes of conversation, he mounted again and rode off. She kept her gaze on him until he disappeared, hoping desperately that he would at least glance back once at her. But he didn't.

She refused to discuss anything with Silas when he questioned her later. She only shook her head and silently served the men and Little Sun their supper, then went into her room. After a sleepless night, she rose early and finished her packing, while Silas loaded the furs. Then she had another heart-rending good-bye to make.

After tying her pack behind the pinto's saddle, she

slowly walked back to the cabin door, where Spirit Eagle stood with Little Sun in his arms.

"He's so young," she murmured, reaching for the little boy. "He may not know me when he sees me again."

"You are wrong, Little Wind," Spirit Eagle said. "He will always remember you. We will talk of you, and you will see him again. Part of your heart is here. You will return."

She snuggled her head against Little Sun's silky hair and shook her head. "I'm not making any promises to anyone right now, my friend. But thank you. I'll like knowing that Little Sun's always going to remember me."

She hugged the little boy as tightly as she dared, and he flung his arms around her neck, squeezing her in return. When he drew back, he patted her on the face, as he had so many times before.

"Cat," he said. "Wuv you, Cat."

"And I love you, little one," she murmured. "Be a good boy, and grow up into a fine, strong man like your father."

He nodded his tiny head. "Me be good, Cat. Good boy."

She forced herself to hand Little Sun back to his father, and Spirit Eagle settled him in the crook of his arm.

"Well," Caitlyn said. "I guess this is good-bye."

"No," Spirit Eagle denied. "We will not say that word. It is only a time when we will not see each other. A time of separation. I will think of you and wish you well. We will always be friends, Little Wind."

Blinking back tears, Caitlyn shook her head but didn't contradict him. She stepped up and kissed him on the cheek, then kissed Little Sun and ruffled his hair. When she started to turn, Spirit Eagle caught her arm.

"As your friend, Little Wind," he murmured, "I have a right to say things others do not. It is also my duty to you, as a friend."

"I'm not going to talk to you about Jon," she said, quickly discerning what he would probably say. "That's my own business."

"You will listen to my words, Little Wind. You will do

as you want with your life, even if I speak, but I *will* speak.''

Caitlyn clenched her teeth and glared at him, but Spirit Eagle went on. ''Morning Star and I had only a short time with each other. We had this time because you helped us have it. There were many things we had to face, many troubles we had to go through. But we faced them together, not alone.''

''This is different,'' Caitlyn said. ''And I'm not going to talk about it with you.''

With a sigh, Spirit Eagle dropped her arm. ''If you need me, I will be there for you, Little Wind.''

''Thank you,'' Caitlyn said in a relenting voice. She glanced at Little Sun and again tears misted her eyes. ''I'll miss you, little one,'' she whispered.

He reached out a chubby arm and patted her face once more. ''Miss you, Cat. Wuv you.''

She didn't know if the little boy realized exactly what their parting this time meant. She'd been gone all day at times over the winter. She hoped he didn't cry for her when she didn't return, as she knew she would weep at times when she missed him.

''I love you, Little Sun.''

After one last caress of his ruddy cheek, she turned and mounted the pinto. Silas walked over as she rode off, and she heard him saying his own farewell in a gruff voice. He would miss them too. But he could return whenever he wanted, while she might be leaving her beloved mountains forever.

Two weeks later, Caitlyn and Silas pulled their horses up on a rise and stared out over a valley floor.

''We'll be able to travel on to St. Louie a little faster after we get rid of these furs, Cat. Looks like rendezvous's in full swing—a few weeks early.''

''Spring came early this year, so I guess the pack trains got an earlier start, Silas,'' Caitlyn said in a weary voice.

She couldn't dredge up even a bit of the excitement she usually felt at attending rendezvous. This year it would be filled with memories—memories of her times there with Pa, and memories of meeting Jon last summer.

"And I've already told you," she said with exasperation for at least the tenth time, "I'm going on to St. Louis alone. I'm not going to Virginia from there, either."

"Got me an invite to Virginie all of my own, Cat." Silas tossed her a smirk through his beard. "Reckon to spend me some time being waited on and pampered 'til I decide it's time to come back out here and check on Little Sun. Spin me some tall yarns with my partner. 'Sides, I gotta take Jon his marker for his share of the furs. We agreed I'd do that afore he lit out."

"Well, you do what you have to do," Caitlyn grumbled around the stab of torment whenever she heard his name. "Let's get on down there and sell our furs before the traders give all the best prices to the trappers who got here ahead of us."

She picked up the lead rope of her pack horse again and kneed her pinto forward. "And I have to find Sky Woman and let her know what happened to Tall Man."

"She probably won't be none too surprised," Silas said as he rode beside her. "That Indian always was meant for a bad end."

"He was still family to her, Silas. We don't get to pick and choose who our family is."

"I ain't quite in agreement with that, Cat. We had us a nice little family going up there on that mountain, 'til you. . . ."

"Damn it, Silas!" Caitlyn turned in her saddle to glare at him. "You don't know a darned thing about my reason for not marrying Jon! And I'm not going to discuss it with you!"

"Yeah, and far's I know, you didn't discuss it with Jon, neither. You growed up into a woman over the past winter, Cat. You sure did. A woman who ain't got the sense God give a goose!"

Caitlyn drew in a furious breath, but Silas held up a hand to forestall her words.

"You ain't got Ol' Mick around to tell you when you're

makin' a bad mistake, Cat. And I figure it's part of the responsibility I took on with you to tell you when you're bein' a dadblamed fool. And I aim to keep on tellin' you it 'til you get it into that danged fool woman's brain of yours!''

"I don't have to listen to you, Silas. Consider me out from under your 'pertection' as of right now! Pa would understand. He told me there would be times when I'd have to hurt people I loved for their own good!''

"So you still love him, huh?'' Silas asked in a milder voice.

Caitlyn's shoulders slumped and she thinned her lips, biting back her retort. She urged the pinto into a trot, but Silas stayed beside her.

"Answer me, Caitlyn O'Neal,'' Silas demanded.

Caitlyn shot him an angry glare. "I still love him! There, does that satisfy you? And because I love him, I'm not going to marry him. Put *that* in your pipe and smoke it! Now, will you leave me alone?''

"Nope,'' Silas said. "I got no intentions of leavin' you alone, Cat. And you can smoke on that 'til it comes out your ears, you're of a mind to.''

"Wasn't almost getting killed over me once enough for you, Silas?'' Caitlyn pleaded.

"Guess not,'' Silas said with a shrug. He faced forward on his horse again and ignored her, whistling a tune that announced them as they rode toward rendezvous.

At least there would be a different campsite this year— a different pond to bathe in. The traders held the annual gathering at various places in the mountains each year, yet somehow word always spread through the mountains as to where the rendezvous site would be that summer.

Caitlyn never understood why they changed the site yearly, since almost the same people came to the trading fair year after year, season after season. The same mountain men, except for those who hadn't made it through the winter, like Pa last year, or a new face here and there, like Jon last summer.

The same Indian tribes, with a few elderly faces missing,

replaced by new babies peering from their mothers' back-boards. The war-like Blackfeet never came, of course. Pa had told her once that the Blackfeet seers believed the whites would eventually overrun their hunting grounds and thought tribes like the Nez Perce and Sioux foolish for allowing the trading with the whites.

She and Pa had discussed that once or twice. He'd told her that the trading with the Indians had been going on since the first white foot stepped onto American shores. And, yes, the land to the east had been taken from the Indians after a lot of bloody wars. In this vast wilderness out here, though, surely there was enough land for the two races to coexist in peace.

She wasn't quite as sure about that this year as last year, before she had read Jon's books and realized just how many people had arrived in America. But she could still almost make herself believe that whites and Indians could live together in peace. The Indians wanted the trade goods brought in—some of them even trapped furs, though they didn't trap as heavily as the white men they allowed free rein in the wilderness.

As they rode closer to the thousands of tipis, traders' tents and mountain men's campsites, Caitlyn glanced at the mountains beyond. Even this huge gathering was only a tiny speck in all the vastness around them. Surely there was enough land here for everyone.

Caitlyn finally gave up fighting the memories that rode with her. When she left again in a day or two, she might never see this land again. She'd gone to Pa's grave one last time, trying without success to gain an answer as to whether she had made the right decision. But the cold cairn didn't respond.

"Reckon this looks like the best spot we'll get to set up camp, Cat," Silas said as he led the way into a grove of trees. "All the spots closer to the tradin' tents are already took. But I can hear water over there, and there's shade here, if it gets hot."

Caitlyn shrugged her shoulders and dismounted. Even if somewhat inconvenient, the camp would serve for a day or so—all the longer she would be here. She could get a map from one of the traders to show her the trail back to St. Louis. Probably, though, all she would really have to do would be to follow their recently-flattened path out here.

She had a vague idea about where St. Louis lay—somewhere east, on a river called the Mississippi. And Jon had said it could take them up to two months to travel that far.

While Silas cut pine boughs and fashioned two lean-tos where they could sleep that night, Caitlyn unloaded the horses and gathered firewood. Now and then, hints of the rendezvous activities drifted toward them on the wind. A shout of laughter, rifle shots from a marksman contest, the smell of food from the cooking tents. Her stomach growled—not really from hunger, since she and Silas had shared breakfast a couple hours earlier. But there would be food at the tents that she hadn't tasted all winter. Fresh ham and bacon—maybe some eggs.

A vision of the orange Jon had promised to buy her last summer wavered in the flames as she fed the fire. Guess he had forgotten, because they'd left rendezvous without that treat. Maybe she would get one for herself, she thought as she swallowed against the moisture in her mouth, recalling Jon telling her how delicious that fruit was.

"Gonna get me a bath and a change of clothes afore I go down there and find me a jug, Cat," Silas said. "How 'bout you?"

Caitlyn glanced down at her tattered dress. Even the sturdy buckskin clothing showed signs of wear and tear every spring.

"I've got on a good enough best dress for now. I'll find another one already made up at an Indian tent."

"You wear that dress down there, Cat, you sit down and sew up that rip on the front of it first. Otherwise, you'll wait here in camp 'til I go find you somethin' more decent to wear."

"Silas, you're not going to order me around again this year! I'll do what I please!"

"You just try goin' down there 'mong all them men with that torn up dress on. I ain't so old I can't haul your little

fanny back here and spank some sense into you—at least
'bout that, even if you won't listen 'bout the other thing.''

"Leave it alone, Silas.''

"Nope. Ain't gonna do it.'' Silas propped his hands on
his hips and thrust out his chest. "Done told you that. Now,
you wanna stand here talkin' 'bout Jon, or you gonna find
something decent to wear, so I don't have to tie you to a
tree while I'm gone?''

"You'd probably try to do it, too, wouldn't you?''

"Wouldn't try—it'd get done. You give me your word
you'll stay here while I get my bath.''

Caitlyn shot him a smirk of defiance and Silas moved
faster than she would have thought possible. He grabbed
her by the waist and started dragging her toward a tree. She
fought and twisted in his grasp, but the old man had muscles of steel from all his years in the wilderness.

Suddenly picturing in her mind what they must look
like—this old, gray-bearded reprobate dragging a young
woman with him—she collapsed in giggles. Ceasing her
resistance, she swatted at Silas's hands.

"All right, all right,'' she said around her giggles. "I'll
wait until we get our baths, Silas.''

Silas stepped back from her with a frown. "And?''

"And I'll find something decent to wear,'' Caitlyn
agreed.

"Your word, Cat.''

"Dash nab it, Silas! Go get your darned bath and let me
get ready, too. Otherwise, you're gonna be waiting until
hell freezes over before you get your jug!''

Silas crossed his arms over his chest and stood without
moving. He glanced at the tree, then back at Caitlyn.

"You've got my dadblasted word!'' Caitlyn shouted
after a second.

Silas stifled the chuckle in his chest as he dropped his
arms and walked away. If that's what it took to bring Caitlyn out of those danged doldrums she'd been lost in the
last few weeks, he'd fight and argue with her every waking
moment. He much preferred the Cat who forgot her proper
English and reminded him of the little ruffian he had first

seen to that silent, morose Cat.

And maybe if he got her mind working again instead of leaving her sunk in whatever fool notion made her decide to give up Jon, she'd do some more thinking. Little Sun was gone, and he had an itch to bounce a new baby on his knee while rocking in front of a fireplace. The new baby he wanted had blue eyes, since both Jon and Cat's eyes were blue. He didn't much care whether it was a girl or a boy, but he could get neither until Cat got back with Jon, so Jon could father that baby.

Before they left rendezvous, too, he was going to find out just what stupidity Cat had in her mind that made her send Jon away. Even if he had to still tie her to that tree and wait for her to talk.

As soon as Silas disappeared, Caitlyn dug into her pack, knowing already she only had two choices as to what Silas would find acceptable for her to wear. She hadn't been able to bring herself to leave Jon's shirt behind when she found it stuffed back in a corner of the shelf after he left. But as she held it up, a thrust of hard agony stabbed her.

Still, she only had one dress she would consider wearing—the one Jon bought her last summer. She hadn't worn it much over the winter, thinking it too nice to work in. It would tear her up even more to wear that dress. Every swish of fringe on her legs would remind her of Jon.

Her britches were in fair repair, and the shirt would hang down far enough to cover that stain on the front of them. She'd shoved the beaded belt into one of the pockets on the pack.

Hearing a footstep, Caitlyn jumped to her feet and whirled, her hand going to the knife on her belt. The tall Indian who walked toward her smiled and held his hands out to his sides.

"Hello, Reach for the Moon," Caitlyn said, returning his smile and dropping her hand from the knife. "How have you been?"

"I have had a good winter," Reach for the Moon said. "I do not see your wedding present here."

Caitlyn quickly explained that she had left Dog with Little Sun, then offered the Sioux a seat.

Reach for the Moon shook his head. "I have come to see Swift Feet. I saw you both riding down the ridge earlier."

"He's over there in that stream, taking a bath."

The Sioux walked away, and Caitlyn knelt again by her pack.

Fifteen minutes or so later, Caitlyn stalked around the campsite, waiting for Silas to return. Darn it, he and Reach for the Moon could talk just as well back here, while she washed herself. She'd heard bursts of laughter twice, and just knew the two men were sitting over there enjoying themselves, while she stewed at the delay.

Caitlyn finally grabbed up her clothing and a bar of soap. Just as she started toward the stream to hurry Silas along, he and Reach for the Moon reappeared. Silas wore the shirt she had made him for Christmas, the matching one from the trio she had decorated for him, Little Sun . . . and Jon.

"You can go wash now, Cat," Silas said, sneaking a mysterious smirk at his companion. "What'd you decide to wear?"

"Something that will cover me to your satisfaction, Silas," she replied. "I'll be back in a lot shorter time than it took you to bathe."

Silas planted himself in the path and shook his head. "Not 'til you show me what you're wearin', Cat."

"Dang it, Silas. . . . " Caitlyn swallowed her exasperation when Silas crossed his arms over his chest again. With a glare of defiance at him for his audacity in attempting to judge her choice, she shook out the white shirt, pulled the britches from her shoulder and held them up.

"Nope. That won't do, Cat." Caitlyn's eyes narrowed further when Silas glanced up at the tall Sioux. "Won't do at all, will it, Reach for the Moon?"

"No," the Indian agreed. "But you have much to learn about how to get a woman to do what you want, Swift Feet. It is no wonder you do not have a woman to warm your bed."

"Get out of my way, both of you," Caitlyn ground out.

Instead of moving, Reach for the Moon pulled something from his shirt pocket. He held it out on his palm under Silas's nose, and the old man sniffed at it.

"Smells right perty," Silas said. "Not that I'd wanna wash myself with a piece of soap that smelled like roses, but Cat here might like it."

Reach for the Moon quirked an eyebrow at Caitlyn, and she stared longingly at the bar of soap in his hand—thought of the bar of raw lye soap wrapped in her towel with her comb.

"Where'd you get that?" Silas asked as he watched Caitlyn closely. "Been tradin' already?"

"It was given to me by someone," Reach for the Moon explained. "And I would gift it to Mick's daughter. But a woman who uses this should look like a woman, as she smells. She should not wear a man's clothing."

Caitlyn gave Reach for the Moon a grudging smile and wadded up the shirt and britches. "You could learn a thing or two about getting your own way from him, Silas."

"Person ain't never too old to learn, Cat," Silas said with another mysterious smirk. "Or too young."

Shaking her head at the two men, Caitlyn went back to her pack. Instead of the dress Jon had given her, though, she drew out the dress Sky Woman had thrust into her hands before they parted. Removing it from the layer of protective buckskin, she held up the white doeskin dress, decorated with pale blue beads and porcupine quills dyed to match.

"Will this do?" she asked.

"Perfect," Silas said.

He and Reach for the Moon stepped to the side of the path as Caitlyn approached. The Sioux handed Caitlyn the soap, and she walked a few steps past them before she turned, holding the soap safely behind her.

"Thank you," she told the Indian. "Now, what's going on here that you two aren't telling me?"

"Why, Cat," Silas said in a wounded voice. "We just want you to look nice when we go into rendezvous. Don't you remember me sayin' you'd growed up into a woman over the winter?''

"I also remember you telling me what sort of woman you thought I'd grown into, Silas.''

"Aw, Cat, maybe I was wrong. We all make mistakes now and then.''

Caitlyn glared suspiciously at the two men, but finally turned and headed for the stream, sniffing deeply of the bar of rose-scented soap as she walked. Behind her, she could have sworn she heard two snorts of muffled laughter, but she wouldn't give them the satisfaction of turning to confront them again.

Chapter Thirty-two

Caitlyn combed through one final snarl and shook her hair back over her shoulders. Although she had washed it yesterday, she almost gave in to the temptation of rewashing it with the scented soap. It would take too long to dry, though, and she had already lingered longer than it had taken Silas to bathe, lathering her body once, then unable to refrain from doing it again.

She debated braiding her hair, but left it loose. Laying the comb down on the rock beside her soiled clothing, she ran her hands down the sides of the white doeskin and fiercely gulped back a sob. She had meant to wear this dress if she and Jon found a minister before they arrived in St. Louis, where she could get more proper attire. But now that she had made the mistake of letting Silas and Reach for the Moon see it, she'd have a devil of a time convincing them that she wanted to change again.

One thing she would do before she left rendezvous was give this dress back to Sky Woman as a final symbol of her plans for a life with Jon having ended. She had enough memories—she didn't need any physical reminders of her lost dreams.

Silas didn't try to hide the jug when Caitlyn walked into the campsite and saw him and the Sioux sitting by the fire. He just winked at Caitlyn and said, "Reach for the Moon brought me a present, too. Left it behind a tree 'til he could give it to me in private."

"Well, maybe I'd like a drink," Caitlyn said.

"Reckon that'll be all right, 'specially today," Silas said as he stood and held out the tin cup in his hand. When Caitlyn shot him a distrustful look, he hurried on to say, "It's our first day at rendezvous. First day always gets celebrated with a drink."

"More than one, usually," Caitlyn said with a tolerant smile as she accepted the cup. She took a tentative sip, almost spitting out the bitter brew before she could swallow it. But when Silas laughed and reached for the cup, she shook her head and finished the inch or so of liquor.

"You sure do look perty, Cat," Silas said after Caitlyn lowered the cup.

"Thank you," Caitlyn murmured. "Now, can we go on in and check out what the furs are bringing this summer?"

"We can go on in," Silas agreed. "Say, you gonna wear some shoes with that dress?"

Caitlyn closed her eyes briefly in annoyance, but then handed Silas the cup and walked over to her pack. With the moccasins that matched the dress in her hand, she started to sit down to pull them on.

"Whoa, Cat!" Silas jumped forward and grabbed her arm. "Here. Sit on this blanket over here. You don't wanna get that perty dress dirty on the ground."

He led her over to the blanket he'd been sitting on and gently shoved her to the ground. Racing over to the damp towel she had tossed over a limb to dry, he carried it back to her.

"Better wipe your feet off," he said. "They got sort of dirty walking back here from the stream."

Caitlyn gritted her teeth and took the towel. Was this the same Silas that she'd had to threaten to lock outside if he didn't at least take his weekly bath? As he stood beside her, she caught a faint hint of a smell and paused in wiping off her feet.

"Since when did you start wearing after-shave, Silas? You don't even shave."

"Oh, Jon left some at the cabin and I thought it might make me smell good to the women," Silas told her, clasping his hands behind his back and rocking back and forth as he gazed over her head instead of into her face.

Caitlyn shoved her feet into the moccasins and stood. "I'm going into rendezvous. Right now. Are you two coming?"

"Sure are." Silas picked up the jug again. "Reckon we're as ready as we can ever be." He slipped Reach for the Moon a sly look. "All three of us."

Tossing her head and sending the shimmering mass of raven hair dancing down her back, Caitlyn snorted at them and strode out of the campsite. As she passed the first wigwam on the edge of the gathering, Reach for the Moon's daughter stepped out of the entrance and smiled shyly at her. Caitlyn returned her smile, and the girl walked over to her father, joining their small group.

A few seconds later, Caitlyn's steps faltered and slowed. It must be that darned dress. The Indian women wore tan buckskin, and her white dress stood out like a beacon. Every person she passed—some she knew, some she didn't—smiled or waved at her. A couple of the women hid a giggle behind a raised hand.

Ahead of her, Caitlyn noticed people beginning to gather in groups lining the path she walked. Glancing over her shoulder, she stumbled to a stop. The silent group trailing behind her numbered close to 50 people.

She flashed Silas an irritated glare. "What's going on here?"

Silas ignored her and pulled his pipe from his shirt pocket. "Dern, I forgot I'm out of tobaccy. You got any, Reach for the Moon?"

The Sioux handed him a pouch, and Silas busied himself opening the drawstring and poking his pipe inside.

Caitlyn gritted her teeth and turned around. She walked a few more feet, then caught sight of a trader's flag flying over a tent behind the people lining her path. Excusing herself, she shoved through the crowd and went over to the tent.

The lone man behind the wooden shelf displaying the trade goods ducked under the counter as she approached.

"Sorry, miss," he said, tipping his hat to her. "We're closed right now, until after the wedding."

"What wedding?" Caitlyn asked with a frown.

Silas grabbed her arm and pulled her after him, and Reach for the Moon fell in on her other side.

"Stop it, Silas," she demanded. "Where do you think you're taking me?"

"Figured we might as well go watch this wedding," Silas replied. "Won't get no tradin' done 'til after it's over."

"Silas, I'm not interested in going to a wedding." She jerked her arm free and heard Reach for the Moon give a deep sigh beside her. The tall Sioux bent and scooped her into his arms.

"Put me down, dash nab it!" Caitlyn struggled and pounded on Reach for the Moon's chest, but he continued to stride forward. One of her moccasins went flying, and Silas shook his head as he grabbed it up and followed them.

"Put me down!" Caitlyn screeched, then suddenly fell silent as she realized her voice was the only sound in the stillness. She stiffened in the Sioux's arms and stared around her.

"She does not go willingly to her man," a voice murmured in Nez Perce, "but her beauty will make taming her worth the fight."

Caitlyn glared at the man as they passed. Then she glanced up at Reach for the Moon in horror.

"What did he mean?" she asked.

But Sky Woman stepped out of the crowd, and Reach for the Moon gratefully set Caitlyn on the ground and backed away. Silas shoved her moccasin into her hand and followed the Sioux, chortling under his breath and dancing a little jig that sent up dust puffs.

"My daughter, I knew you would be beautiful on this day," Sky Woman said, holding out her arms for Caitlyn.

With a whimper of confusion, Caitlyn ran into her embrace. She hugged the woman she had called mother tightly for several seconds, before stepping back and allowing her turmoil and embarrassment to show on her face.

"My mother, I don't know what they're doing to me. Please. Take me somewhere we can talk."

"There is another waiting to speak to you first, daughter. He has waited many days, and he is anxious to see you. Go now."

Sky Woman took Caitlyn by the shoulders and turned her around, giving her a little shove. Caitlyn stared wildly around her, unsure which direction to go. Then she felt Sky Woman's hand on her shoulder again.

"Wait, daughter. Here."

Sky Woman knelt, and Caitlyn glanced down and lifted her foot to slip the moccasin back on. When she looked up again, Jon stood barely six feet away.

"Hello, darlin'," he murmured.

Caitlyn's mouth went dry, and she licked her lips with a tongue as powdery as the dust Silas had kicked up. She fought the urge to run to him with every bit of willpower she could dredge up, but her willpower fell far short. With a glad cry, she ran into his arms.

Jon grabbed her up and whirled her around, but when he set her down and she turned her face up for his kiss, he covered her mouth with a finger.

"The next kiss I give you is going to be as my wife, sweetheart. There's a minister waiting over there for us."

"Jon, I can't . . ." she began with a whimper of pain.

"Listen to me for once in your life, Caitlyn," Jon ordered in a stern voice. "And you remember this—this is the last time I expect to have to read your mind and try to figure out what's going on inside your head. From now on, if you refuse to talk to me about something, I'm going to tie you to our bed until you do talk."

"That's better than the tree Silas was going to tie me to," Caitlyn grumbled.

Sneaking a look around her from beneath her lashes, Caitlyn saw the crowd of people still surrounding them, listening avidly to every word.

"Jon, can't we go somewhere else and talk?"

"Nope. These people are going to be part of our life from now on, since I've bought a share in one of the trading companies. We'll be coming out here each summer to trade with them. And they've helped me plan this wedding."

"Jon! But your family at the plantation . . . and . . . Jon, damn it, I *can't* marry . . . !"

Jon threw her over his shoulder and strode through the crowd. Caitlyn screeched and pounded on his back, biting back her next scream when she heard the women's titters and men's laughter behind her. Shoving aside her hair, she craned her neck and saw the crowd following them yet again.

"Darn fool women," she heard Jon mutter. "First you can't get them to talk, then you can't get them to shut up."

"Put me down, Jon Clay," Caitlyn ground out.

Jon complied at once, and Caitlyn staggered a step until she caught her balance. When she glared up at Jon, furious blue daggers of rage spitting from her eyes, he gripped her arms and held her gaze steadily.

"This is a time to listen again, Caitlyn," he said. "There's someone else here you need to meet."

Caitlyn swept her arms up, dislodging Jon's grasp. "I'm not going to marry you, Jon," she said, crossing her arms over her chest and sticking her lower lip out mutinously.

"Oh, lord." Jon raised his eyes skyward for a brief second. "This is going to be some marriage."

"I'm *not* . . . !"

"Ye're surely gonna have yer hands full, son," a soft voice said. "She's the spittin' image of me darlin' Maureen."

Caitlyn gasped. Hair flying, she whirled on the new voice, only to have Jon grab her around the waist and clap one hard palm across her mouth.

"I told you it's time to listen now, damn it," Jon growled. "And listen you will."

Caitlyn couldn't have spoken even without Jon's hand on her mouth. She stared at the tall, white-haired man before her. A dim memory came back to her of this same man and her mother, yelling and screaming at each other in the huge, stone hall of a castle.

The man had been younger then—salt and pepper rather than snow-white hair. But he had the same brilliant blue eyes and stern chin. The voice had roared in anger that time, but she seemed to recall other times, when he spoke as softly as he just had.

"I'm ye're grandda, Caitlyn," he said now in a hesitant voice. "Sean Keefe. Do ye remember me?"

Caitlyn managed to nod her head, and Jon loosened his grasp on her mouth. He eased his hand away, but kept it near her face, ready, she realized, to cover her mouth again if she said the wrong thing.

"I. . . ." She cleared her throat. "I remember. You and my mother fought. I . . . was listening—up on the stairwell."

Tears misted the old man's eyes, and he nodded his head. "I ran her off, and it near broke me heart. Tried to find her, I did, to tell her to come home. Bring her young man with her. And ye, a'course. Didn't . . . didn't know about the other wee one until I learned how she died."

"But you tried to have me killed, too."

"Nay, child," Keefe denied. "T'was another big mistake I made, trustin' ye're cousin Patrick—me only nephew—to handle the search for ye, after I found out two years ago ye were still alive. He would've taken it all after I died, ye see, had I not found me darlin' grandchild."

"I don't know that I believe you," Caitlyn said. "And, even if I do, I don't know that I can forgive you. My mother and father died because you wouldn't accept their marriage and they had to leave Ireland."

The old man's head bowed, and his shoulders shook. A tear crawled down his face, and Caitlyn noticed the discoloration on his weathered cheek, which looked like a fading bruise.

"What happened to his face?" she asked Jon quietly.

"I didn't give him much of a chance to explain himself when I found him here at rendezvous looking for you," Jon replied. "But Sean had already been talking to Reach for the Moon, telling him the real reason he'd been searching for you. Reach for the Moon dragged me off Sean before I could beat him to death."

Caitlyn remained silent, watching her grandfather turn his back and draw out a handkerchief from his pocket.

Jon continued, "Sean found the report Hogan sent back to your cousin, Patrick, after Hogan saw you at rendezvous last summer. When he read it, he realized that his nephew had been trying to find you to kill you, instead of begging you to come back to Ireland."

Jon grasped Caitlyn's shoulders and turned her to face him. "Patrick's dead. They fought, and Patrick pulled a knife, trying to kill Sean. Sean's butler shot Patrick before he could stab Sean. Darlin', then Sean got on the next ship and came over here to find you himself. He arrived in St. Louis in time to come out here with one of the pack trains."

Caitlyn heard her grandfather's gruff voice again, and stiffened when his hand fell on her shoulder.

"I don't blame ye, me wee little darlin'. I can't forgive meself, either. Maureen was the pride o' me heart, and I failed her. Tried to force her to my way, when I knew all along she had her mother's stubbornness and would only marry again for love—like me and your gramma did."

He dropped his hand and Caitlyn said without facing him, "You . . . used to call me that."

"Me wee little darlin'? Ye were, Caitlyn. Ye'll always be that to me, no matter if you hate me forever."

Caitlyn took a deep breath and glanced up at Jon. "I didn't want to marry you because I was afraid whoever was after me would hurt you in their attempts to get at me. I didn't want you to be injured, like Silas."

"I thought it might be something like that," Jon said with a nod. "But from now on, we face things together."

"Yes, Jon," she murmured.

Sean gave a wry chuckle. "Take me words as a weddin'

gift, son,'' he said to Jon. ''The Keefe women only say yes when they really mean it.''

Holding Caitlyn in one arm, Jon clasped Sean's hand when he held it out.

''Will ye at least write to me, Jon?'' Sean asked.

''I'll write,'' Jon promised. ''But aren't you staying for the wedding?''

''No. I won't ruin me wee darlin's day. I'll get started on back. Take care of her, son. And if someday she finds it in her heart to forgive me. . . . ''

''I'll let you know,'' Jon said.

When she finally heard Sean's retreating footsteps, Caitlyn turned to watch him leave. The tall figure walked with shoulders hunched, his hands in his pockets. He looked smaller than she remembered him, when he would reach down and pick her up—toss her into the air with her skirts flying, as her mother laughed tolerantly at the side of the room.

Then her grandfather's eyes would sparkle with laughter, not the tears she had seen a moment ago. His voice would boom out, echoing from the rafters when he called her his wee darlin', instead of cracking with gruff torment.

''Jon,'' she whispered. ''Did he tell you why he refused to give his consent to my mother marrying my stepfather? Why they ran away?''

''Yes. Your stepfather, James, was a younger son, Caitlyn. He didn't have any prospects, and he'd already decided to come to America and try to make his fortune in the fur trade. Sean didn't want your mother to leave—she was his only child. Sean offered James a share in his own holdings—told him that since he didn't have a male heir, it would all be Maureen's someday anyway.''

''Why didn't my stepfather accept it?'' Caitlyn asked.

''Pride, I guess. Male pride takes over instead of common sense sometimes, darlin'.'' He tilted Caitlyn's chin up. ''My own stupid pride sent me away from you, instead of staying there and working things out. Making you tell me what was bothering you. It hurt like hell when you said you wouldn't marry me—hurt my pride that you didn't think I loved you enough to take care of you.''

"I've always loved you, Jon.''

"And I love you, sweetheart. Now, that minister's waiting over there by Sky Woman's wigwam.''

Caitlyn took his hand and walked beside Jon, her head held high and her love shining in her eyes. The crowd parted for them, and more than one man nodded at Jon and gave him a wink. But Jon only had eyes for Caitlyn, who would be his wife forever in just a few more minutes.

They stopped in front of a black-robed man, who stood in front of the wigwam Caitlyn recognized as Sky Woman's. Caitlyn held out her hand to the Indian woman.

"Stand with me, Mother,'' she said softly.

Sky Woman nodded and joined them, as Silas walked up in response to Jon's wave of his free hand.

"Here, boyo,'' Silas said with a sly wink. "Reach for the Moon said for me to give you this from Caitlyn's grandfather.''

Silas handed Jon something, and the glint of sunlight that shot from it drew Catilyn's attention before Jon closed his fingers.

"What's that, Jon?''

"A ring your grandfather brought with him, darlin'. We need a ring, you know.''

Caitlyn picked up Jon's hand and pried at his fingers, but Jon closed his fist tightly.

"Uh uh. You can see it when I slip it on your finger, not before.''

Caitlyn stuck her lip out at him, then gave in grudgingly and faced the minister. The minister began the age-old ceremony, and Caitlyn's eyes filled with tears as she tried to concentrate on his words instead of a half-surfacing, nagging thought in her subconscious. The tears were only for the beauty of the ceremony, she told herself.

She made her replies in a choked voice, and when Jon finally said, "With this ring, I thee wed,'' she glanced at the ring through misty eyes.

"Jon!'' she said with a gasp. "That's one of my mother's rings. I remember her wearing it!''

"Caitlyn, give me your hand," Jon muttered as he heard a titter here and there in the crowd.

"Don't you see, Jon? He kept it for me and brought it all this way. And. . . . "

Caitlyn's eyes widened and she whirled, standing on tiptoe to try to peer over the heads of the crowd.

"Where did he go, Jon?"

"Caitlyn," Jon said through gritted teeth. "Turn your butt back around here so we can finish getting married!"

"I will not!" Caitlyn said with a stamp of her foot. "I want my grandda here when I get married!"

"Damn it, you told him you couldn't forgive him!"

"That was before I realized that it wasn't his fault. You told me that yourself a minute ago, Jon."

"What the hell wasn't his fault?" Jon demanded.

"Mother leaving Ireland," Caitlyn said in an exasperated voice. "Don't you see? She left with my stepfather because she loved him—because he was going, and she wanted to be with him. She would've gone anyway. Grandda didn't run her off, and he was protecting me by not telling me that. He took the blame, rather than letting me know my mother had made her own decision. She died because she wanted to be with my stepfather—not because Grandda ran her off."

"Caitlyn. . . . "

Caitlyn whirled and shoved through the crowd. Once free, she gazed wildly in the direction Sean had gone and saw him sitting on a horse a few hundred yards away.

He hadn't left yet. He was waiting to see her get married.

"Grandda!" Caitlyn pulled the doeskin dress above her knees and started running. "Grandda, wait! Don't go! Please!"

Jon followed more slowly, ignoring the muffled guffaws from the men as they elbowed one another when he passed.

"She will be a fine one, if you can ever tame her," one Indian man shouted after Jon.

Jon turned and smiled at him. "I don't want to tame her," he said. "I love her just fine the way she is."

The Indian nodded his agreement, and Jon started after

Caitlyn again. He watched **Sean dis**mount in time to catch
Caitlyn in his arms and **hug her tigh**tly. Jon walked more
slowly, giving them plenty of **time** to talk before he interrupted them.

But interrupt them he would. That little minx was going
to be his wife before this day was over.

Sean lifted his head as Jon approached, swiping at a hint
of moisture on his face with an embarrassed gesture.

"Son," he said. "I'd like to bring her to you, if that's
all right. Give her away to you."

Jon shrugged his shoulders and shook his head. "Whatever it takes to get her back there and through that ceremony," he said. Then he softened his voice. "I'd be proud
to accept her from you, sir."

"Jon," Caitlyn said excitedly. "Grandda's promised to
stay over here in America for a little while longer. He said
you'd asked him to maybe give your brother some help
running his plantation."

"Well, I'm going to be busy learning the fur trading
business," Jon said. "And since Charlie's divorcing Roxie,
maybe he'll have some sense about managing his money
again."

"Divorcing her? Oh, Jon, why? And what about . . . ?"

"Caitlyn, can't these explanations wait until after the
wedding?" One look at the avid curiosity on Caitlyn's face
told Jon that if he wanted her complete attention during the
ceremony, he should never have brought up the news in
Charlie's letter.

"Charlie caught her with someone," Jon gave in and
explained. "And he's figured out that the boy's mine. He's
keeping custody of him, and only hopes that I'll share him,
since he loves the little guy so much. How do you feel
about being a mother right away, Caitlyn? I know I promised we'd wait until. . . . "

Caitlyn threw her arms around his neck, her lips cutting
off his words and her kiss telling him everything he needed
to know. Despite his vow to wait until they were wed, Jon
returned her kiss hungrily. When he could finally force

himself to break the embrace, she gazed up at him with a merry twinkle in her eyes.

"Got your kiss, didn't you, you little minx?" Jon said around a laugh.

"Uh huh. Well, we're half married. Let's just call it half a kiss, and you can give me the other half in a few minutes."

Jon traced her lips with his finger. "I'll keep the other half warm for you. I love you, Caitlyn."

He glanced at Sean. "Think you can get her back there now, so we can get this over with this time?"

"Over with?" Caitlyn demanded. "Is that how you think about our wedding vows?"

Sean threw his head back and laughed, then wrapped his arm around Caitlyn's waist. "I'll bring her, son." When Caitlyn looked up at him, he amended his words. "That is, long as the wee darlin' wants to come."

"Do you, Caitlyn?" Jon asked softly.

"Yes," she replied with a huge smile. "Yes, Jon. I love you. Let's get married."

Fifteen minutes later, coonskin and wolfskin hats tossed overhead by the mountain men filled the sky, their shouts intermingling with whoops from the Indian men. Caitlyn heard the noise only dimly as she kissed Jon after the minister breathed a sigh of relief and pronounced them man and wife.

But she heard Jon's words clearly, even whispered amid all the noise.

"I love you, Mrs. Clay," he breathed.

"I love you, husband," she replied.

An Angel's Touch

Forever Angels

TRANA MAE SIMMONS

Tess Foster is convinced she has someone watching over her. The thoroughly modern woman has everything: a brilliant career, a rich fiance, and a glamorous life. But when her boyfriend demands she sign a prenuptial agreement, Tess thinks she's lost her happiness forever. Then her guardian angel sneezes and sends the woman of the nineties back to another era: the 1890s.

At first, Tess can't believe her senses. After all, no real man can be as handsome as the cowboy who rescues her from the Oklahoma wilderness. And Tess has never tasted sweeter ecstasy than she finds in Stone Chisum's kisses. But before she will surrender to a marriage made in heaven, Tess has to make sure that her bumbling guardian angel doesn't sneeze again—and ruin her second chance at love.

_52021-4 $4.99 US/$5.99 CAN

Dorchester Publishing Co., Inc.
65 Commerce Road
Stamford, CT 06902

Please add $1.75 for shipping and handling for the first book and $.50 for each book thereafter. NY, NYC, PA and CT residents, please add appropriate sales tax. No cash, stamps, or C.O.D.s. All orders shipped within 6 weeks via postal service book rate. Canadian orders require $2.00 extra postage and must be paid in U.S. dollars through a U.S. banking facility.

Name _____

Address _____

City _____ State _____ Zip _____

I have enclosed $_____ in payment for the checked book(s). Payment <u>must</u> accompany all orders.☐ Please send a free catalog.

HISTORICAL ROMANCE
BITTERSWEET PROMISES
By Trana Mae Simmons

Cody Garret likes everything in its place: his horse in its stable, his six-gun in its holster, his money in the bank. But the rugged cowpoke's life is turned head over heels when a robbery throws Shanna Van Alystyne into his arms. With a spirit as fiery as the blazing sun, and a temper to match, Shanna is the most downright thrilling woman ever to set foot in Liberty, Missouri. No matter what it takes, Cody will besiege Shanna's hesitant heart and claim her heavenly love.

_51934-8 $4.99 US/$5.99 CAN

CONTEMPORARY ROMANCE
SNOWBOUND WEEKEND/GAMBLER'S LOVE
By Amii Lorin

In *Snowbound Weekend,* romance is the last thing on Jennifer Lengle's mind when she sets off for a ski trip. But trapped by a blizzard in a roadside inn, Jen finds herself drawn to sophisticated Adam Banner, with his seductive words and his outrageous promises...promises that can be broken as easily as her innocent heart.

And in *Gambler's Love,* Vichy Sweigart's heart soars when she meets handsome Ben Larkin in Atlantic City. But Ben is a gambler, and Vichy knows from experience that such a man can hurt her badly. She is willing to risk everything she has for love, but the odds are high—and her heart is at stake.

_51935-6   (two unforgettable romances in one volume) Only $4.99

LEIGH GREENWOOD'S
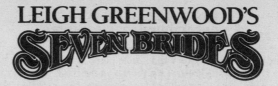
SEVEN BRIDES

FROST FLOWER

SONYA BIRMINGHAM

Out in the wilds of Red Oak Hollow, pretty Misty Malone has come across plenty of critters, but none surprises her more than a knocked-out, buck-naked stranger. Taught by her granny to cure ills with herbs, Misty knows a passel of cures that will heal the unknown man, yet does she dare give him the most potent remedy of all—her sweet Ozark love?

After being robbed, stripped, and left for dead, Adam Davenport awakes to a vision in buckskins who makes his heart race like white lightning. But since the Malones and the Davenports have been feuding longer than a coon's age, the St. Louis doctor's only chance to win Misty is to hide his real name—and pray that a dash of mountain magic and a heap of good loving will hold the rustic beauty down when she finds out the truth.

__3775-0 $4.99 US/$5.99 CAN

An Angel's Touch

Where angels go, love is sure to follow.

Time Heals by Susan Collier. Tired of her nagging relatives, Maeve Fredrickson asks for the impossible: to be a thousand miles and a hundred years away from them. Then a heavenly being grants her wish, and she awakens in frontier Montana. Saved from the wilderness by a handsome widower, Maeve loses her heart to her rescuer—and her temper over the antics of his three less-than-angelic children. As her angel prods her to fight for Seth, Maeve can only pray for the strength to claim a love made in paradise.

_52030-3 $4.99 US/$5.99 CAN

Longer Than Forever by Bronwyn Wolfe. Patrick is in trouble, alone in turn-of-the-century Chicago, and unjustly jailed with little hope for survival. Then the honey-haired beauty comes to him, as if she has heard his prayers. Lauren has all but given up on finding true love when she feels the green-eyed stranger's call—summoning her across boundaries of time and space to join him in a struggle against all odds; uniting them in a love that will last longer than forever.

_52042-7 $5.99 US/$7.99 CAN

Dorchester Publishing Co., Inc.
65 Commerce Road
Stamford, CT 06902

Please add $1.75 for shipping and handling for the first book and $.50 for each book thereafter. NY, NYC, PA and CT residents, please add appropriate sales tax. No cash, stamps, or C.O.D.s. All orders shipped within 6 weeks via postal service book rate. Canadian orders require $2.00 extra postage and must be paid in U.S. dollars through a U.S. banking facility.

Name _____

Address _____

City _____ State _____ Zip _____

I have enclosed $_____ in payment for the checked book(s).
Payment <u>must</u> accompany all orders. ☐ Please send a free catalog.

Sherrilyn Kenyon

"Sherrilyn Kenyon is a bright new star!"
—Affaire de Coeur

An Angel's Touch Romance: Daemon's Angel. Cast to the mortal realm by an evil sorceress, Arina has more than her share of problems. She is trapped in a temptress's body and doomed to lose any man she desires. Yet even as Arina yearns for the safety of the pearly gates, she finds paradise in the arms of a Norman mercenary. But to savor the joys of life with Daemon, she will have to battle demons and risk her very soul for love.

_52026-5 $4.99 US/$5.99 CAN

Futuristic Romance: Paradise City. Fleeing her past, Alix wants a life free of trouble. Yet no sooner has the spaceship expert signed on with Captain Devyn Kell than they are outrunning the authorities and heading toward Paradise City, where even assassins aren't safe. But Alix doesn't know what danger is until Devyn's burning kiss awakens her restless spirit with a taste of heaven.

_51969-0 $4.99 US/$5.99 CAN

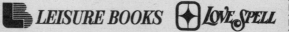